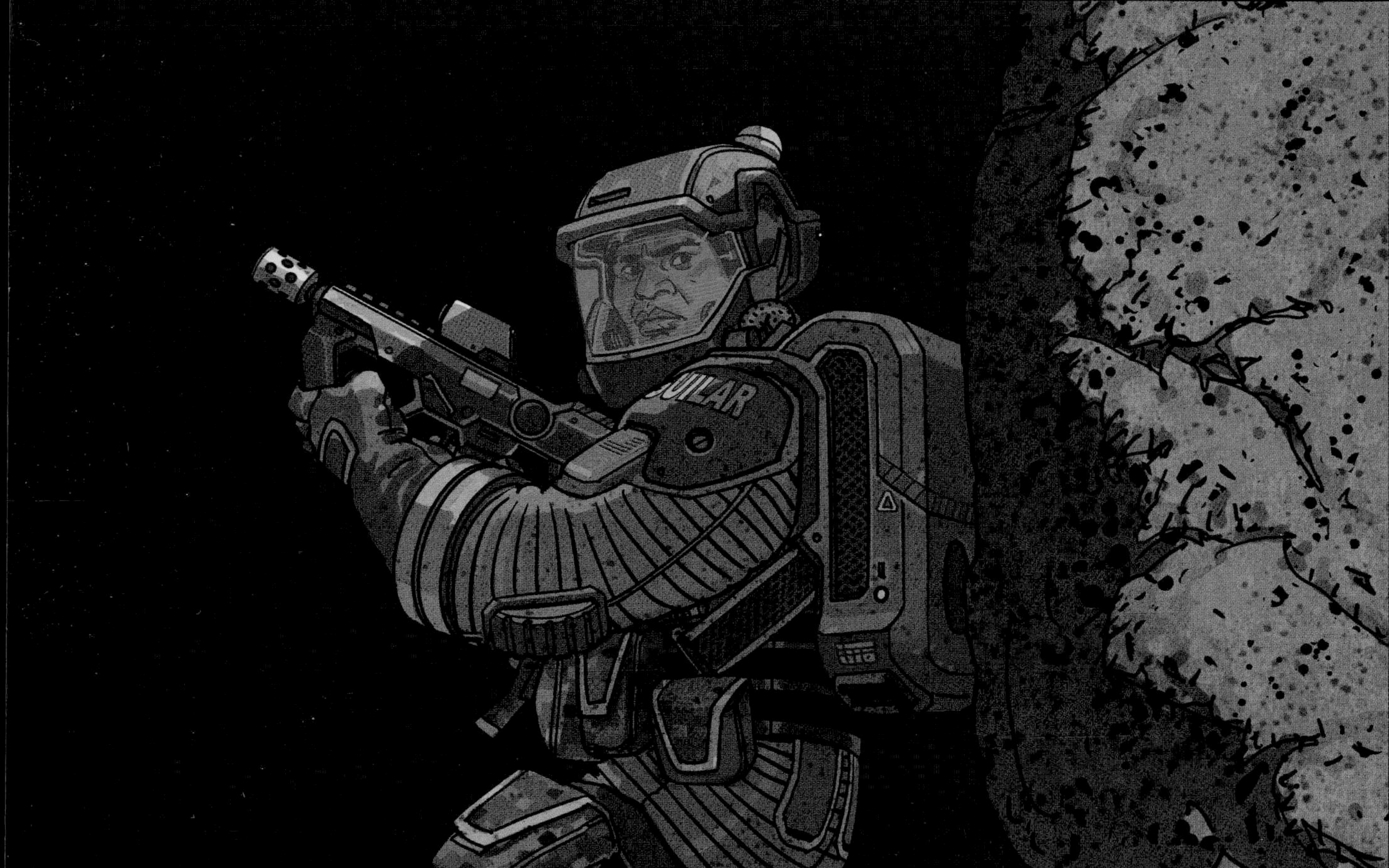

JERRY FRISSEN & PHILIPPE SCOFFONI

EXO

HUMANOIDS

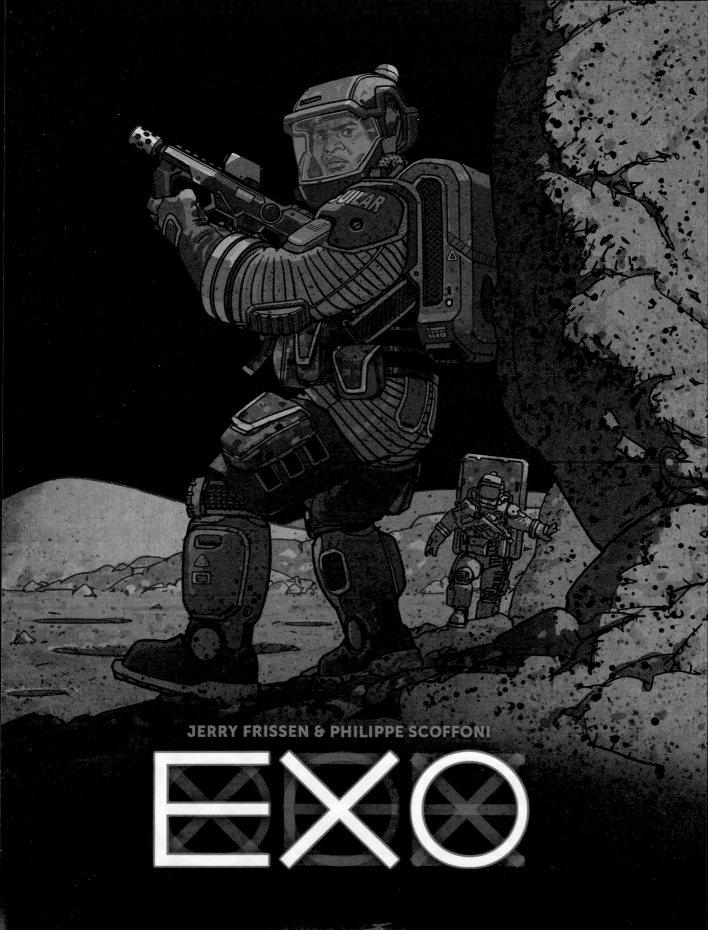

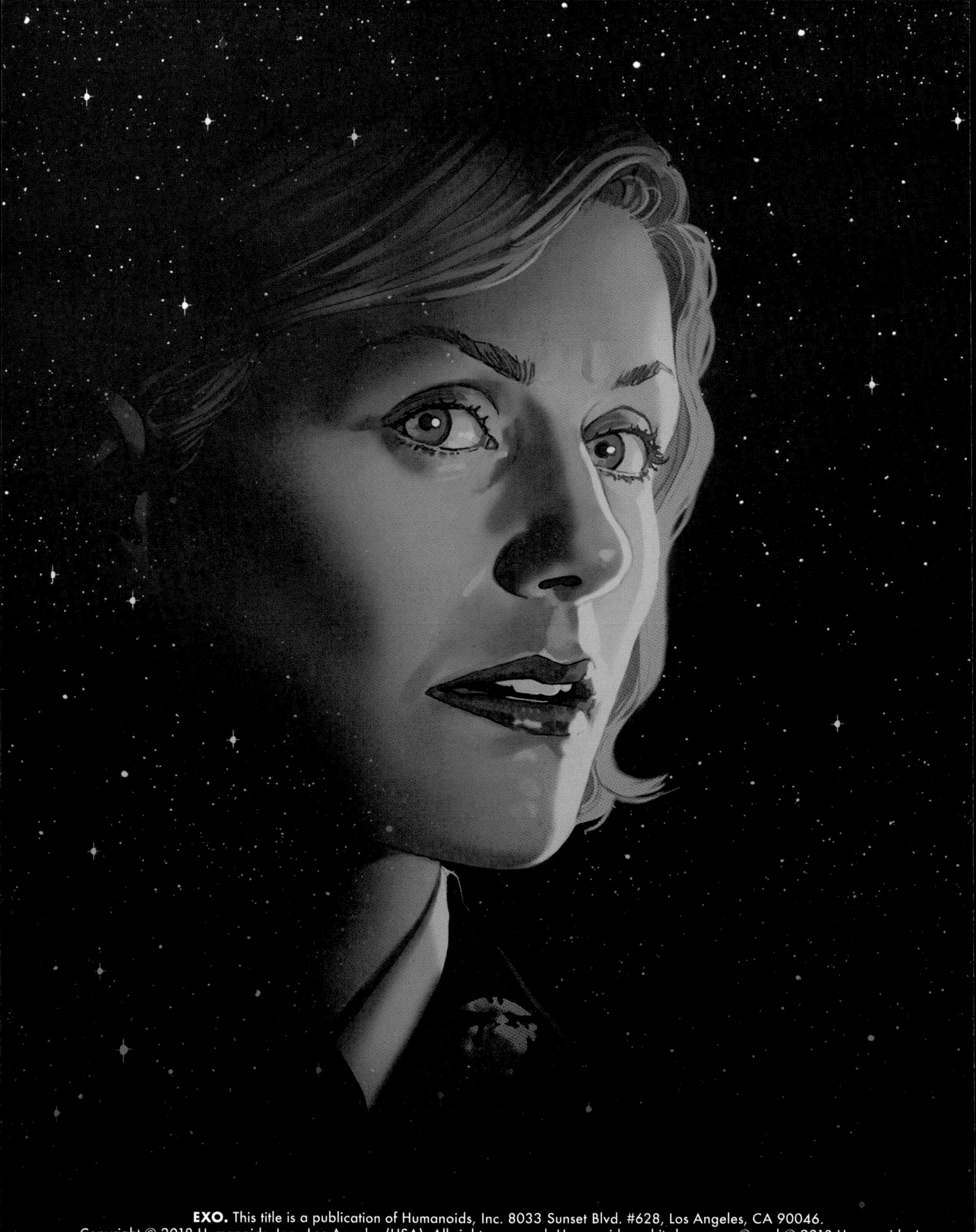

Jerry Frissen
Writer

Philippe Scoffoni
Artist & Colorist

Vincent Grière
Flatter

Mark Bence
Translator

Jerry Frissen
Senior Art Director

Alex Donoghue
U.S. Edition Editor

Bruno Lecigne &
Camille Thélot-Vernoux
Original Edition Editors

Fabrice Giger
Publisher

Rights & Licensing - licensing@humanoids.com
Press and Social Media - pr@humanoids.com

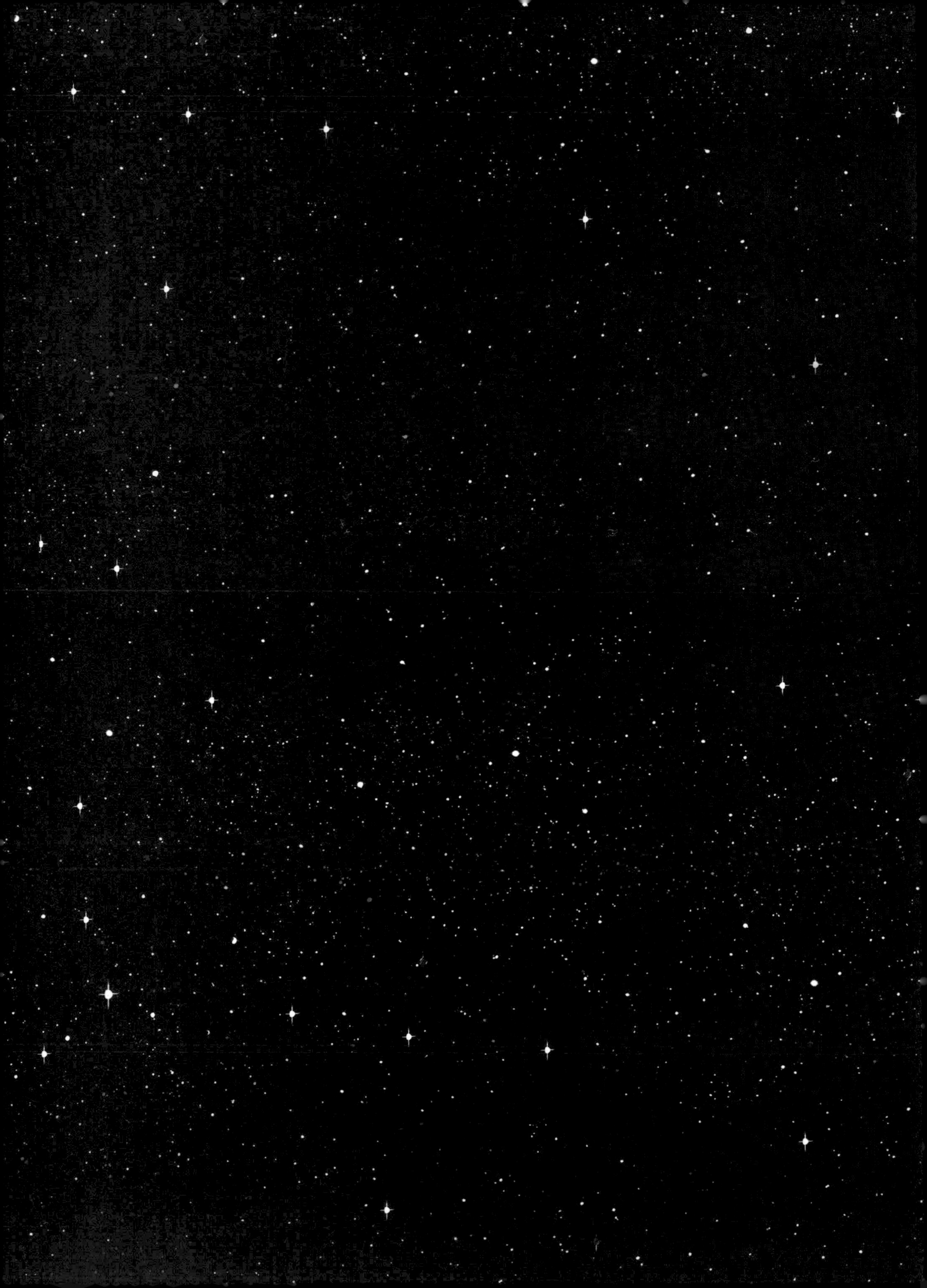

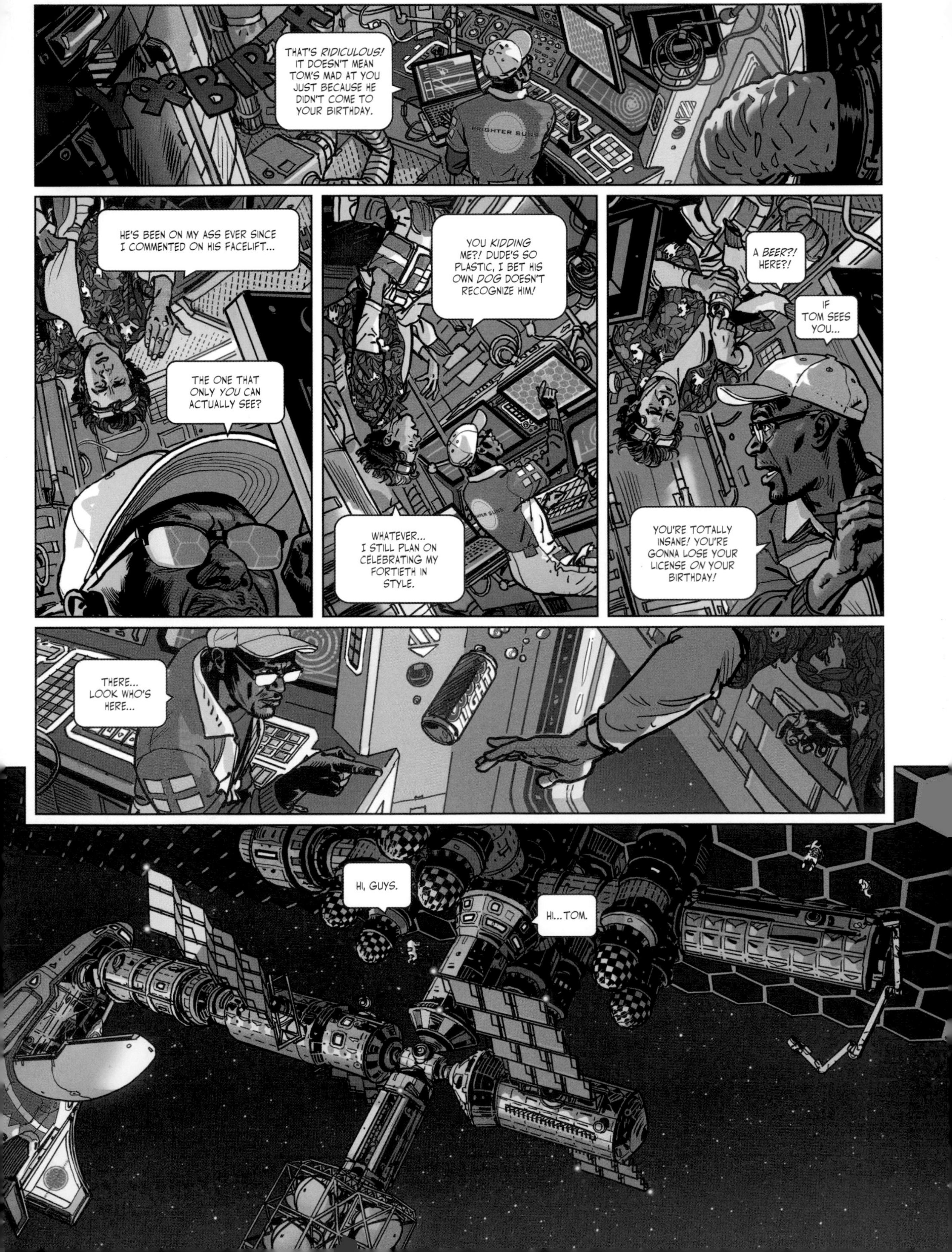
THAT'S RIDICULOUS! IT DOESN'T MEAN TOM'S MAD AT YOU JUST BECAUSE HE DIDN'T COME TO YOUR BIRTHDAY.
HE'S BEEN ON MY ASS EVER SINCE I COMMENTED ON HIS FACELIFT...
THE ONE THAT ONLY YOU CAN ACTUALLY SEE?
YOU KIDDING ME?! DUDE'S SO PLASTIC, I BET HIS OWN DOG DOESN'T RECOGNIZE HIM!
WHATEVER... I STILL PLAN ON CELEBRATING MY FORTIETH IN STYLE.
A BEER?! HERE?!
IF TOM SEES YOU...
YOU'RE TOTALLY INSANE! YOU'RE GONNA LOSE YOUR LICENSE ON YOUR BIRTHDAY!
THERE... LOOK WHO'S HERE...
HI, GUYS.
HI...TOM.

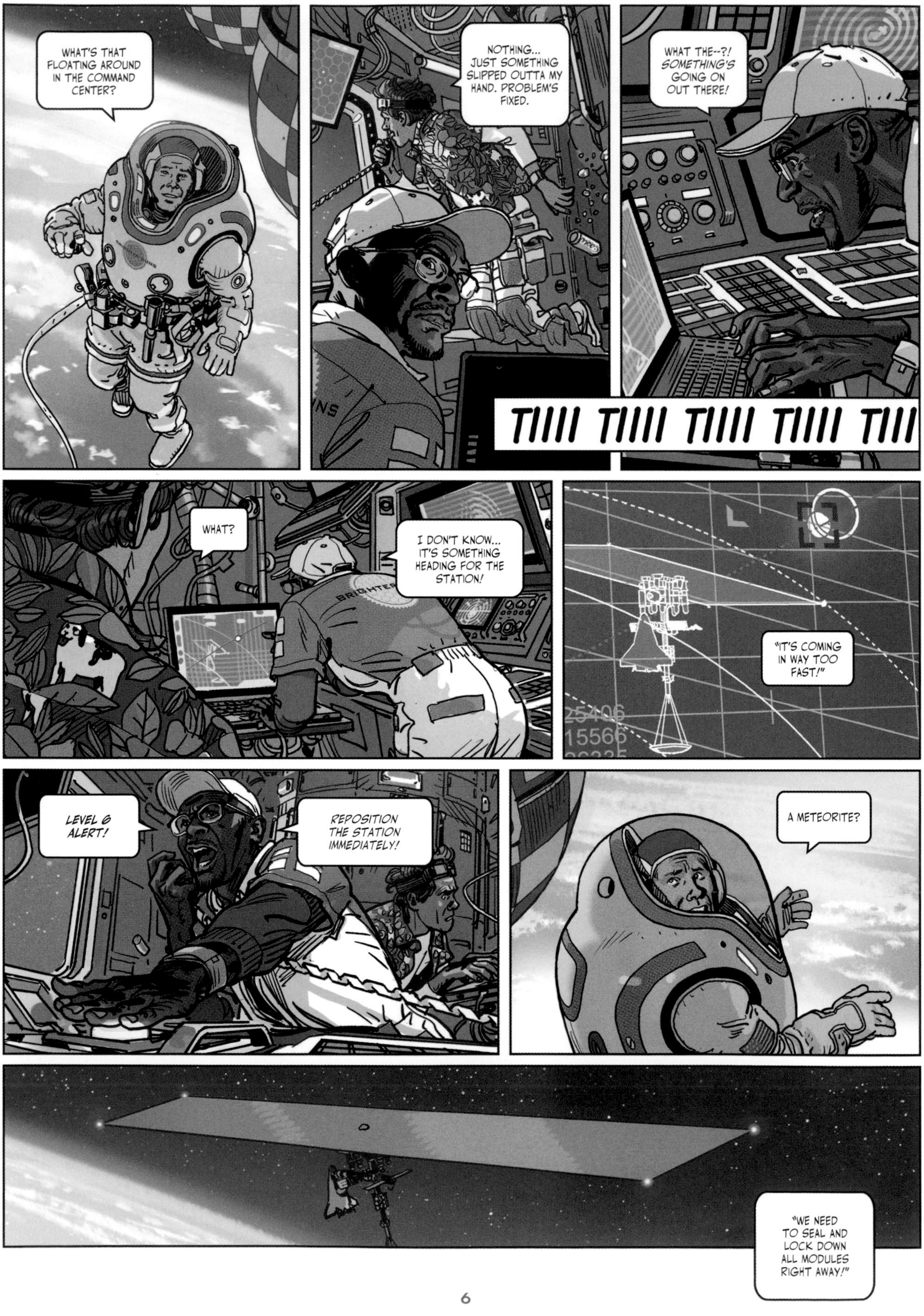

WHAT'S THAT FLOATING AROUND IN THE COMMAND CENTER?
NOTHING... JUST SOMETHING SLIPPED OUTTA MY HAND. PROBLEM'S FIXED.
WHAT THE--?! SOMETHING'S GOING ON OUT THERE!
TIIII TIIII TIIII TIIII TIII
WHAT?
I DON'T KNOW... IT'S SOMETHING HEADING FOR THE STATION!
"IT'S COMING IN WAY TOO FAST!"
LEVEL 6 ALERT!
REPOSITION THE STATION IMMEDIATELY!
A METEORITE?
"WE NEED TO SEAL AND LOCK DOWN ALL MODULES RIGHT AWAY!"

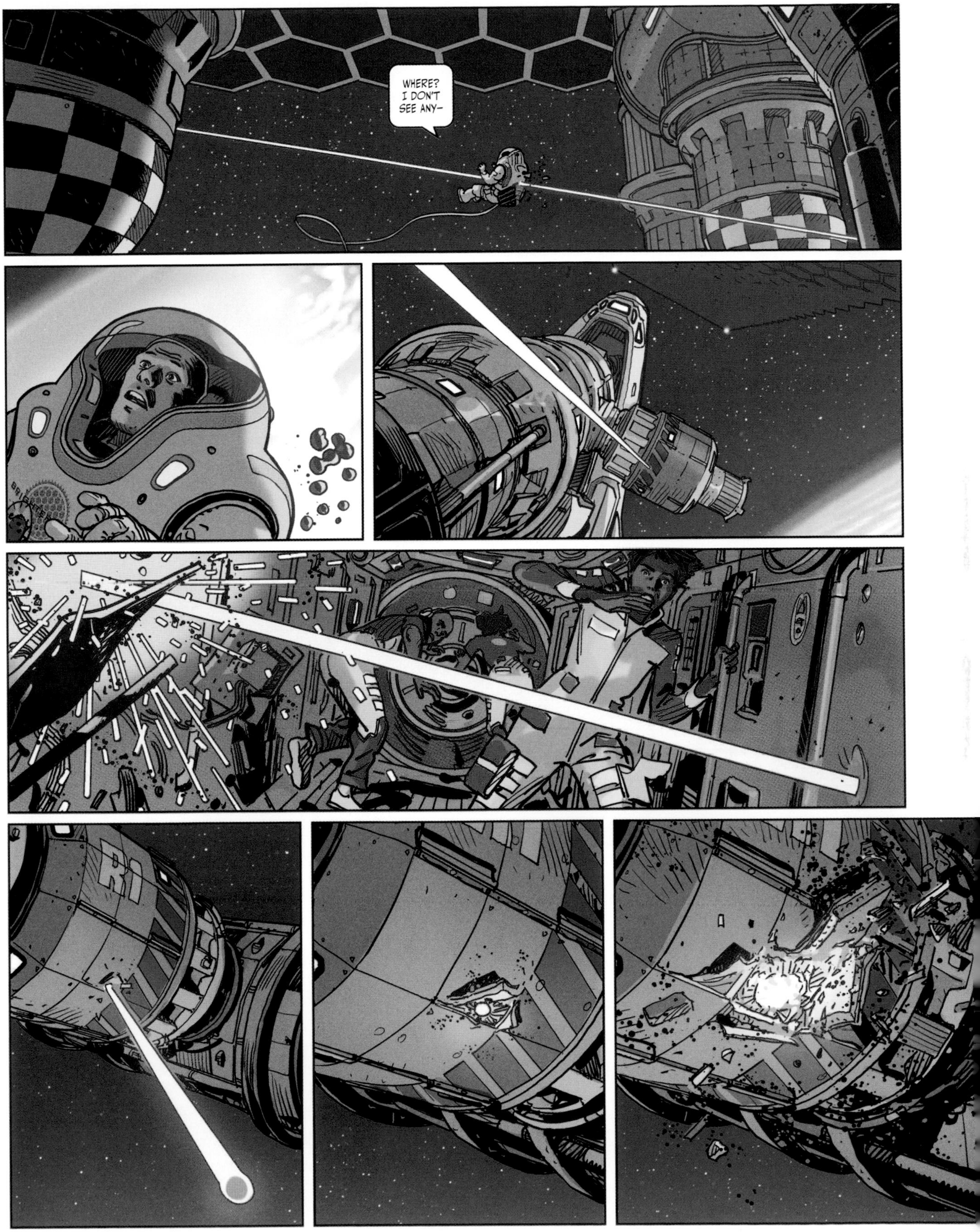
WHERE? I DON'T SEE ANY–
R1

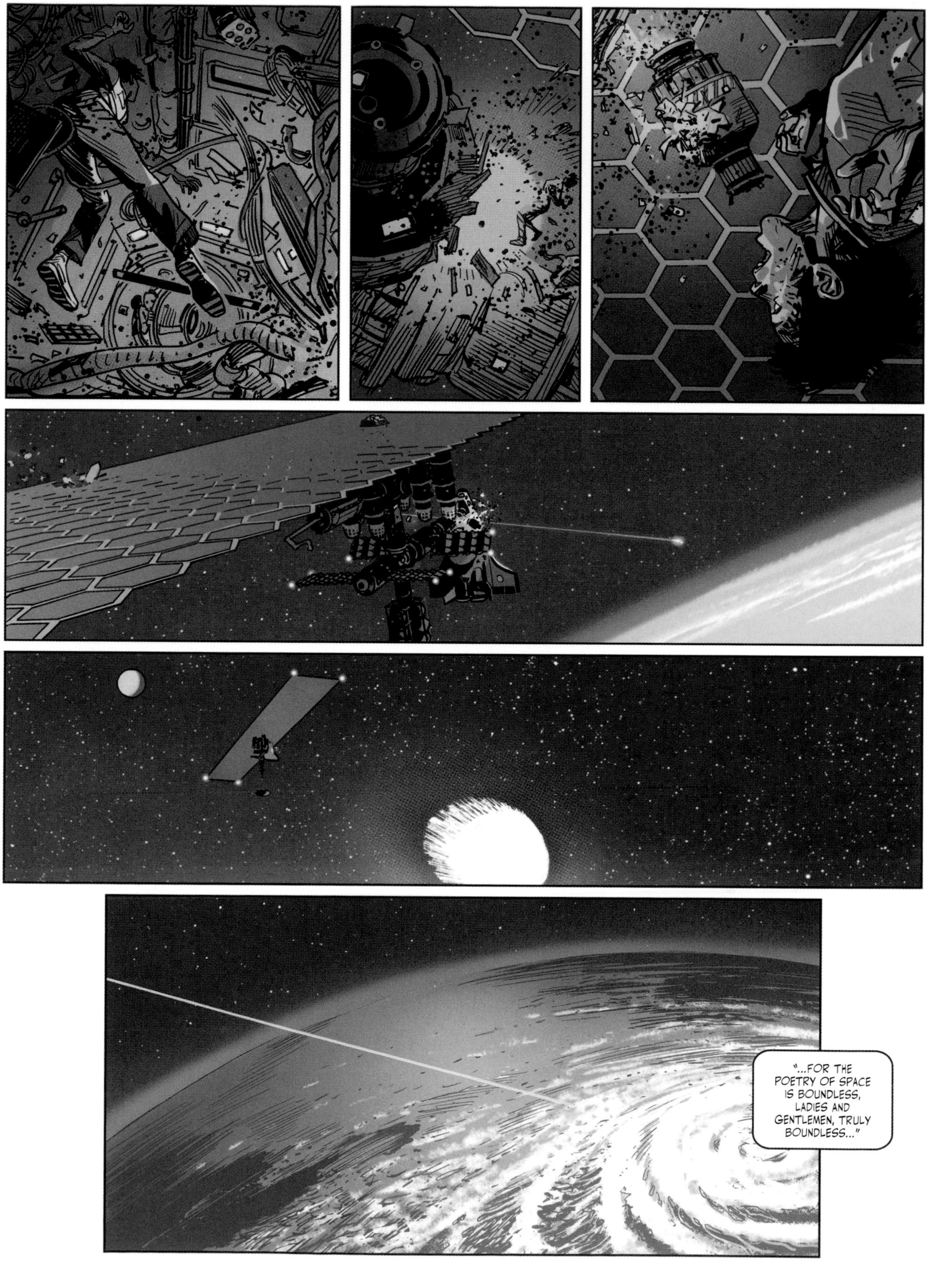
"...FOR THE POETRY OF SPACE IS BOUNDLESS, LADIES AND GENTLEMEN, TRULY BOUNDLESS..."

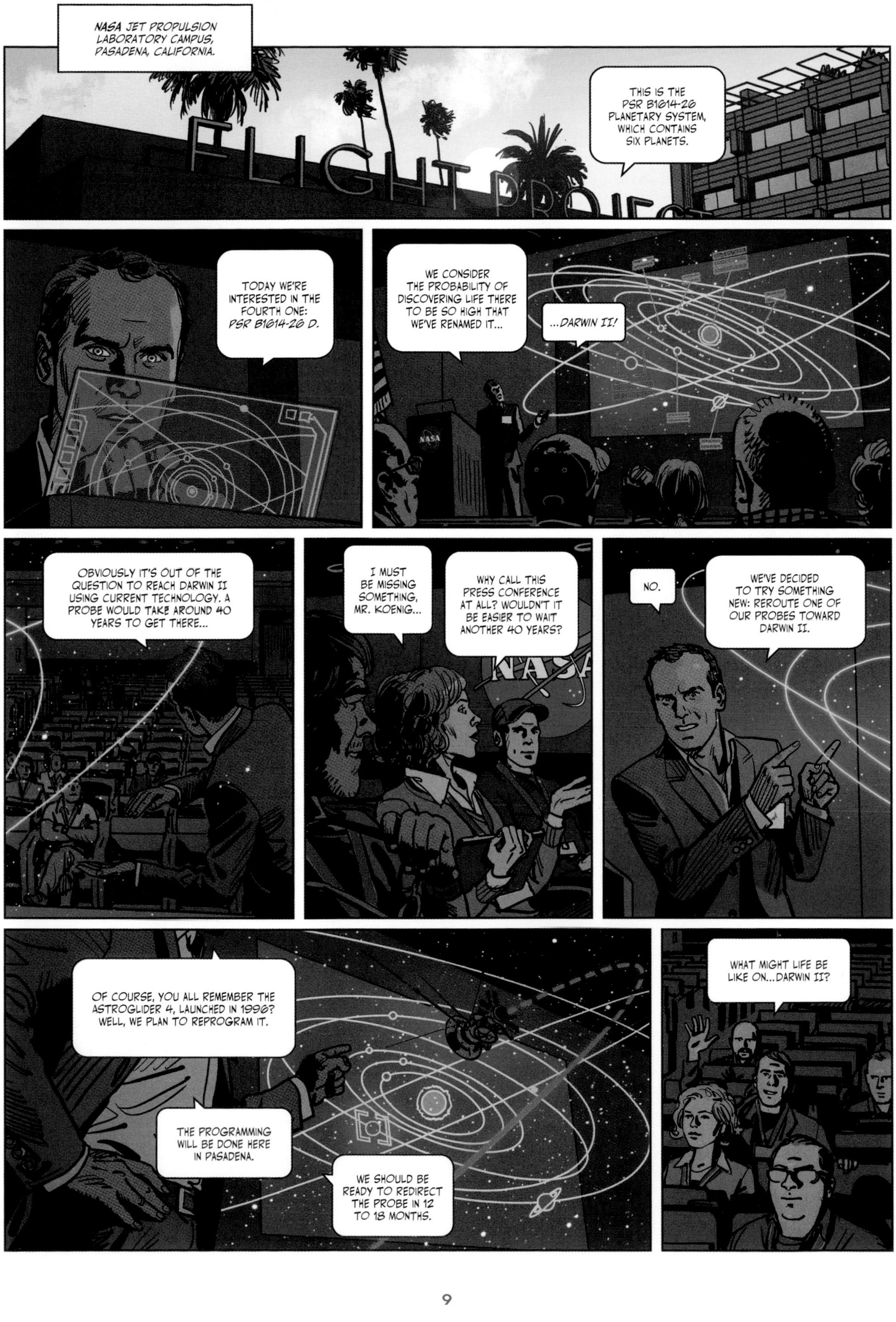
NASA JET PROPULSION LABORATORY CAMPUS, PASADENA, CALIFORNIA.
FLIGHT PROJECT
THIS IS THE PSR B1614-26 PLANETARY SYSTEM, WHICH CONTAINS SIX PLANETS.
TODAY WE'RE INTERESTED IN THE FOURTH ONE: PSR B1614-26 D.
WE CONSIDER THE PROBABILITY OF DISCOVERING LIFE THERE TO BE SO HIGH THAT WE'VE RENAMED IT...
...DARWIN II!
NASA
OBVIOUSLY IT'S OUT OF THE QUESTION TO REACH DARWIN II USING CURRENT TECHNOLOGY. A PROBE WOULD TAKE AROUND 40 YEARS TO GET THERE...
I MUST BE MISSING SOMETHING, MR. KOENIG...
WHY CALL THIS PRESS CONFERENCE AT ALL? WOULDN'T IT BE EASIER TO WAIT ANOTHER 40 YEARS?
NASA
NO.
WE'VE DECIDED TO TRY SOMETHING NEW: REROUTE ONE OF OUR PROBES TOWARD DARWIN II.
OF COURSE, YOU ALL REMEMBER THE ASTROGLIDER 4, LAUNCHED IN 1996? WELL, WE PLAN TO REPROGRAM IT.
THE PROGRAMMING WILL BE DONE HERE IN PASADENA.
WE SHOULD BE READY TO REDIRECT THE PROBE IN 12 TO 18 MONTHS.
WHAT MIGHT LIFE BE LIKE ON...DARWIN II?

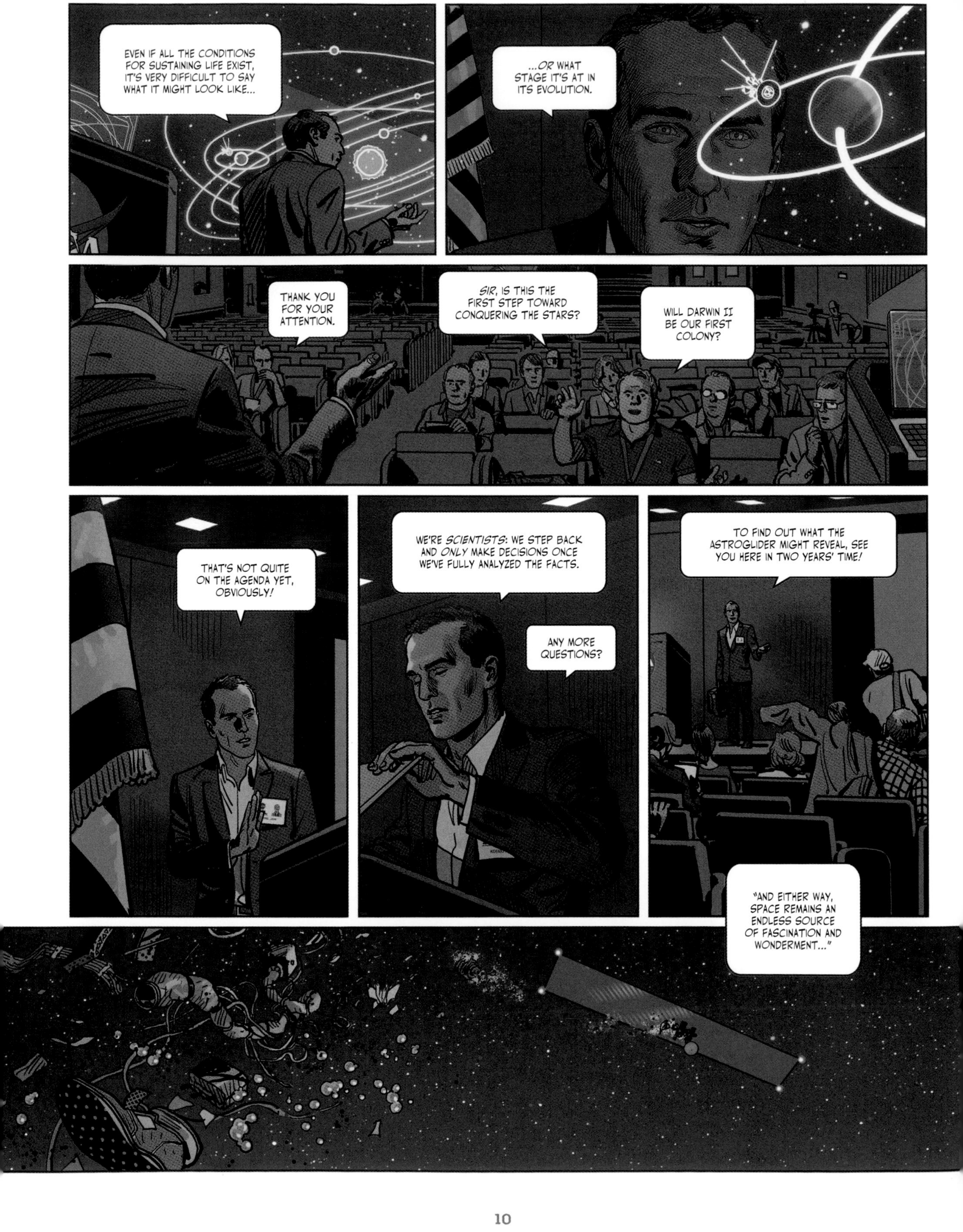

EVEN IF ALL THE CONDITIONS FOR SUSTAINING LIFE EXIST, IT'S VERY DIFFICULT TO SAY WHAT IT MIGHT LOOK LIKE...
...OR WHAT STAGE IT'S AT IN ITS EVOLUTION.
THANK YOU FOR YOUR ATTENTION.
SIR, IS THIS THE FIRST STEP TOWARD CONQUERING THE STARS?
WILL DARWIN II BE OUR FIRST COLONY?
THAT'S NOT QUITE ON THE AGENDA YET, OBVIOUSLY!
WE'RE SCIENTISTS: WE STEP BACK AND ONLY MAKE DECISIONS ONCE WE'VE FULLY ANALYZED THE FACTS.
ANY MORE QUESTIONS?
TO FIND OUT WHAT THE ASTROGLIDER MIGHT REVEAL, SEE YOU HERE IN TWO YEARS' TIME!
"AND EITHER WAY, SPACE REMAINS AN ENDLESS SOURCE OF FASCINATION AND WONDERMENT..."

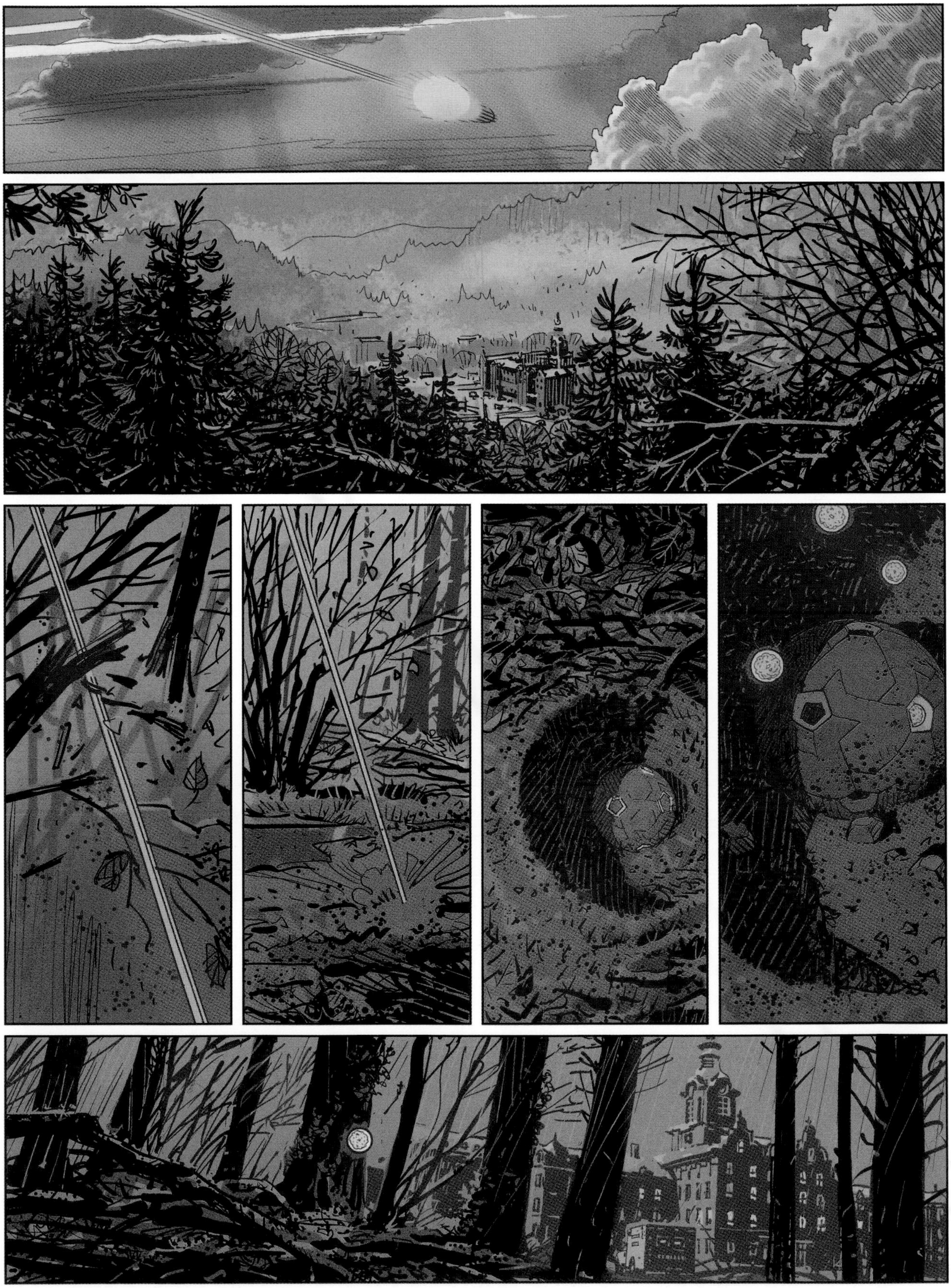

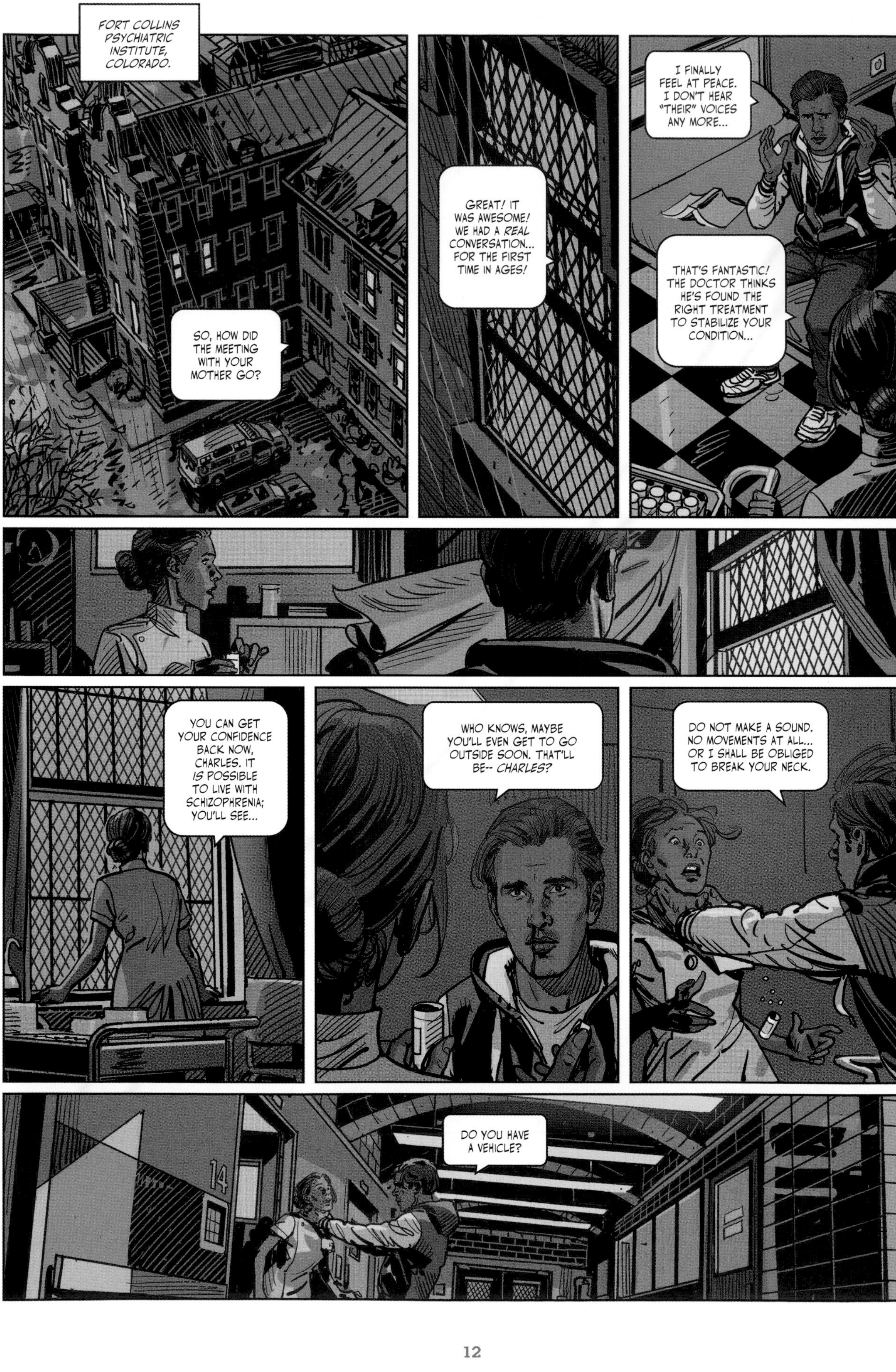
FORT COLLINS PSYCHIATRIC INSTITUTE, COLORADO.
SO, HOW DID THE MEETING WITH YOUR MOTHER GO?
GREAT! IT WAS AWESOME! WE HAD A REAL CONVERSATION... FOR THE FIRST TIME IN AGES!
I FINALLY FEEL AT PEACE. I DON'T HEAR "THEIR" VOICES ANY MORE...
THAT'S FANTASTIC! THE DOCTOR THINKS HE'S FOUND THE RIGHT TREATMENT TO STABILIZE YOUR CONDITION...
YOU CAN GET YOUR CONFIDENCE BACK NOW, CHARLES. IT IS POSSIBLE TO LIVE WITH SCHIZOPHRENIA; YOU'LL SEE...
WHO KNOWS, MAYBE YOU'LL EVEN GET TO GO OUTSIDE SOON. THAT'LL BE-- CHARLES?
DO NOT MAKE A SOUND. NO MOVEMENTS AT ALL... OR I SHALL BE OBLIGED TO BREAK YOUR NECK.
14
DO YOU HAVE A VEHICLE?

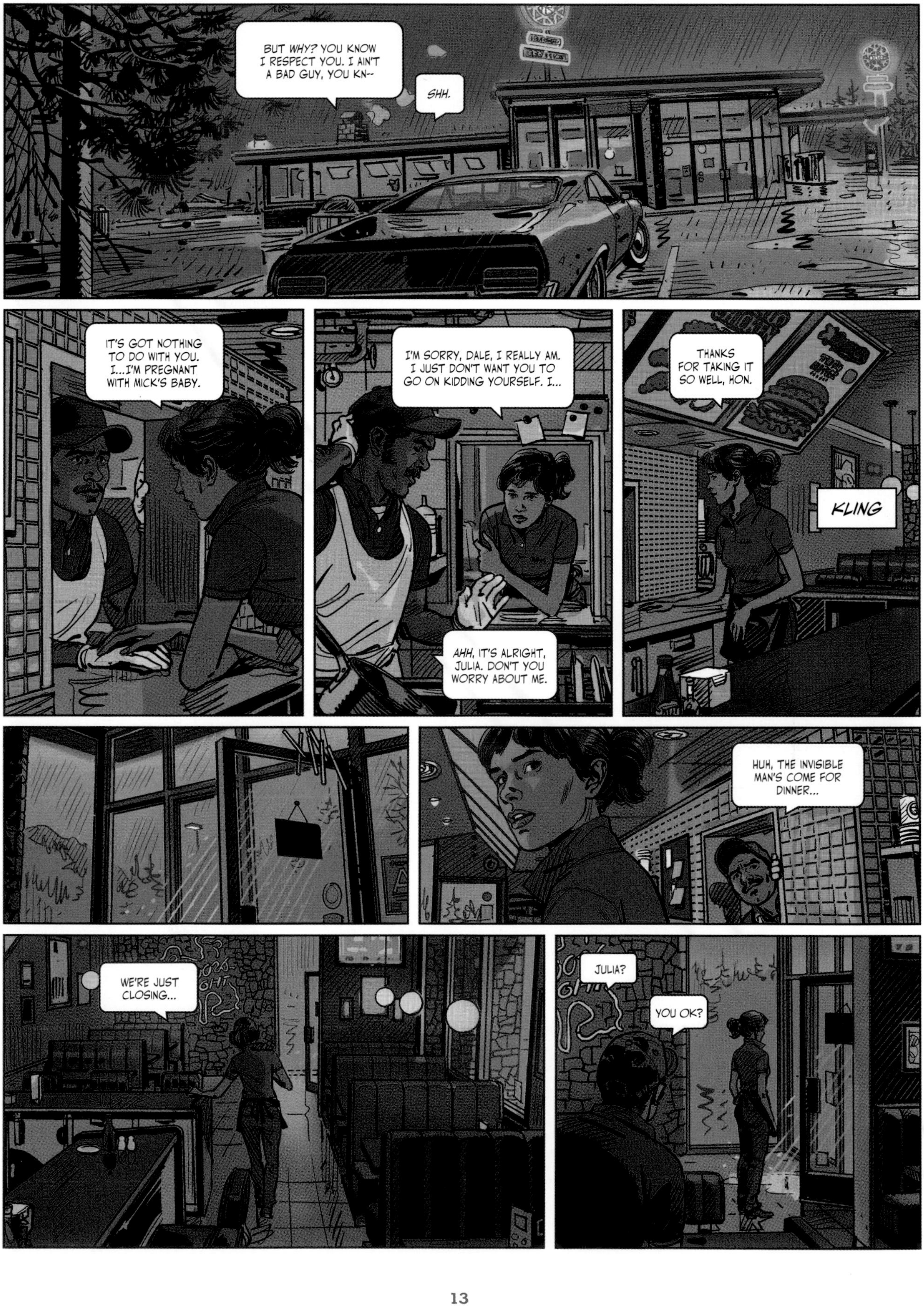
BUT *WHY?* YOU KNOW I RESPECT YOU. I AIN'T A BAD GUY, YOU KN--
SHH.
IT'S GOT NOTHING TO DO WITH YOU. I...I'M PREGNANT WITH MICK'S BABY.
I'M SORRY, DALE, I REALLY AM. I JUST DON'T WANT YOU TO GO ON KIDDING YOURSELF. I...
AHH, IT'S ALRIGHT, JULIA. DON'T YOU WORRY ABOUT ME.
THANKS FOR TAKING IT SO WELL, HON.
KLING
HUH, THE INVISIBLE MAN'S COME FOR DINNER...
WE'RE JUST CLOSING...
JULIA?
YOU OK?

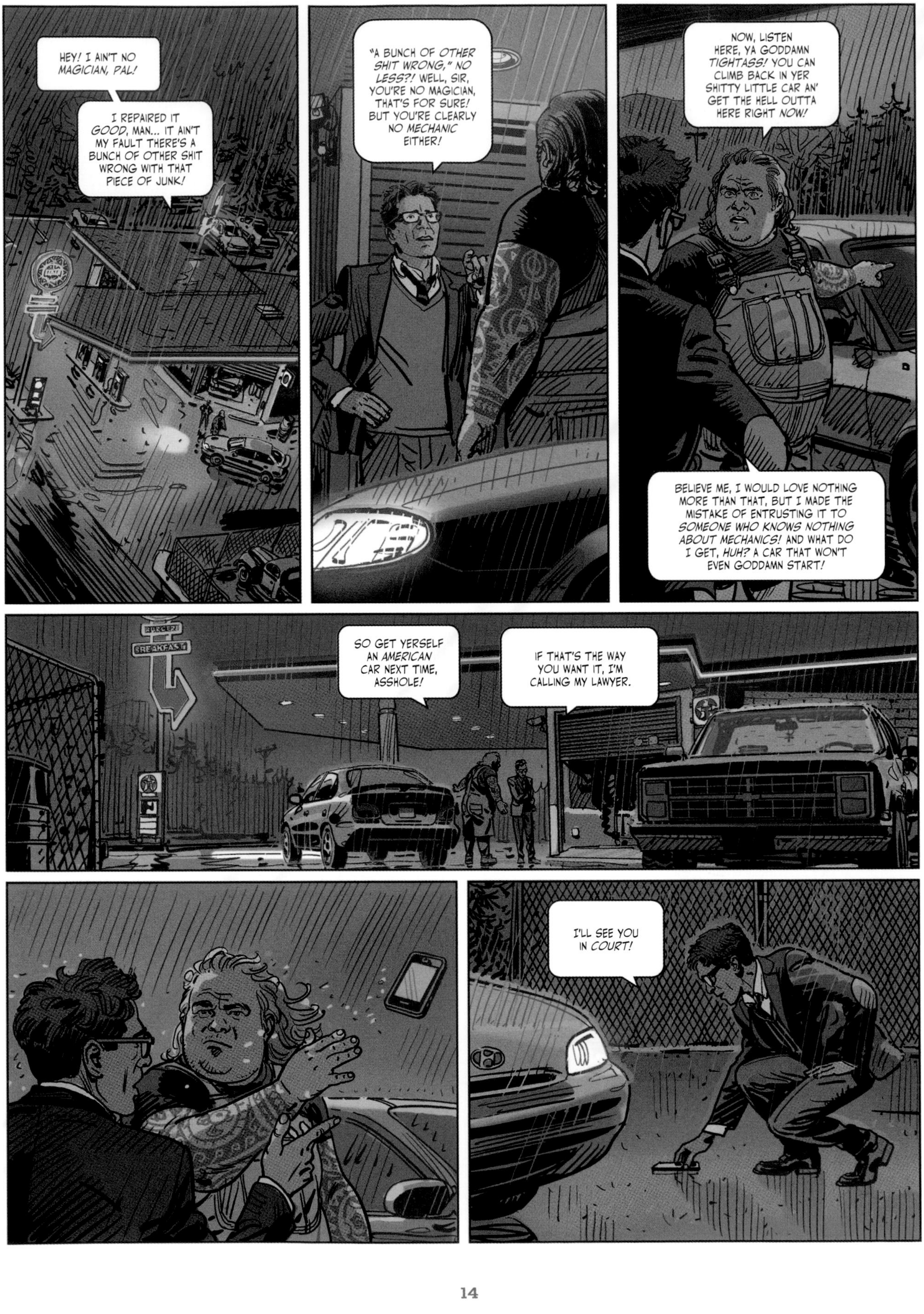
HEY! I AIN'T NO MAGICIAN, PAL!
I REPAIRED IT GOOD, MAN... IT AIN'T MY FAULT THERE'S A BUNCH OF OTHER SHIT WRONG WITH THAT PIECE OF JUNK!
"A BUNCH OF OTHER SHIT WRONG," NO LESS?! WELL, SIR, YOU'RE NO MAGICIAN, THAT'S FOR SURE! BUT YOU'RE CLEARLY NO MECHANIC EITHER!
NOW, LISTEN HERE, YA GODDAMN TIGHTASS! YOU CAN CLIMB BACK IN YER SHITTY LITTLE CAR AN' GET THE HELL OUTTA HERE RIGHT NOW!
BELIEVE ME, I WOULD LOVE NOTHING MORE THAN THAT, BUT I MADE THE MISTAKE OF ENTRUSTING IT TO SOMEONE WHO KNOWS NOTHING ABOUT MECHANICS! AND WHAT DO I GET, HUH? A CAR THAT WON'T EVEN GODDAMN START!
BURGER
BREAKFAST
SO GET YERSELF AN AMERICAN CAR NEXT TIME, ASSHOLE!
IF THAT'S THE WAY YOU WANT IT, I'M CALLING MY LAWYER.
I'LL SEE YOU IN COURT!

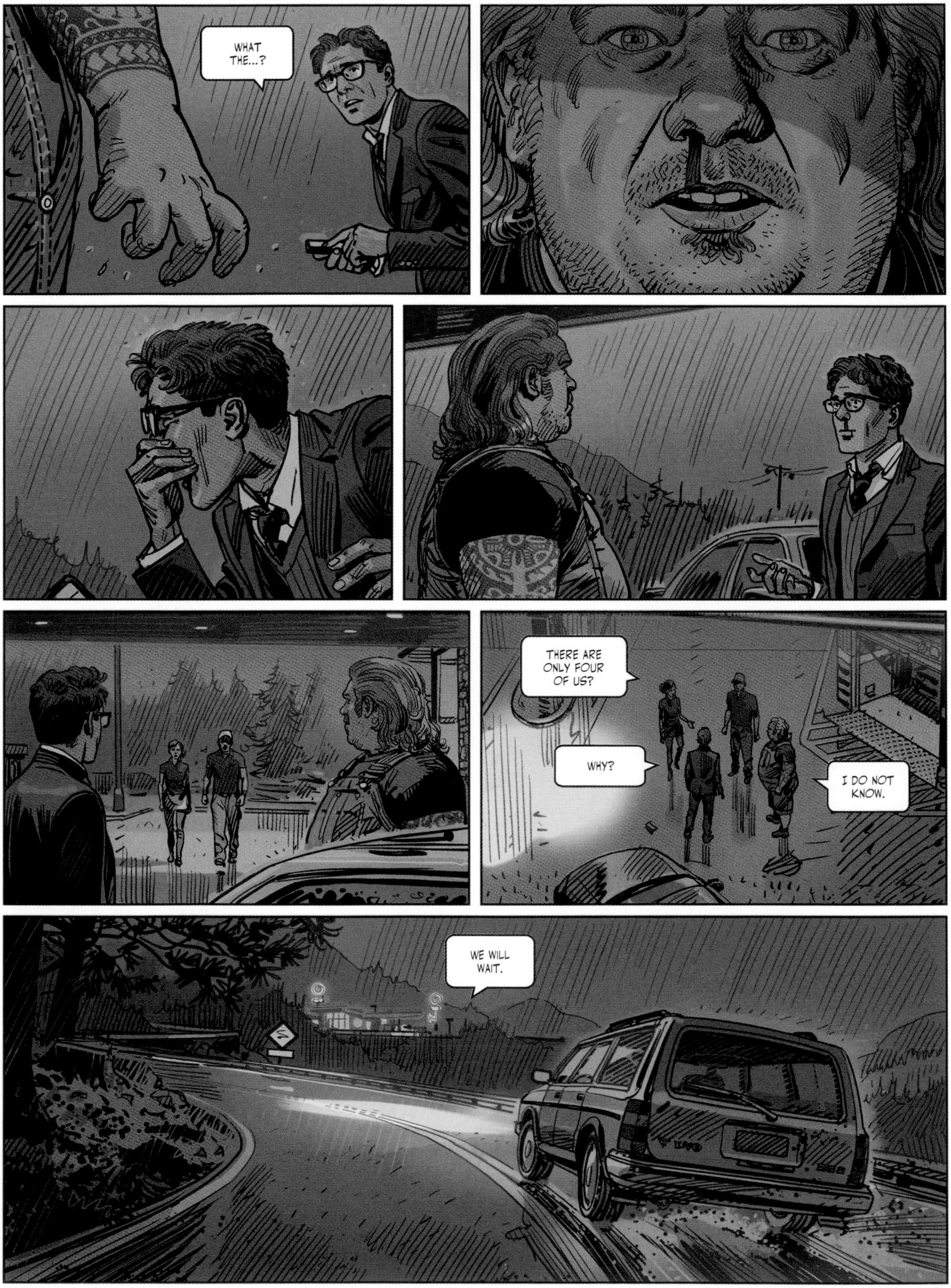
WHAT THE...?
THERE ARE ONLY FOUR OF US?
WHY?
I DO NOT KNOW.
WE WILL WAIT.

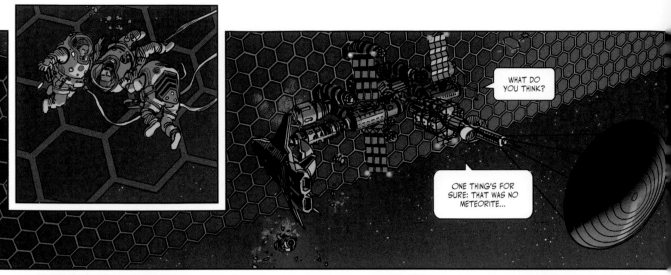

WHAT DO YOU THINK?

ONE THING'S FOR SURE: THAT WAS NO METEORITE...

SO WHAT THE HELL DO WE DO IN SITUATIONS LIKE THIS?

WE JUST FOLLOW THE INSTRUCTIONS...

HERE!

ALIEN ENCOUNTER

TYPE 1

TYPE 2
A UFO event in which a physical effect is alleged

TYPE 3
UFO encounters in which a creature is present

DDE

WARNING

Bloecher subtypes:
B: An entity is observed only in...
C: An entity is observed...

ALIEN...?

DO YOU REALLY THINK--?

KNOW WHAT I SEE ON THAT SCREEN? A PROJECTILE! A GODDAMN MISSILE!

THAT DAMN THING KILLED OUR CREWMATES!

SOMEONE TOOK A SHOT AT US, GIL!

"SO WE KEY IN THE CODE AND WE WAIT FOR BACKUP, THEN HOPE IT SHOWS UP BEFORE THE NEXT ATTACK..."

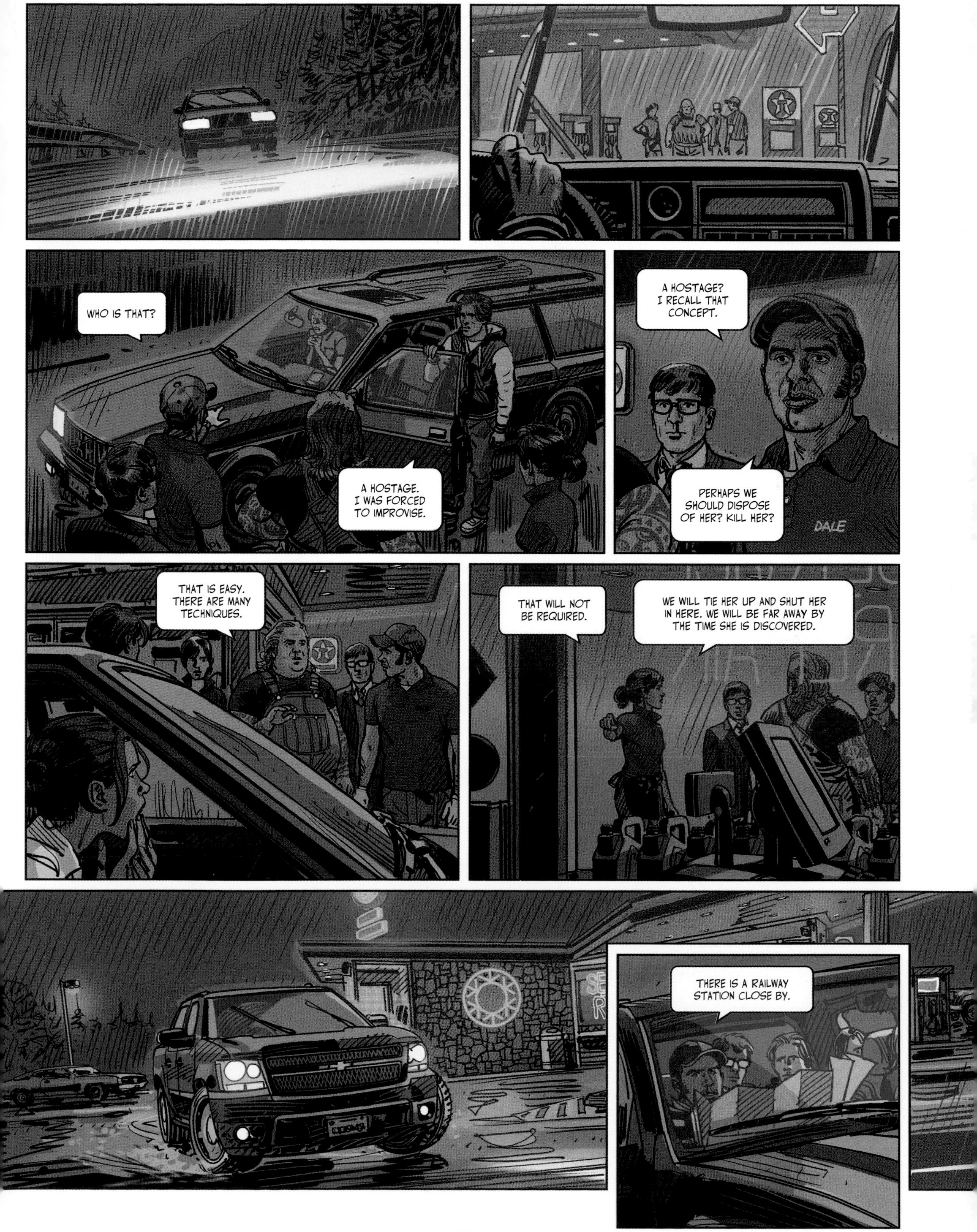
WHO IS THAT?
A HOSTAGE. I WAS FORCED TO IMPROVISE.
A HOSTAGE? I RECALL THAT CONCEPT.
PERHAPS WE SHOULD DISPOSE OF HER? KILL HER?
DALE
THAT IS EASY. THERE ARE MANY TECHNIQUES.
THAT WILL NOT BE REQUIRED.
WE WILL TIE HER UP AND SHUT HER IN HERE. WE WILL BE FAR AWAY BY THE TIME SHE IS DISCOVERED.
THERE IS A RAILWAY STATION CLOSE BY.

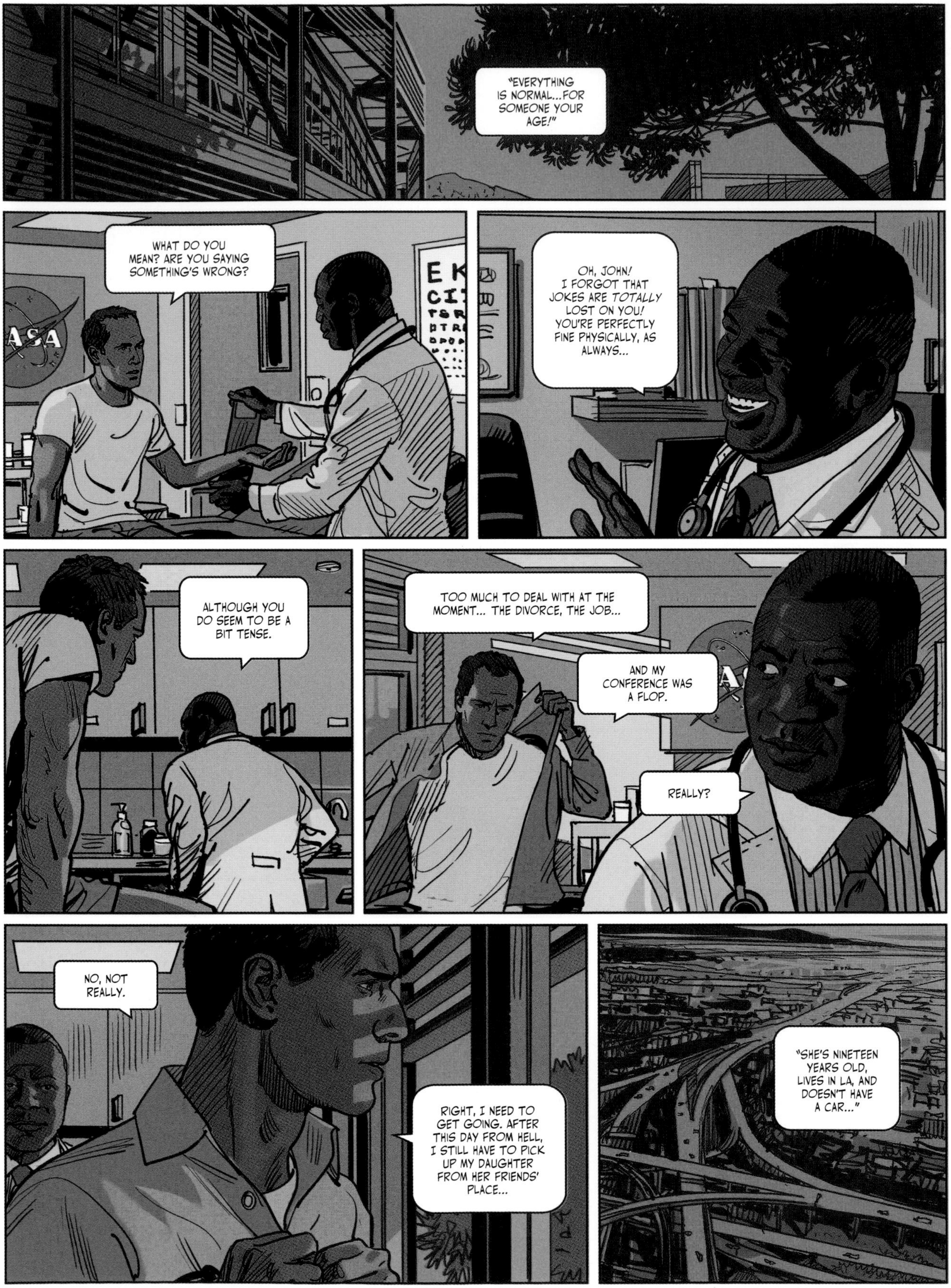
"EVERYTHING IS NORMAL...FOR SOMEONE YOUR AGE!"
WHAT DO YOU MEAN? ARE YOU SAYING SOMETHING'S WRONG?
OH, JOHN! I FORGOT THAT JOKES ARE *TOTALLY* LOST ON YOU! YOU'RE PERFECTLY FINE PHYSICALLY, AS ALWAYS...
ALTHOUGH YOU DO SEEM TO BE A BIT TENSE.
TOO MUCH TO DEAL WITH AT THE MOMENT... THE DIVORCE, THE JOB...
AND MY CONFERENCE WAS A FLOP.
REALLY?
NO, NOT REALLY.
RIGHT, I NEED TO GET GOING. AFTER THIS DAY FROM HELL, I STILL HAVE TO PICK UP MY DAUGHTER FROM HER FRIENDS' PLACE...
"SHE'S NINETEEN YEARS OLD, LIVES IN LA, AND DOESN'T HAVE A CAR..."

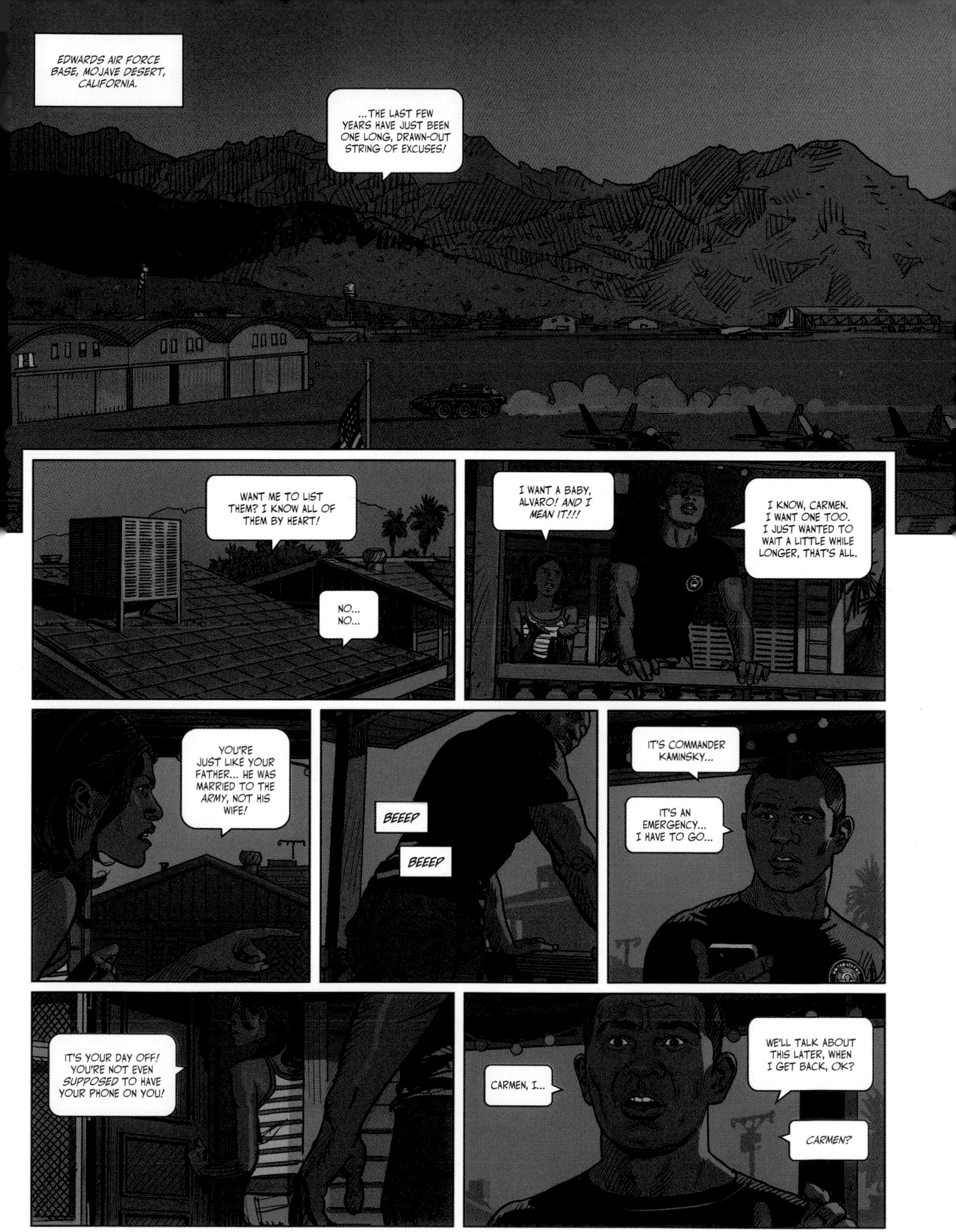
EDWARDS AIR FORCE BASE, MOJAVE DESERT, CALIFORNIA.
...THE LAST FEW YEARS HAVE JUST BEEN ONE LONG, DRAWN-OUT STRING OF EXCUSES!
WANT ME TO LIST THEM? I KNOW ALL OF THEM BY HEART!
NO... NO...
I WANT A BABY, ALVARO! AND I MEAN IT!!!
I KNOW, CARMEN. I WANT ONE TOO. I JUST WANTED TO WAIT A LITTLE WHILE LONGER, THAT'S ALL.
YOU'RE JUST LIKE YOUR FATHER... HE WAS MARRIED TO THE ARMY, NOT HIS WIFE!
BEEEP
BEEEP
IT'S COMMANDER KAMINSKY...
IT'S AN EMERGENCY... I HAVE TO GO...
IT'S YOUR DAY OFF! YOU'RE NOT EVEN SUPPOSED TO HAVE YOUR PHONE ON YOU!
CARMEN, I...
WE'LL TALK ABOUT THIS LATER, WHEN I GET BACK, OK?
CARMEN?

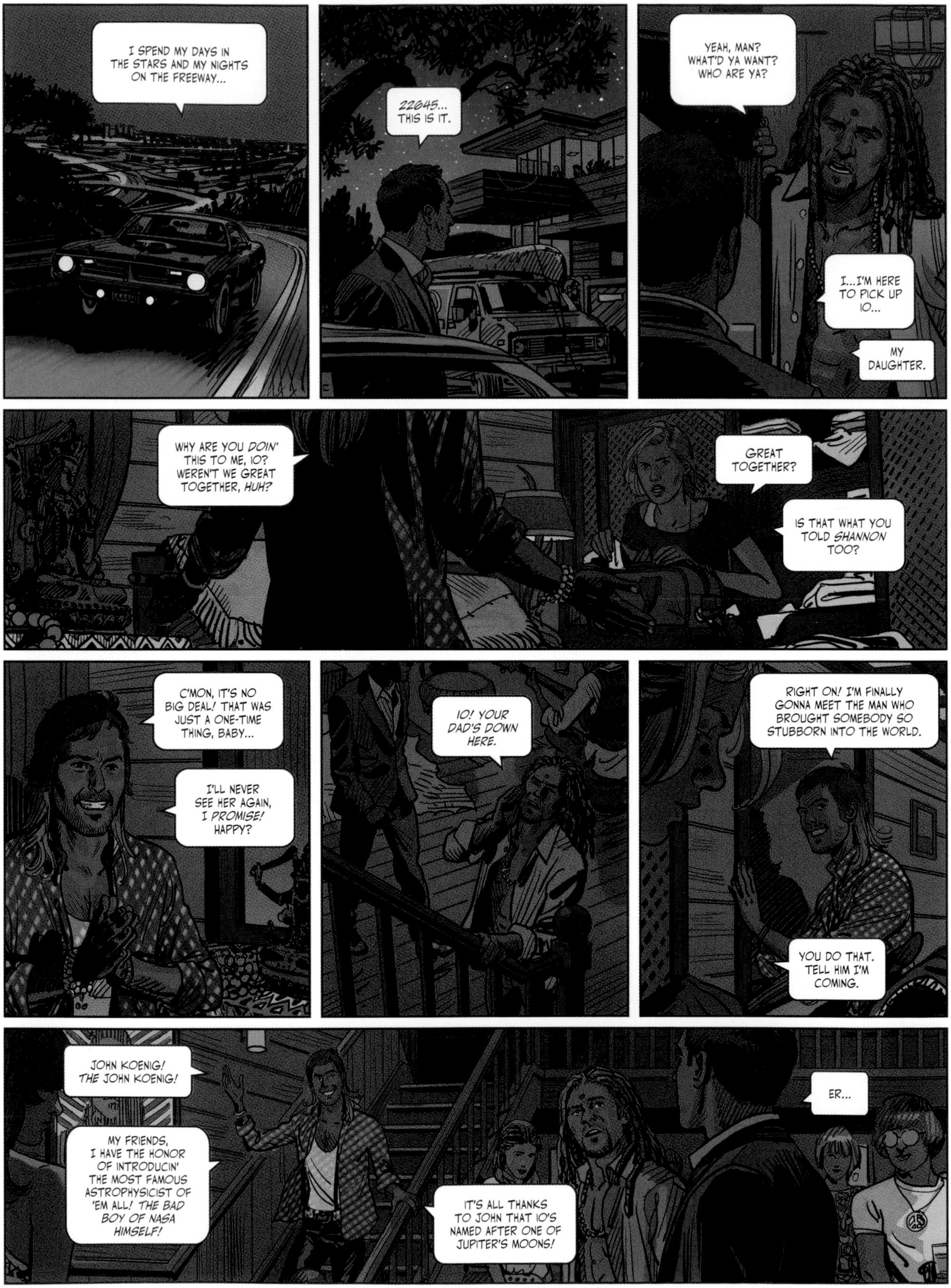
I SPEND MY DAYS IN THE STARS AND MY NIGHTS ON THE FREEWAY...
22645... THIS IS IT.
YEAH, MAN? WHAT'D YA WANT? WHO ARE YA?
I...I'M HERE TO PICK UP IO...
MY DAUGHTER.
WHY ARE YOU *DOIN'* THIS TO ME, IO? WEREN'T WE GREAT TOGETHER, *HUH?*
GREAT TOGETHER?
IS THAT WHAT YOU TOLD *SHANNON* TOO?
C'MON, IT'S NO BIG DEAL! THAT WAS JUST A ONE-TIME THING, BABY...
I'LL NEVER SEE HER AGAIN, *I PROMISE!* HAPPY?
IO! YOUR DAD'S DOWN HERE.
RIGHT ON! I'M FINALLY GONNA MEET THE MAN WHO BROUGHT SOMEBODY SO STUBBORN INTO THE WORLD.
YOU DO THAT. TELL HIM I'M COMING.
JOHN KOENIG! THE JOHN KOENIG!
MY FRIENDS, I HAVE THE HONOR OF INTRODUCIN' THE MOST FAMOUS ASTROPHYSICIST OF 'EM ALL! *THE BAD BOY OF NASA HIMSELF!*
ER...
IT'S ALL THANKS TO JOHN THAT IO'S NAMED AFTER ONE OF JUPITER'S MOONS!

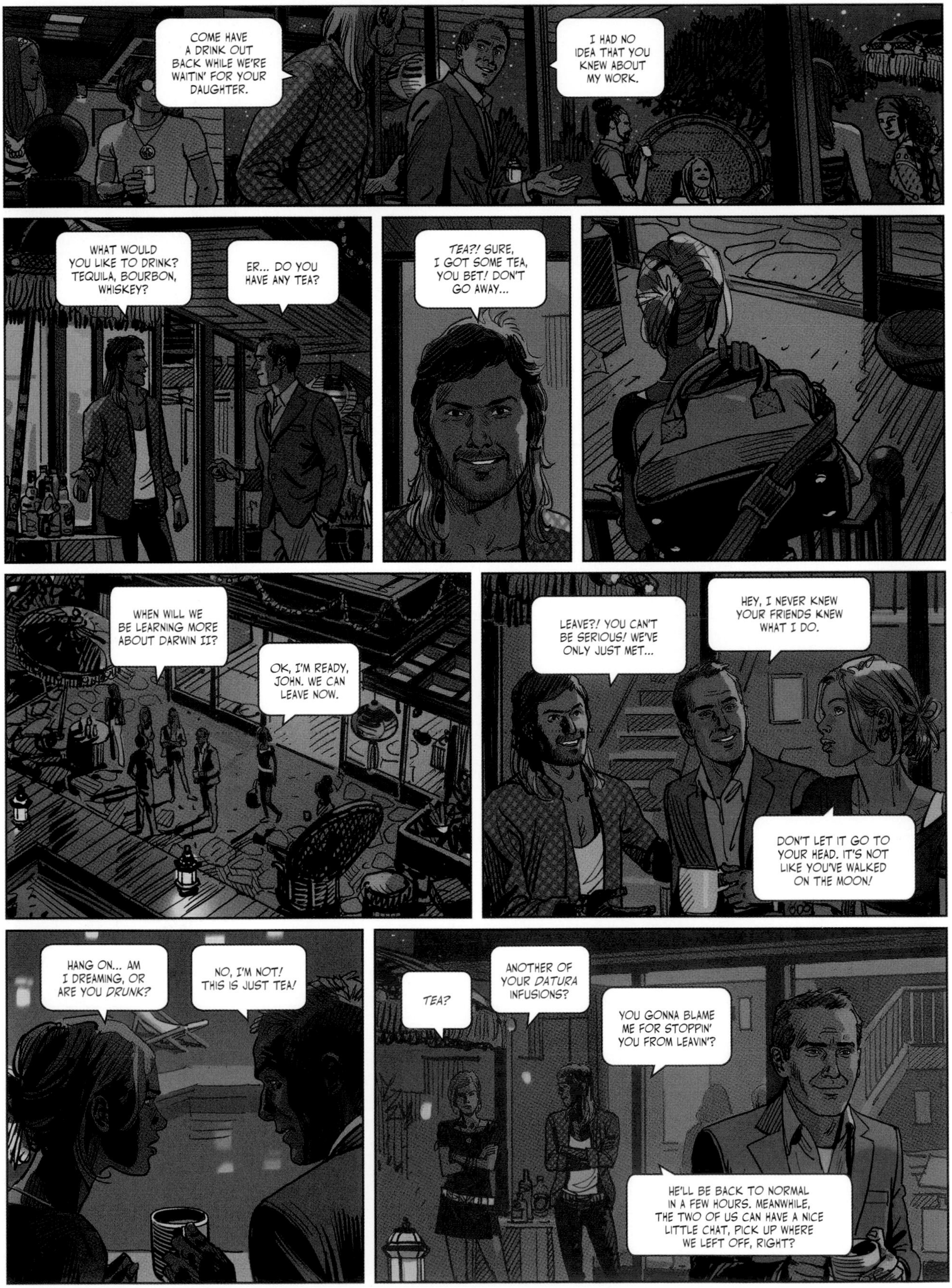
COME HAVE A DRINK OUT BACK WHILE WE'RE WAITIN' FOR YOUR DAUGHTER.
I HAD NO IDEA THAT YOU KNEW ABOUT MY WORK.
WHAT WOULD YOU LIKE TO DRINK? TEQUILA, BOURBON, WHISKEY?
ER... DO YOU HAVE ANY TEA?
TEA?! SURE, I GOT SOME TEA, YOU BET! DON'T GO AWAY...
WHEN WILL WE BE LEARNING MORE ABOUT DARWIN II?
OK, I'M READY, JOHN. WE CAN LEAVE NOW.
LEAVE?! YOU CAN'T BE SERIOUS! WE'VE ONLY JUST MET...
HEY, I NEVER KNEW YOUR FRIENDS KNEW WHAT I DO.
DON'T LET IT GO TO YOUR HEAD. IT'S NOT LIKE YOU'VE WALKED ON THE MOON!
HANG ON... AM I DREAMING, OR ARE YOU *DRUNK*?
NO, I'M NOT! THIS IS JUST TEA!
TEA?
ANOTHER OF YOUR *DATURA* INFUSIONS?
YOU GONNA BLAME ME FOR STOPPIN' YOU FROM LEAVIN'?
HE'LL BE BACK TO NORMAL IN A FEW HOURS. MEANWHILE, THE TWO OF US CAN HAVE A NICE LITTLE CHAT, PICK UP WHERE WE LEFT OFF, RIGHT?

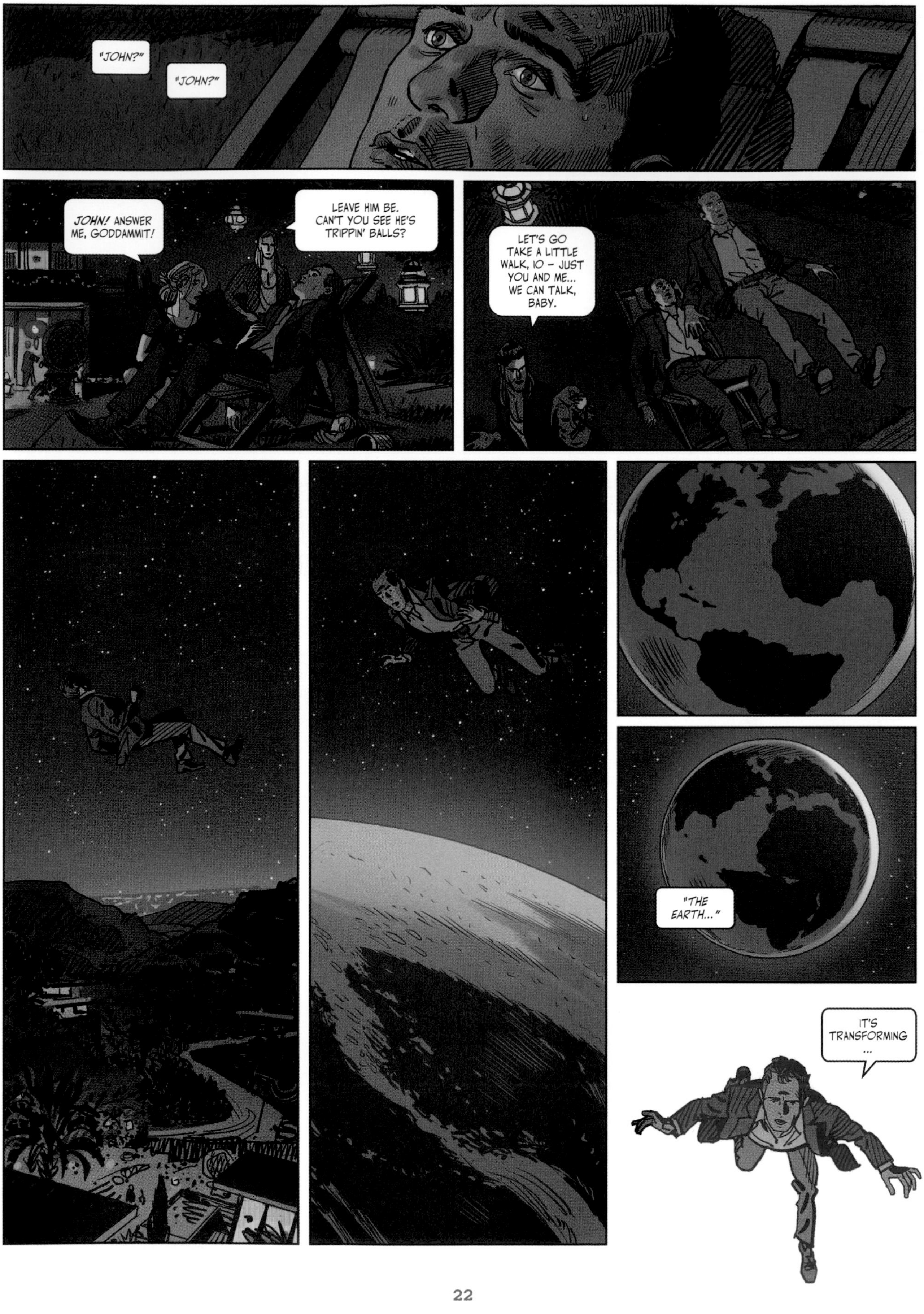
"JOHN?"
"JOHN?"
JOHN! ANSWER ME, GODDAMMIT!
LEAVE HIM BE. CAN'T YOU SEE HE'S TRIPPIN' BALLS?
LET'S GO TAKE A LITTLE WALK, IO – JUST YOU AND ME... WE CAN TALK, BABY.
"THE EARTH..."
IT'S TRANSFORMING ...

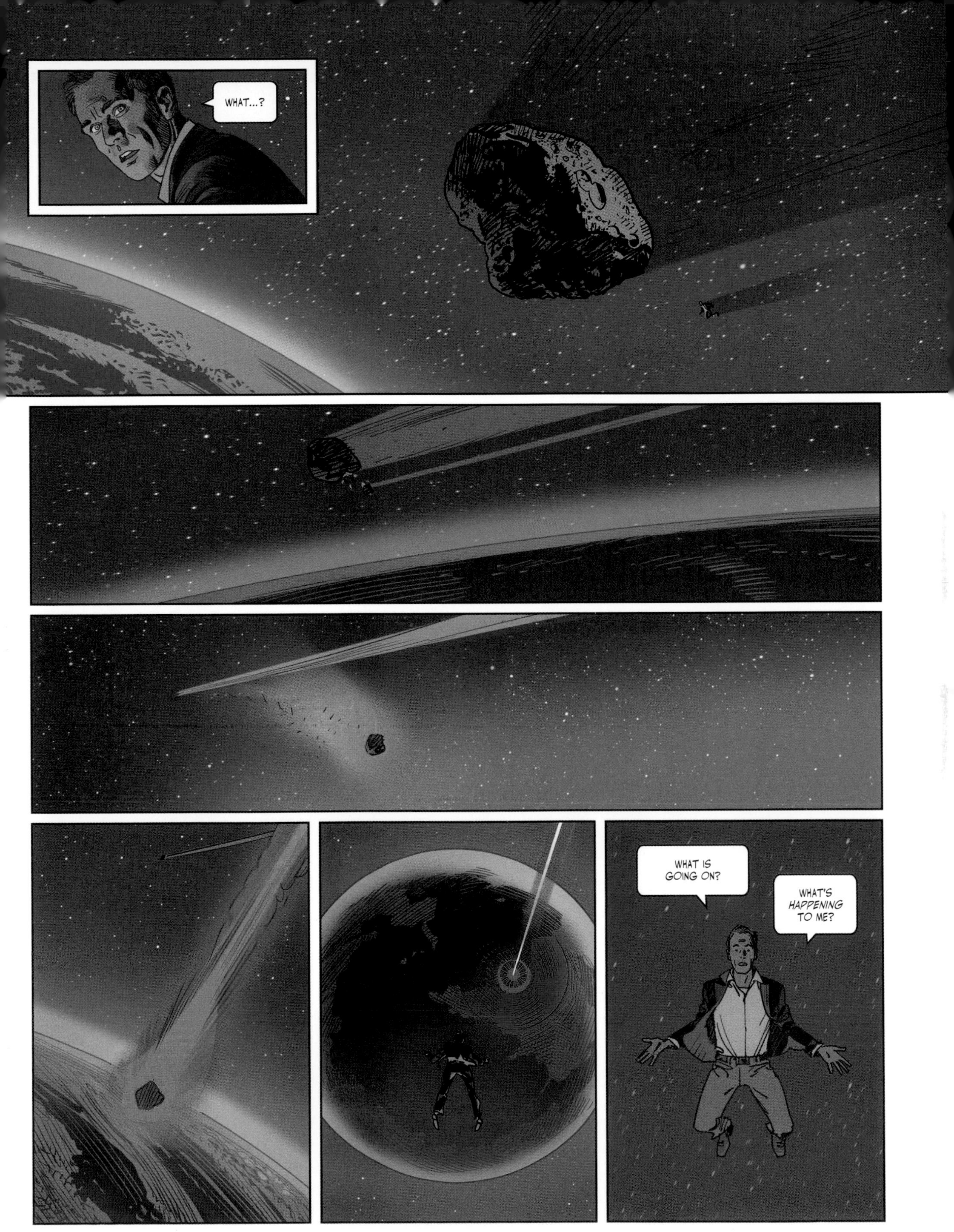
WHAT...?
WHAT IS GOING ON?
WHAT'S HAPPENING TO ME?

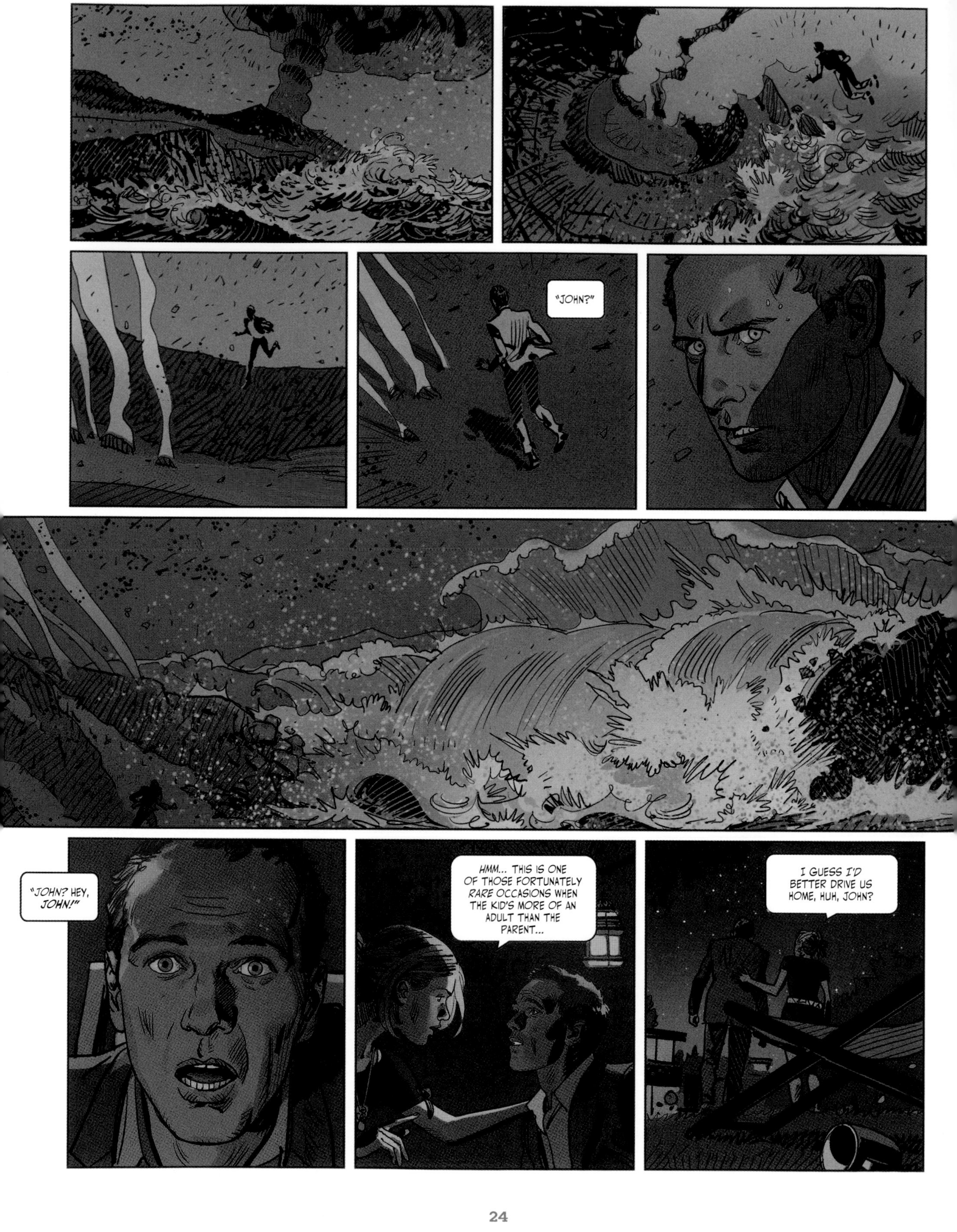

"JOHN?"
"JOHN? HEY, JOHN!"
HMM... THIS IS ONE OF THOSE FORTUNATELY RARE OCCASIONS WHEN THE KID'S MORE OF AN ADULT THAN THE PARENT...
I GUESS I'D BETTER DRIVE US HOME, HUH, JOHN?

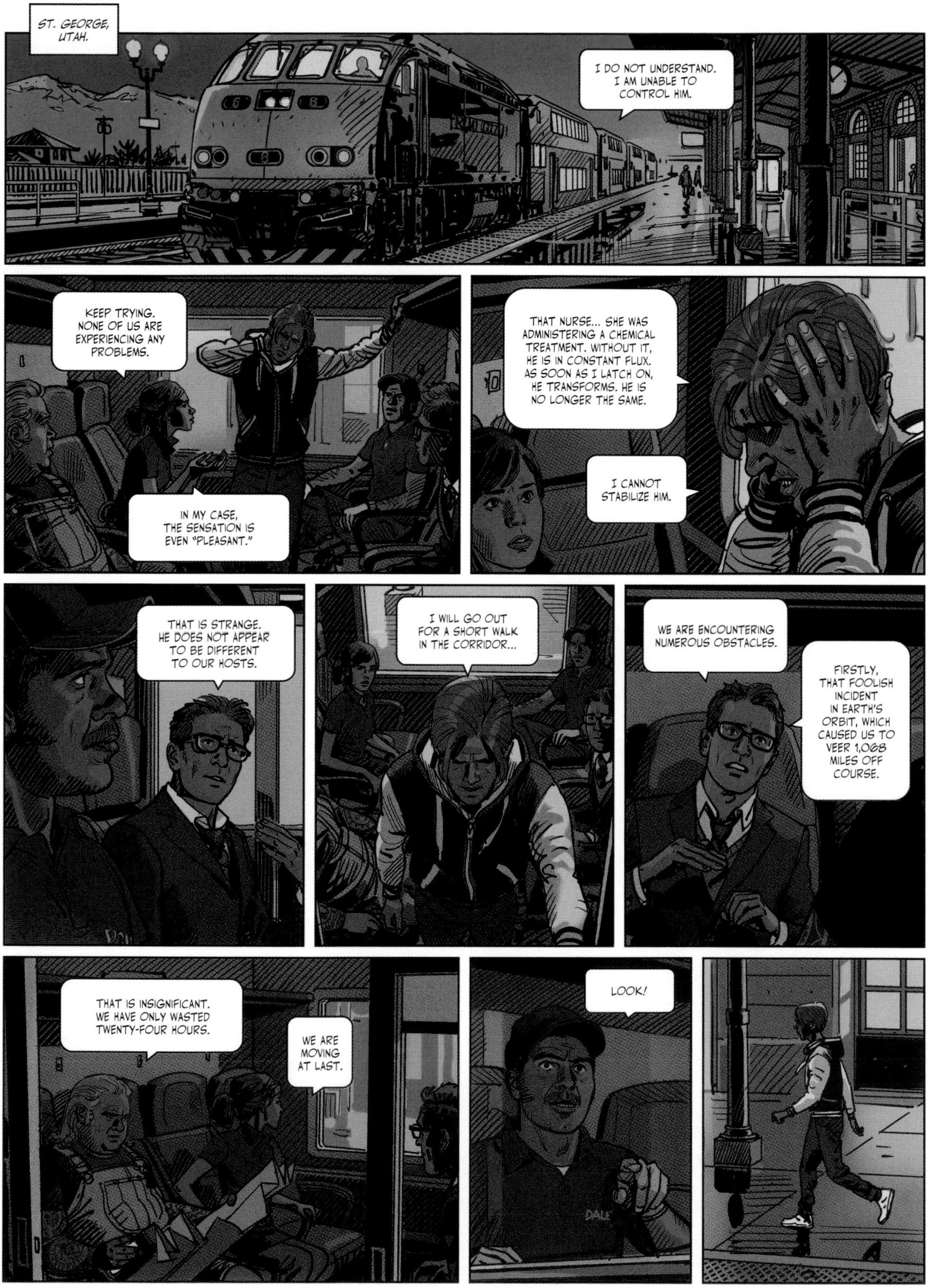
ST. GEORGE, UTAH.
I DO NOT UNDERSTAND. I AM UNABLE TO CONTROL HIM.
KEEP TRYING. NONE OF US ARE EXPERIENCING ANY PROBLEMS.
IN MY CASE, THE SENSATION IS EVEN "PLEASANT."
THAT NURSE... SHE WAS ADMINISTERING A CHEMICAL TREATMENT. WITHOUT IT, HE IS IN CONSTANT FLUX. AS SOON AS I LATCH ON, HE TRANSFORMS. HE IS NO LONGER THE SAME.
I CANNOT STABILIZE HIM.
THAT IS STRANGE. HE DOES NOT APPEAR TO BE DIFFERENT TO OUR HOSTS.
I WILL GO OUT FOR A SHORT WALK IN THE CORRIDOR...
WE ARE ENCOUNTERING NUMEROUS OBSTACLES.
FIRSTLY, THAT FOOLISH INCIDENT IN EARTH'S ORBIT, WHICH CAUSED US TO VEER 1,068 MILES OFF COURSE.
THAT IS INSIGNIFICANT. WE HAVE ONLY WASTED TWENTY-FOUR HOURS.
WE ARE MOVING AT LAST.
LOOK!
DALE

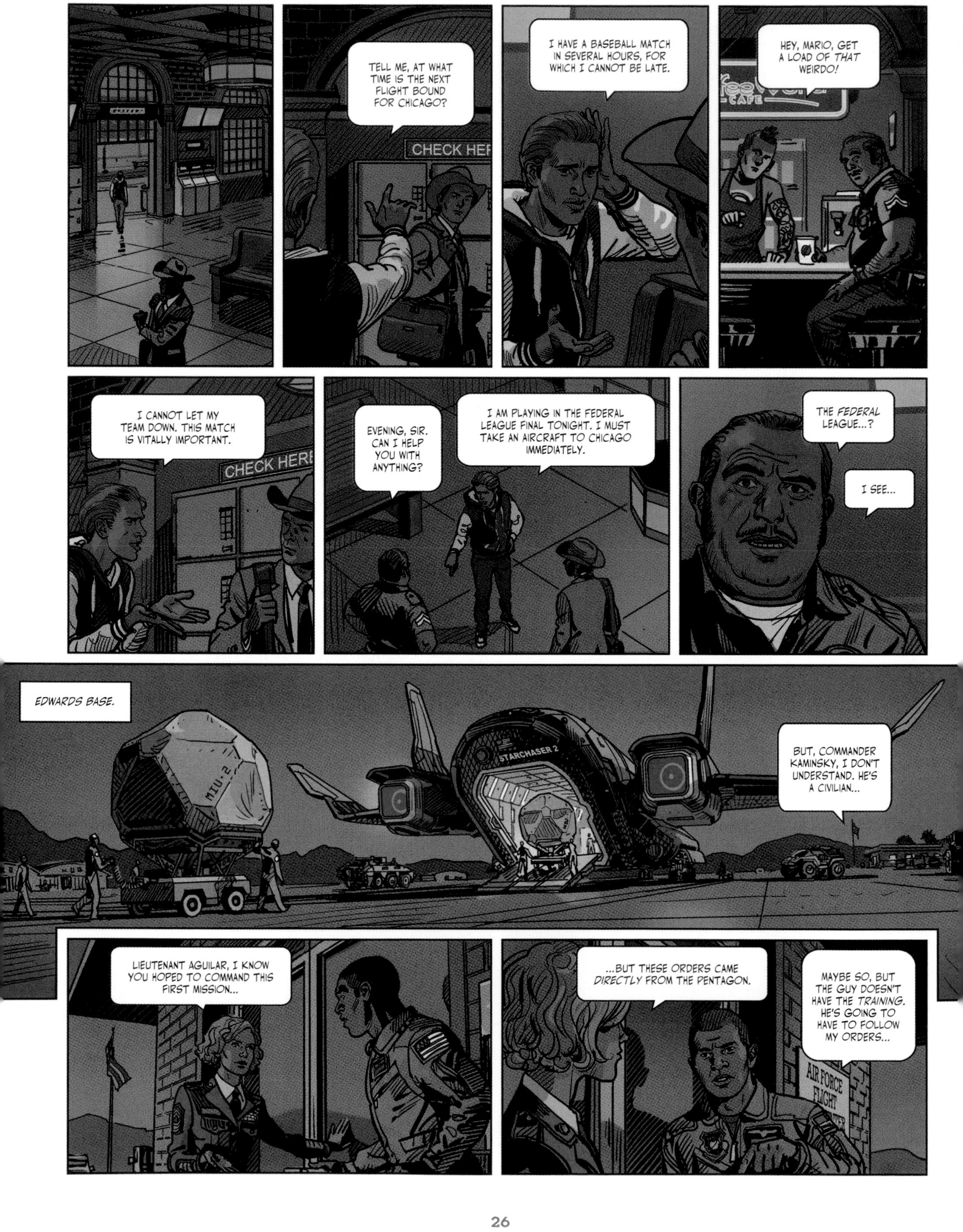
TELL ME, AT WHAT TIME IS THE NEXT FLIGHT BOUND FOR CHICAGO?
CHECK HERE
I HAVE A BASEBALL MATCH IN SEVERAL HOURS, FOR WHICH I CANNOT BE LATE.
HEY, MARIO, GET A LOAD OF *THAT* WEIRDO!
CAFE
I CANNOT LET MY TEAM DOWN. THIS MATCH IS VITALLY IMPORTANT.
CHECK HERE
EVENING, SIR. CAN I HELP YOU WITH ANYTHING?
I AM PLAYING IN THE FEDERAL LEAGUE FINAL TONIGHT. I MUST TAKE AN AIRCRAFT TO CHICAGO IMMEDIATELY.
THE *FEDERAL* LEAGUE...?
I SEE...
EDWARDS BASE.
MIU-2
STARCHASER 2
BUT, COMMANDER KAMINSKY, I DON'T UNDERSTAND. HE'S A CIVILIAN...
LIEUTENANT AGUILAR, I KNOW YOU HOPED TO COMMAND THIS FIRST MISSION...
...BUT THESE ORDERS CAME *DIRECTLY* FROM THE PENTAGON.
MAYBE SO, BUT THE GUY DOESN'T HAVE THE *TRAINING*. HE'S GOING TO HAVE TO FOLLOW MY ORDERS...
AIR FORCE FLIGHT

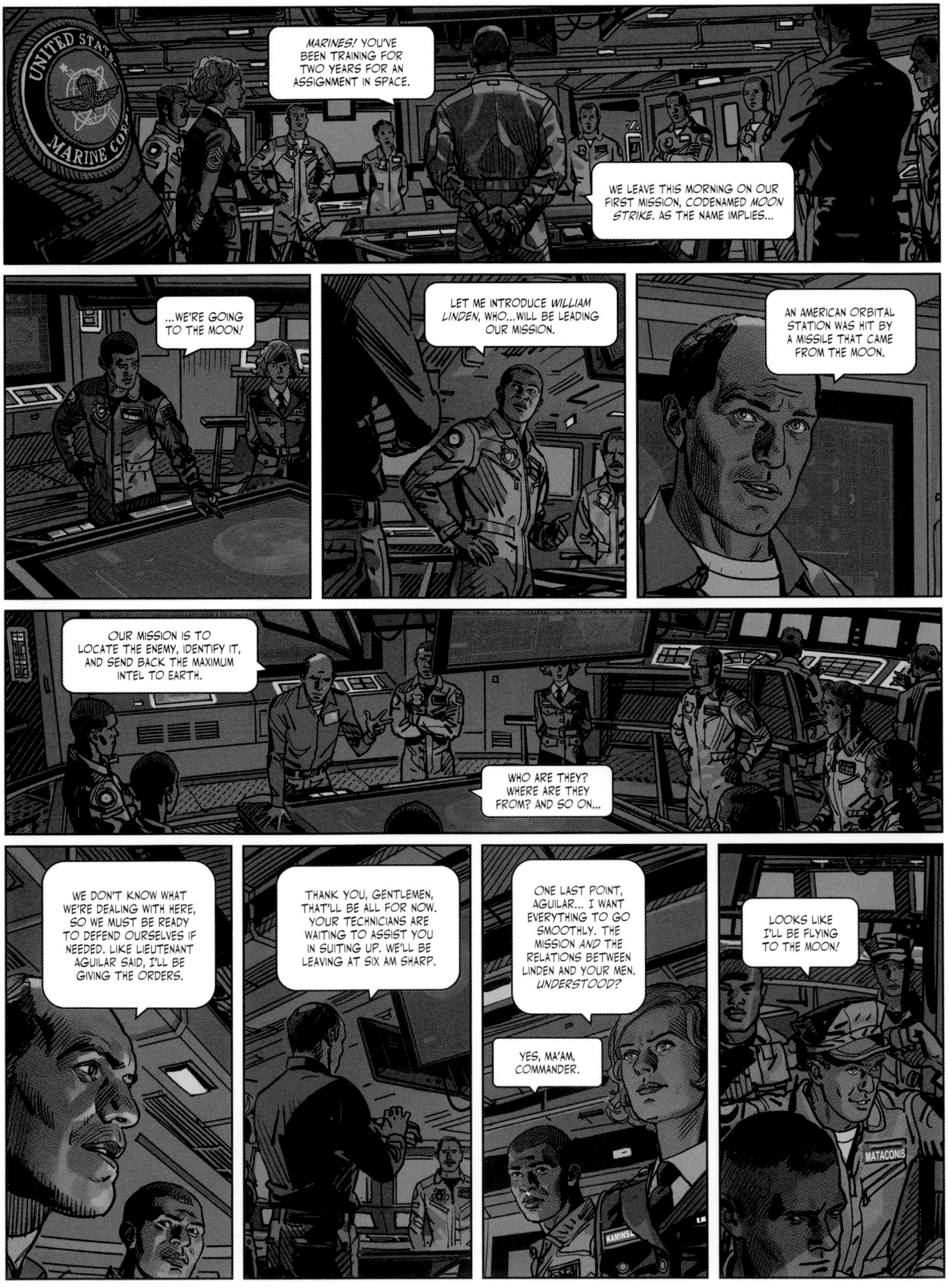
UNITED STATES MARINE CORPS
MARINES! YOU'VE BEEN TRAINING FOR TWO YEARS FOR AN ASSIGNMENT IN SPACE.
WE LEAVE THIS MORNING ON OUR FIRST MISSION, CODENAMED *MOON STRIKE*. AS THE NAME IMPLIES...
...WE'RE GOING TO THE MOON!
LET ME INTRODUCE *WILLIAM LINDEN*, WHO...WILL BE LEADING OUR MISSION.
AN AMERICAN ORBITAL STATION WAS HIT BY A MISSILE THAT CAME FROM THE MOON.
OUR MISSION IS TO LOCATE THE ENEMY, IDENTIFY IT, AND SEND BACK THE MAXIMUM INTEL TO EARTH.
WHO ARE THEY? WHERE ARE THEY FROM? AND SO ON...
WE DON'T KNOW WHAT WE'RE DEALING WITH HERE, SO WE MUST BE READY TO DEFEND OURSELVES IF NEEDED. LIKE LIEUTENANT AGUILAR SAID, I'LL BE GIVING THE ORDERS.
THANK YOU, GENTLEMEN, THAT'LL BE ALL FOR NOW. YOUR TECHNICIANS ARE WAITING TO ASSIST YOU IN SUITING UP. WE'LL BE LEAVING AT SIX AM SHARP.
ONE LAST POINT, AGUILAR... I WANT EVERYTHING TO GO SMOOTHLY. THE MISSION *AND* THE RELATIONS BETWEEN LINDEN AND YOUR MEN. *UNDERSTOOD?*
YES, MA'AM, COMMANDER.
KAMINSKI
LOOKS LIKE I'LL BE FLYING TO THE MOON!
MATACONIS

QUIT FEEDING ME THE SAME LINE! THE FEDERAL LEAGUE COLLAPSED BACK IN 1915!

WHO ARE YOU?

MARIO?

WE HAVE AN ID: *CHARLES WEBSTER*, PATIENT AT A PSYCHIATRIC HOSPITAL IN FORT COLLINS, COLORADO.

HE ESCAPED... WITH A HOSTAGE. A NURSE.

JEEZ, MARIO, YOU REALLY WORKED THE GUY OVER! DIDN'T I TELL YOU TO TAKE IT EASY?

WHAT? I NEVER *TOUCHED* HIM! HE BANGED HIS OWN HEAD WHILE HE WAS SQUIRMING AROUND...

AND HE'S BEEN BLEEDING LIKE THAT FOR AN HOUR.

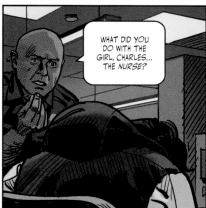

WHAT DID YOU DO WITH THE GIRL, CHARLES... THE *NURSE*?

I DO NOT NEED THE NURSE. I NEED TO TAKE AN AIRCRAFT.

OK. MENTAL CASE. NOSEBLEED... SEND HIM BACK TO COLORADO. THEY'LL KNOW WHAT TO DO.

UNION STATION, LOS ANGELES.

TRACK

28

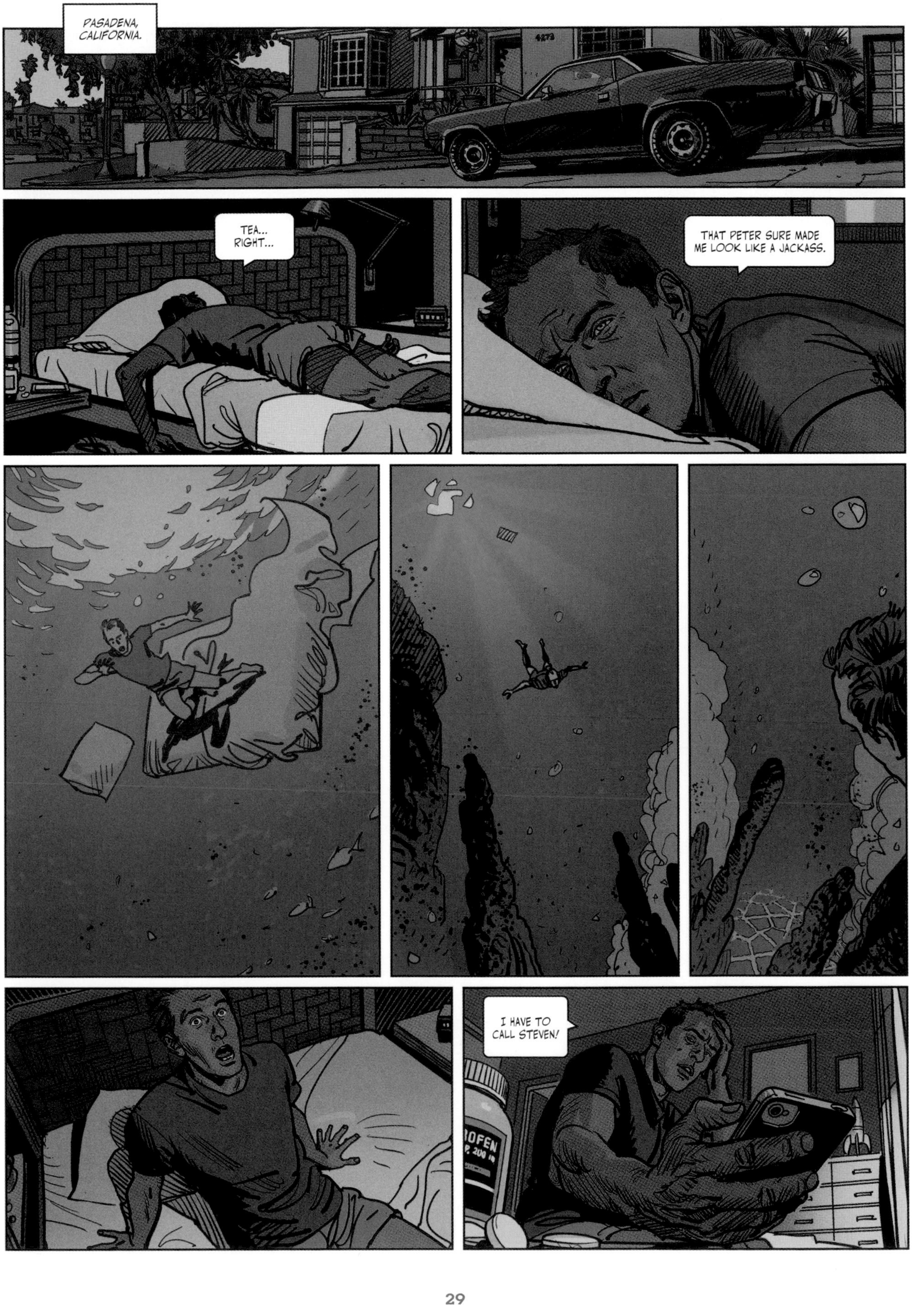
PASADENA, CALIFORNIA.
TEA... RIGHT...
THAT PETER SURE MADE ME LOOK LIKE A JACKASS.
I HAVE TO CALL STEVEN!

JOHN...I SEE NO REAL CAUSE FOR CONCERN. YOU HAD YOUR MEDICAL YESTERDAY, REMEMBER? I PUT YOU DOWN AS "FIT FOR SERVICE."

YES... I KNOW, BUT I--

YOU'RE EXHAUSTING YOURSELF! YOU'RE LIVING IN THE STARS. COME BACK DOWN TO EARTH, MAN.

NOW, FOLLOW MY EXAMPLE AND TRY TO MAKE THE MOST OF THE FEW...ER...MINUTES OF SLEEP YOU STILL HAVE LEFT BEFORE YOU HAVE TO GO TO WORK, AGREED?

WHAT IS THE MATTER WITH ME?

DING DONG

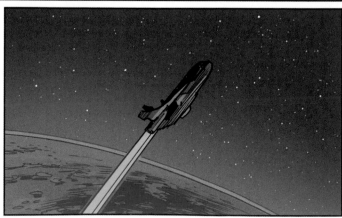

OK, MARINES, GET TO WORK!

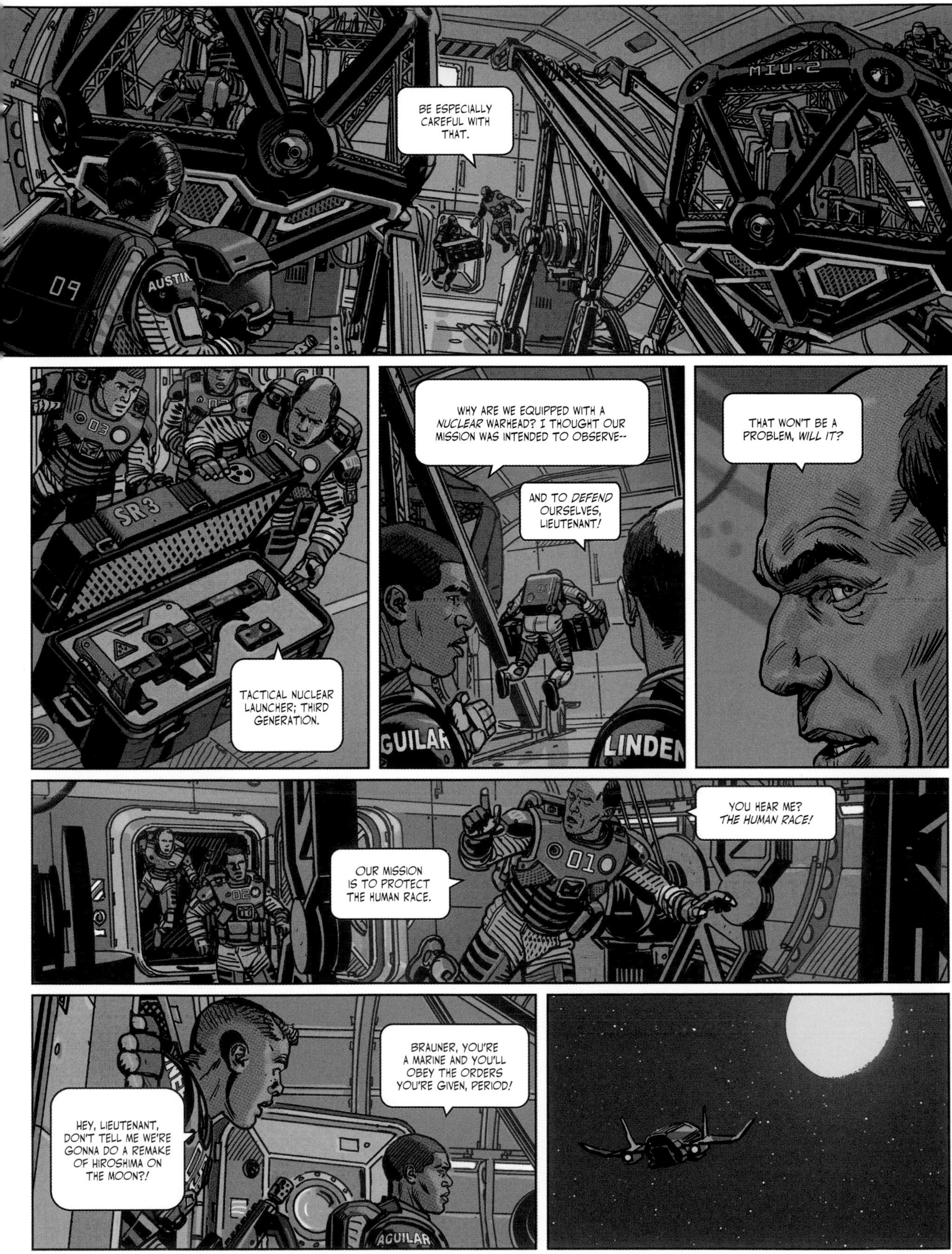

MIU-2
BE ESPECIALLY CAREFUL WITH THAT.
09
AUSTIN
SR 3
TACTICAL NUCLEAR LAUNCHER; THIRD GENERATION.
WHY ARE WE EQUIPPED WITH A *NUCLEAR* WARHEAD? I THOUGHT OUR MISSION WAS INTENDED TO OBSERVE--
AND TO *DEFEND* OURSELVES, LIEUTENANT!
GUILAR
LINDEN
THAT WON'T BE A PROBLEM, *WILL IT?*
OUR MISSION IS TO PROTECT THE HUMAN RACE.
YOU HEAR ME? *THE HUMAN RACE!*
01
BRAUNER, YOU'RE A MARINE AND YOU'LL OBEY THE ORDERS YOU'RE GIVEN, PERIOD!
HEY, LIEUTENANT, DON'T TELL ME WE'RE GONNA DO A REMAKE OF HIROSHIMA ON THE MOON?!
AGUILAR

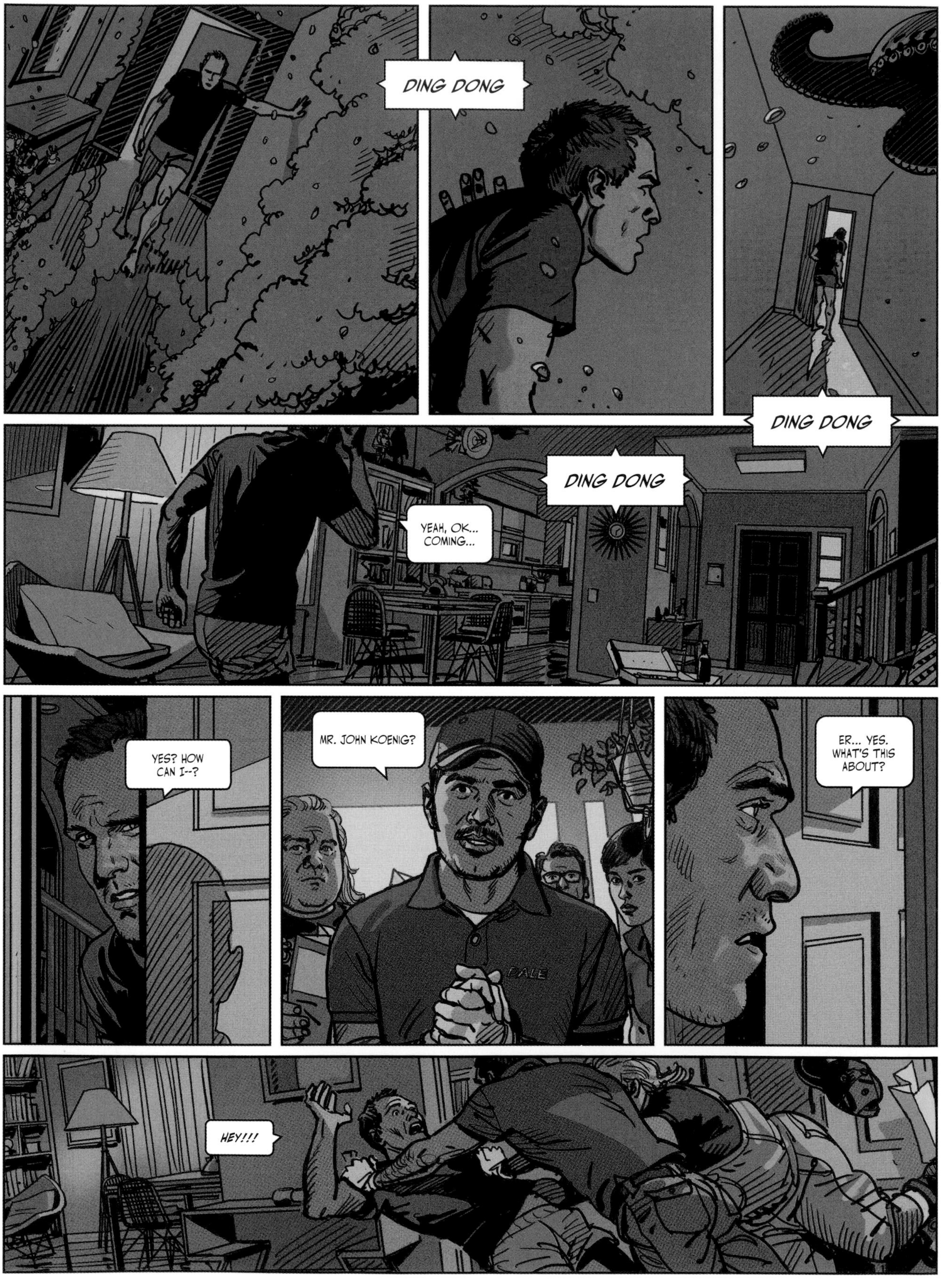
DING DONG
DING DONG
DING DONG
YEAH, OK... COMING...
YES? HOW CAN I--?
MR. JOHN KOENIG?
ER... YES. WHAT'S THIS ABOUT?
HEY!!!

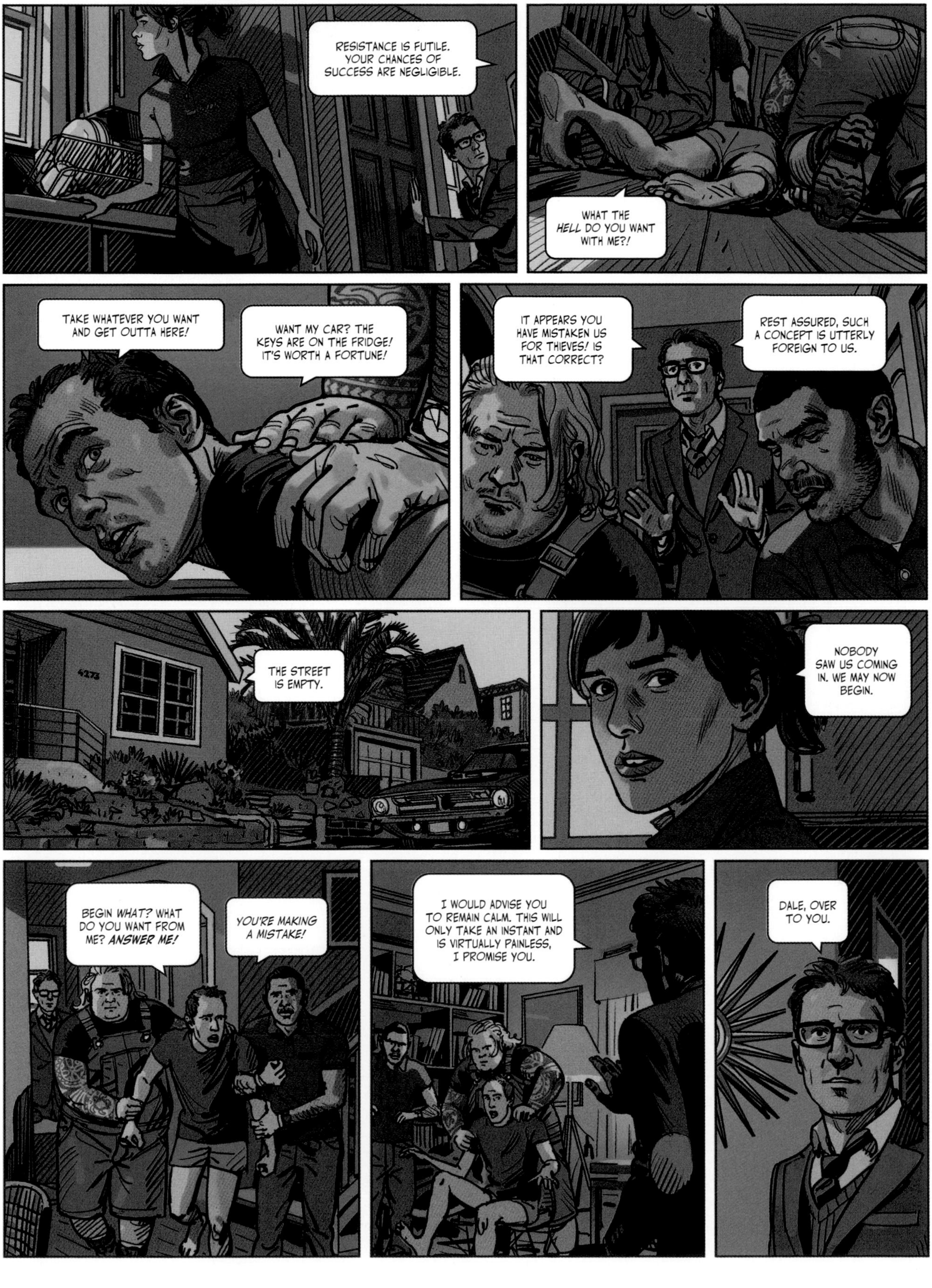
RESISTANCE IS FUTILE. YOUR CHANCES OF SUCCESS ARE NEGLIGIBLE.
WHAT THE *HELL* DO YOU WANT WITH ME?!
TAKE WHATEVER YOU WANT AND GET OUTTA HERE!
WANT MY CAR? THE KEYS ARE ON THE FRIDGE! IT'S WORTH A FORTUNE!
IT APPEARS YOU HAVE MISTAKEN US FOR THIEVES! IS THAT CORRECT?
REST ASSURED, SUCH A CONCEPT IS UTTERLY FOREIGN TO US.
4273
THE STREET IS EMPTY.
NOBODY SAW US COMING IN. WE MAY NOW BEGIN.
BEGIN *WHAT*? WHAT DO YOU WANT FROM ME? ***ANSWER ME!***
YOU'RE MAKING A MISTAKE!
I WOULD ADVISE YOU TO REMAIN CALM. THIS WILL ONLY TAKE AN INSTANT AND IS VIRTUALLY PAINLESS, I PROMISE YOU.
DALE, OVER TO YOU.

WHAT DO YOU WANT FROM ME, YOU BUNCH OF FREAKS?!

HUUUU...

OH, SHIT! OH, SHIT...

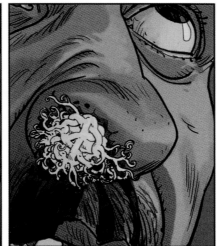

WHAT'S GOING ON IN HERE?

DALE?

HUUURRR...

DALE?!

DALE IS DECEASED. THE TRANSFER FAILED.

MIU 1, SALMA? THIS IS MIU 2, ALVARO. PREPARING TO BEGIN COUNTDOWN. ALL CLEAR?

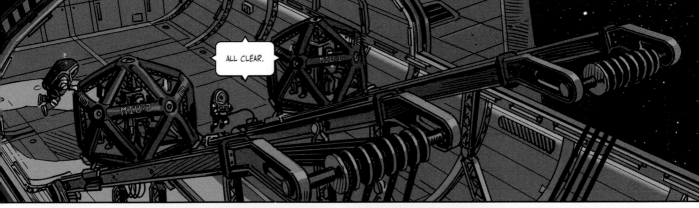

ALL CLEAR.

THE RETROROCKETS WILL ONLY FIRE FOR A 12-SECOND BURN AT 900 FEET ALTITUDE. THE LANDING MAY BE A LITTLE ROUGH...

UNDERSTOOD. READY FOR LAUNCH.

AND REMINDER — NO RADIO COMMUNICATIONS BEFORE LANDING. IF YOU NEED TO TALK TO EACH OTHER, USE THE INTERCOM.

I'LL SEE YOU ALL ON THE MOON!

GOOD LUCK, GUYS!

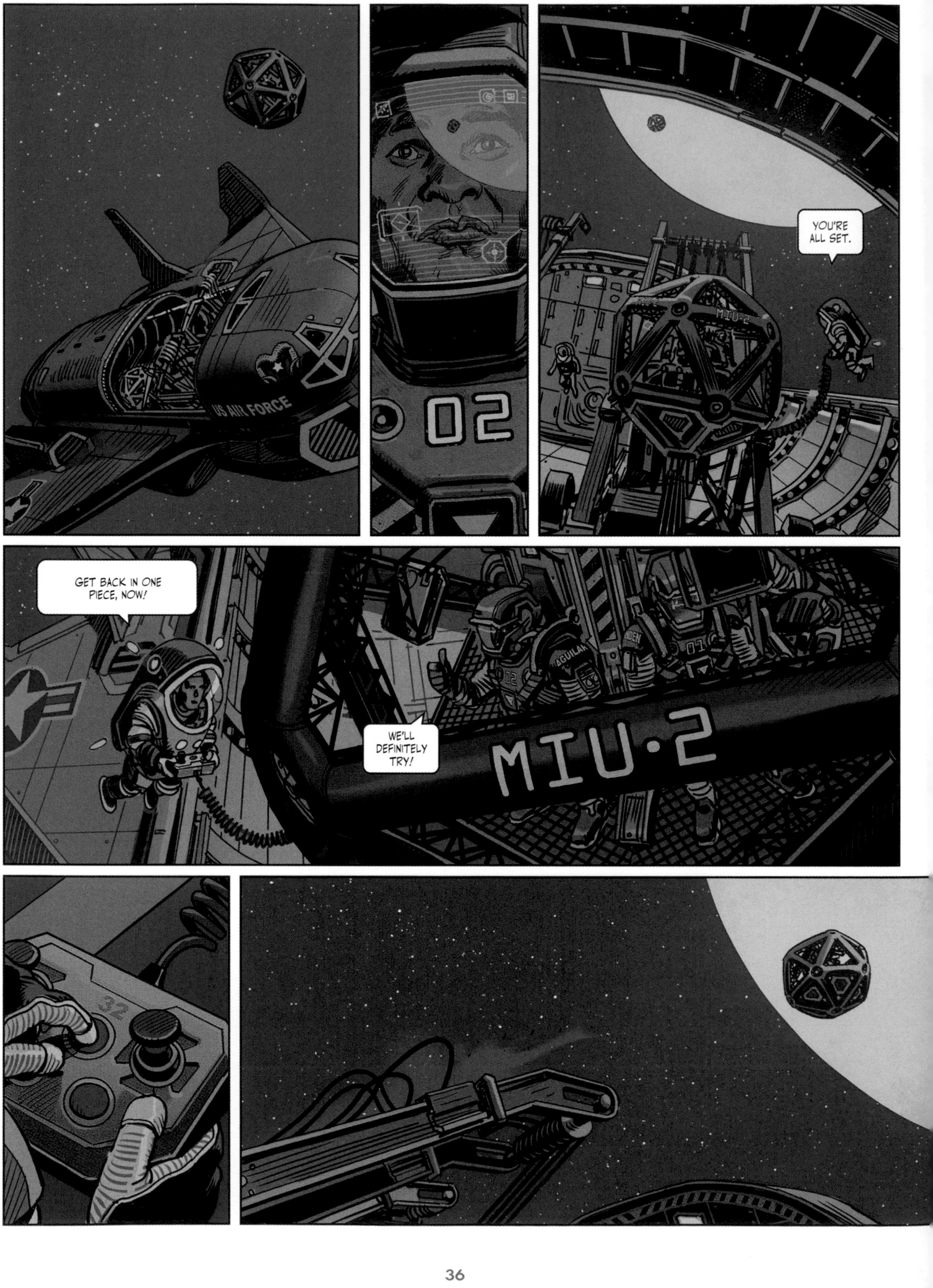
US AIR FORCE
02
YOU'RE ALL SET.
MIU-2
GET BACK IN ONE PIECE, NOW!
WE'LL DEFINITELY TRY!
MIU·2
AGUILAR
02
32

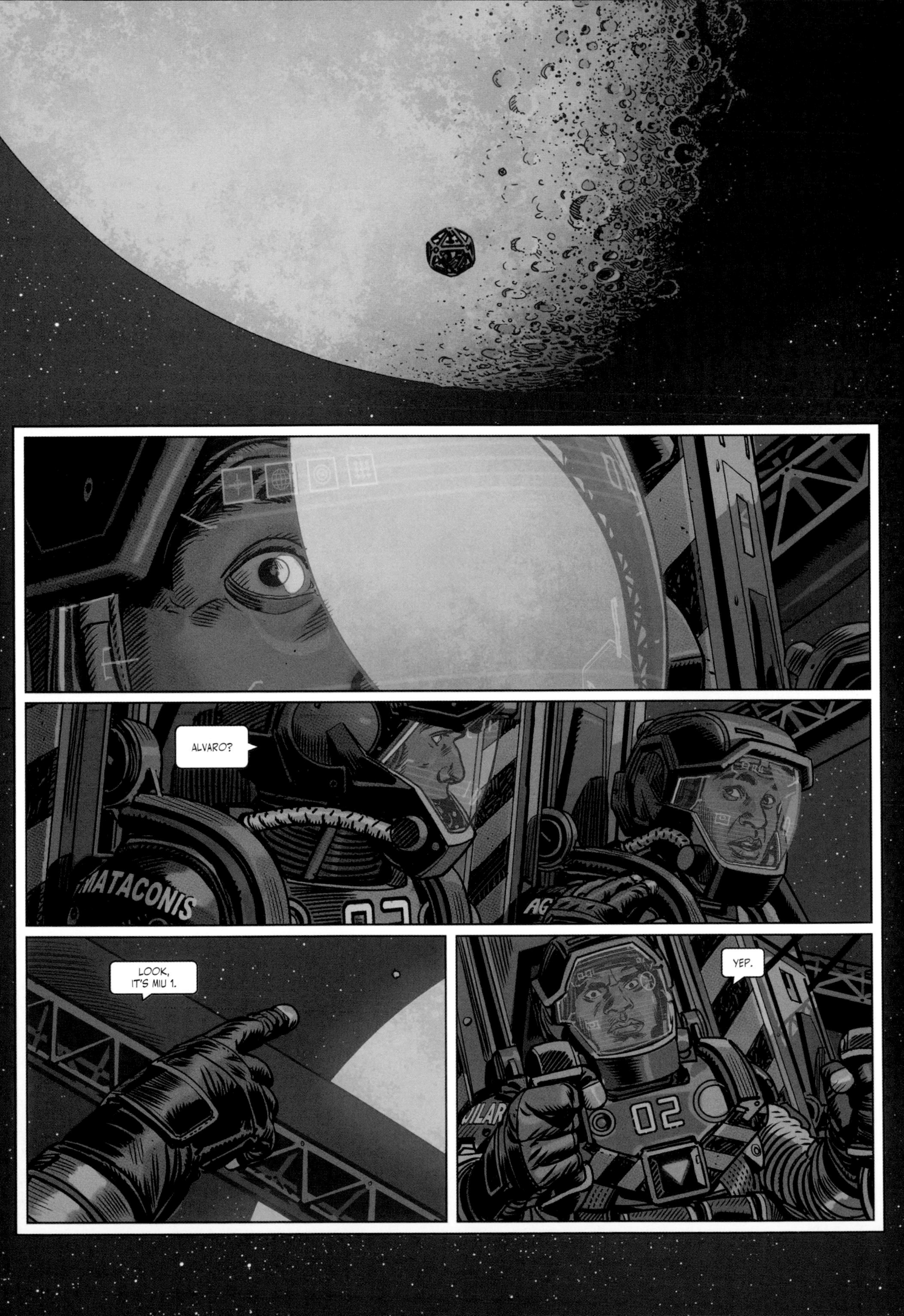
ALVARO?
MATACONIS
07
AG
LOOK, IT'S MIU 1.
YEP.
02

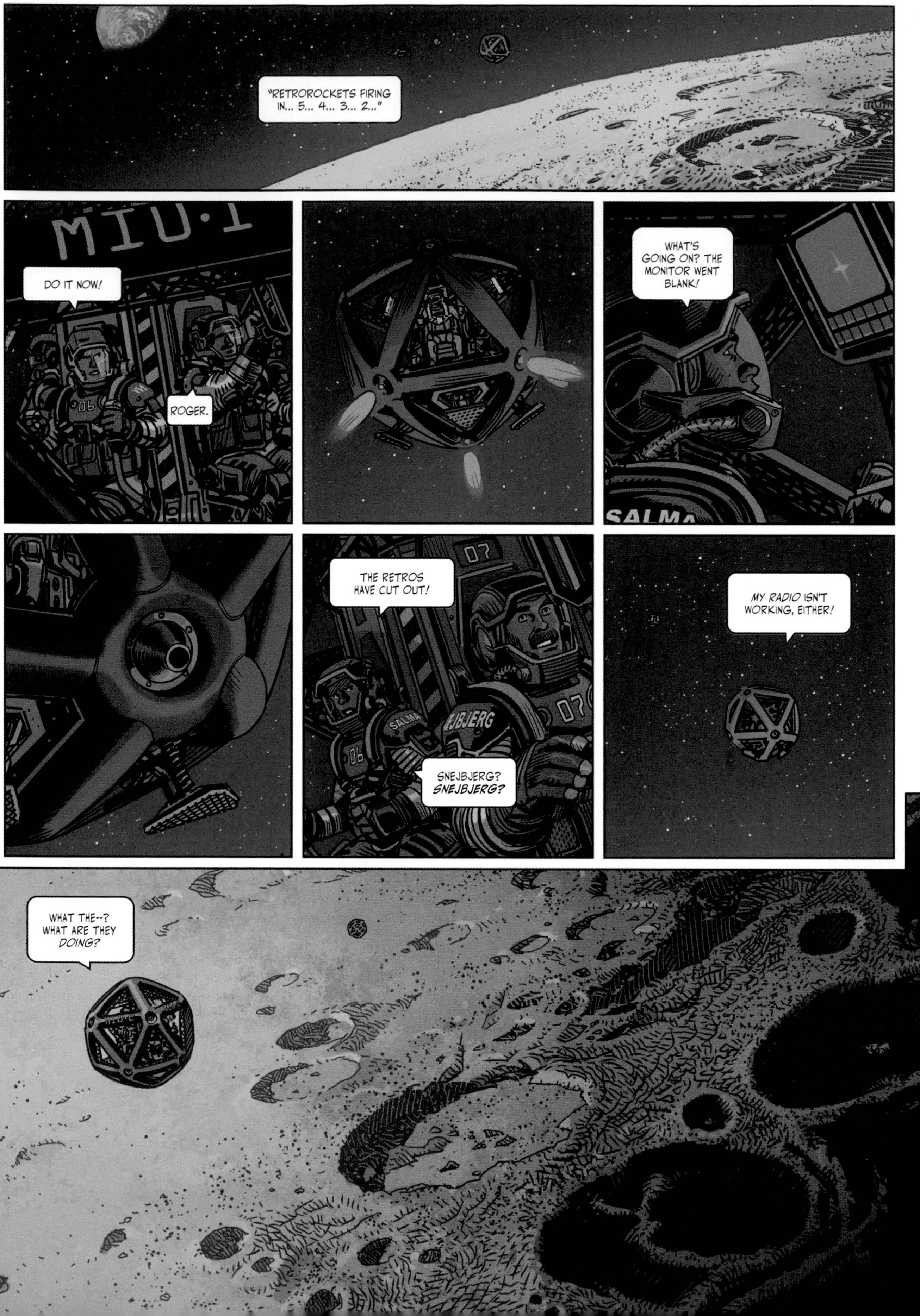
"RETROROCKETS FIRING IN... 5... 4... 3... 2..."
DO IT NOW!
ROGER.
WHAT'S GOING ON? THE MONITOR WENT BLANK!
THE RETROS HAVE CUT OUT!
SNEJBJERG? *SNEJBJERG?*
MY RADIO ISN'T WORKING, EITHER!
WHAT THE--? WHAT ARE THEY *DOING?*

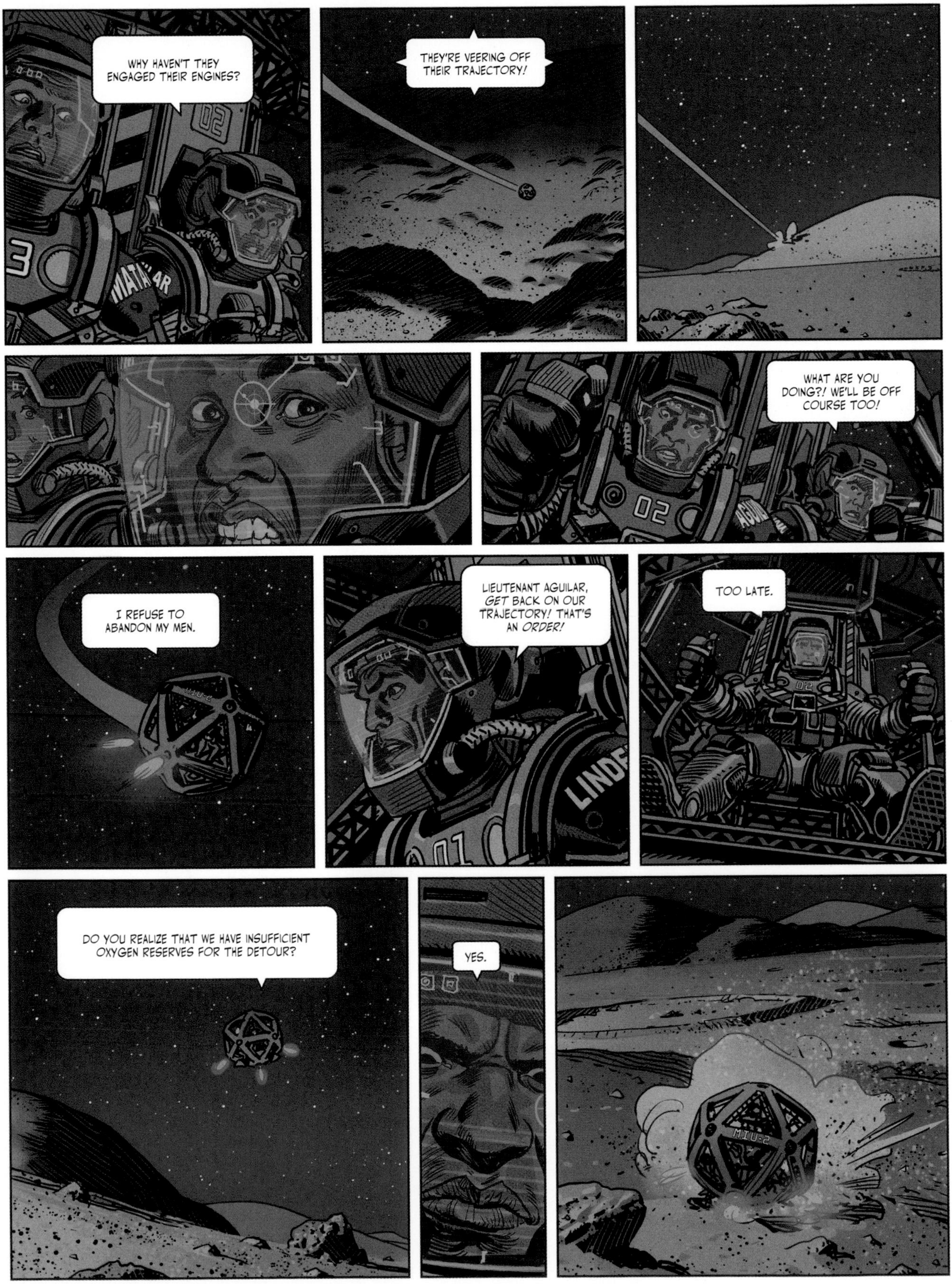
WHY HAVEN'T THEY ENGAGED THEIR ENGINES?
THEY'RE VEERING OFF THEIR TRAJECTORY!
WHAT ARE YOU DOING?! WE'LL BE OFF COURSE TOO!
I REFUSE TO ABANDON MY MEN.
LIEUTENANT AGUILAR, GET BACK ON OUR TRAJECTORY! THAT'S AN ORDER!
TOO LATE.
DO YOU REALIZE THAT WE HAVE INSUFFICIENT OXYGEN RESERVES FOR THE DETOUR?
YES.

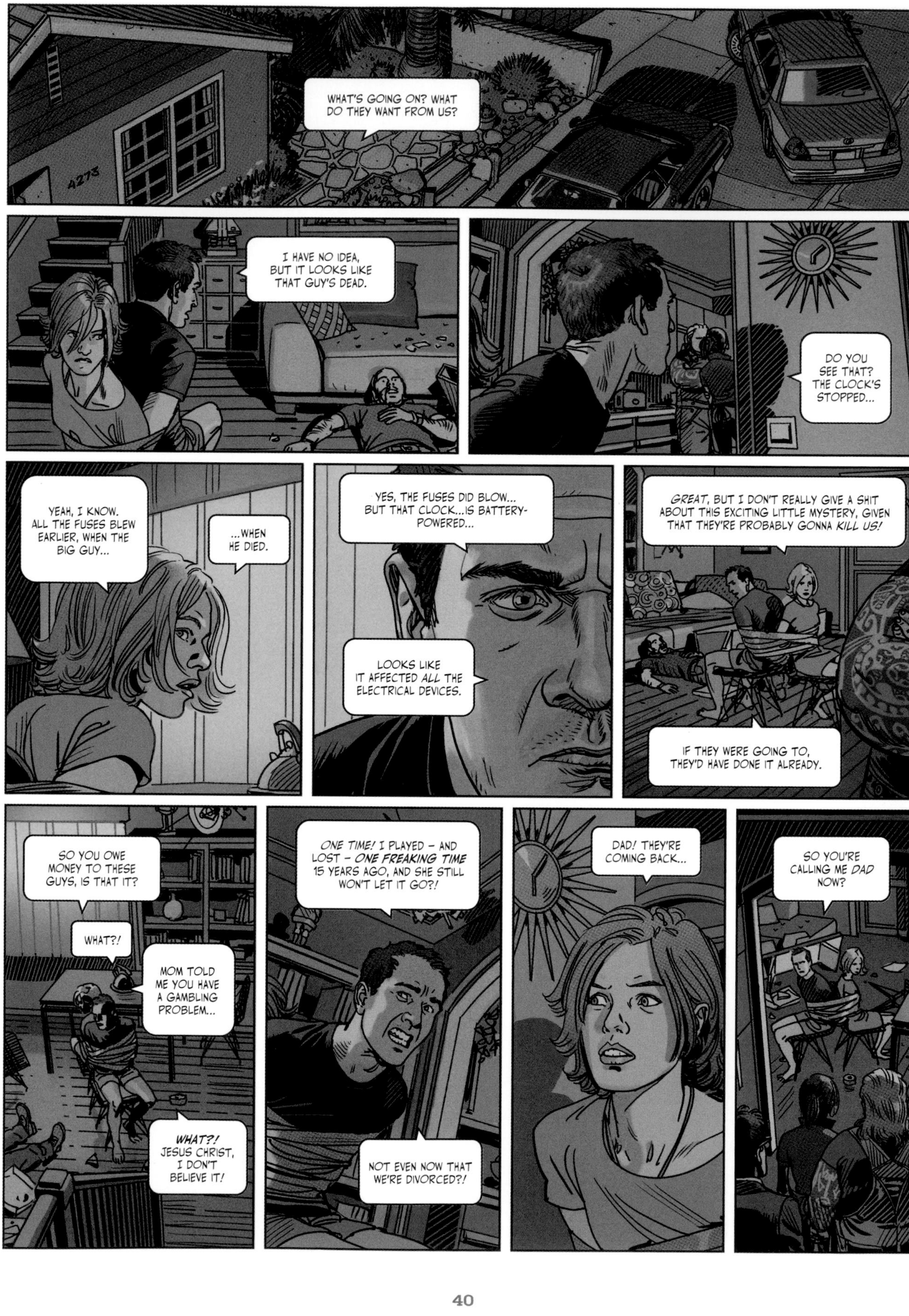

WHAT'S GOING ON? WHAT DO THEY WANT FROM US?
I HAVE NO IDEA, BUT IT LOOKS LIKE THAT GUY'S DEAD.
DO YOU SEE THAT? THE CLOCK'S STOPPED...
YEAH, I KNOW. ALL THE FUSES BLEW EARLIER, WHEN THE BIG GUY...
...WHEN HE DIED.
YES, THE FUSES DID BLOW... BUT THAT CLOCK...IS BATTERY-POWERED...
LOOKS LIKE IT AFFECTED *ALL* THE ELECTRICAL DEVICES.
GREAT, BUT I DON'T REALLY GIVE A SHIT ABOUT THIS EXCITING LITTLE MYSTERY, GIVEN THAT THEY'RE PROBABLY GONNA *KILL US!*
IF THEY WERE GOING TO, THEY'D HAVE DONE IT ALREADY.
SO YOU OWE MONEY TO THESE GUYS, IS THAT IT?
WHAT?!
MOM TOLD ME YOU HAVE A GAMBLING PROBLEM...
WHAT?! JESUS CHRIST, I DON'T BELIEVE IT!
ONE TIME! I PLAYED – AND LOST – ***ONE FREAKING TIME*** 15 YEARS AGO, AND SHE STILL WON'T LET IT GO?!
NOT EVEN NOW THAT WE'RE DIVORCED?!
DAD! THEY'RE COMING BACK...
SO YOU'RE CALLING ME *DAD* NOW?

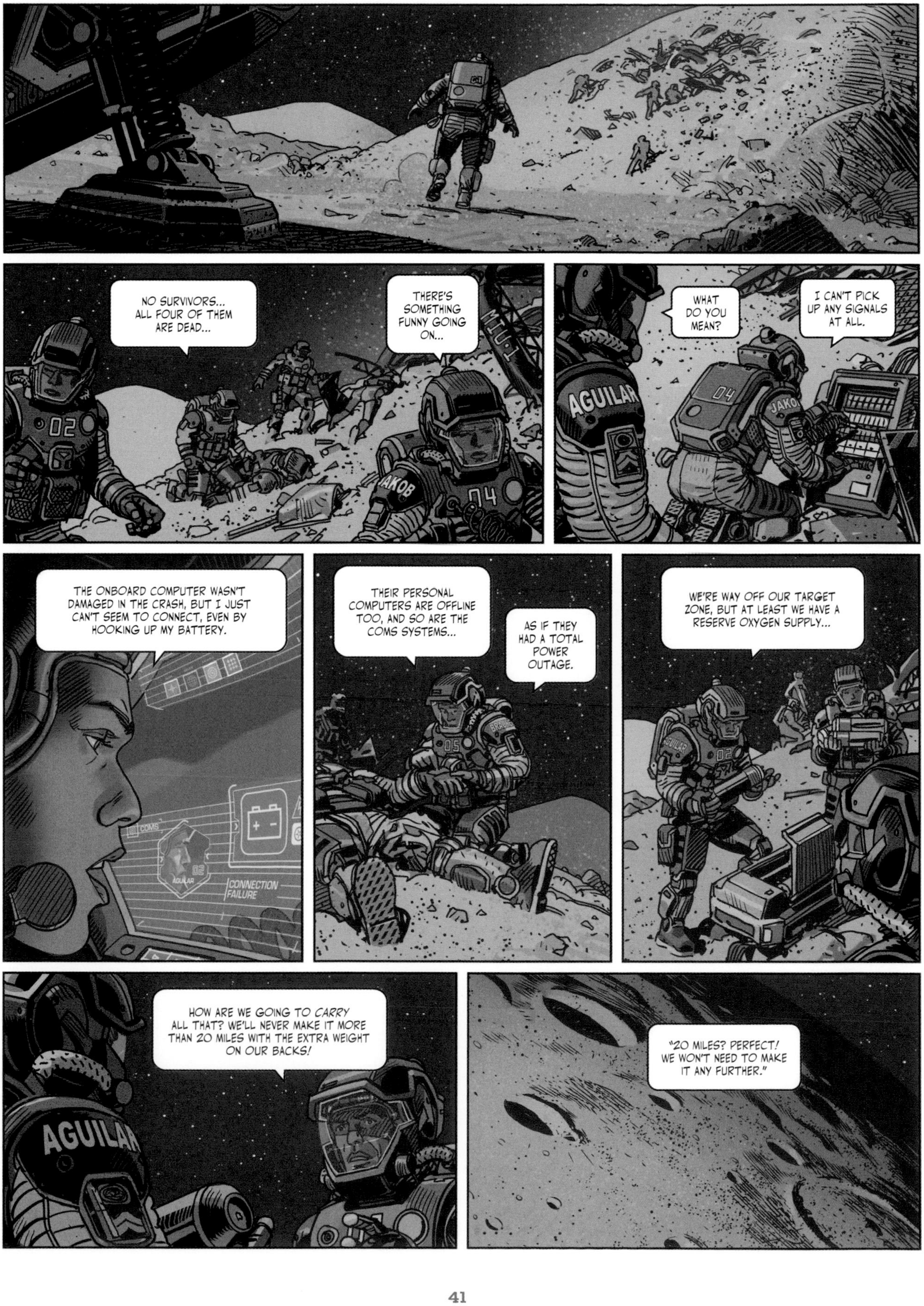

NO SURVIVORS... ALL FOUR OF THEM ARE DEAD...
THERE'S SOMETHING FUNNY GOING ON...
M.I.U.-1
AGUILAR
04
JAKOB
WHAT DO YOU MEAN?
I CAN'T PICK UP ANY SIGNALS AT ALL.
THE ONBOARD COMPUTER WASN'T DAMAGED IN THE CRASH, BUT I JUST CAN'T SEEM TO CONNECT, EVEN BY HOOKING UP MY BATTERY.
COMS
AGUILAR
02
CONNECTION FAILURE
THEIR PERSONAL COMPUTERS ARE OFFLINE TOO, AND SO ARE THE COMS SYSTEMS...
AS IF THEY HAD A TOTAL POWER OUTAGE.
WE'RE WAY OFF OUR TARGET ZONE, BUT AT LEAST WE HAVE A RESERVE OXYGEN SUPPLY...
HOW ARE WE GOING TO *CARRY* ALL THAT? WE'LL NEVER MAKE IT MORE THAN 20 MILES WITH THE EXTRA WEIGHT ON OUR BACKS!
AGUILAR
"20 MILES? PERFECT! WE WON'T NEED TO MAKE IT ANY FURTHER."

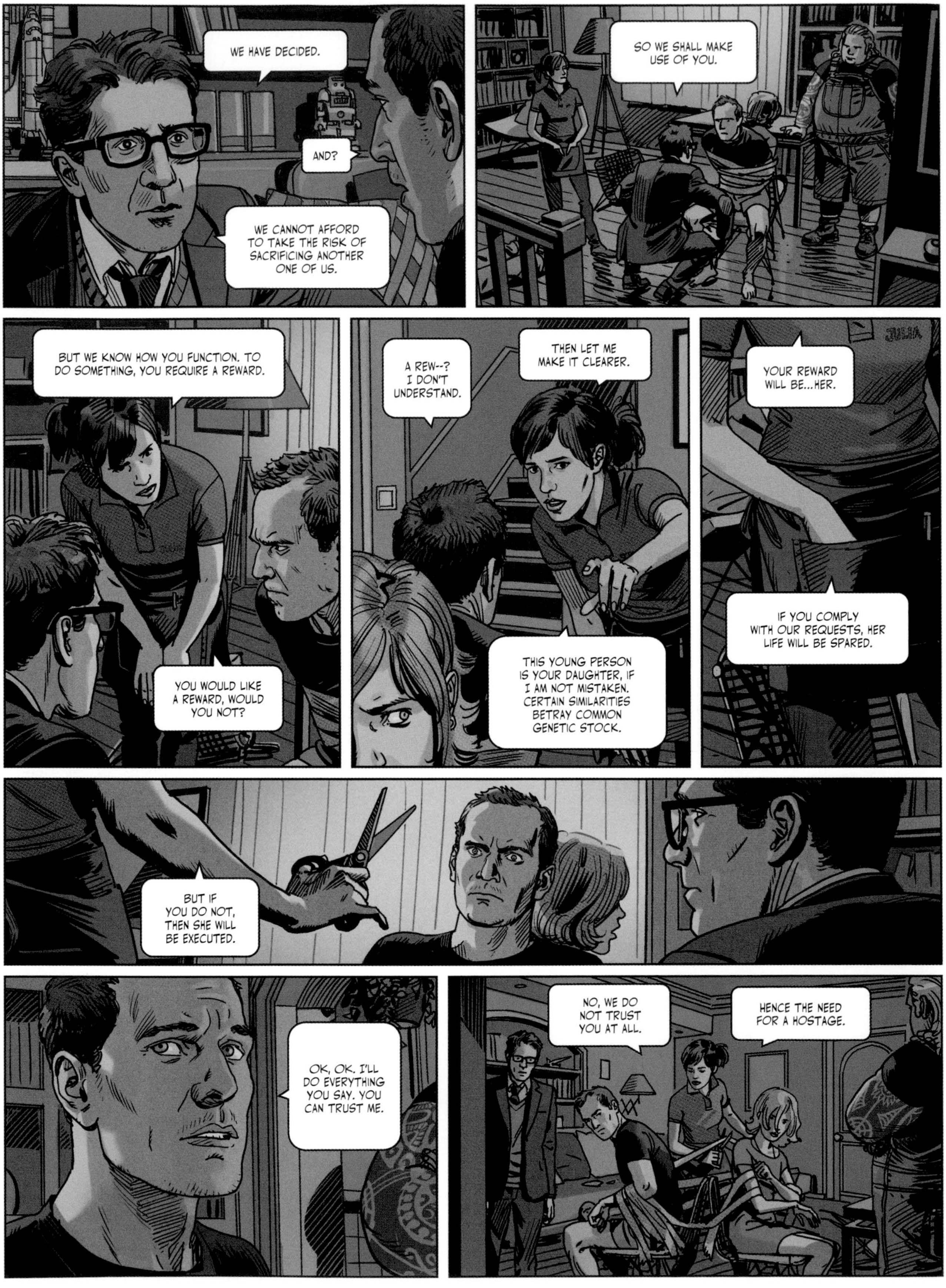
WE HAVE DECIDED.
AND?
WE CANNOT AFFORD TO TAKE THE RISK OF SACRIFICING ANOTHER ONE OF US.
SO WE SHALL MAKE USE OF YOU.
BUT WE KNOW HOW YOU FUNCTION. TO DO SOMETHING, YOU REQUIRE A REWARD.
YOU WOULD LIKE A REWARD, WOULD YOU NOT?
A REW--? I DON'T UNDERSTAND.
THEN LET ME MAKE IT CLEARER.
THIS YOUNG PERSON IS YOUR DAUGHTER, IF I AM NOT MISTAKEN. CERTAIN SIMILARITIES BETRAY COMMON GENETIC STOCK.
JULIA
YOUR REWARD WILL BE...HER.
IF YOU COMPLY WITH OUR REQUESTS, HER LIFE WILL BE SPARED.
BUT IF YOU DO NOT, THEN SHE WILL BE EXECUTED.
OK, OK. I'LL DO EVERYTHING YOU SAY. YOU CAN TRUST ME.
NO, WE DO NOT TRUST YOU AT ALL.
HENCE THE NEED FOR A HOSTAGE.

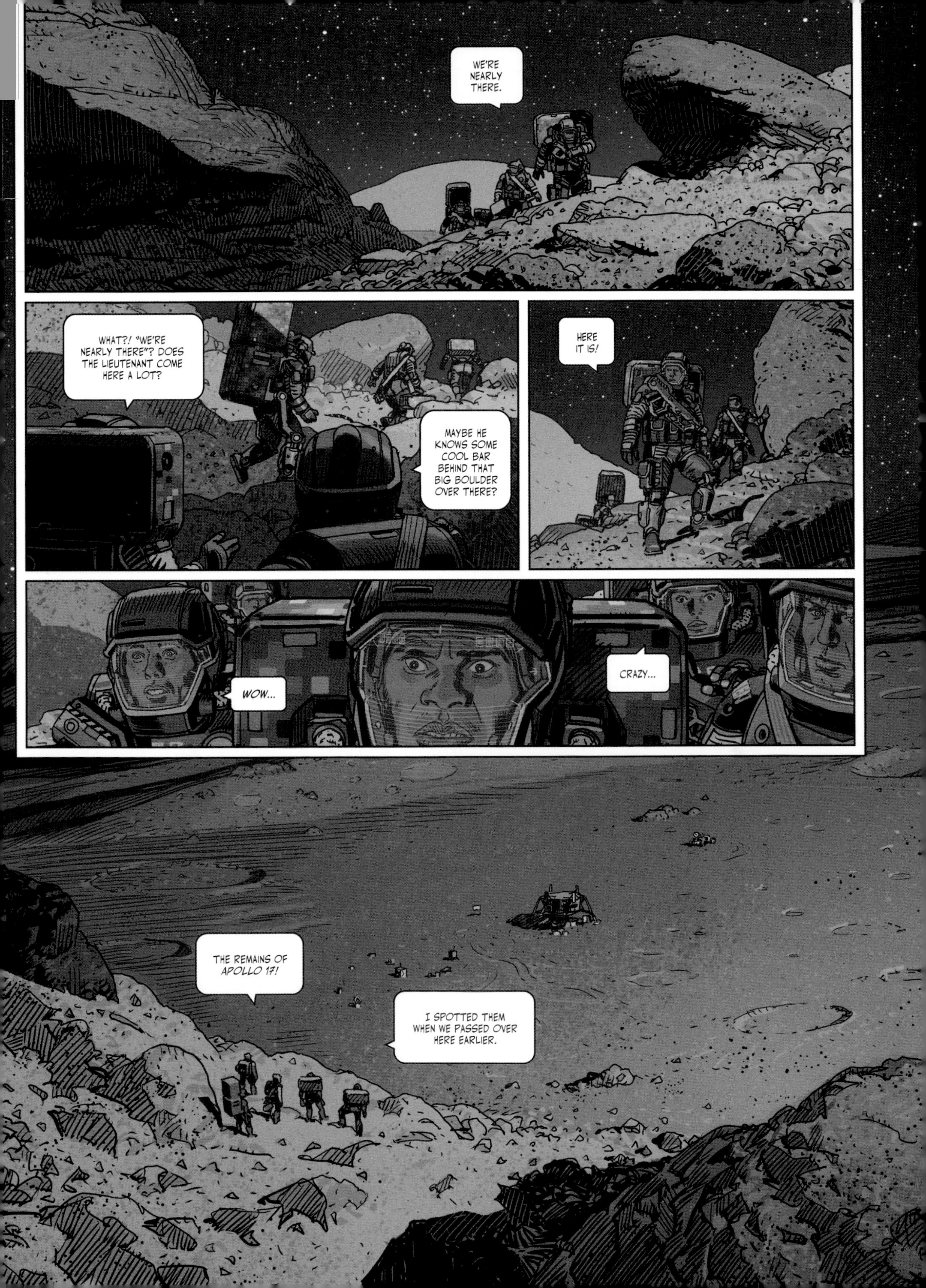
WE'RE NEARLY THERE.
WHAT?! "WE'RE NEARLY THERE"? DOES THE LIEUTENANT COME HERE A LOT?
MAYBE HE KNOWS SOME COOL BAR BEHIND THAT BIG BOULDER OVER THERE?
HERE IT IS!
WOW...
CRAZY...
THE REMAINS OF *APOLLO 17!*
I SPOTTED THEM WHEN WE PASSED OVER HERE EARLIER.

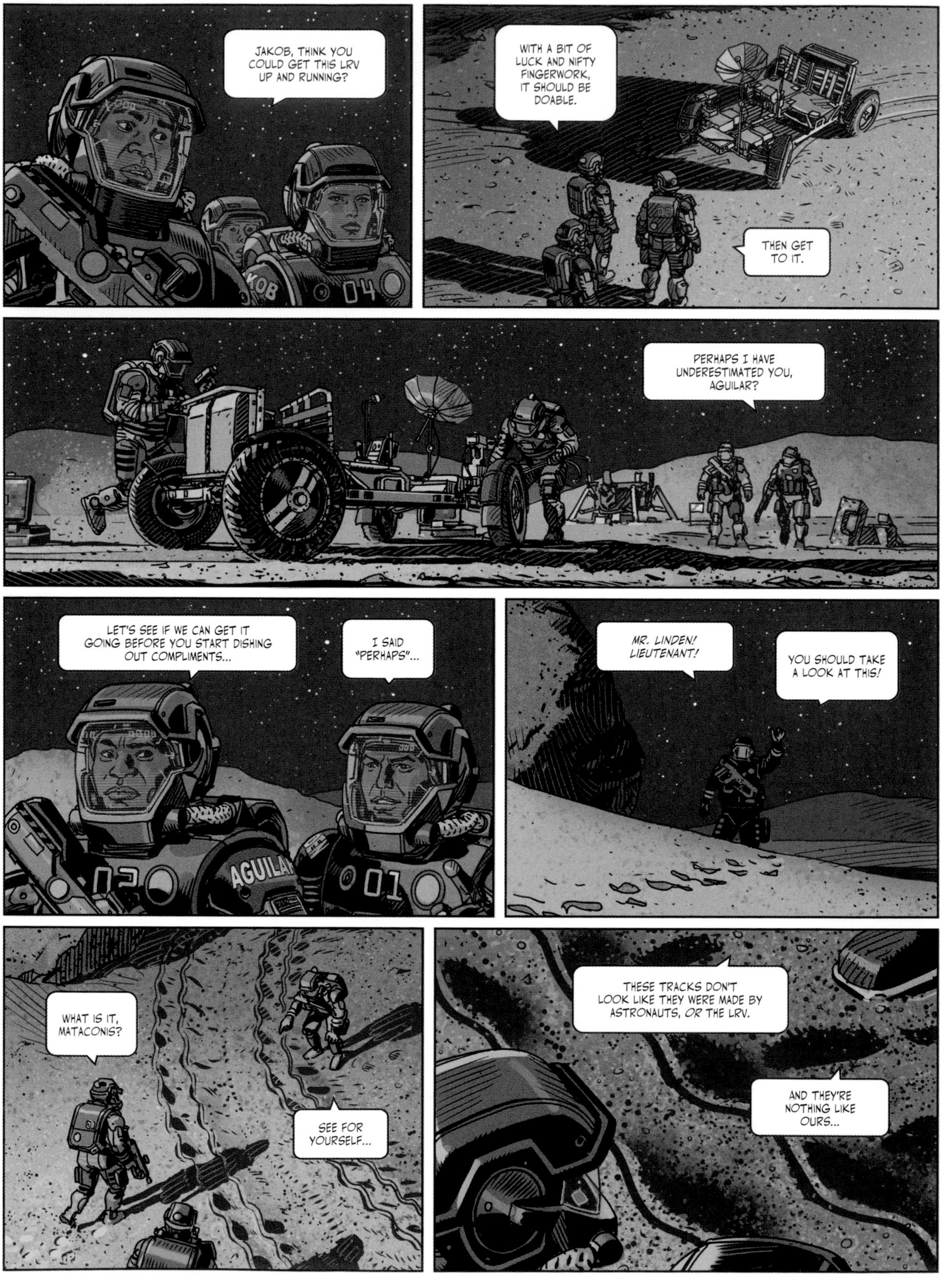
JAKOB, THINK YOU COULD GET THIS LRV UP AND RUNNING?
WITH A BIT OF LUCK AND NIFTY FINGERWORK, IT SHOULD BE DOABLE.
THEN GET TO IT.
PERHAPS I HAVE UNDERESTIMATED YOU, AGUILAR?
LET'S SEE IF WE CAN GET IT GOING BEFORE YOU START DISHING OUT COMPLIMENTS...
I SAID "PERHAPS"...
MR. LINDEN! LIEUTENANT!
YOU SHOULD TAKE A LOOK AT THIS!
WHAT IS IT, MATACONIS?
SEE FOR YOURSELF...
THESE TRACKS DON'T LOOK LIKE THEY WERE MADE BY ASTRONAUTS, OR THE LRV.
AND THEY'RE NOTHING LIKE OURS...

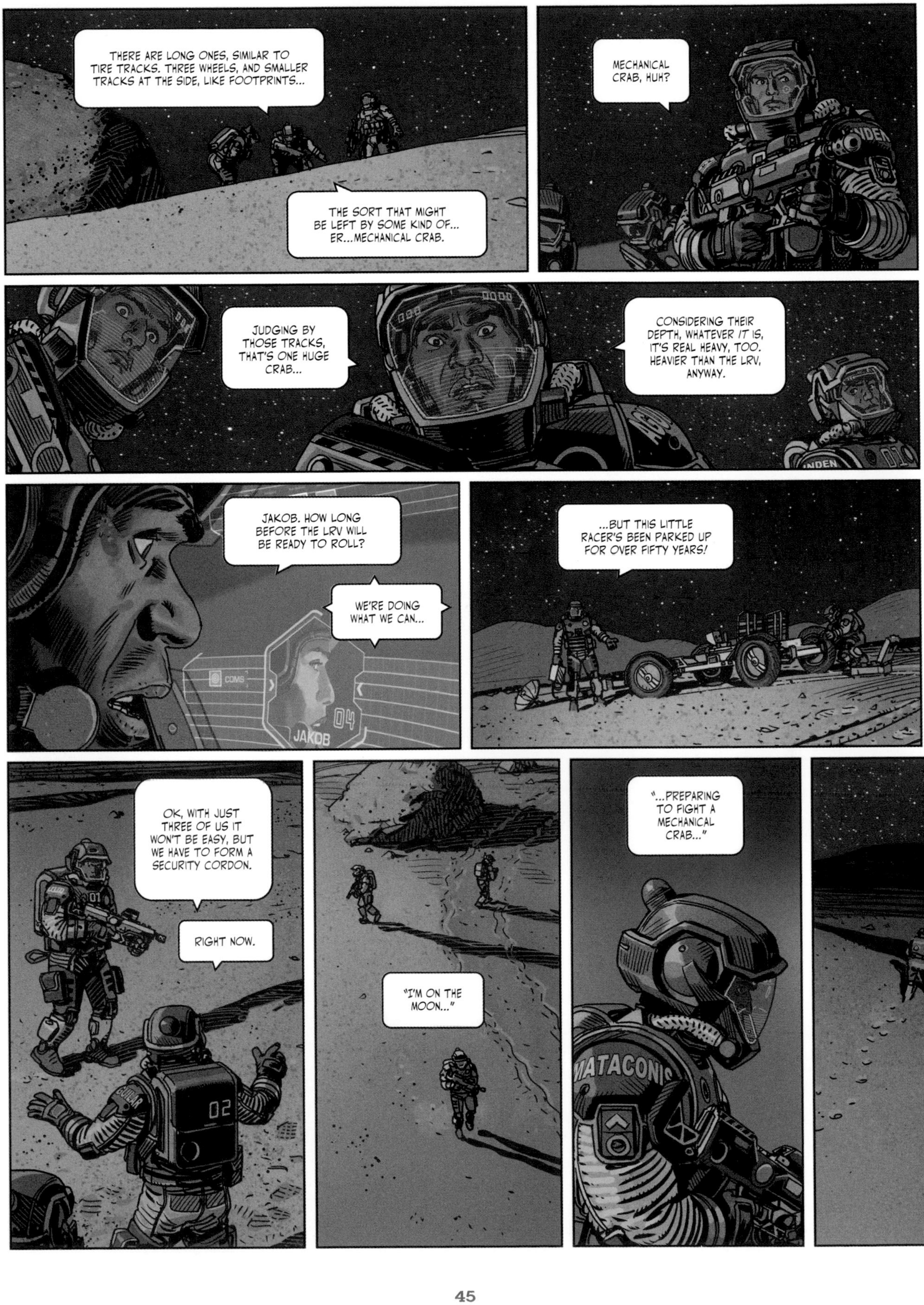
THERE ARE LONG ONES, SIMILAR TO TIRE TRACKS. THREE WHEELS, AND SMALLER TRACKS AT THE SIDE, LIKE FOOTPRINTS...
THE SORT THAT MIGHT BE LEFT BY SOME KIND OF... ER...MECHANICAL CRAB.
MECHANICAL CRAB, HUH?
JUDGING BY THOSE TRACKS, THAT'S ONE HUGE CRAB...
CONSIDERING THEIR DEPTH, WHATEVER *IT* IS, IT'S REAL HEAVY, TOO. HEAVIER THAN THE LRV, ANYWAY.
JAKOB. HOW LONG BEFORE THE LRV WILL BE READY TO ROLL?
WE'RE DOING WHAT WE CAN...
COMS
04
JAKOB
...BUT THIS LITTLE RACER'S BEEN PARKED UP FOR OVER FIFTY YEARS!
OK, WITH JUST THREE OF US IT WON'T BE EASY, BUT WE HAVE TO FORM A SECURITY CORDON.
RIGHT NOW.
02
"I'M ON THE MOON..."
"...PREPARING TO FIGHT A MECHANICAL CRAB..."
MATACONIS

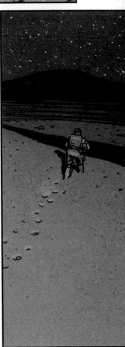

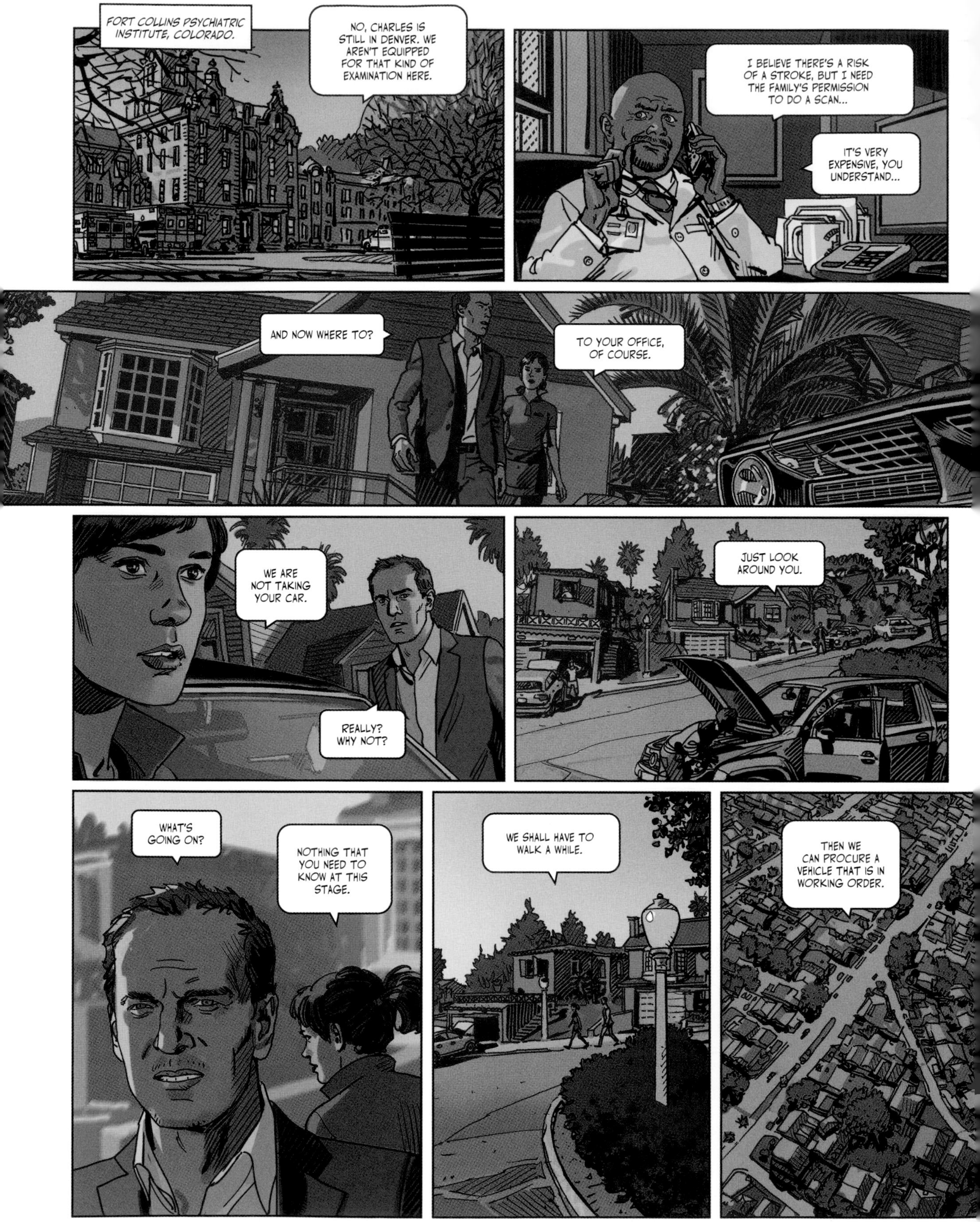
FORT COLLINS PSYCHIATRIC INSTITUTE, COLORADO.
NO, CHARLES IS STILL IN DENVER. WE AREN'T EQUIPPED FOR THAT KIND OF EXAMINATION HERE.
I BELIEVE THERE'S A RISK OF A STROKE, BUT I NEED THE FAMILY'S PERMISSION TO DO A SCAN...
IT'S VERY EXPENSIVE, YOU UNDERSTAND...
AND NOW WHERE TO?
TO YOUR OFFICE, OF COURSE.
WE ARE NOT TAKING YOUR CAR.
REALLY? WHY NOT?
JUST LOOK AROUND YOU.
WHAT'S GOING ON?
NOTHING THAT YOU NEED TO KNOW AT THIS STAGE.
WE SHALL HAVE TO WALK A WHILE.
THEN WE CAN PROCURE A VEHICLE THAT IS IN WORKING ORDER.

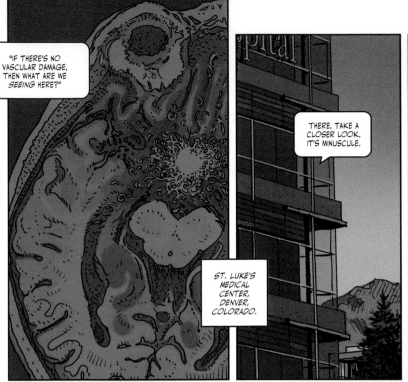

"IF THERE'S NO VASCULAR DAMAGE, THEN WHAT ARE WE *SEEING* HERE?"

THERE, TAKE A CLOSER LOOK. IT'S MINUSCULE.

ST. LUKE'S MEDICAL CENTER, DENVER, COLORADO.

IT'S... *WOW!*

I'VE NEVER SEEN ANYTHING LIKE THIS! WHAT *IS* IT?

NO IDEA.

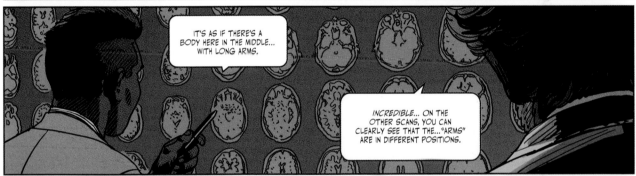

IT'S AS IF THERE'S A BODY HERE IN THE MIDDLE... WITH LONG ARMS.

INCREDIBLE... ON THE OTHER SCANS, YOU CAN CLEARLY SEE THAT THE..."ARMS" ARE IN DIFFERENT POSITIONS.

THIS THING'S MOVING. IT'S *ALIVE!*

THIS THING... JUST CAN'T BE HUMAN!

DON'T JUMP TO CONCLUSIONS, IF YOU DON'T MIND!

WHERE ARE YOU GOING?

I'M GOING TO CALL HIS DOCTOR AND ASK HIM TO COME SEE US...

... TO EXPLAIN TO HIM THAT CHARLES WEBSTER'S THE ONE WHO'S SICK IN THE HEAD, *NOT US!*

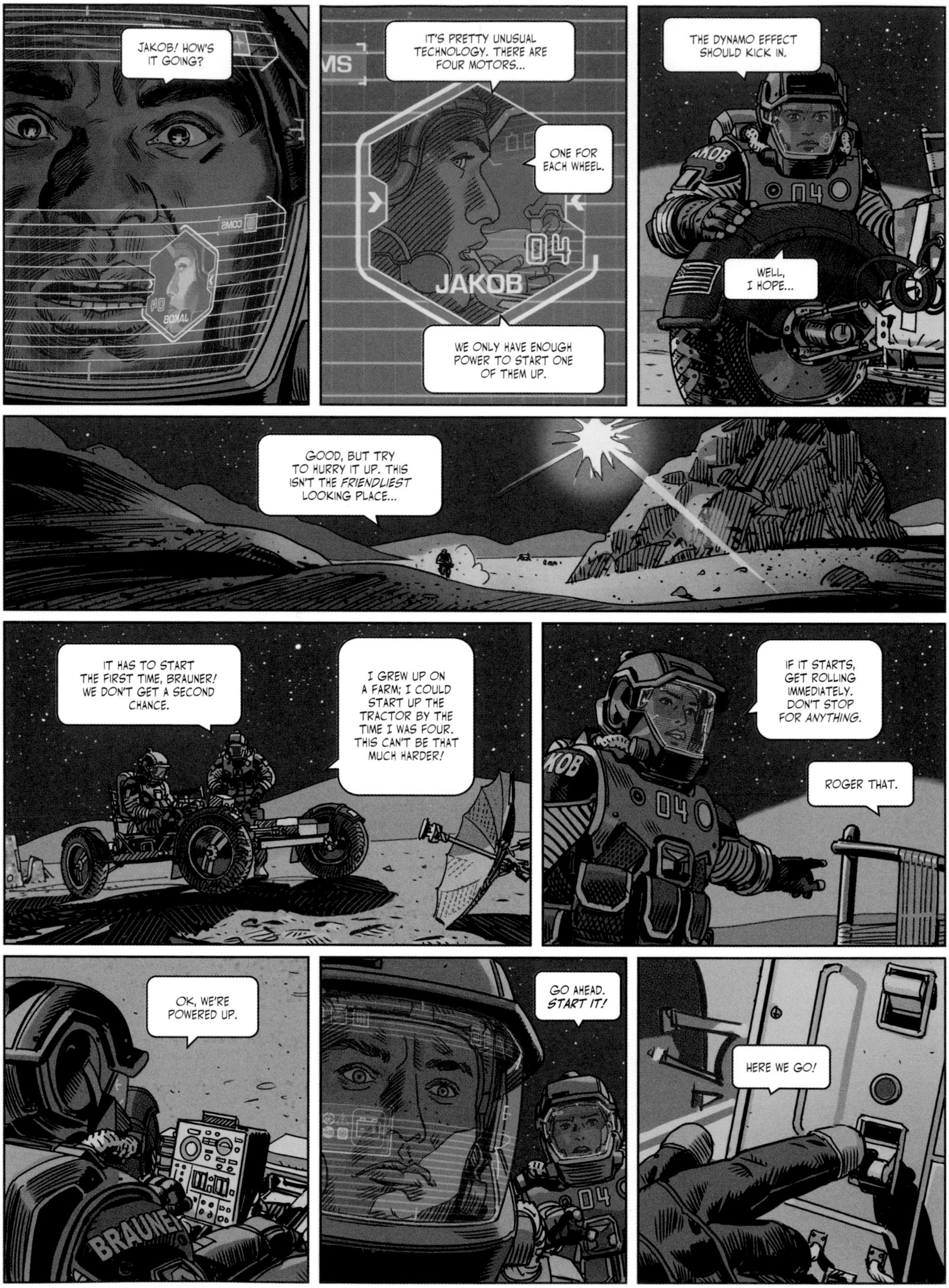
JAKOB! HOW'S IT GOING?
IT'S PRETTY UNUSUAL TECHNOLOGY. THERE ARE FOUR MOTORS...
ONE FOR EACH WHEEL.
JAKOB
04
WE ONLY HAVE ENOUGH POWER TO START ONE OF THEM UP.
THE DYNAMO EFFECT SHOULD KICK IN.
WELL, I HOPE...
GOOD, BUT TRY TO HURRY IT UP. THIS ISN'T THE *FRIENDLIEST* LOOKING PLACE...
IT HAS TO START THE FIRST TIME, BRAUNER! WE DON'T GET A SECOND CHANCE.
I GREW UP ON A FARM; I COULD START UP THE TRACTOR BY THE TIME I WAS FOUR. THIS CAN'T BE THAT MUCH HARDER!
IF IT STARTS, GET ROLLING IMMEDIATELY. DON'T STOP FOR *ANYTHING*.
ROGER THAT.
OK, WE'RE POWERED UP.
GO AHEAD. ***START IT!***
HERE WE GO!

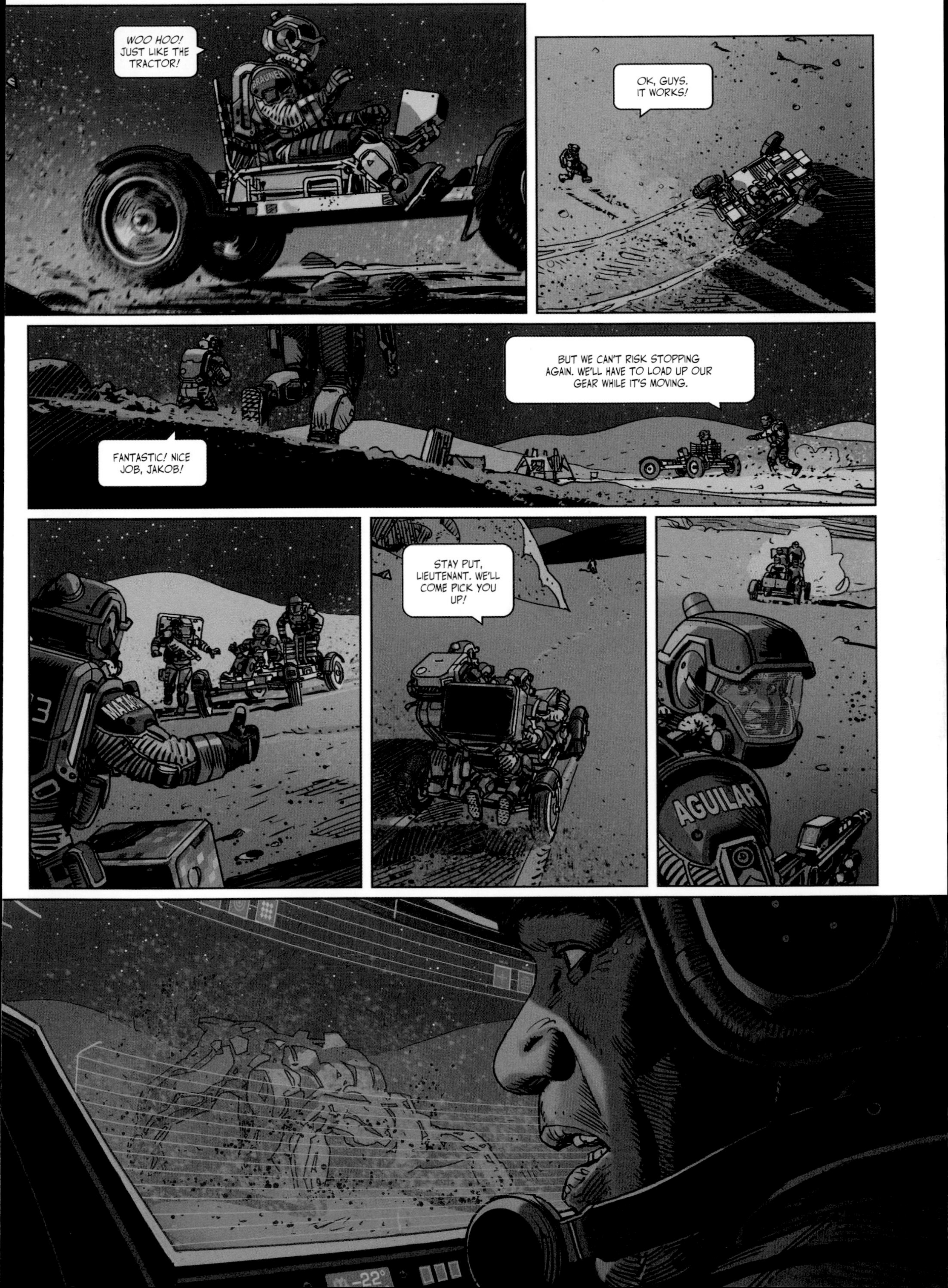
WOO HOO! JUST LIKE THE TRACTOR!
BRAUNER
OK, GUYS. IT WORKS!
BUT WE CAN'T RISK STOPPING AGAIN. WE'LL HAVE TO LOAD UP OUR GEAR WHILE IT'S MOVING.
FANTASTIC! NICE JOB, JAKOB!
STAY PUT, LIEUTENANT. WE'LL COME PICK YOU UP!
AGUILAR
-22°

"CALM DOWN. DRIVE CAREFULLY."

SORRY, I GUESS I'LL PROBABLY BE CALMER ONCE I'VE GOTTEN USED TO STEALING CARS...

WE WILL NOT NEED TO STEAL ANY MORE VEHICLES.

SO I GATHERED... IRONY ISN'T REALLY YOUR THING, IS IT?

THAT CONCEPT IS OF NO USE TO ME.

HOW ABOUT YOU TELL ME WHO YOU ARE, AND WHAT YOU WANT?

WHO AM I? IT IS DIFFICULT TO GIVE A SIMPLE REPLY.

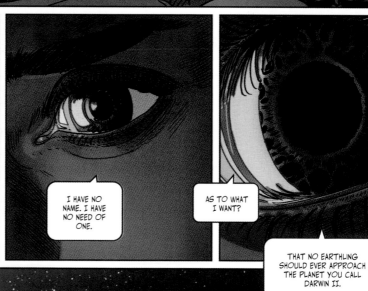

I HAVE NO NAME. I HAVE NO NEED OF ONE.

AS TO WHAT I WANT?

THAT NO EARTHLING SHOULD EVER APPROACH THE PLANET YOU CALL DARWIN II.

"OTHERWISE, YOU SHALL ALL DIE..."

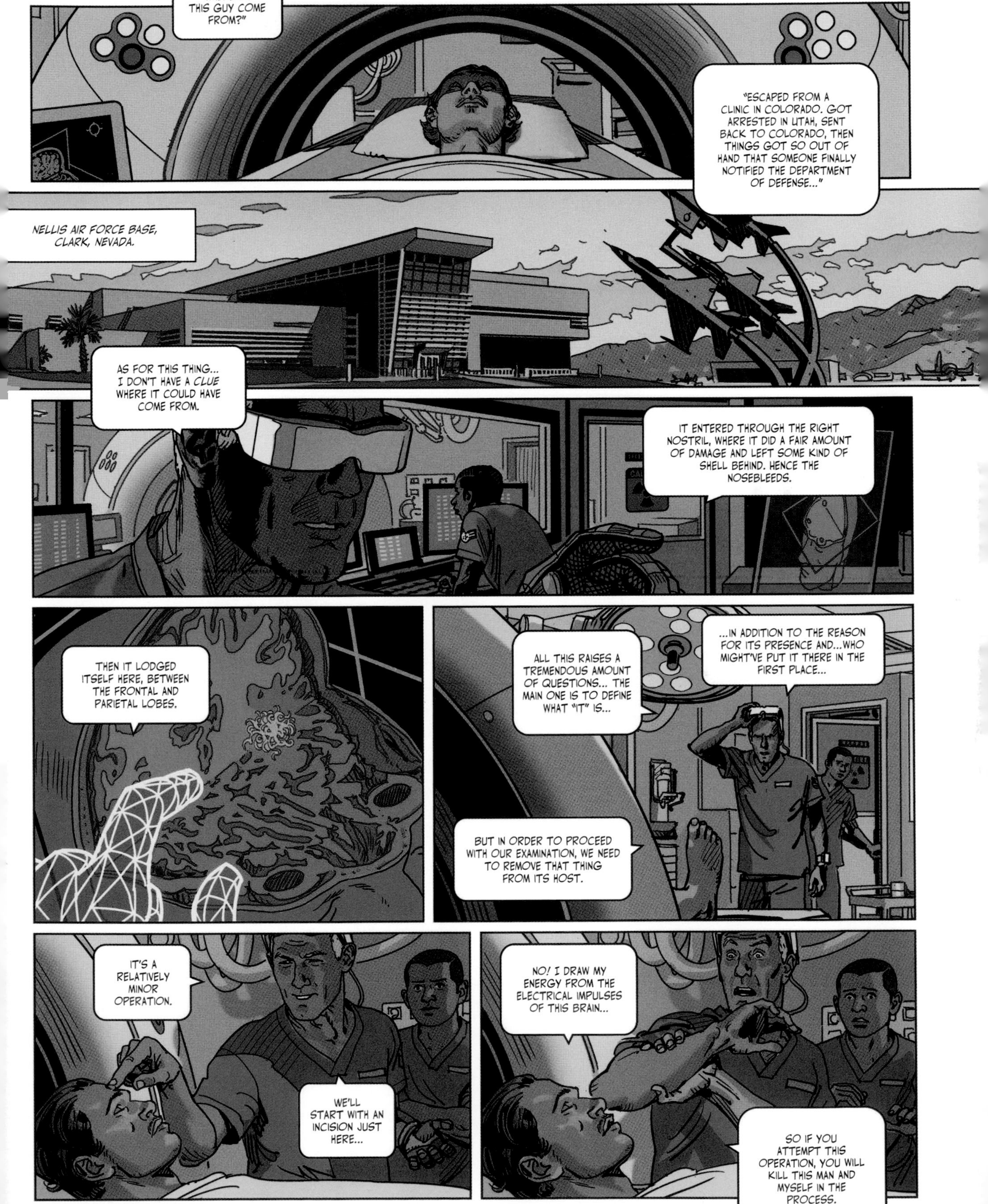
"WHERE DID THIS GUY COME FROM?"
"ESCAPED FROM A CLINIC IN COLORADO. GOT ARRESTED IN UTAH, SENT BACK TO COLORADO, THEN THINGS GOT SO OUT OF HAND THAT SOMEONE FINALLY NOTIFIED THE DEPARTMENT OF DEFENSE..."
NELLIS AIR FORCE BASE, CLARK, NEVADA.
AS FOR THIS THING... I DON'T HAVE A CLUE WHERE IT COULD HAVE COME FROM.
IT ENTERED THROUGH THE RIGHT NOSTRIL, WHERE IT DID A FAIR AMOUNT OF DAMAGE AND LEFT SOME KIND OF SHELL BEHIND. HENCE THE NOSEBLEEDS.
THEN IT LODGED ITSELF HERE, BETWEEN THE FRONTAL AND PARIETAL LOBES.
ALL THIS RAISES A TREMENDOUS AMOUNT OF QUESTIONS... THE MAIN ONE IS TO DEFINE WHAT "IT" IS...
...IN ADDITION TO THE REASON FOR ITS PRESENCE AND...WHO MIGHT'VE PUT IT THERE IN THE FIRST PLACE...
BUT IN ORDER TO PROCEED WITH OUR EXAMINATION, WE NEED TO REMOVE THAT THING FROM ITS HOST.
IT'S A RELATIVELY MINOR OPERATION.
WE'LL START WITH AN INCISION JUST HERE...
NO! I DRAW MY ENERGY FROM THE ELECTRICAL IMPULSES OF THIS BRAIN...
SO IF YOU ATTEMPT THIS OPERATION, YOU WILL KILL THIS MAN AND MYSELF IN THE PROCESS.

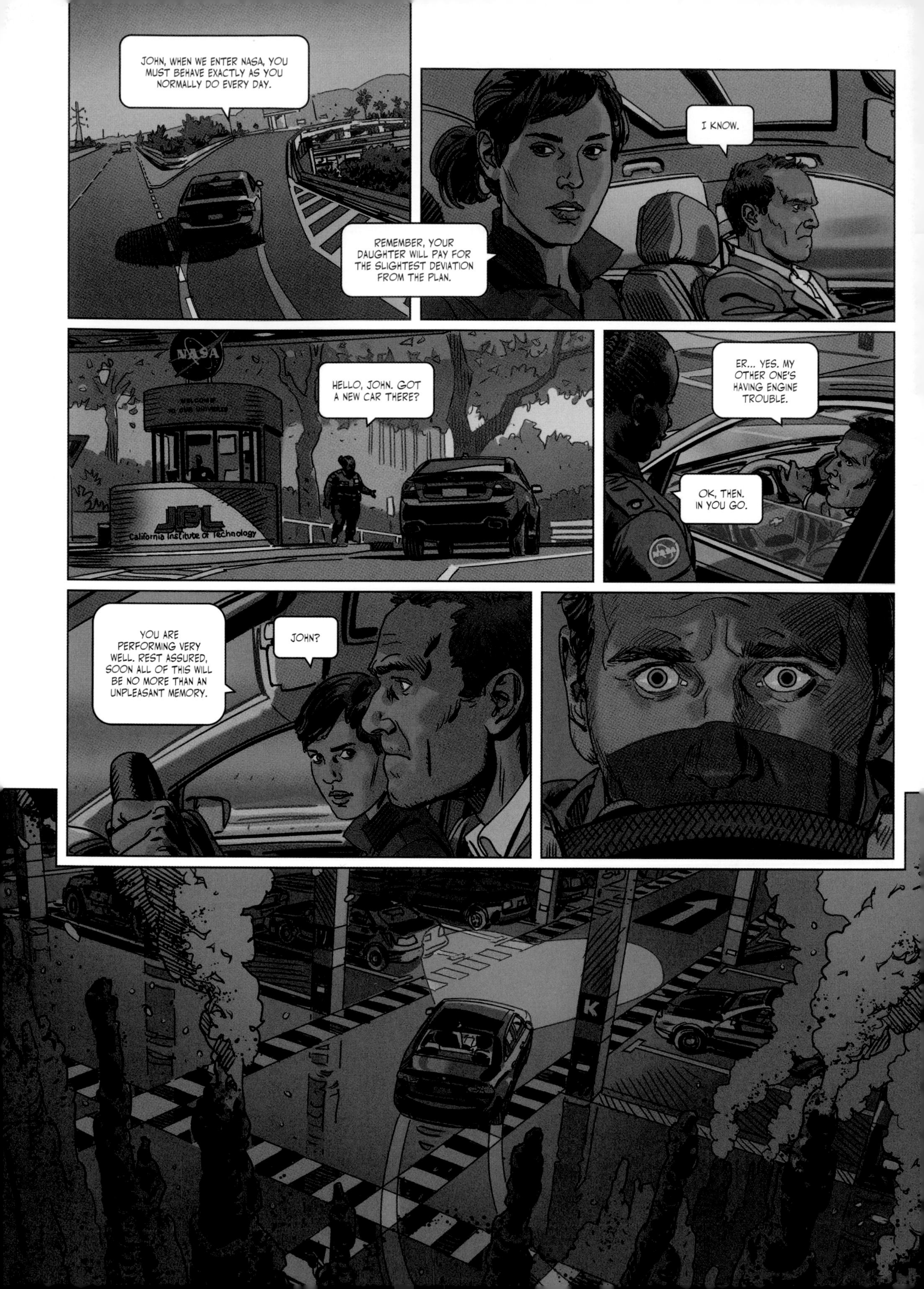

JOHN, WHEN WE ENTER NASA, YOU MUST BEHAVE EXACTLY AS YOU NORMALLY DO EVERY DAY.
I KNOW.
REMEMBER, YOUR DAUGHTER WILL PAY FOR THE SLIGHTEST DEVIATION FROM THE PLAN.
NASA
JPL
California Institute of Technology
HELLO, JOHN. GOT A NEW CAR THERE?
ER... YES. MY OTHER ONE'S HAVING ENGINE TROUBLE.
OK, THEN. IN YOU GO.
YOU ARE PERFORMING VERY WELL. REST ASSURED, SOON ALL OF THIS WILL BE NO MORE THAN AN UNPLEASANT MEMORY.
JOHN?
K

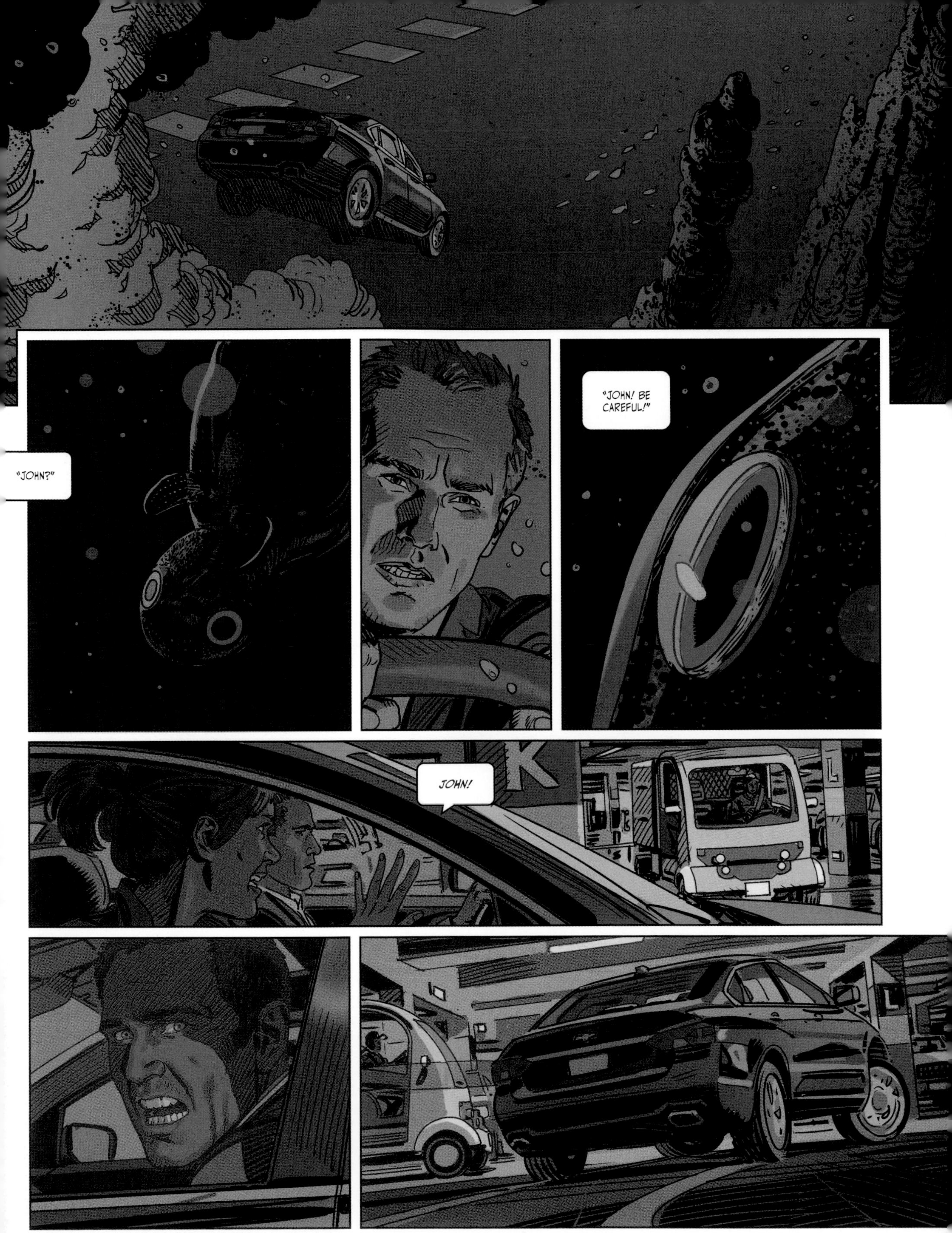
"JOHN?"
"JOHN! BE CAREFUL!"
JOHN!

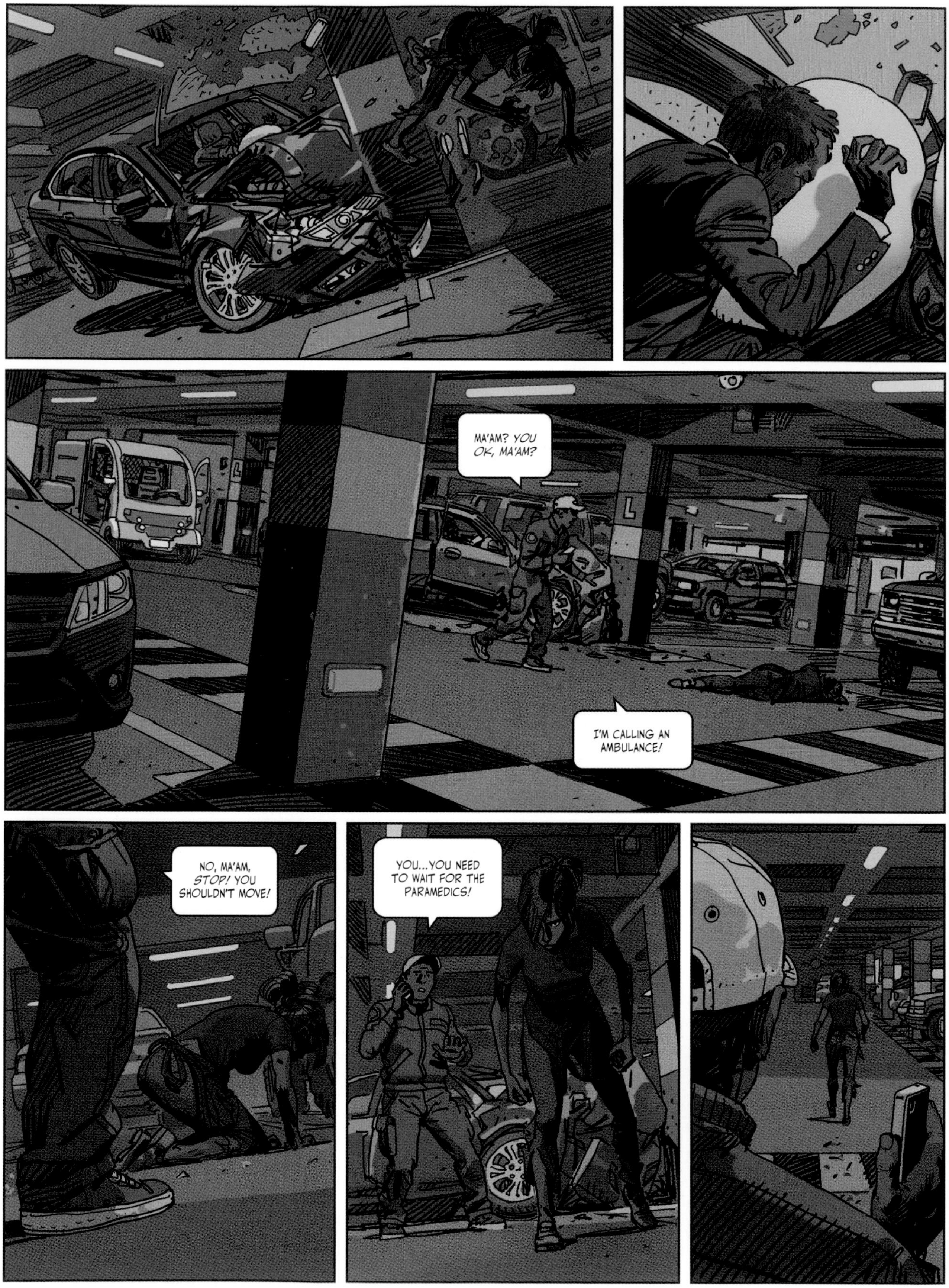
MA'AM? YOU OK, MA'AM?
I'M CALLING AN AMBULANCE!
NO, MA'AM, STOP! YOU SHOULDN'T MOVE!
YOU...YOU NEED TO WAIT FOR THE PARAMEDICS!

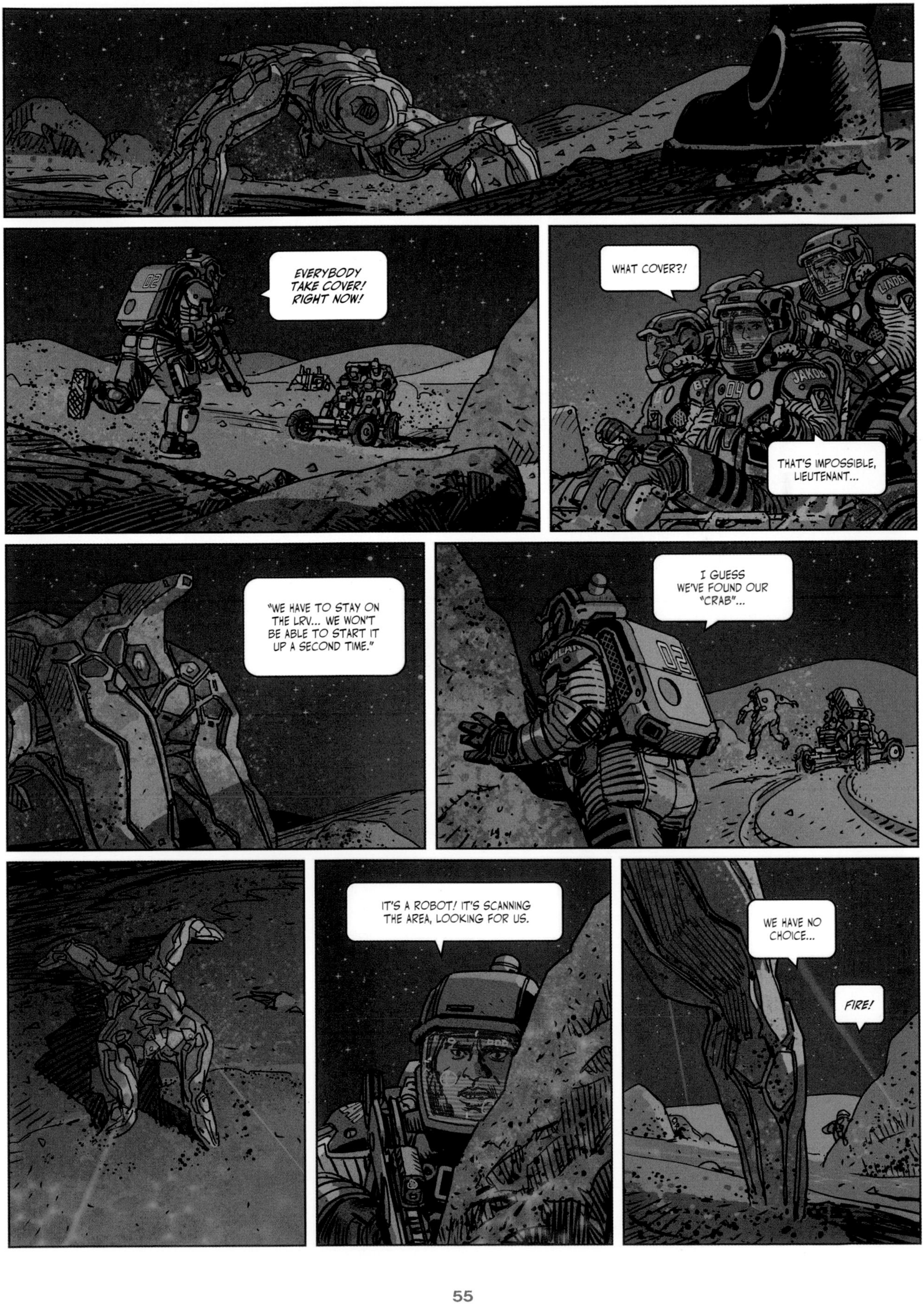
EVERYBODY TAKE COVER! RIGHT NOW!
WHAT COVER?!
THAT'S IMPOSSIBLE, LIEUTENANT...
"WE HAVE TO STAY ON THE LRV... WE WON'T BE ABLE TO START IT UP A SECOND TIME."
I GUESS WE'VE FOUND OUR "CRAB"...
IT'S A ROBOT! IT'S SCANNING THE AREA, LOOKING FOR US.
WE HAVE NO CHOICE...
FIRE!

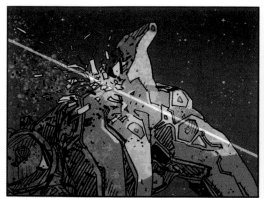

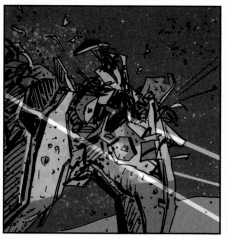

CEASE FIRE!

OK, HE'S REGAINING CONSCIOUSNESS.

YOU'LL BE ALL RIGHT, SIR. WE'LL GET YOU OUT OF THERE.

SECURITY

NEVER SEEN SOMEONE CRASH THIS BAD IN A PARKING LOT...

WHO IS THIS PUBLIC MENACE, ANYWAY?

JOHN SOMETHING... SOME BIG SHOT.

HE OUGHTA *UBER* TO WORK!

A BRACE? DID I BREAK MY NECK?

NO, DON'T YOU WORRY, SIR. IT'S JUST STANDARD PROCEDURE.

I... JULIA?! WHERE'S THE WOMAN WHO WAS WITH ME?

NO IDEA. GUESS SHE JUST UPPED AND LEFT WITHOUT A WORD.

WE *HAVE* TO CATCH HER! SHE'S A TERRORIST!

SHE'LL DESTROY EVERYTHING! CALL *THE COPS!*

ALRIGHT, BUT CALM DOWN!

SO THERE YOU ARE... THAT WAS PROBABLY THE FIRST CONTACT BETWEEN HUMANS AND AN EXTRATERRESTRIAL ENTITY...

...AND IT WAS A BATTLE.

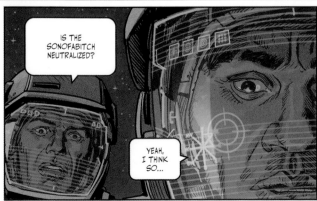

IS THE SONOFABITCH NEUTRALIZED?

YEAH, I THINK SO...

I'LL TAKE THIS BACK...

57

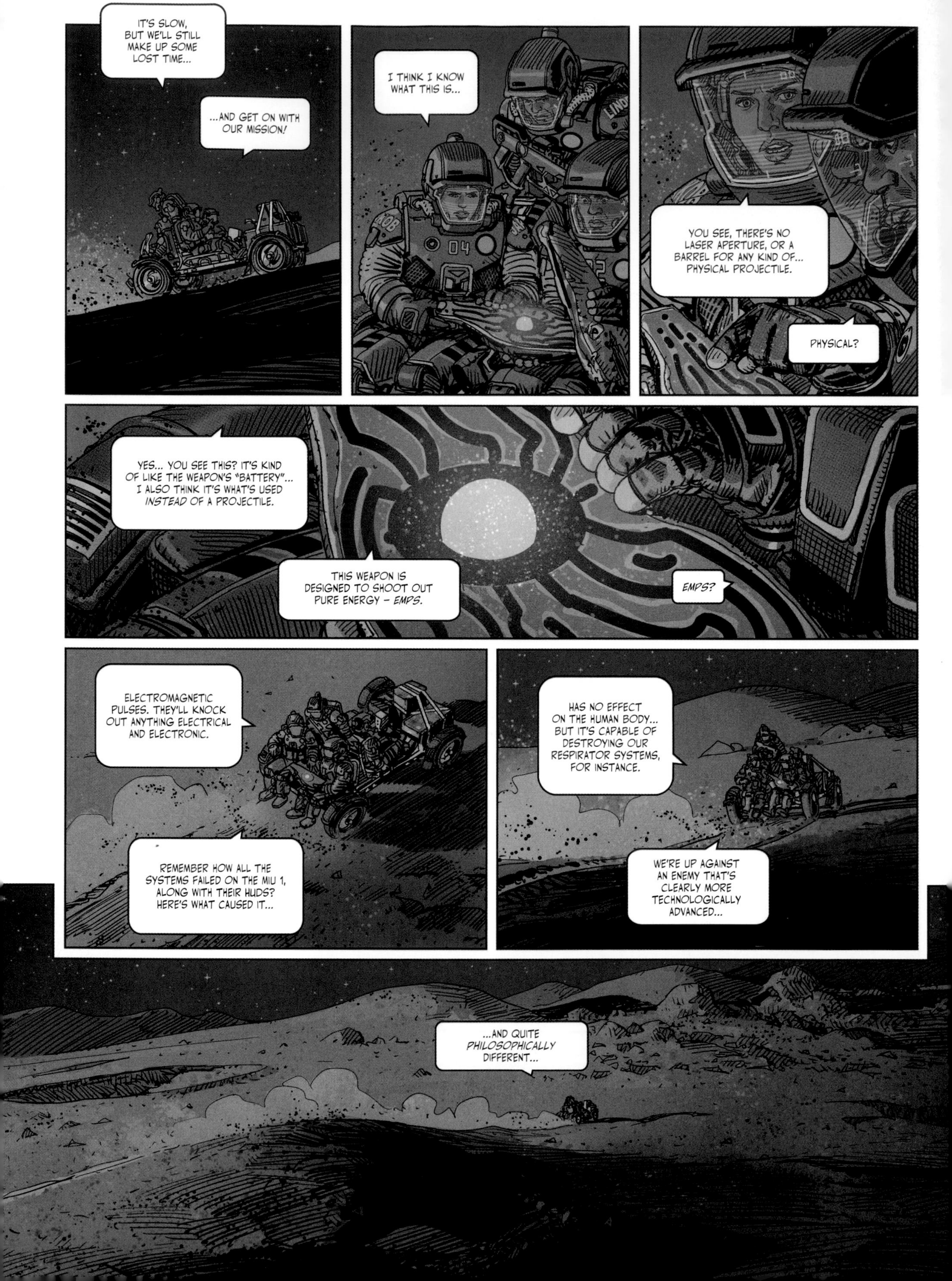
IT'S SLOW, BUT WE'LL STILL MAKE UP SOME LOST TIME...
...AND GET ON WITH OUR MISSION!
I THINK I KNOW WHAT THIS IS...
YOU SEE, THERE'S NO LASER APERTURE, OR A BARREL FOR ANY KIND OF... PHYSICAL PROJECTILE.
PHYSICAL?
YES... YOU SEE THIS? IT'S KIND OF LIKE THE WEAPON'S "BATTERY"... I ALSO THINK IT'S WHAT'S USED *INSTEAD* OF A PROJECTILE.
THIS WEAPON IS DESIGNED TO SHOOT OUT PURE ENERGY – *EMPS*.
EMPS?
ELECTROMAGNETIC PULSES. THEY'LL KNOCK OUT ANYTHING ELECTRICAL AND ELECTRONIC.
REMEMBER HOW ALL THE SYSTEMS FAILED ON THE MIU 1, ALONG WITH THEIR HUDS? HERE'S WHAT CAUSED IT...
HAS NO EFFECT ON THE HUMAN BODY... BUT IT'S CAPABLE OF DESTROYING OUR RESPIRATOR SYSTEMS, FOR INSTANCE.
WE'RE UP AGAINST AN ENEMY THAT'S CLEARLY MORE TECHNOLOGICALLY ADVANCED...
...AND QUITE *PHILOSOPHICALLY* DIFFERENT...

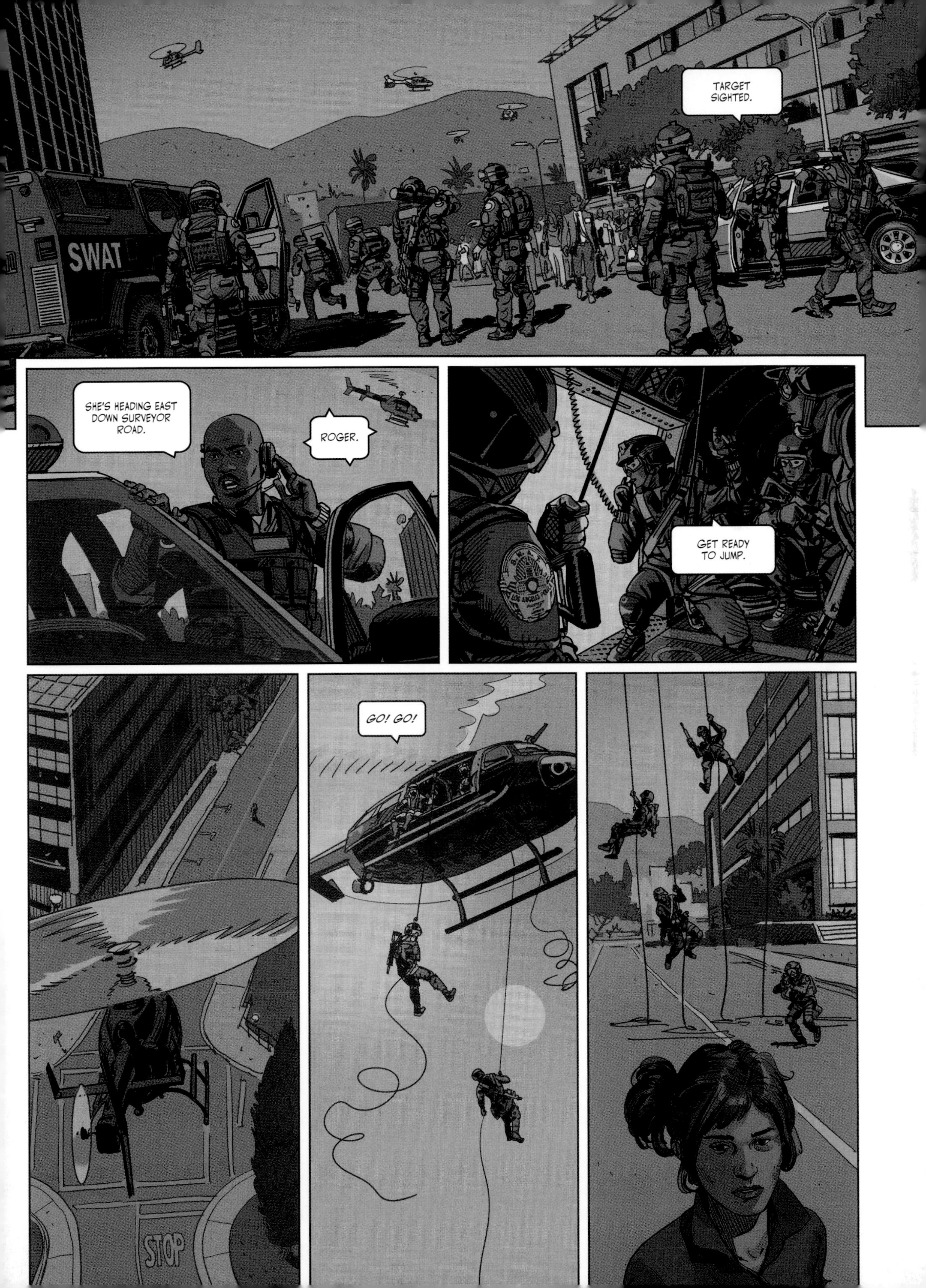
TARGET SIGHTED.
SWAT
SHE'S HEADING EAST DOWN SURVEYOR ROAD.
ROGER.
GET READY TO JUMP.
GO! GO!
STOP

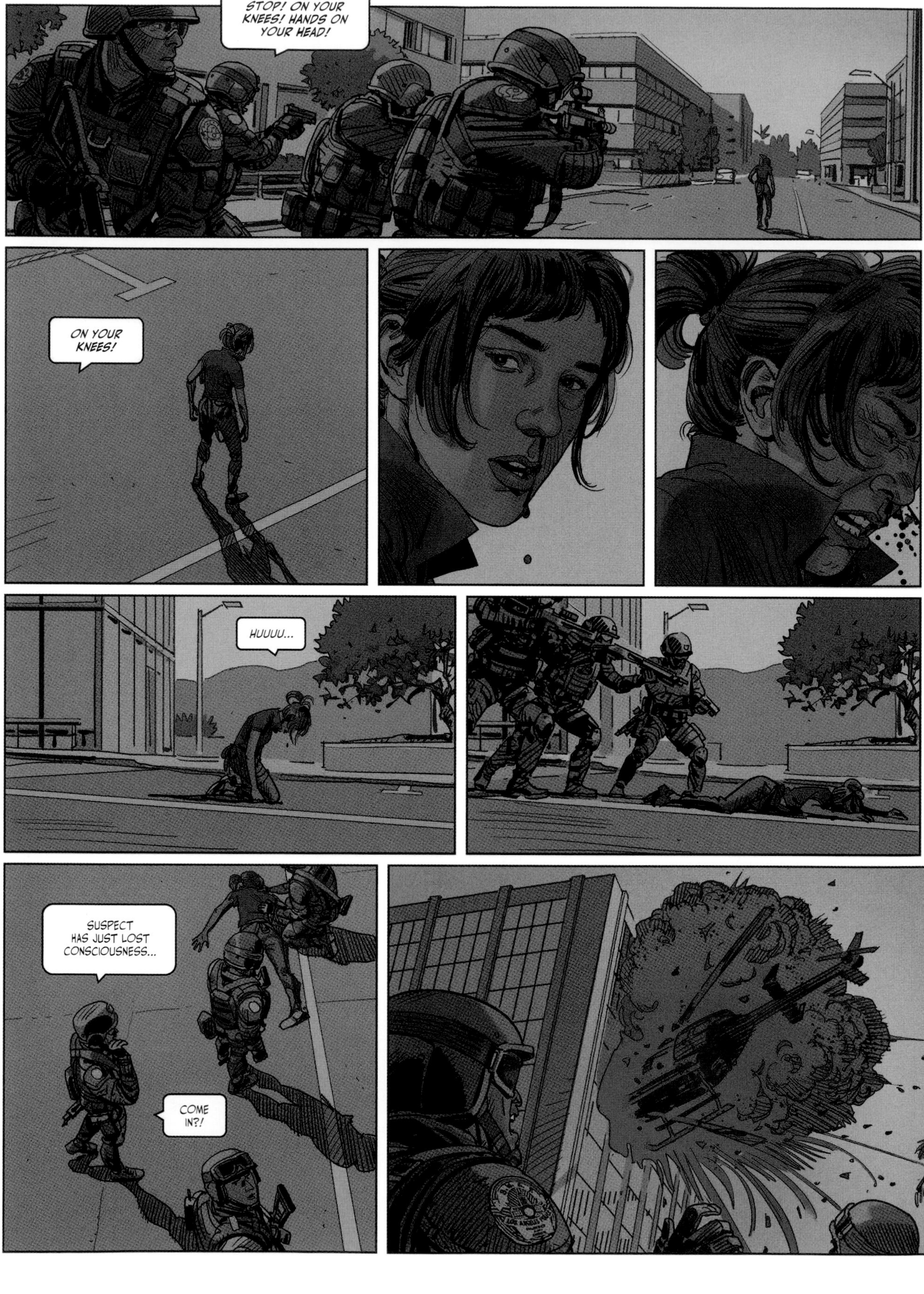
STOP! ON YOUR KNEES! HANDS ON YOUR HEAD!
ON YOUR KNEES!
HUUUU...
SUSPECT HAS JUST LOST CONSCIOUSNESS...
COME IN?!

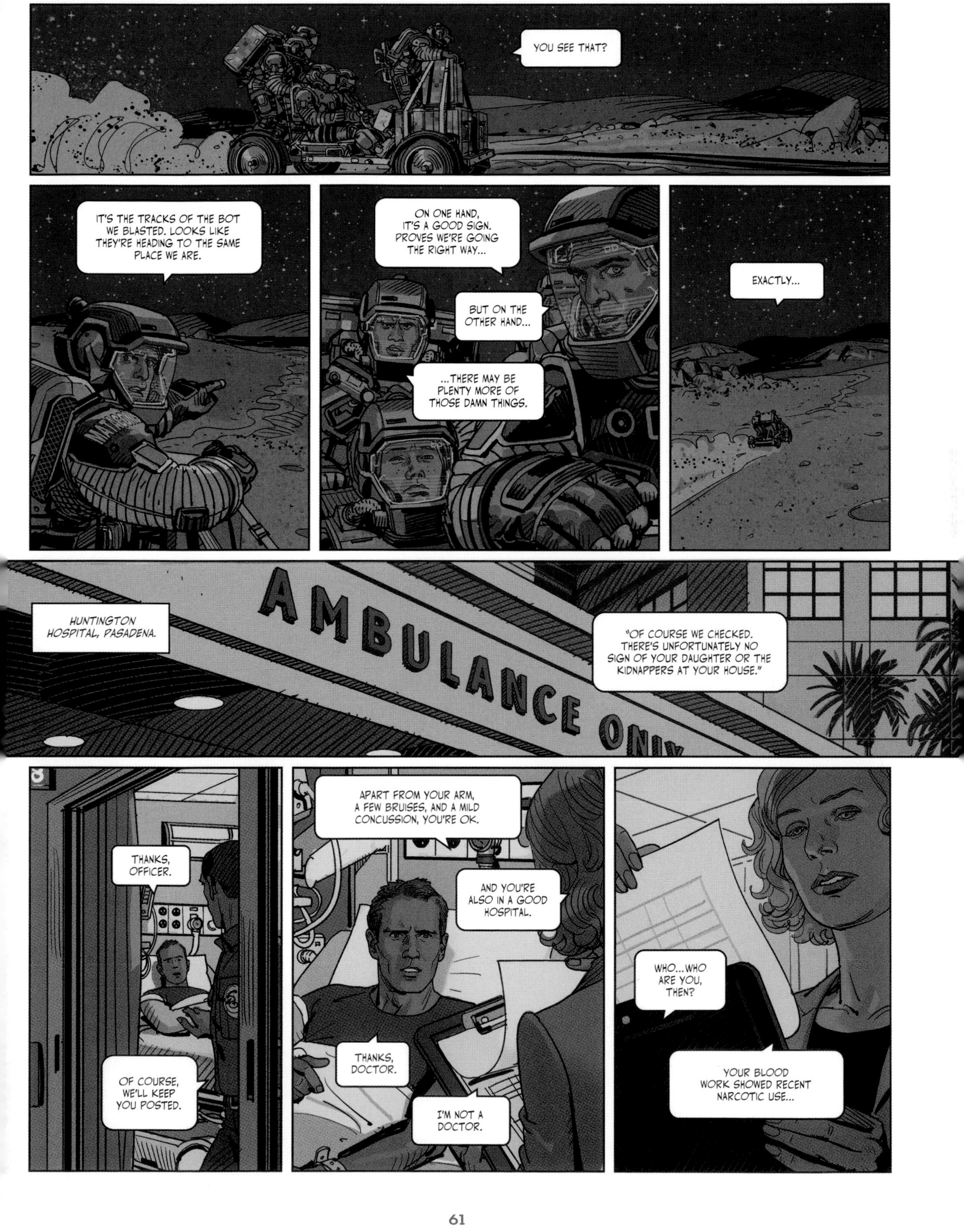
YOU SEE THAT?
IT'S THE TRACKS OF THE BOT WE BLASTED. LOOKS LIKE THEY'RE HEADING TO THE SAME PLACE WE ARE.
ON ONE HAND, IT'S A GOOD SIGN. PROVES WE'RE GOING THE RIGHT WAY...
BUT ON THE OTHER HAND...
...THERE MAY BE PLENTY MORE OF THOSE DAMN THINGS.
EXACTLY...
AMBULANCE ONLY
HUNTINGTON HOSPITAL, PASADENA.
"OF COURSE WE CHECKED. THERE'S UNFORTUNATELY NO SIGN OF YOUR DAUGHTER OR THE KIDNAPPERS AT YOUR HOUSE."
THANKS, OFFICER.
OF COURSE, WE'LL KEEP YOU POSTED.
APART FROM YOUR ARM, A FEW BRUISES, AND A MILD CONCUSSION, YOU'RE OK.
AND YOU'RE ALSO IN A GOOD HOSPITAL.
THANKS, DOCTOR.
I'M NOT A DOCTOR.
WHO...WHO ARE YOU, THEN?
YOUR BLOOD WORK SHOWED RECENT NARCOTIC USE...

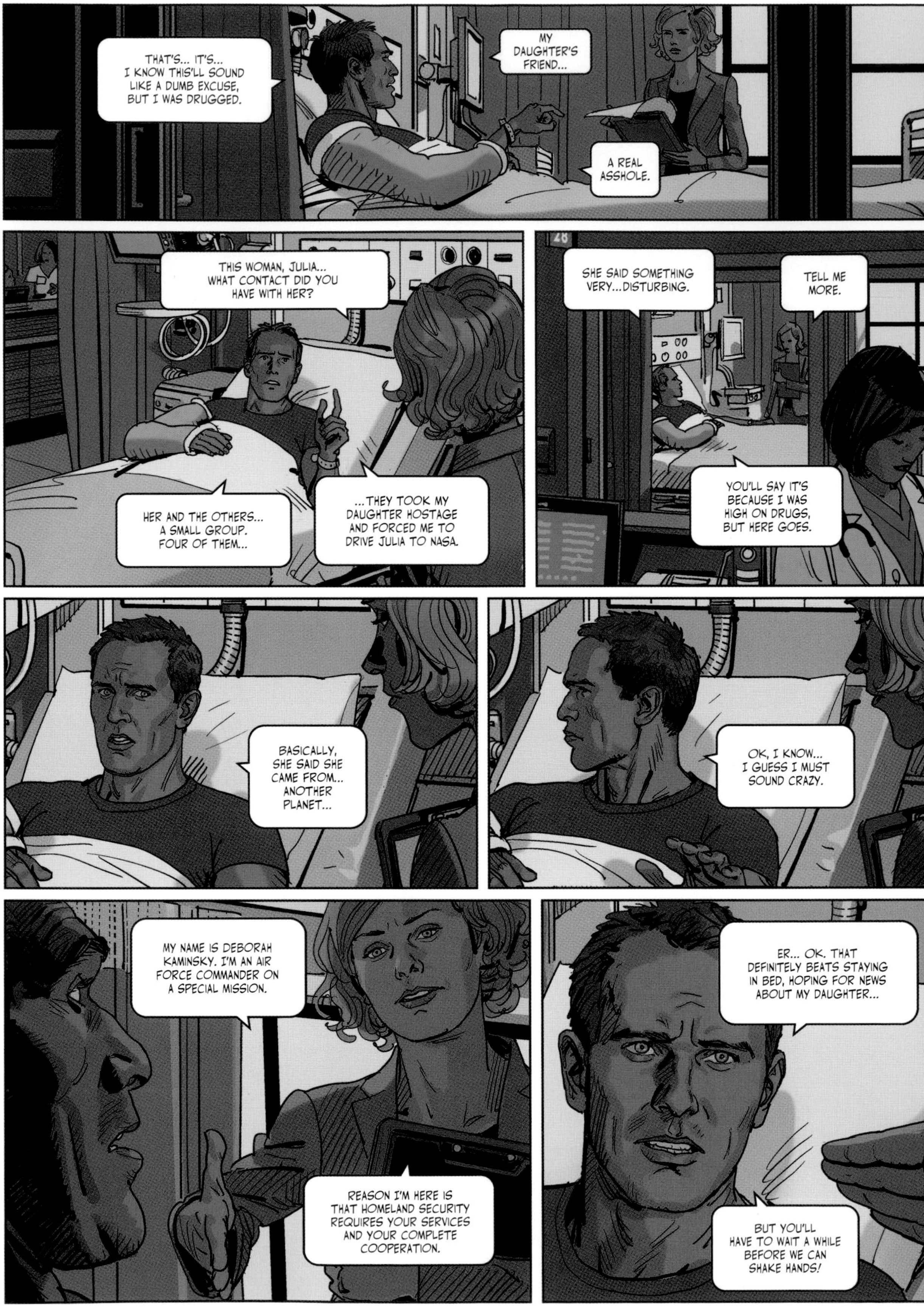
THAT'S... IT'S... I KNOW THIS'LL SOUND LIKE A DUMB EXCUSE, BUT I WAS DRUGGED.
MY DAUGHTER'S FRIEND...
A REAL ASSHOLE.
THIS WOMAN, JULIA... WHAT CONTACT DID YOU HAVE WITH HER?
HER AND THE OTHERS... A SMALL GROUP. FOUR OF THEM...
...THEY TOOK MY DAUGHTER HOSTAGE AND FORCED ME TO DRIVE JULIA TO NASA.
SHE SAID SOMETHING VERY...DISTURBING.
TELL ME MORE.
YOU'LL SAY IT'S BECAUSE I WAS HIGH ON DRUGS, BUT HERE GOES.
BASICALLY, SHE SAID SHE CAME FROM... ANOTHER PLANET...
OK, I KNOW... I GUESS I MUST SOUND CRAZY.
MY NAME IS DEBORAH KAMINSKY. I'M AN AIR FORCE COMMANDER ON A SPECIAL MISSION.
REASON I'M HERE IS THAT HOMELAND SECURITY REQUIRES YOUR SERVICES AND YOUR COMPLETE COOPERATION.
ER... OK. THAT DEFINITELY BEATS STAYING IN BED, HOPING FOR NEWS ABOUT MY DAUGHTER...
BUT YOU'LL HAVE TO WAIT A WHILE BEFORE WE CAN SHAKE HANDS!

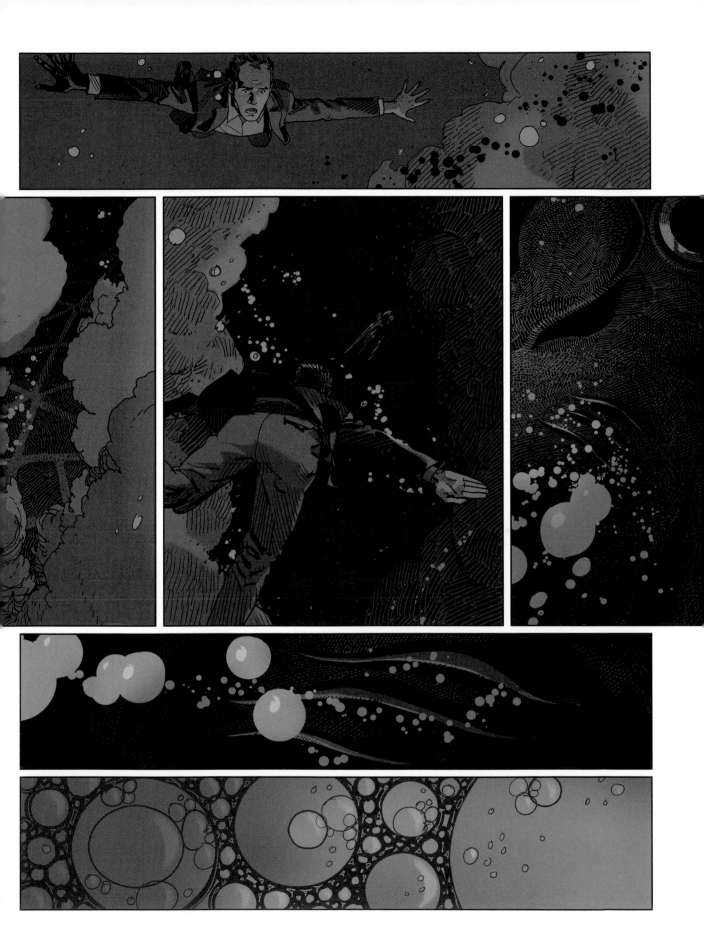

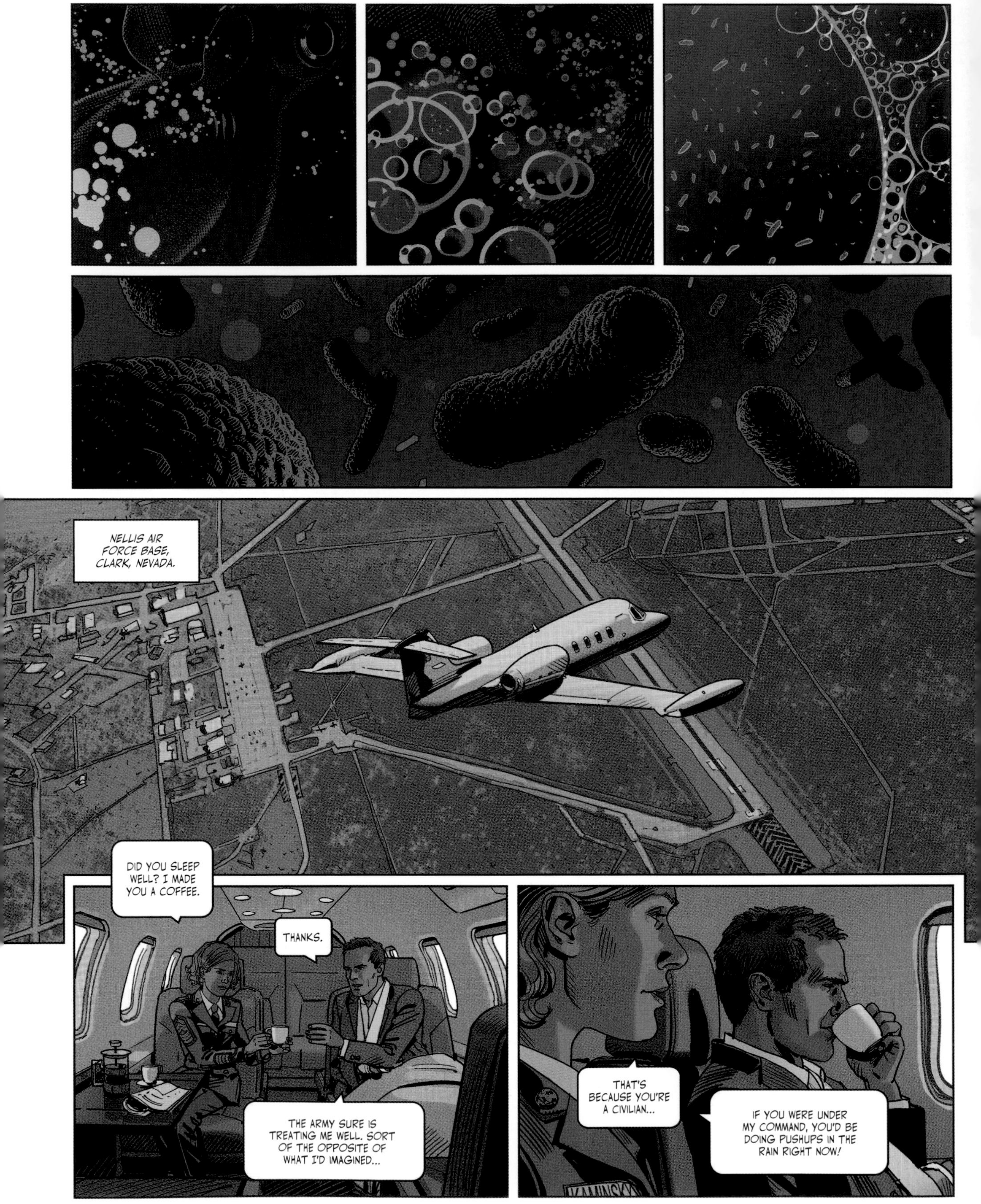
NELLIS AIR FORCE BASE, CLARK, NEVADA.
DID YOU SLEEP WELL? I MADE YOU A COFFEE.
THANKS.
THE ARMY SURE IS TREATING ME WELL. SORT OF THE OPPOSITE OF WHAT I'D IMAGINED...
THAT'S BECAUSE YOU'RE A CIVILIAN...
IF YOU WERE UNDER MY COMMAND, YOU'D BE DOING PUSHUPS IN THE RAIN RIGHT NOW!

DO YOU RECOGNIZE THESE PEOPLE?

YES, JULIA AND THE ONE WHO DIED IN MY LIVING ROOM...

JULIA CARPENTER AND DALE ROTHS. BOTH RESTAURANT EMPLOYEES FROM FORT COLLINS, COLORADO.

NOT EXTRATERRESTRIALS AT ALL.

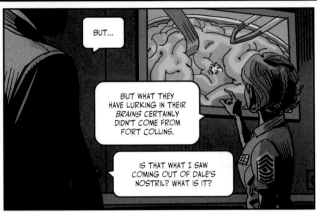

BUT...

BUT WHAT THEY HAVE LURKING IN THEIR *BRAINS* CERTAINLY DIDN'T COME FROM FORT COLLINS.

IS THAT WHAT I SAW COMING OUT OF DALE'S NOSTRIL? WHAT IS IT?

IT'S DIFFICULT TO SAY AT THIS STAGE. WE'LL NEED TO RUN SOME TESTS.

AS IT IS, I COULDN'T TELL YOU IF IT'S A NANOBOT OR A MINIATURE ALIEN.

EITHER WAY, IT SEEMS TO BE DEACTIVATED OR...DEAD. DEPENDS ON--

WHEN DO YOU THINK YOU'LL HAVE FINISHED ANALYZING THAT...THING?

KAMINSKY

"A FULL ANALYSIS COULD TAKE MONTHS OR EVEN MUCH, MUCH LONGER..."

"WE'VE NEVER SEEN *ANYTHING* LIKE IT BEFORE..."

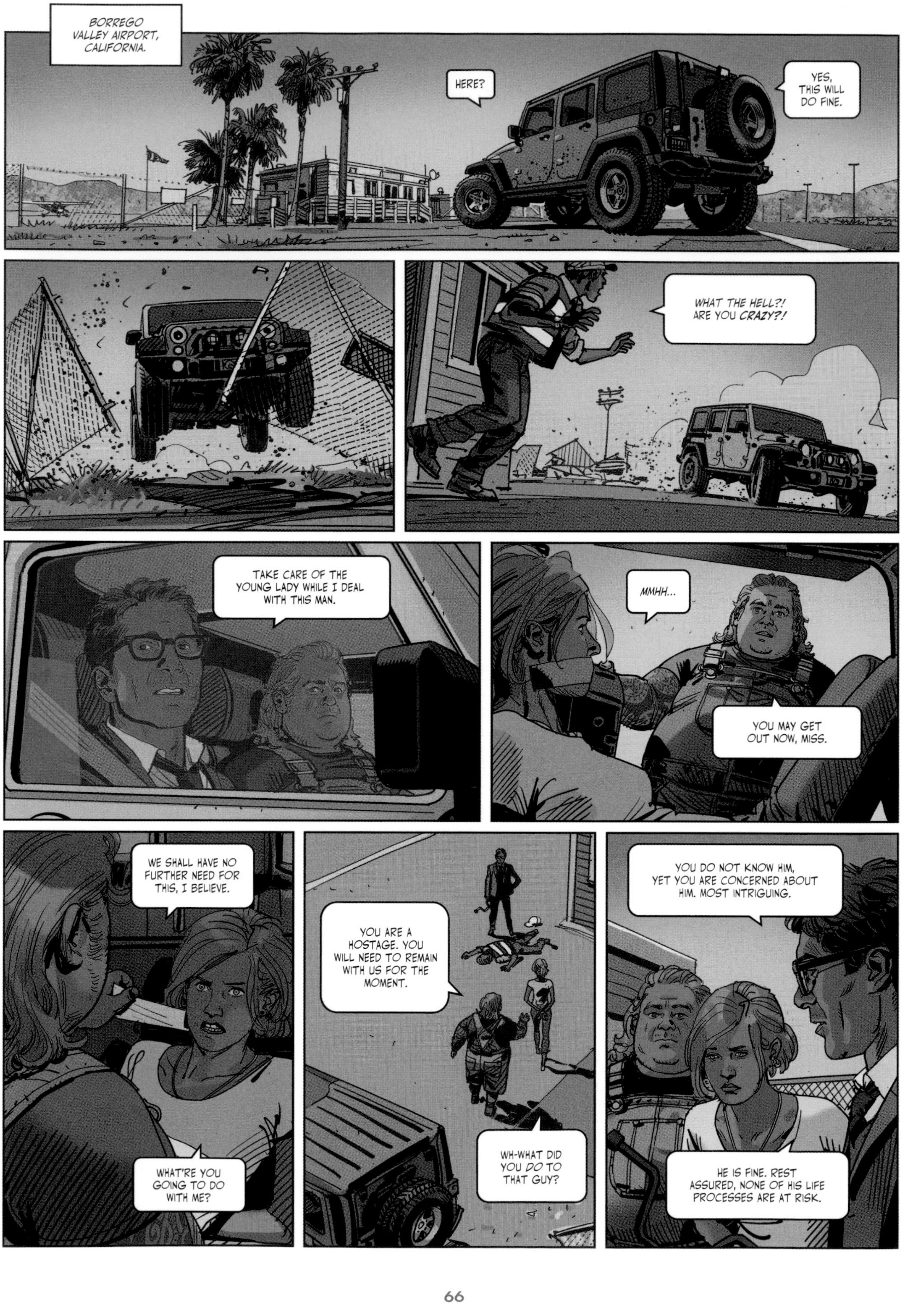
BORREGO VALLEY AIRPORT, CALIFORNIA.
HERE?
YES, THIS WILL DO FINE.
WHAT THE HELL?! ARE YOU CRAZY?!
TAKE CARE OF THE YOUNG LADY WHILE I DEAL WITH THIS MAN.
MMHH...
YOU MAY GET OUT NOW, MISS.
WE SHALL HAVE NO FURTHER NEED FOR THIS, I BELIEVE.
WHAT'RE YOU GOING TO DO WITH ME?
YOU ARE A HOSTAGE. YOU WILL NEED TO REMAIN WITH US FOR THE MOMENT.
WH-WHAT DID YOU DO TO THAT GUY?
YOU DO NOT KNOW HIM, YET YOU ARE CONCERNED ABOUT HIM. MOST INTRIGUING.
HE IS FINE. REST ASSURED, NONE OF HIS LIFE PROCESSES ARE AT RISK.

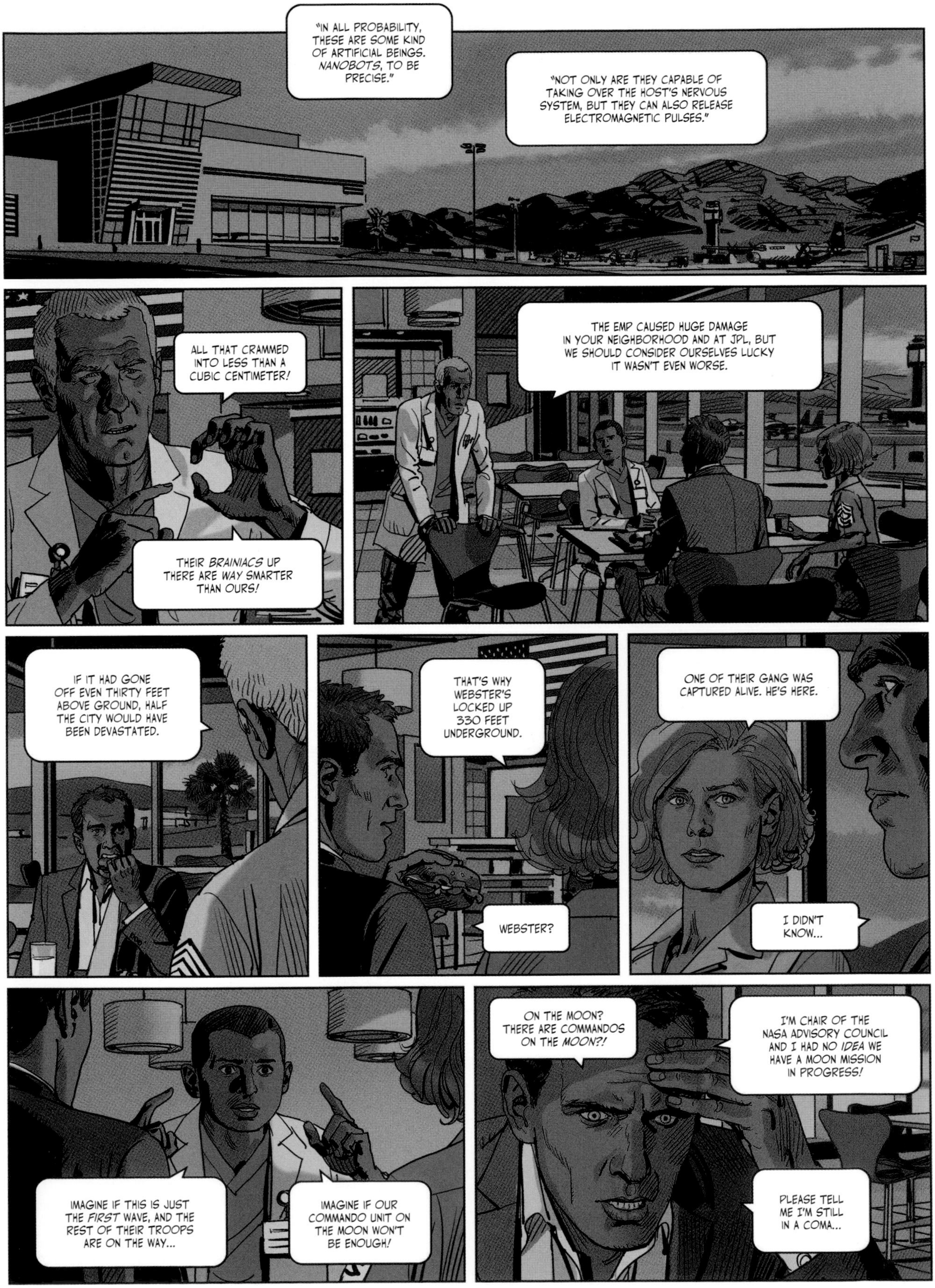
"IN ALL PROBABILITY, THESE ARE SOME KIND OF ARTIFICIAL BEINGS. *NANOBOTS*, TO BE PRECISE."
"NOT ONLY ARE THEY CAPABLE OF TAKING OVER THE HOST'S NERVOUS SYSTEM, BUT THEY CAN ALSO RELEASE ELECTROMAGNETIC PULSES."
ALL THAT CRAMMED INTO LESS THAN A CUBIC CENTIMETER!
THEIR *BRAINIACS* UP THERE ARE *WAY* SMARTER THAN OURS!
THE EMP CAUSED HUGE DAMAGE IN YOUR NEIGHBORHOOD AND AT JPL, BUT WE SHOULD CONSIDER OURSELVES LUCKY IT WASN'T EVEN WORSE.
IF IT HAD GONE OFF EVEN THIRTY FEET ABOVE GROUND, HALF THE CITY WOULD HAVE BEEN DEVASTATED.
THAT'S WHY WEBSTER'S LOCKED UP 330 FEET UNDERGROUND.
WEBSTER?
ONE OF THEIR GANG WAS CAPTURED ALIVE. HE'S HERE.
I DIDN'T KNOW...
IMAGINE IF THIS IS JUST THE *FIRST* WAVE, AND THE REST OF THEIR TROOPS ARE ON THE WAY...
IMAGINE IF OUR COMMANDO UNIT ON THE MOON WON'T BE ENOUGH!
ON THE MOON? THERE ARE COMMANDOS ON THE *MOON*?!
I'M CHAIR OF THE NASA ADVISORY COUNCIL AND I HAD NO *IDEA* WE HAVE A MOON MISSION IN PROGRESS!
PLEASE TELL ME I'M STILL IN A COMA...

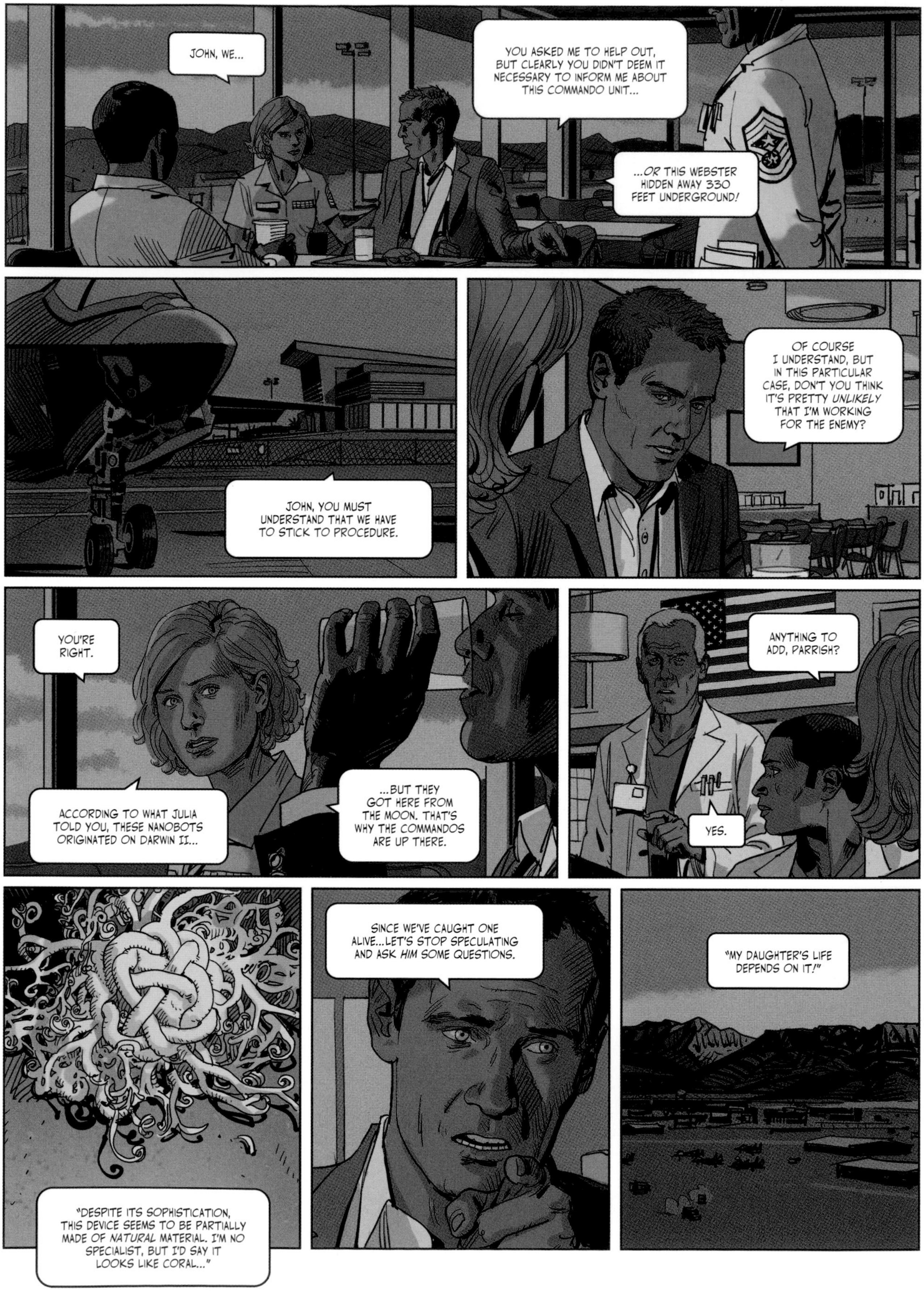
JOHN, WE...
YOU ASKED ME TO HELP OUT, BUT CLEARLY YOU DIDN'T DEEM IT NECESSARY TO INFORM ME ABOUT THIS COMMANDO UNIT...
...*OR* THIS WEBSTER HIDDEN AWAY 330 FEET UNDERGROUND!
JOHN, YOU MUST UNDERSTAND THAT WE HAVE TO STICK TO PROCEDURE.
OF COURSE I UNDERSTAND, BUT IN THIS PARTICULAR CASE, DON'T YOU THINK IT'S PRETTY *UNLIKELY* THAT I'M WORKING FOR THE ENEMY?
YOU'RE RIGHT.
ACCORDING TO WHAT JULIA TOLD YOU, THESE NANOBOTS ORIGINATED ON DARWIN II...
...BUT THEY GOT HERE FROM THE MOON. THAT'S WHY THE COMMANDOS ARE UP THERE.
ANYTHING TO ADD, PARRISH?
YES.
"DESPITE ITS SOPHISTICATION, THIS DEVICE SEEMS TO BE PARTIALLY MADE OF *NATURAL* MATERIAL. I'M NO SPECIALIST, BUT I'D SAY IT LOOKS LIKE CORAL..."
SINCE WE'VE CAUGHT ONE ALIVE...LET'S STOP SPECULATING AND ASK *HIM* SOME QUESTIONS.
"MY DAUGHTER'S LIFE DEPENDS ON IT!"

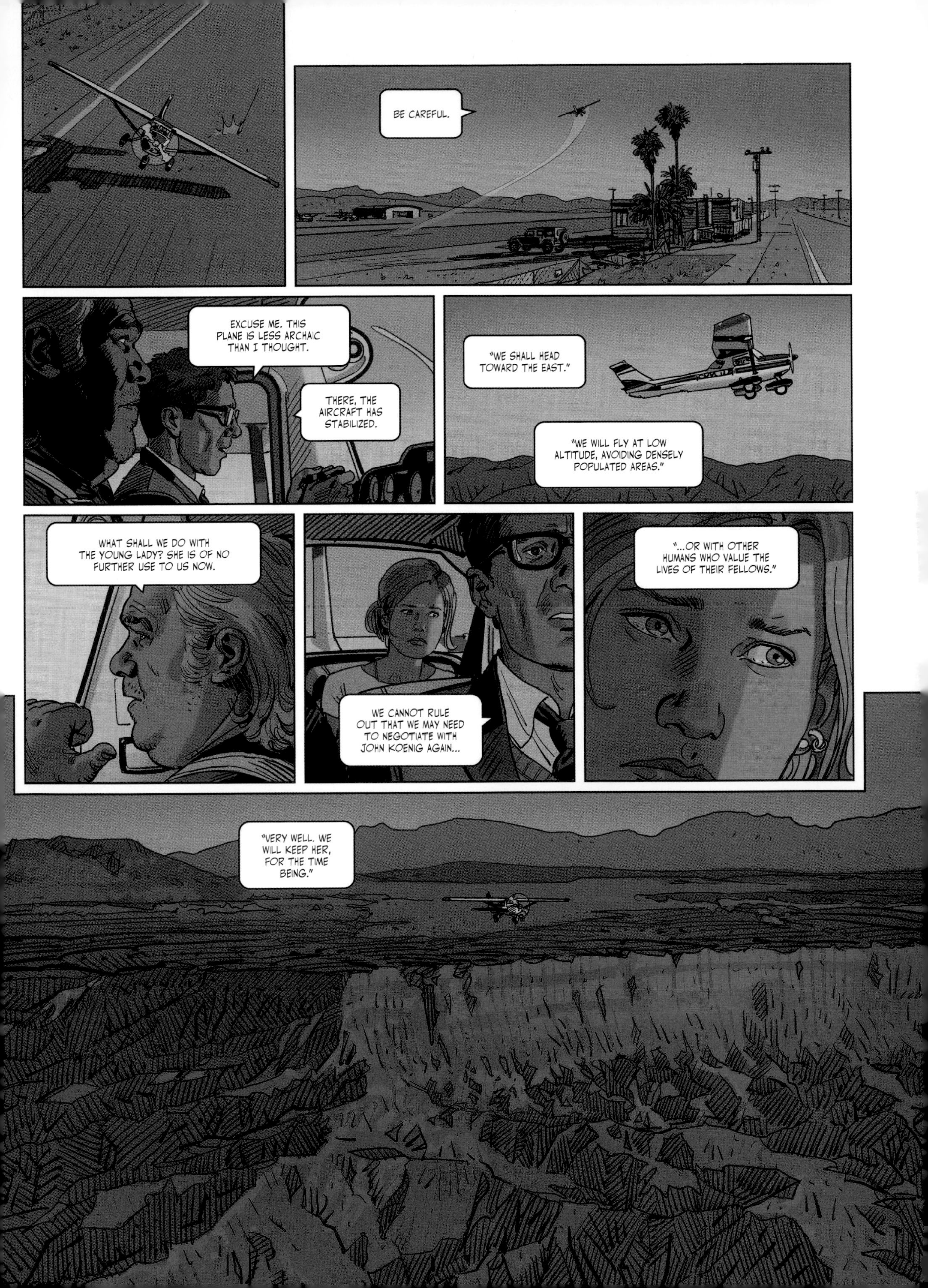
BE CAREFUL.
EXCUSE ME. THIS PLANE IS LESS ARCHAIC THAN I THOUGHT.
THERE, THE AIRCRAFT HAS STABILIZED.
"WE SHALL HEAD TOWARD THE EAST."
"WE WILL FLY AT LOW ALTITUDE, AVOIDING DENSELY POPULATED AREAS."
WHAT SHALL WE DO WITH THE YOUNG LADY? SHE IS OF NO FURTHER USE TO US NOW.
WE CANNOT RULE OUT THAT WE MAY NEED TO NEGOTIATE WITH JOHN KOENIG AGAIN...
"...OR WITH OTHER HUMANS WHO VALUE THE LIVES OF THEIR FELLOWS."
"VERY WELL. WE WILL KEEP HER, FOR THE TIME BEING."

SLOW DOWN, BRAUNER.

LINDEN?

YES?

IN A FEW MINUTES, WE'LL CROSS OVER TO THE DARK SIDE OF THE MOON AND LOSE CONTACT WITH EARTH.

WE'LL ONLY BE ABLE TO COMMUNICATE ONCE WE GET *BACK* FROM THE DARK SIDE.

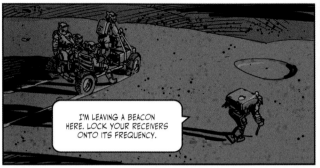

I'M LEAVING A BEACON HERE. LOCK YOUR RECEIVERS ONTO ITS FREQUENCY.

FROM HERE ON OUT, WE SWITCH TO NIGHT VISION. ADJUST YOUR HUDS.

WE'RE CLOSING IN ON THE GATES OF HELL, GUYS...

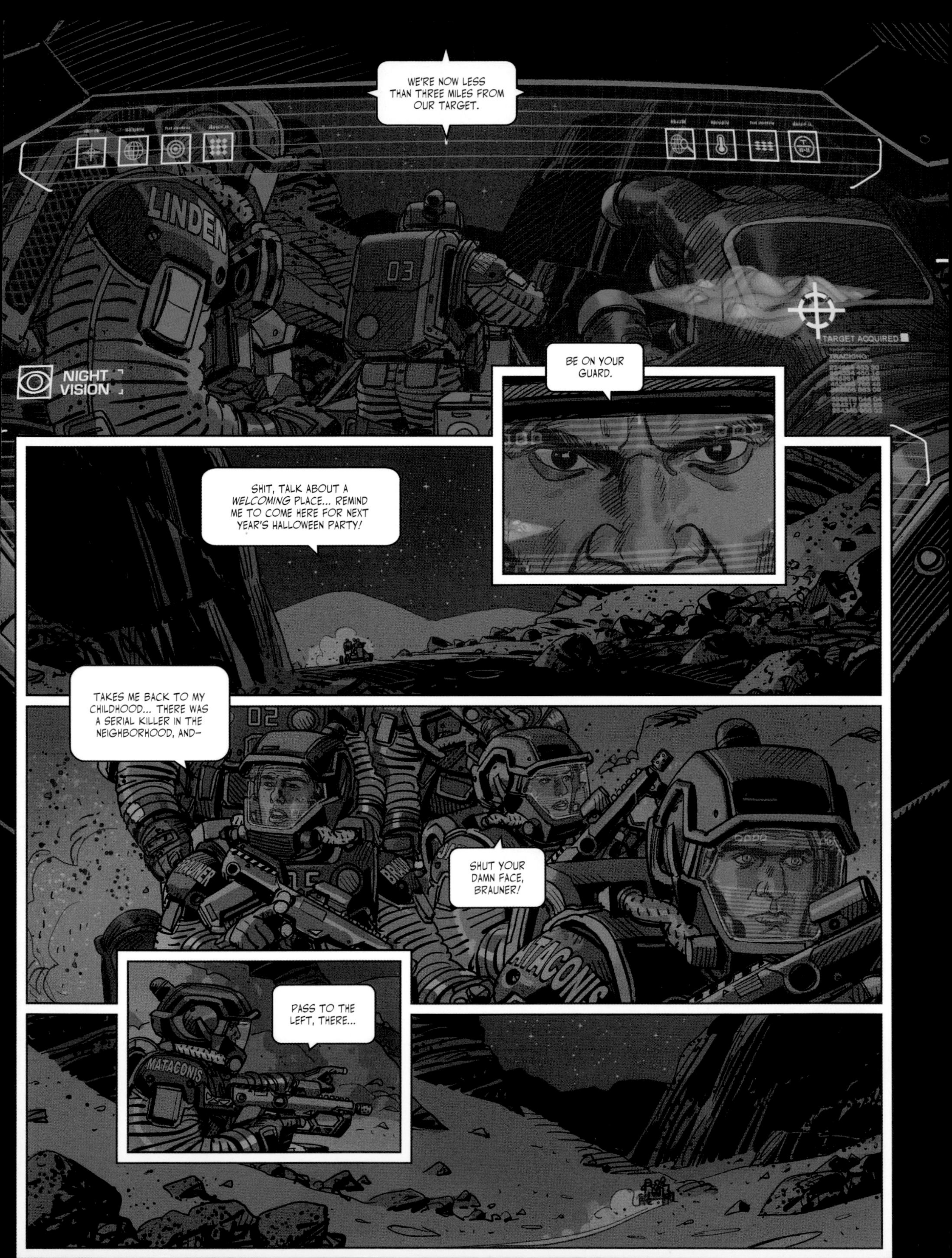
WE'RE NOW LESS THAN THREE MILES FROM OUR TARGET.
LINDEN
03
NIGHT VISION
TARGET ACQUIRED
TRACKING:
BE ON YOUR GUARD.
SHIT, TALK ABOUT A *WELCOMING* PLACE... REMIND ME TO COME HERE FOR NEXT YEAR'S HALLOWEEN PARTY!
TAKES ME BACK TO MY CHILDHOOD... THERE WAS A SERIAL KILLER IN THE NEIGHBORHOOD, AND–
02
SHUT YOUR DAMN FACE, BRAUNER!
PASS TO THE LEFT, THERE...
MATACONIS

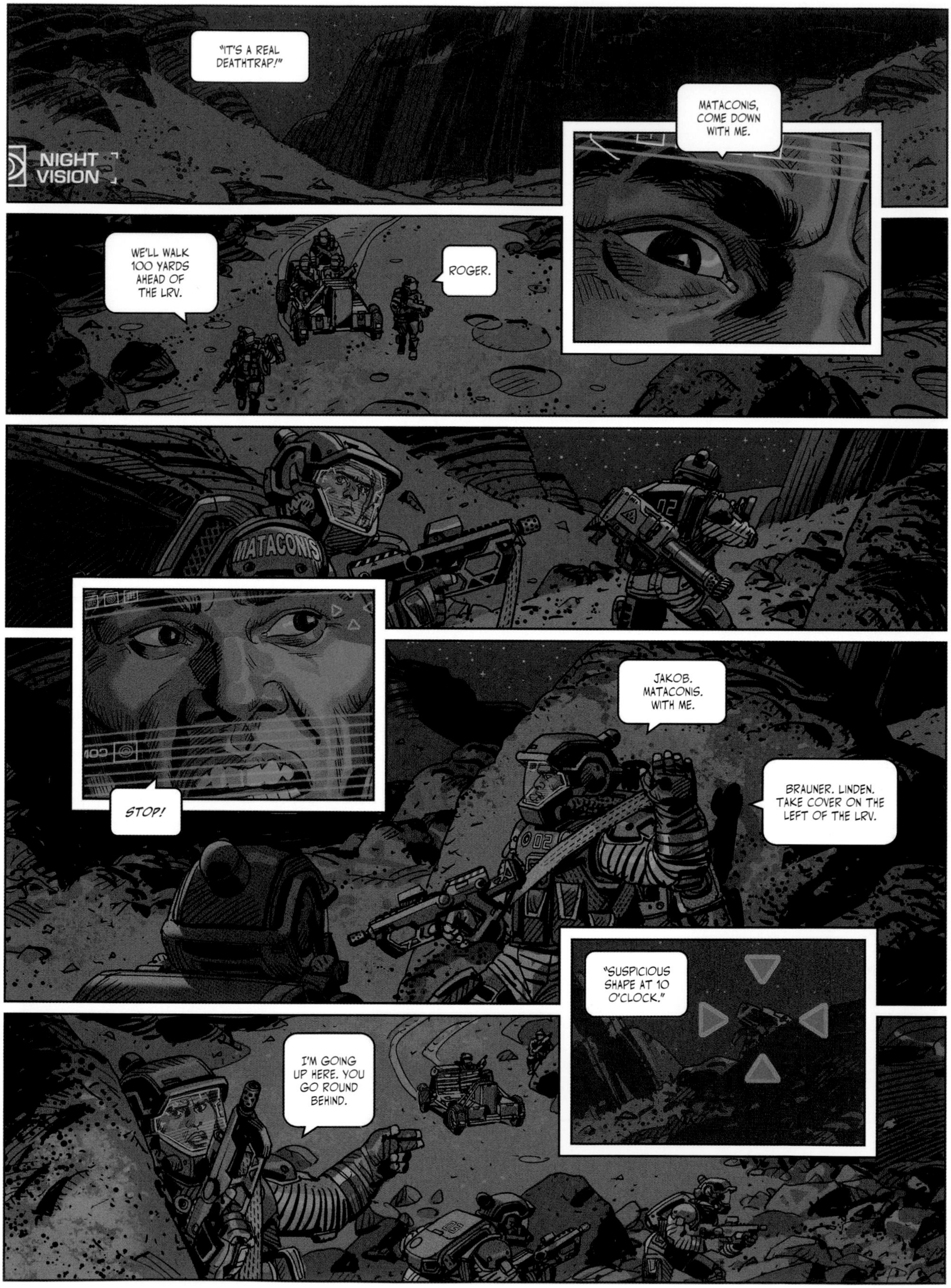
"IT'S A REAL DEATHTRAP!"
NIGHT VISION
MATACONIS, COME DOWN WITH ME.
WE'LL WALK 100 YARDS AHEAD OF THE LRV.
ROGER.
MATACONIS
STOP!
JAKOB. MATACONIS. WITH ME.
BRAUNER. LINDEN. TAKE COVER ON THE LEFT OF THE LRV.
"SUSPICIOUS SHAPE AT 10 O'CLOCK."
I'M GOING UP HERE. YOU GO ROUND BEHIND.

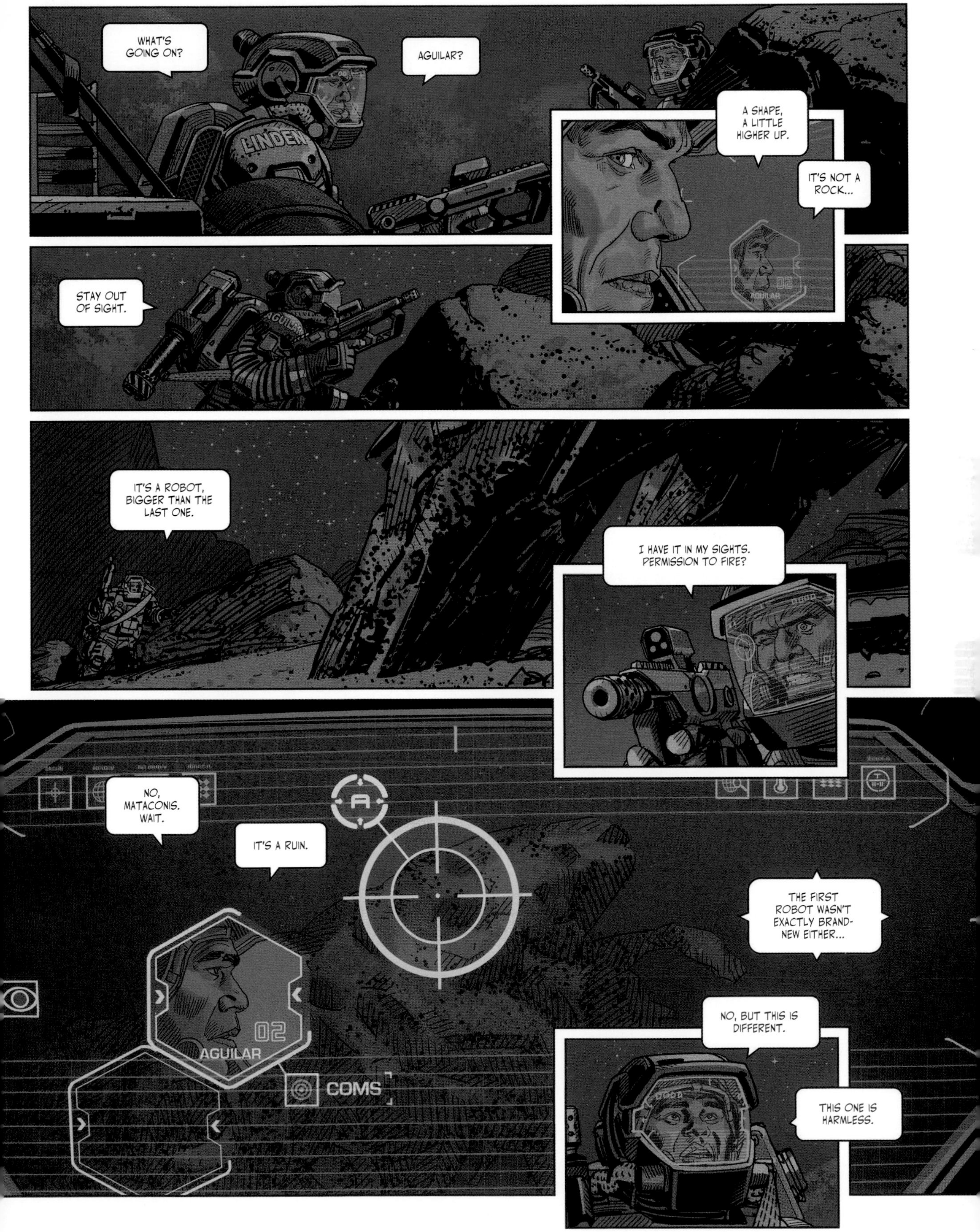
WHAT'S GOING ON?
LINDEN
AGUILAR?
A SHAPE, A LITTLE HIGHER UP.
IT'S NOT A ROCK...
02
AGUILAR
STAY OUT OF SIGHT.
AGUILAR
IT'S A ROBOT, BIGGER THAN THE LAST ONE.
I HAVE IT IN MY SIGHTS. PERMISSION TO FIRE?
NO, MATACONIS. WAIT.
IT'S A RUIN.
THE FIRST ROBOT WASN'T EXACTLY BRAND-NEW EITHER...
02
AGUILAR
COMS
NO, BUT THIS IS DIFFERENT.
THIS ONE IS HARMLESS.

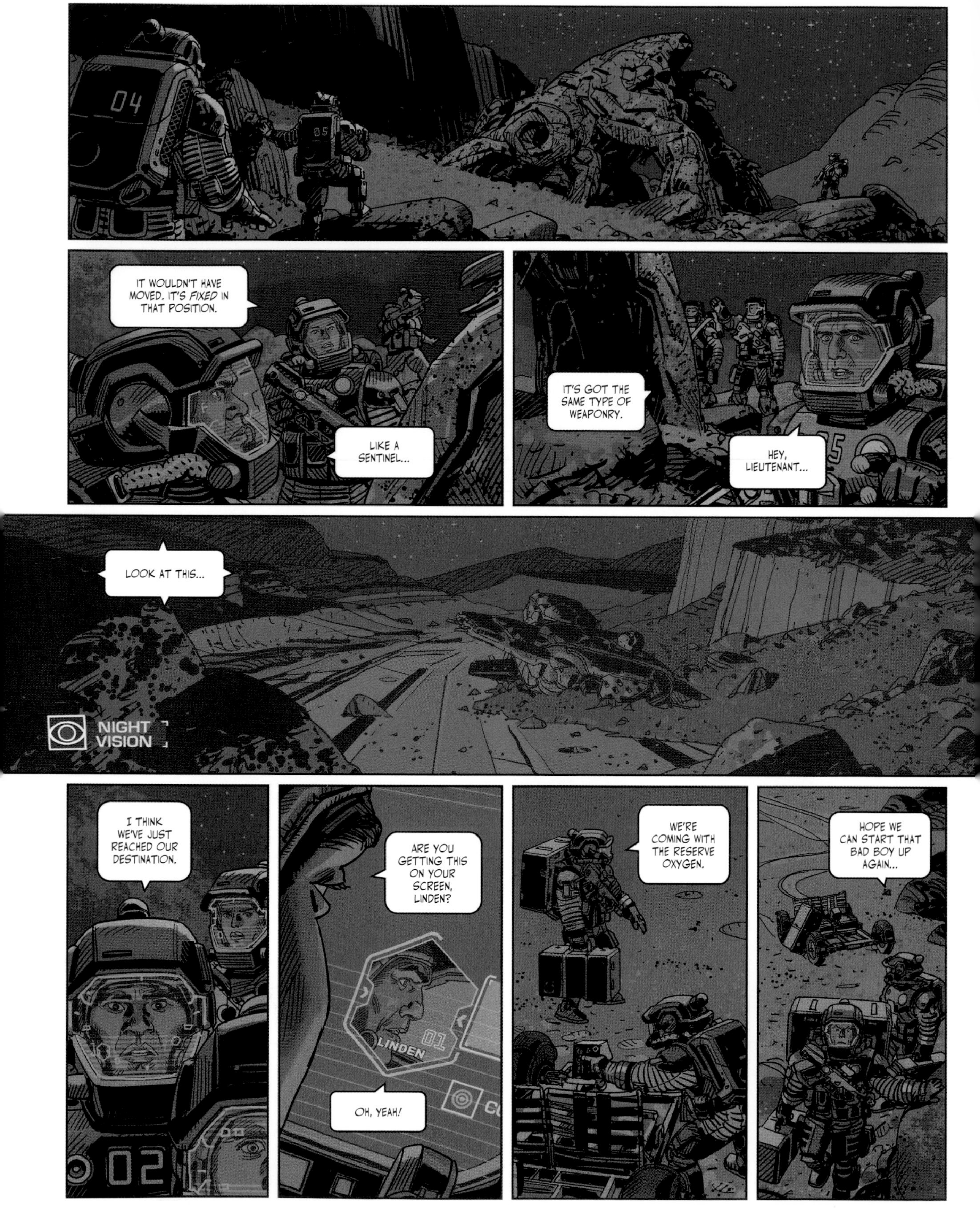
IT WOULDN'T HAVE MOVED. IT'S *FIXED* IN THAT POSITION.
LIKE A SENTINEL...
IT'S GOT THE SAME TYPE OF WEAPONRY.
HEY, LIEUTENANT...
LOOK AT THIS...
NIGHT VISION
I THINK WE'VE JUST REACHED OUR DESTINATION.
02
ARE YOU GETTING THIS ON YOUR SCREEN, LINDEN?
LINDEN
01
OH, YEAH!
WE'RE COMING WITH THE RESERVE OXYGEN.
HOPE WE CAN START THAT BAD BOY UP AGAIN...

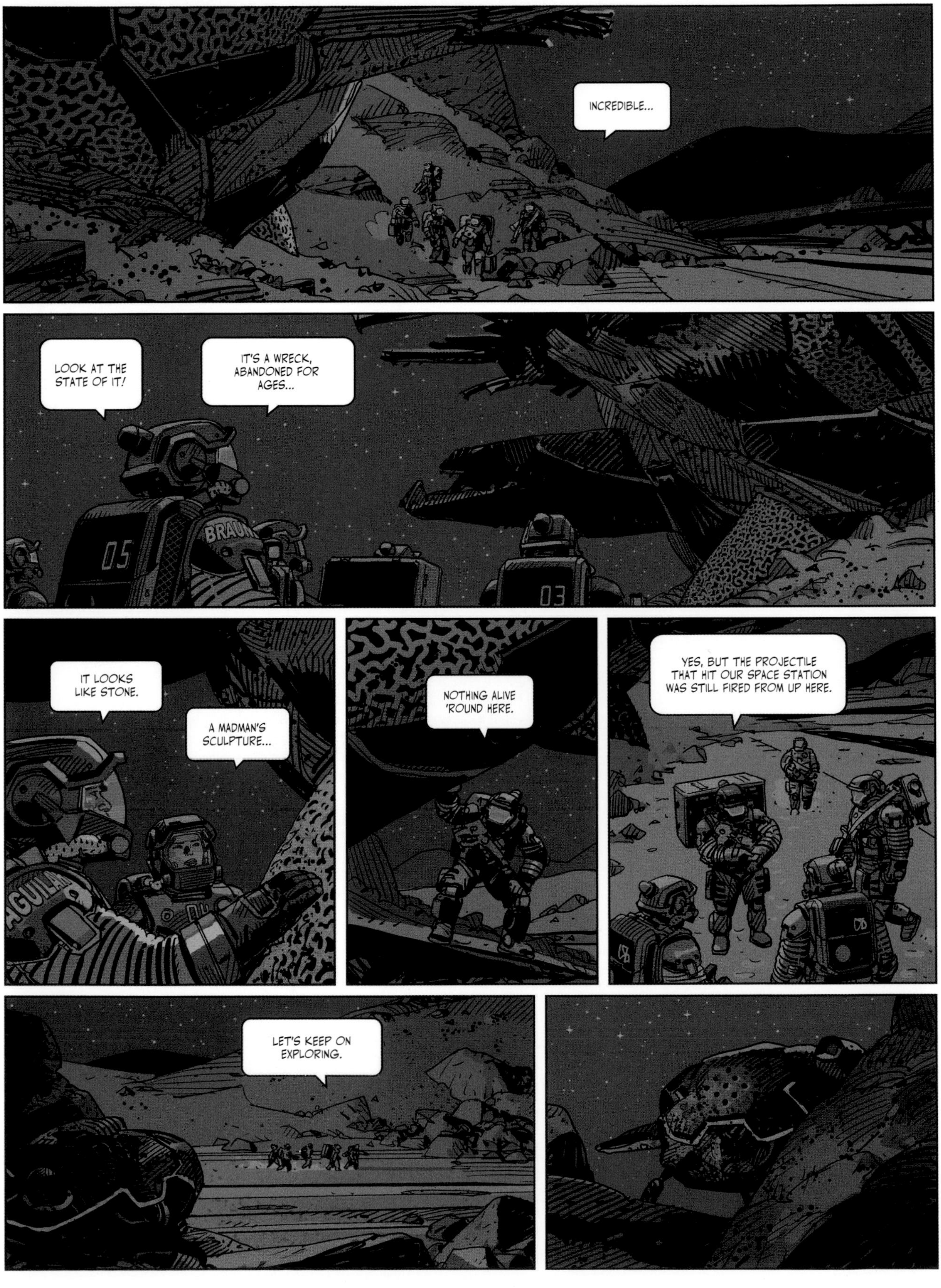
INCREDIBLE...
LOOK AT THE STATE OF IT!
IT'S A WRECK, ABANDONED FOR AGES...
BRAUN
05
03
IT LOOKS LIKE STONE.
A MADMAN'S SCULPTURE...
NOTHING ALIVE 'ROUND HERE.
YES, BUT THE PROJECTILE THAT HIT OUR SPACE STATION WAS STILL FIRED FROM UP HERE.
LET'S KEEP ON EXPLORING.

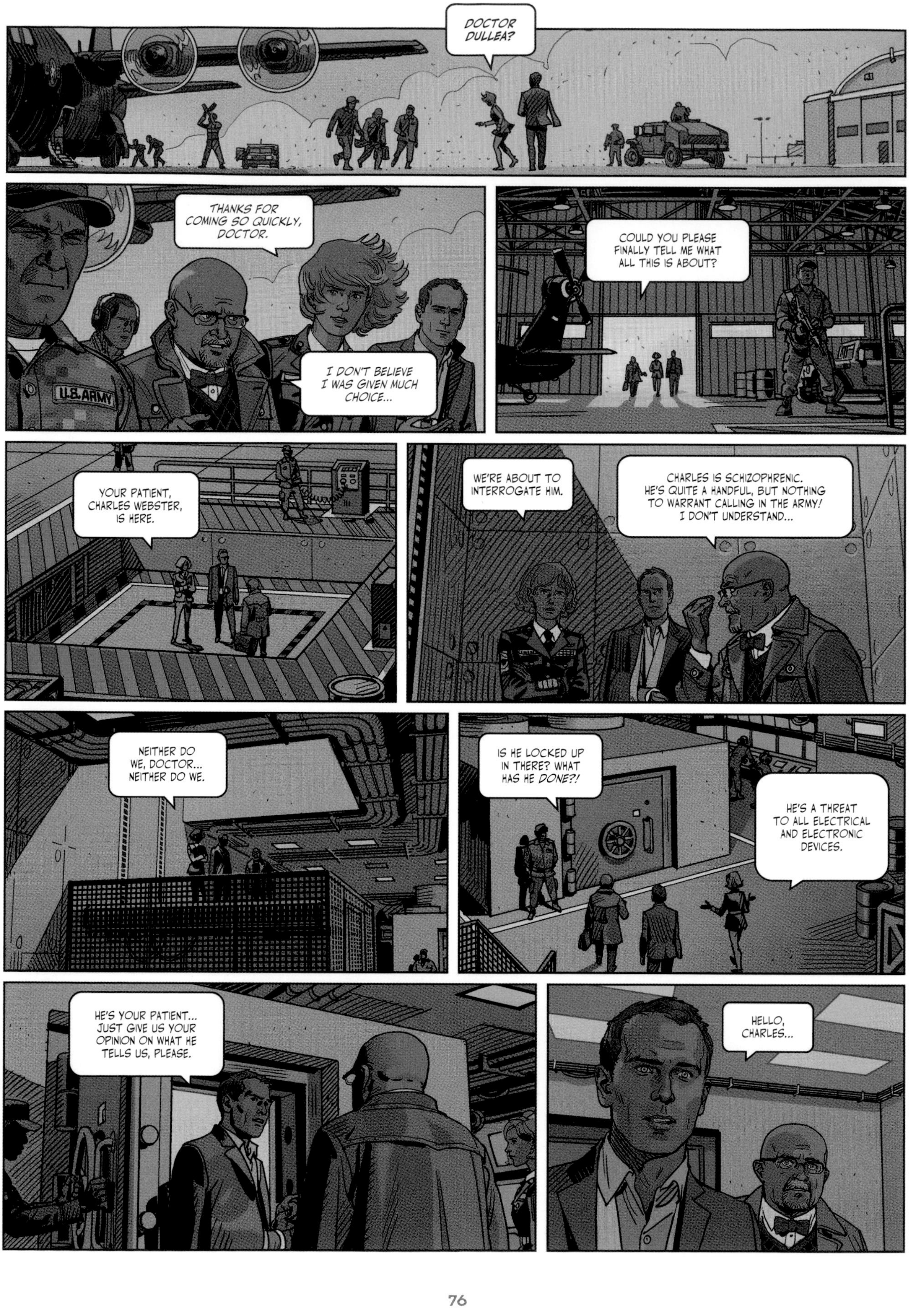

DOCTOR DULLEA?
THANKS FOR COMING SO QUICKLY, DOCTOR.
I DON'T BELIEVE I WAS GIVEN MUCH CHOICE...
U.S. ARMY
COULD YOU PLEASE FINALLY TELL ME WHAT ALL THIS IS ABOUT?
YOUR PATIENT, CHARLES WEBSTER, IS HERE.
WE'RE ABOUT TO INTERROGATE HIM.
CHARLES IS SCHIZOPHRENIC. HE'S QUITE A HANDFUL, BUT NOTHING TO WARRANT CALLING IN THE ARMY! I DON'T UNDERSTAND...
NEITHER DO WE, DOCTOR... NEITHER DO WE.
IS HE LOCKED UP IN THERE? WHAT HAS HE DONE?!
HE'S A THREAT TO ALL ELECTRICAL AND ELECTRONIC DEVICES.
HE'S YOUR PATIENT... JUST GIVE US YOUR OPINION ON WHAT HE TELLS US, PLEASE.
HELLO, CHARLES...

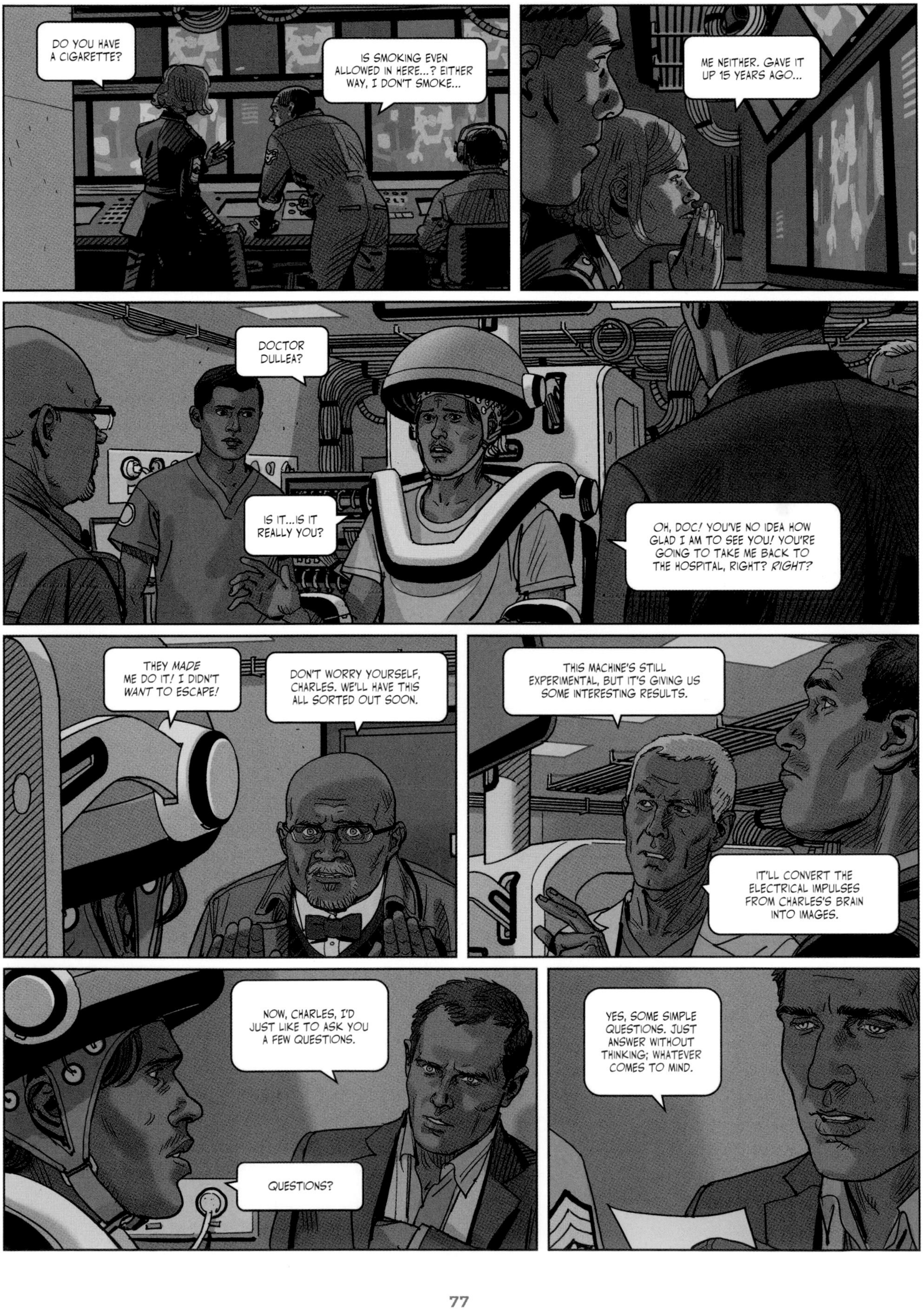
DO YOU HAVE A CIGARETTE?
IS SMOKING EVEN ALLOWED IN HERE...? EITHER WAY, I DON'T SMOKE...
ME NEITHER. GAVE IT UP 15 YEARS AGO...
DOCTOR DULLEA?
IS IT...IS IT REALLY YOU?
OH, DOC! YOU'VE NO IDEA HOW GLAD I AM TO SEE YOU! YOU'RE GOING TO TAKE ME BACK TO THE HOSPITAL, RIGHT? *RIGHT?*
THEY *MADE* ME DO IT! I DIDN'T *WANT* TO ESCAPE!
DON'T WORRY YOURSELF, CHARLES. WE'LL HAVE THIS ALL SORTED OUT SOON.
THIS MACHINE'S STILL EXPERIMENTAL, BUT IT'S GIVING US SOME INTERESTING RESULTS.
IT'LL CONVERT THE ELECTRICAL IMPULSES FROM CHARLES'S BRAIN INTO IMAGES.
NOW, CHARLES, I'D JUST LIKE TO ASK YOU A FEW QUESTIONS.
QUESTIONS?
YES, SOME SIMPLE QUESTIONS. JUST ANSWER WITHOUT THINKING; WHATEVER COMES TO MIND.

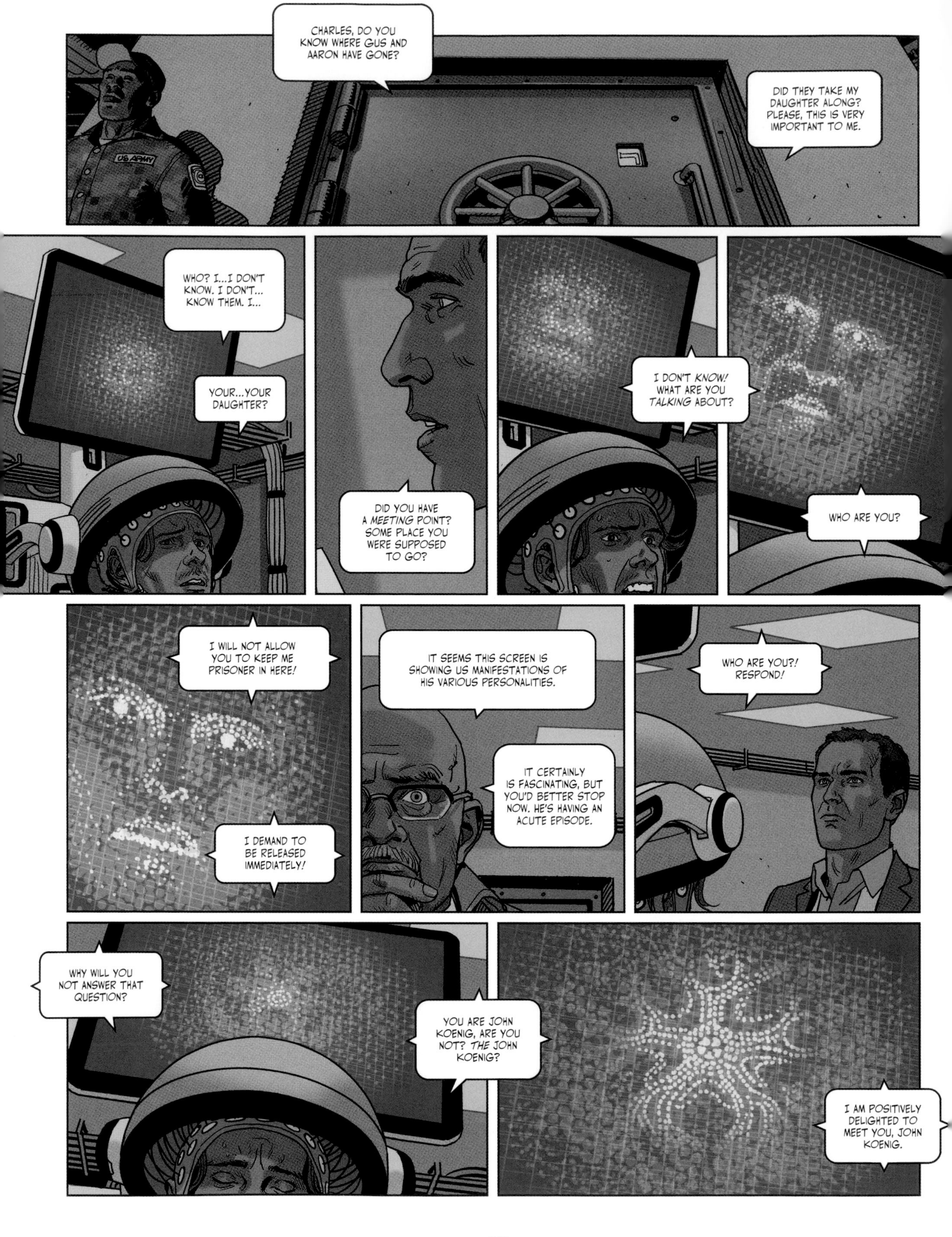
CHARLES, DO YOU KNOW WHERE GUS AND AARON HAVE GONE?
DID THEY TAKE MY DAUGHTER ALONG? PLEASE, THIS IS VERY IMPORTANT TO ME.
US ARMY
WHO? I...I DON'T KNOW. I DON'T... KNOW THEM. I...
YOUR...YOUR DAUGHTER?
DID YOU HAVE A *MEETING* POINT? SOME PLACE YOU WERE SUPPOSED TO GO?
I DON'T *KNOW!* WHAT ARE YOU *TALKING* ABOUT?
WHO ARE YOU?
I WILL NOT ALLOW YOU TO KEEP ME PRISONER IN HERE!
I DEMAND TO BE RELEASED IMMEDIATELY!
IT SEEMS THIS SCREEN IS SHOWING US MANIFESTATIONS OF HIS VARIOUS PERSONALITIES.
IT CERTAINLY IS FASCINATING, BUT YOU'D BETTER STOP NOW. HE'S HAVING AN ACUTE EPISODE.
WHO ARE YOU?! RESPOND!
WHY WILL YOU NOT ANSWER THAT QUESTION?
YOU ARE JOHN KOENIG, ARE YOU NOT? *THE* JOHN KOENIG?
I AM POSITIVELY DELIGHTED TO MEET YOU, JOHN KOENIG.

YES, I AM JOHN KOENIG.

AND YOU? WHO ARE YOU?

MY NAME? CALL ME SAM. IT WILL BE MORE PRACTICAL.

SAM?

I'VE NEVER HEARD OF A "SAM." IT ISN'T ONE OF HIS USUAL PERSONALITIES.

THIS IS A NEW INCARNATION. I'M AFRAID HE'S REGRESSING.

WHY NOT ANESTHETIZE CHARLES, SO THAT I MAY HAVE A MORE STRAIGHTFORWARD CONVERSATION WITH JOHN KOENIG?

DO AS HE SAYS.

I DON'T REALLY KNOW THE CORRECT DOSAGE FOR THIS KIND OF OPERATION...

NO NEED TO BE CONCERNED.

THE MAIN THING IS TO PACIFY CHARLES'S BRAIN FOR SEVERAL MOMENTS.

IT IS EXTREMELY DIFFICULT TO CONTROL HIM.

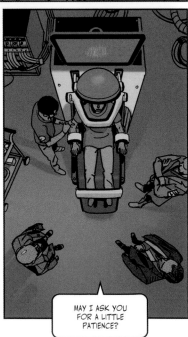

MAY I ASK YOU FOR A LITTLE PATIENCE?

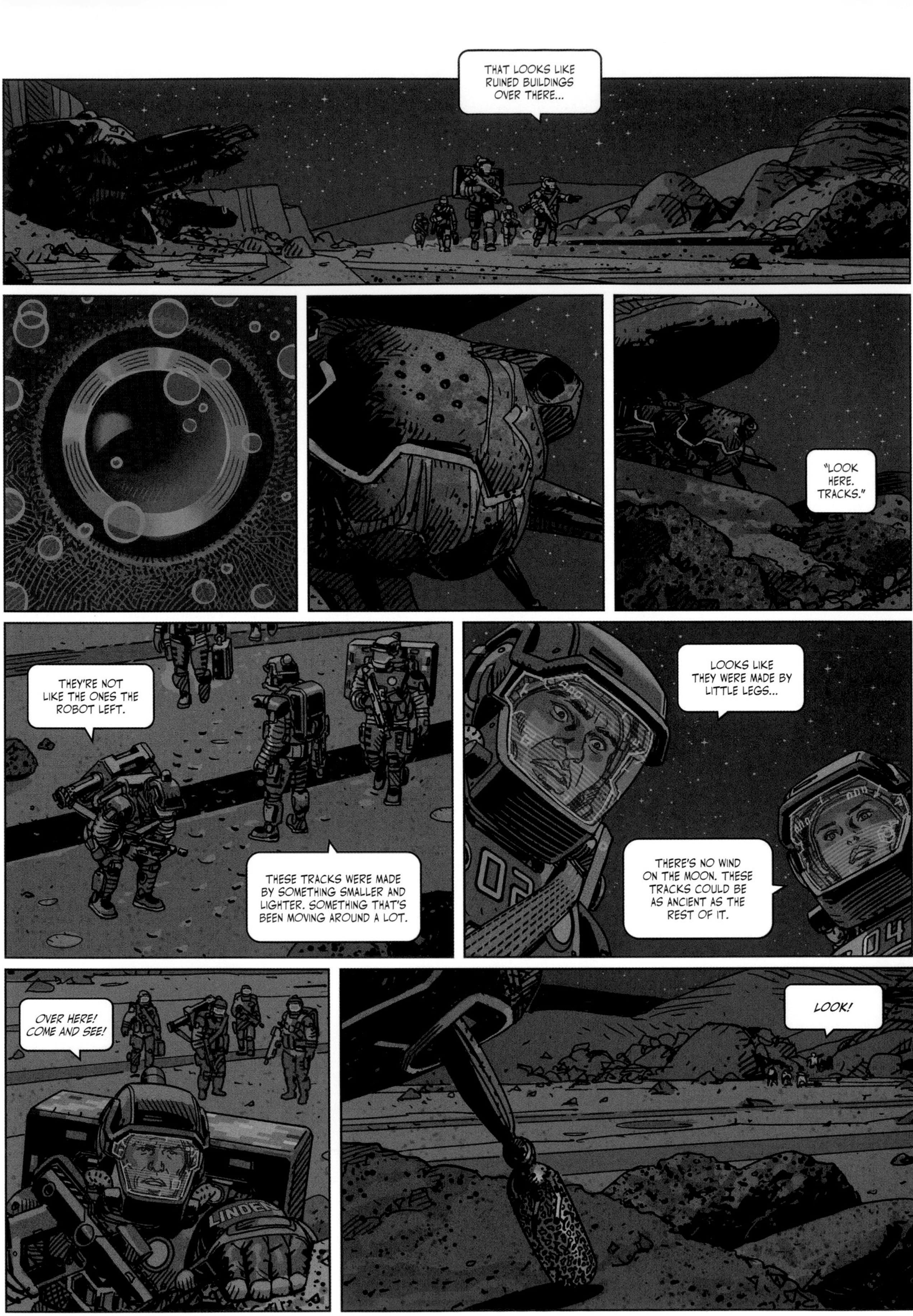
THAT LOOKS LIKE RUINED BUILDINGS OVER THERE...
"LOOK HERE. TRACKS."
THEY'RE NOT LIKE THE ONES THE ROBOT LEFT.
THESE TRACKS WERE MADE BY SOMETHING SMALLER AND LIGHTER. SOMETHING THAT'S BEEN MOVING AROUND A LOT.
LOOKS LIKE THEY WERE MADE BY LITTLE LEGS...
THERE'S NO WIND ON THE MOON. THESE TRACKS COULD BE AS ANCIENT AS THE REST OF IT.
OVER HERE! COME AND SEE!
LINDE
LOOK!

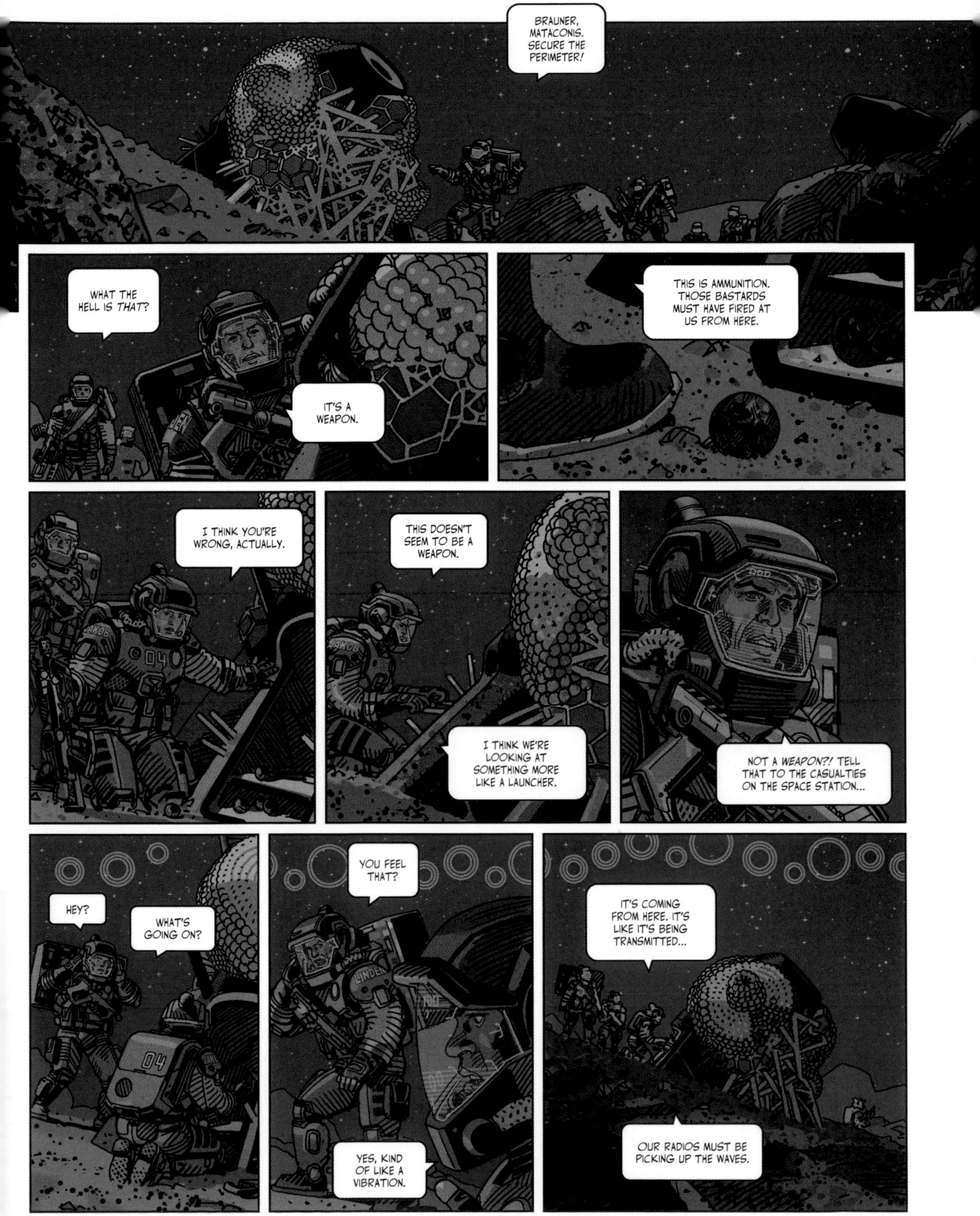

BRAUNER, MATACONIS. SECURE THE PERIMETER!
WHAT THE HELL IS THAT?
IT'S A WEAPON.
THIS IS AMMUNITION. THOSE BASTARDS MUST HAVE FIRED AT US FROM HERE.
I THINK YOU'RE WRONG, ACTUALLY.
THIS DOESN'T SEEM TO BE A WEAPON.
I THINK WE'RE LOOKING AT SOMETHING MORE LIKE A LAUNCHER.
NOT A WEAPON?! TELL THAT TO THE CASUALTIES ON THE SPACE STATION...
HEY?
WHAT'S GOING ON?
YOU FEEL THAT?
YES, KIND OF LIKE A VIBRATION.
IT'S COMING FROM HERE. IT'S LIKE IT'S BEING TRANSMITTED...
OUR RADIOS MUST BE PICKING UP THE WAVES.

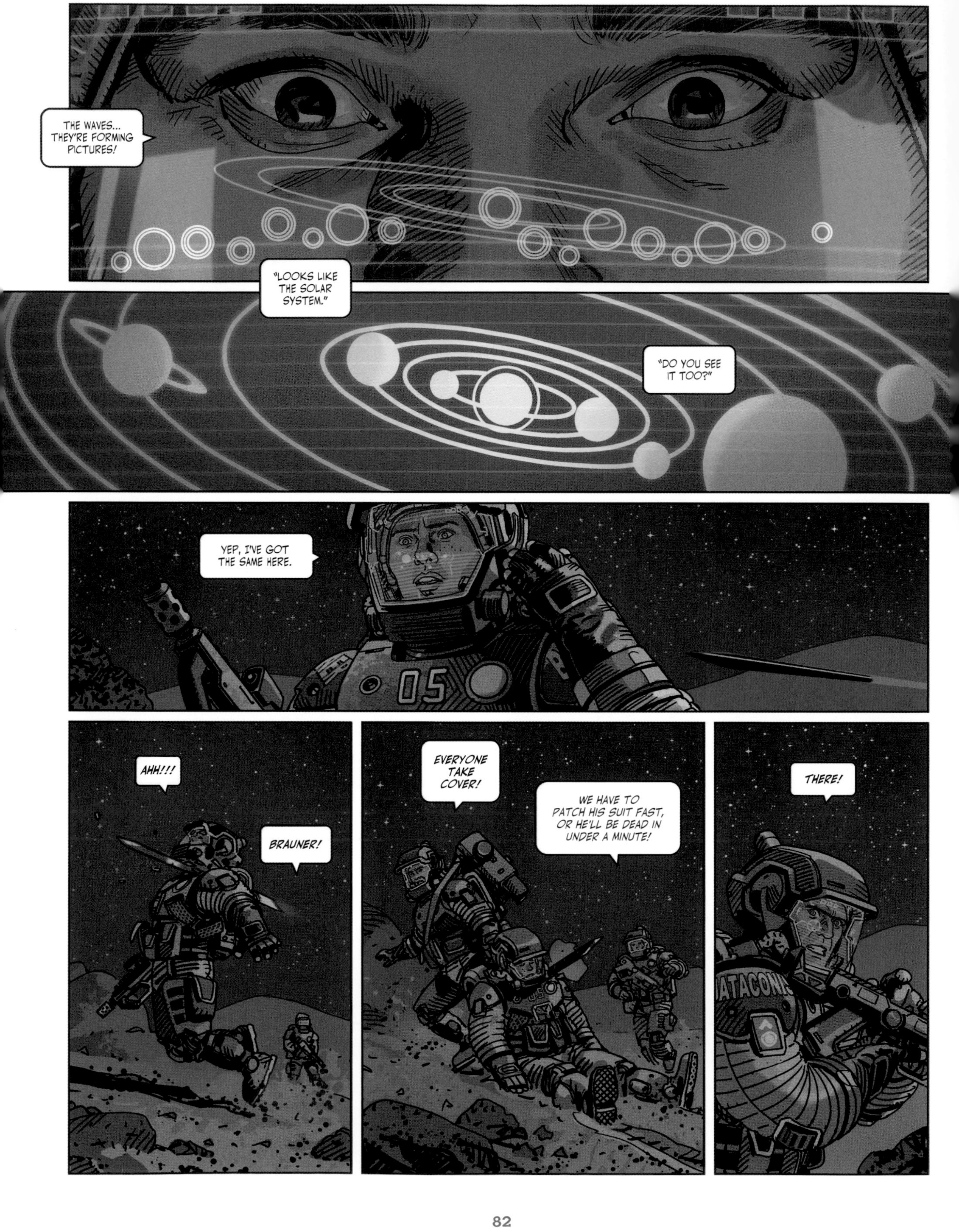
THE WAVES... THEY'RE FORMING PICTURES!
"LOOKS LIKE THE SOLAR SYSTEM."
"DO YOU SEE IT TOO?"
YEP, I'VE GOT THE SAME HERE.
AHH!!!
BRAUNER!
EVERYONE TAKE COVER!
WE HAVE TO PATCH HIS SUIT FAST, OR HE'LL BE DEAD IN UNDER A MINUTE!
THERE!

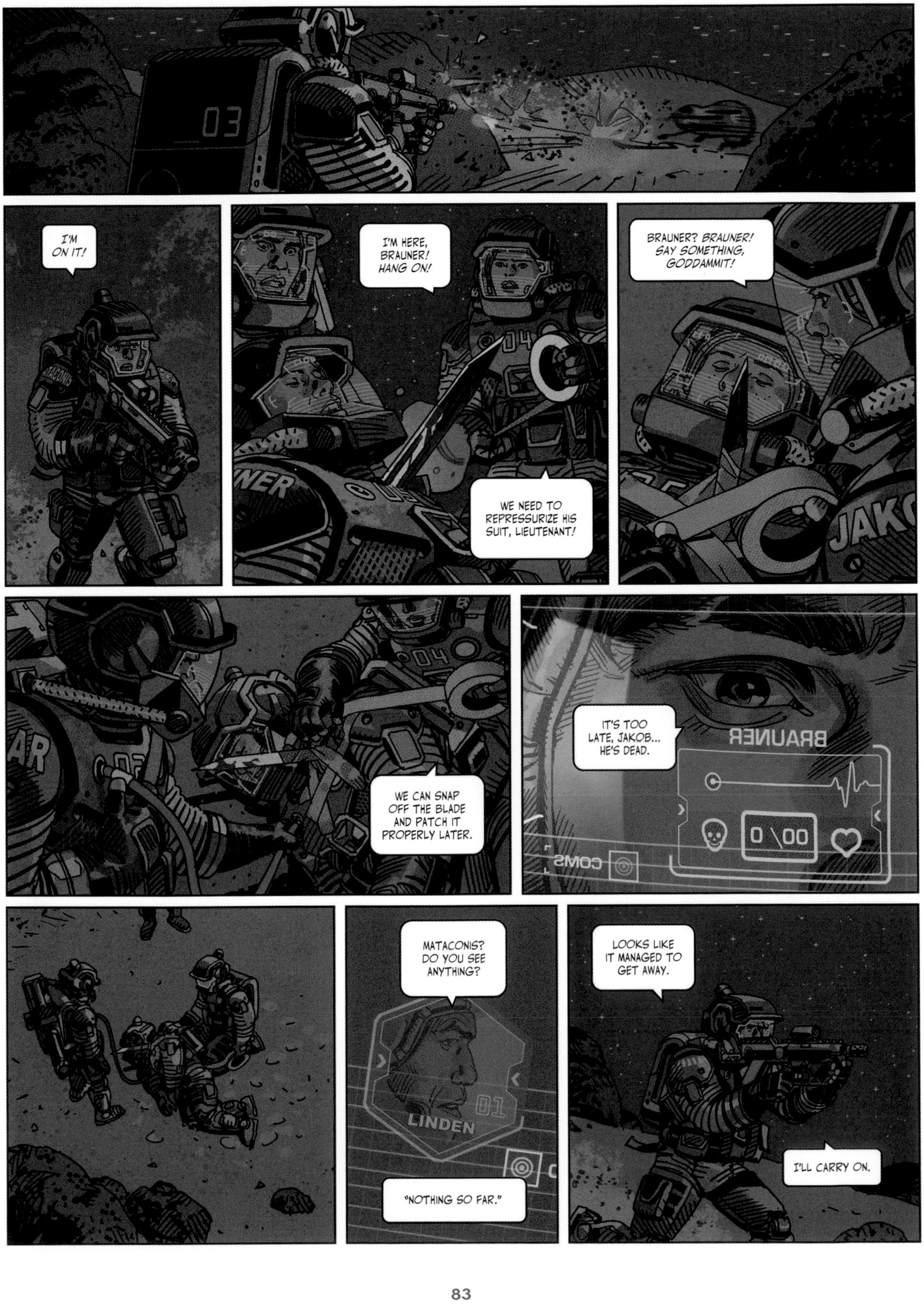

I'M ON IT!
I'M HERE, BRAUNER! HANG ON!
WE NEED TO REPRESSURIZE HIS SUIT, LIEUTENANT!
BRAUNER? BRAUNER! SAY SOMETHING, GODDAMMIT!
WE CAN SNAP OFF THE BLADE AND PATCH IT PROPERLY LATER.
IT'S TOO LATE, JAKOB... HE'S DEAD.
BRAUNER
COMS
MATACONIS? DO YOU SEE ANYTHING?
LINDEN
"NOTHING SO FAR."
LOOKS LIKE IT MANAGED TO GET AWAY.
I'LL CARRY ON.

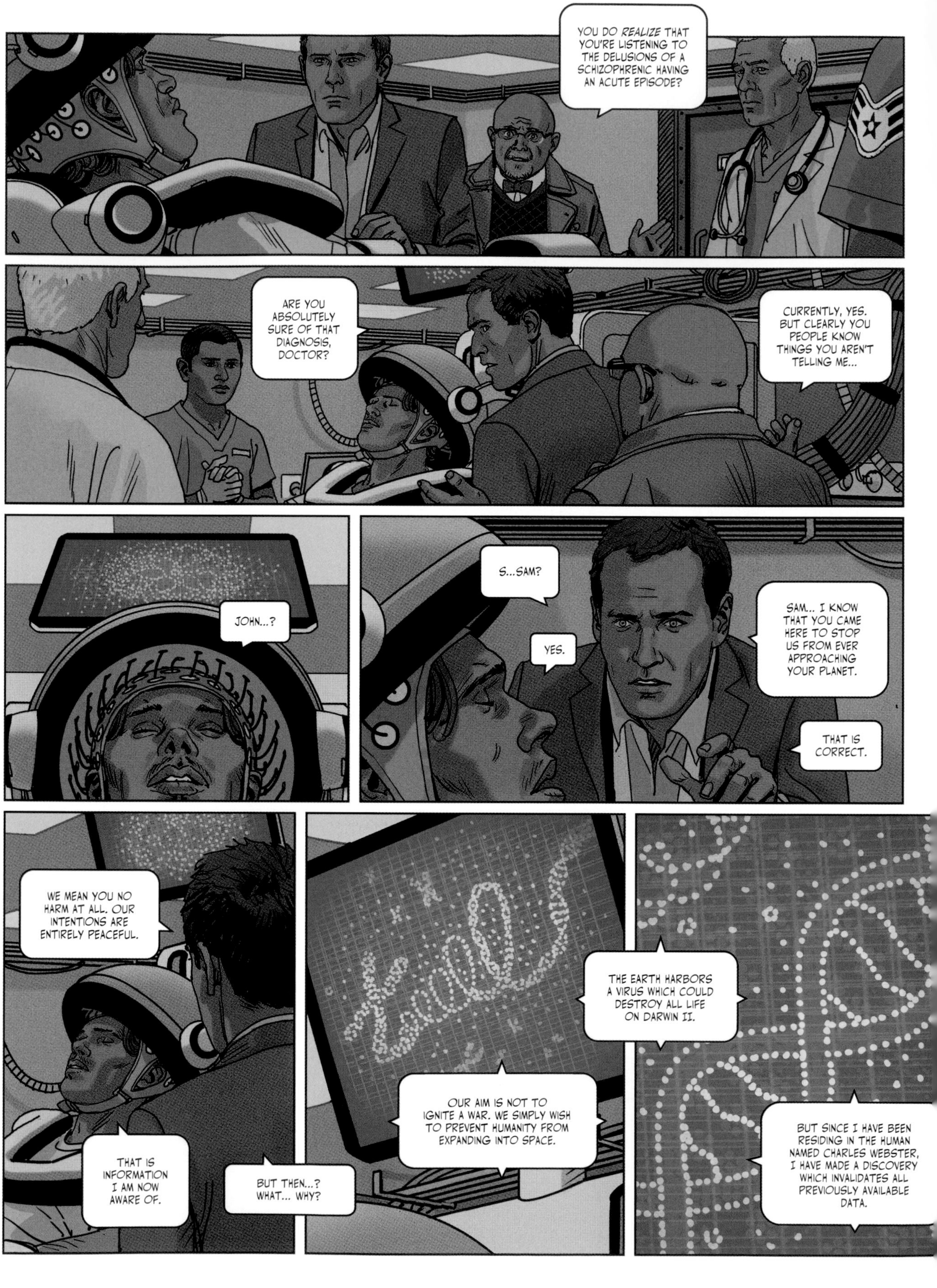
YOU DO *REALIZE* THAT YOU'RE LISTENING TO THE DELUSIONS OF A SCHIZOPHRENIC HAVING AN ACUTE EPISODE?
ARE YOU ABSOLUTELY SURE OF THAT DIAGNOSIS, DOCTOR?
CURRENTLY, YES. BUT CLEARLY YOU PEOPLE KNOW THINGS YOU AREN'T TELLING ME...
JOHN...?
S...SAM?
YES.
SAM... I KNOW THAT YOU CAME HERE TO STOP US FROM EVER APPROACHING YOUR PLANET.
THAT IS CORRECT.
WE MEAN YOU NO HARM AT ALL. OUR INTENTIONS ARE ENTIRELY PEACEFUL.
THAT IS INFORMATION I AM NOW AWARE OF.
BUT THEN...? WHAT... WHY?
OUR AIM IS NOT TO IGNITE A WAR. WE SIMPLY WISH TO PREVENT HUMANITY FROM EXPANDING INTO SPACE.
THE EARTH HARBORS A VIRUS WHICH COULD DESTROY ALL LIFE ON DARWIN II.
BUT SINCE I HAVE BEEN RESIDING IN THE HUMAN NAMED CHARLES WEBSTER, I HAVE MADE A DISCOVERY WHICH INVALIDATES ALL PREVIOUSLY AVAILABLE DATA.

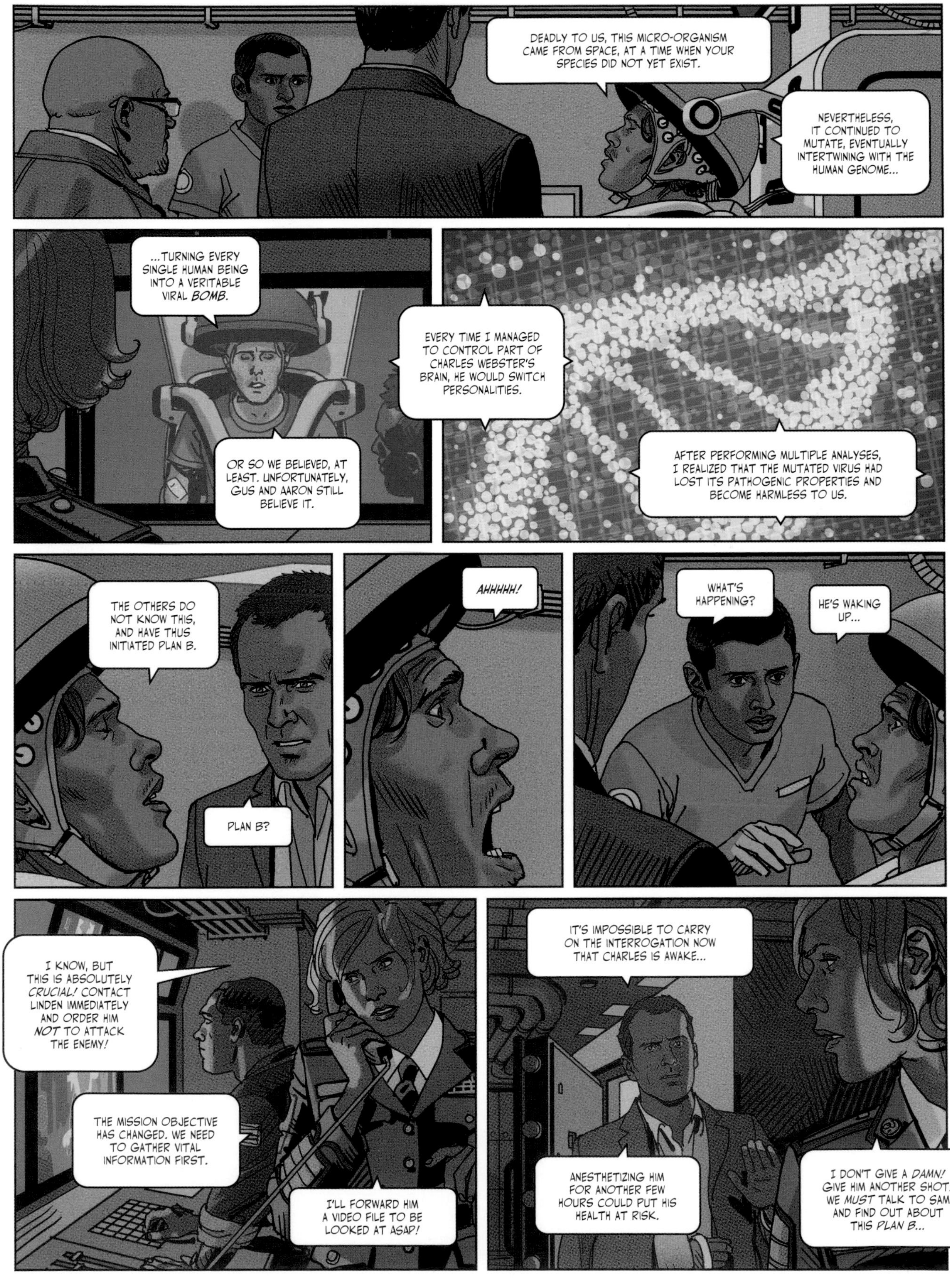
DEADLY TO US, THIS MICRO-ORGANISM CAME FROM SPACE, AT A TIME WHEN YOUR SPECIES DID NOT YET EXIST.
NEVERTHELESS, IT CONTINUED TO MUTATE, EVENTUALLY INTERTWINING WITH THE HUMAN GENOME...
...TURNING EVERY SINGLE HUMAN BEING INTO A VERITABLE VIRAL *BOMB.*
OR SO WE BELIEVED, AT LEAST. UNFORTUNATELY, GUS AND AARON STILL BELIEVE IT.
EVERY TIME I MANAGED TO CONTROL PART OF CHARLES WEBSTER'S BRAIN, HE WOULD SWITCH PERSONALITIES.
AFTER PERFORMING MULTIPLE ANALYSES, I REALIZED THAT THE MUTATED VIRUS HAD LOST ITS PATHOGENIC PROPERTIES AND BECOME HARMLESS TO US.
THE OTHERS DO NOT KNOW THIS, AND HAVE THUS INITIATED PLAN B.
PLAN B?
AHHHHH!
WHAT'S HAPPENING?
HE'S WAKING UP...
I KNOW, BUT THIS IS ABSOLUTELY *CRUCIAL!* CONTACT LINDEN IMMEDIATELY AND ORDER HIM *NOT* TO ATTACK THE ENEMY!
THE MISSION OBJECTIVE HAS CHANGED. WE NEED TO GATHER VITAL INFORMATION FIRST.
I'LL FORWARD HIM A VIDEO FILE TO BE LOOKED AT ASAP!
IT'S IMPOSSIBLE TO CARRY ON THE INTERROGATION NOW THAT CHARLES IS AWAKE...
ANESTHETIZING HIM FOR ANOTHER FEW HOURS COULD PUT HIS HEALTH AT RISK.
I DON'T GIVE A *DAMN!* GIVE HIM ANOTHER SHOT! WE *MUST* TALK TO SAM AND FIND OUT ABOUT THIS *PLAN B...*

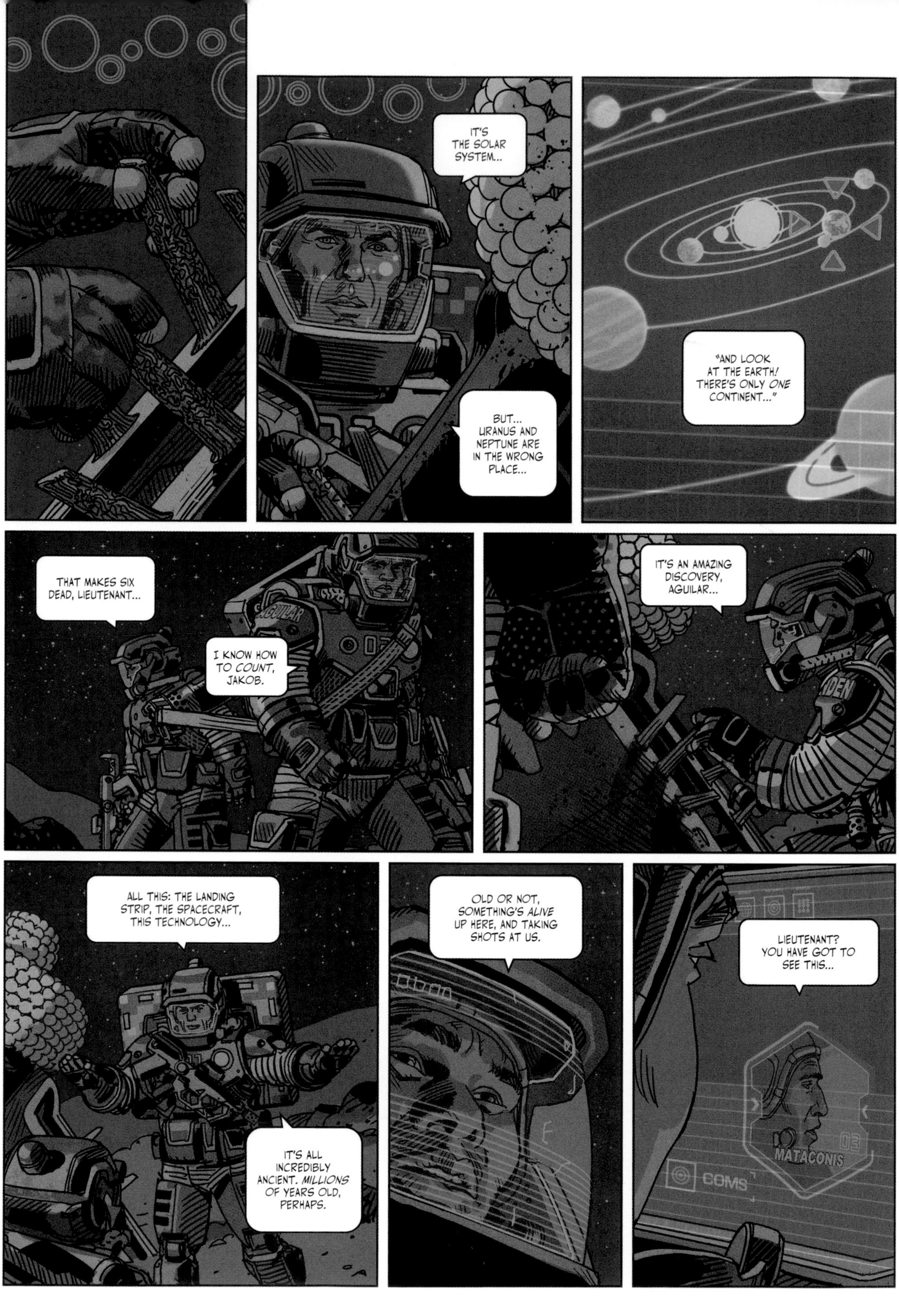
IT'S THE SOLAR SYSTEM...
BUT... URANUS AND NEPTUNE ARE IN THE WRONG PLACE...
"AND LOOK AT THE EARTH! THERE'S ONLY ONE CONTINENT..."
THAT MAKES SIX DEAD, LIEUTENANT...
I KNOW HOW TO COUNT, JAKOB.
AGUILAR
IT'S AN AMAZING DISCOVERY, AGUILAR...
ALL THIS: THE LANDING STRIP, THE SPACECRAFT, THIS TECHNOLOGY...
IT'S ALL INCREDIBLY ANCIENT. MILLIONS OF YEARS OLD, PERHAPS.
OLD OR NOT, SOMETHING'S ALIVE UP HERE, AND TAKING SHOTS AT US.
LIEUTENANT? YOU HAVE GOT TO SEE THIS...
MATACONIS
03
COMS

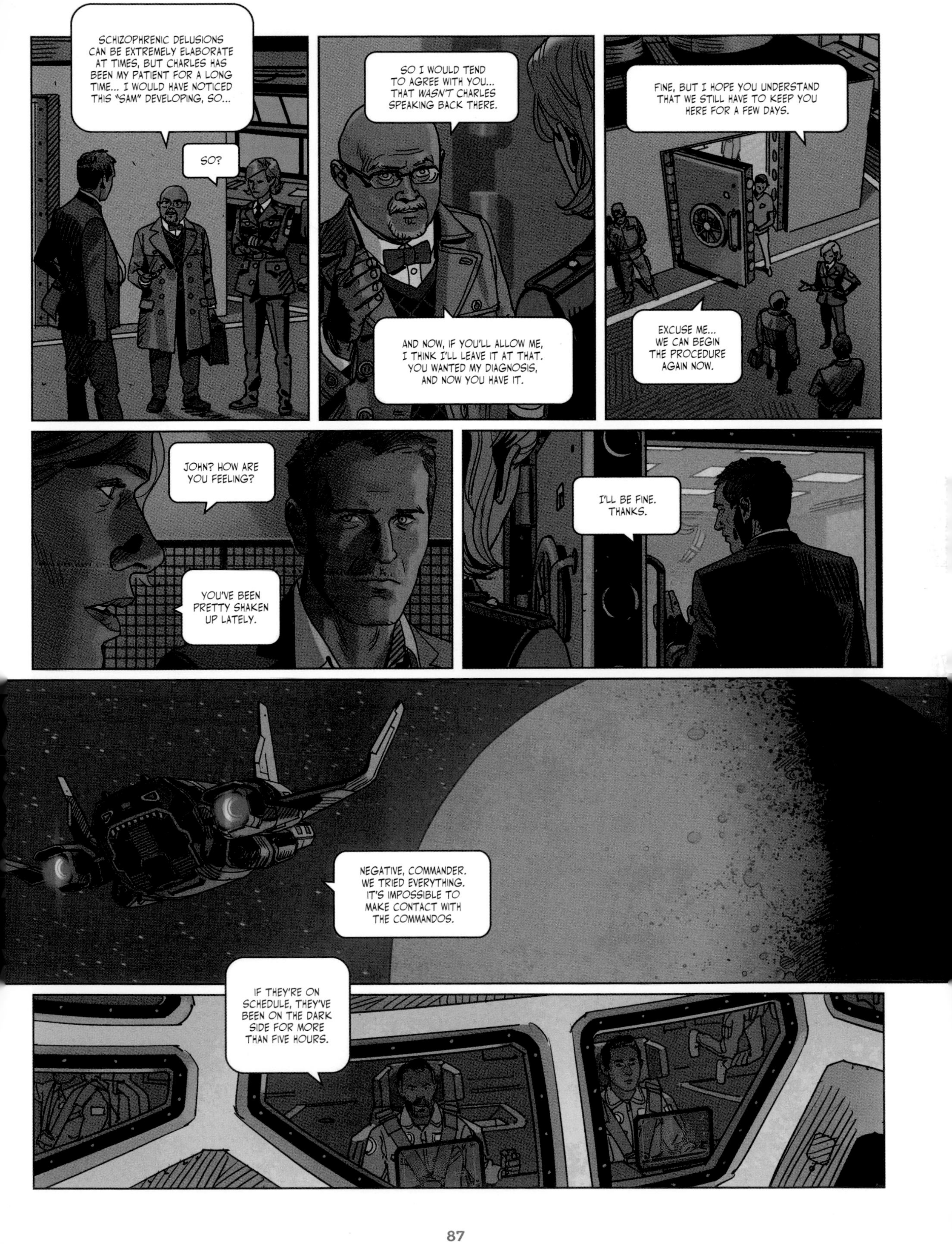
SCHIZOPHRENIC DELUSIONS CAN BE EXTREMELY ELABORATE AT TIMES, BUT CHARLES HAS BEEN MY PATIENT FOR A LONG TIME... I WOULD HAVE NOTICED THIS "SAM" DEVELOPING, SO...
SO?
SO I WOULD TEND TO AGREE WITH YOU... THAT WASN'T CHARLES SPEAKING BACK THERE.
AND NOW, IF YOU'LL ALLOW ME, I THINK I'LL LEAVE IT AT THAT. YOU WANTED MY DIAGNOSIS, AND NOW YOU HAVE IT.
FINE, BUT I HOPE YOU UNDERSTAND THAT WE STILL HAVE TO KEEP YOU HERE FOR A FEW DAYS.
EXCUSE ME... WE CAN BEGIN THE PROCEDURE AGAIN NOW.
JOHN? HOW ARE YOU FEELING?
YOU'VE BEEN PRETTY SHAKEN UP LATELY.
I'LL BE FINE. THANKS.
NEGATIVE, COMMANDER. WE TRIED EVERYTHING. IT'S IMPOSSIBLE TO MAKE CONTACT WITH THE COMMANDOS.
IF THEY'RE ON SCHEDULE, THEY'VE BEEN ON THE DARK SIDE FOR MORE THAN FIVE HOURS.

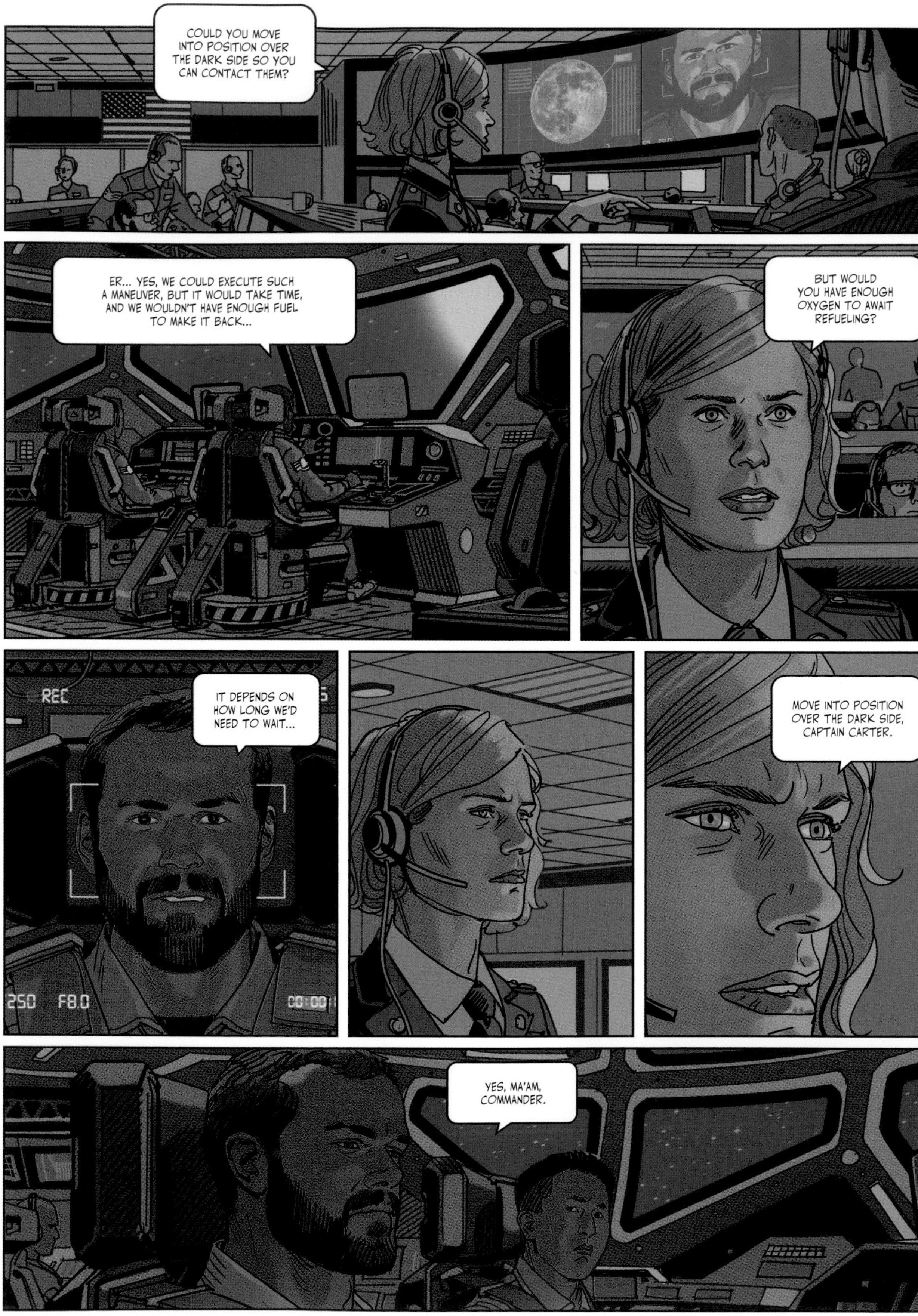
COULD YOU MOVE INTO POSITION OVER THE DARK SIDE SO YOU CAN CONTACT THEM?
ER... YES, WE COULD EXECUTE SUCH A MANEUVER, BUT IT WOULD TAKE TIME, AND WE WOULDN'T HAVE ENOUGH FUEL TO MAKE IT BACK...
BUT WOULD YOU HAVE ENOUGH OXYGEN TO AWAIT REFUELING?
REC
IT DEPENDS ON HOW LONG WE'D NEED TO WAIT...
250 F8.0
MOVE INTO POSITION OVER THE DARK SIDE, CAPTAIN CARTER.
YES, MA'AM, COMMANDER.

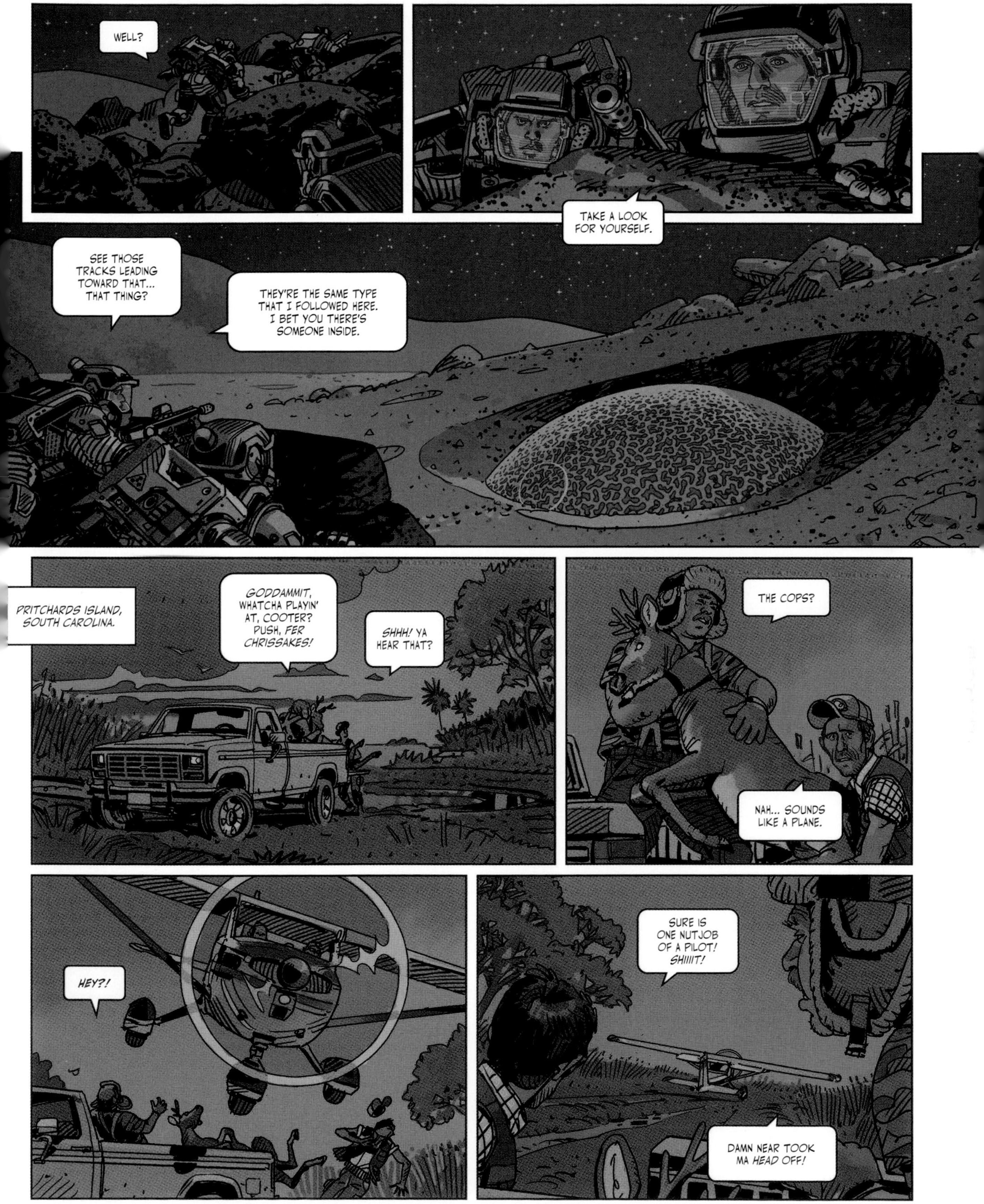
WELL?
TAKE A LOOK FOR YOURSELF.
SEE THOSE TRACKS LEADING TOWARD THAT... THAT THING?
THEY'RE THE SAME TYPE THAT I FOLLOWED HERE. I BET YOU THERE'S SOMEONE INSIDE.
PRITCHARDS ISLAND, SOUTH CAROLINA.
GODDAMMIT, WHATCHA PLAYIN' AT, COOTER? PUSH, FER CHRISSAKES!
SHHH! YA HEAR THAT?
THE COPS?
NAH... SOUNDS LIKE A PLANE.
HEY?!
SURE IS ONE NUTJOB OF A PILOT! SHIIIIT!
DAMN NEAR TOOK MA HEAD OFF!

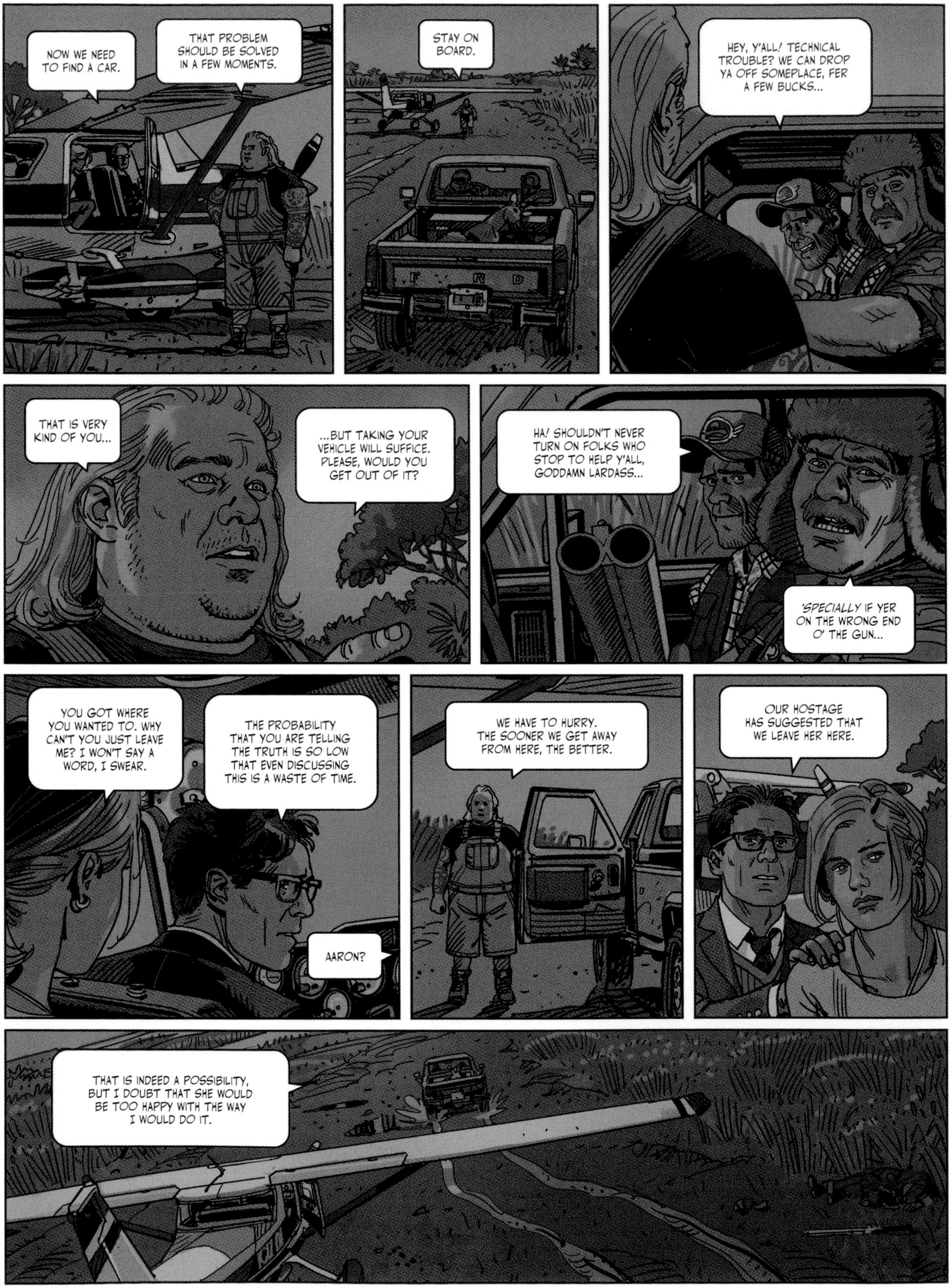
NOW WE NEED TO FIND A CAR.
THAT PROBLEM SHOULD BE SOLVED IN A FEW MOMENTS.
STAY ON BOARD.
HEY, Y'ALL! TECHNICAL TROUBLE? WE CAN DROP YA OFF SOMEPLACE, FER A FEW BUCKS...
THAT IS VERY KIND OF YOU...
...BUT TAKING YOUR VEHICLE WILL SUFFICE. PLEASE, WOULD YOU GET OUT OF IT?
HA! SHOULDN'T NEVER TURN ON FOLKS WHO STOP TO HELP Y'ALL, GODDAMN LARDASS...
'SPECIALLY IF YER ON THE WRONG END O' THE GUN...
YOU GOT WHERE YOU WANTED TO. WHY CAN'T YOU JUST LEAVE ME? I WON'T SAY A WORD, I SWEAR.
THE PROBABILITY THAT YOU ARE TELLING THE TRUTH IS SO LOW THAT EVEN DISCUSSING THIS IS A WASTE OF TIME.
AARON?
WE HAVE TO HURRY. THE SOONER WE GET AWAY FROM HERE, THE BETTER.
OUR HOSTAGE HAS SUGGESTED THAT WE LEAVE HER HERE.
THAT IS INDEED A POSSIBILITY, BUT I DOUBT THAT SHE WOULD BE TOO HAPPY WITH THE WAY I WOULD DO IT.

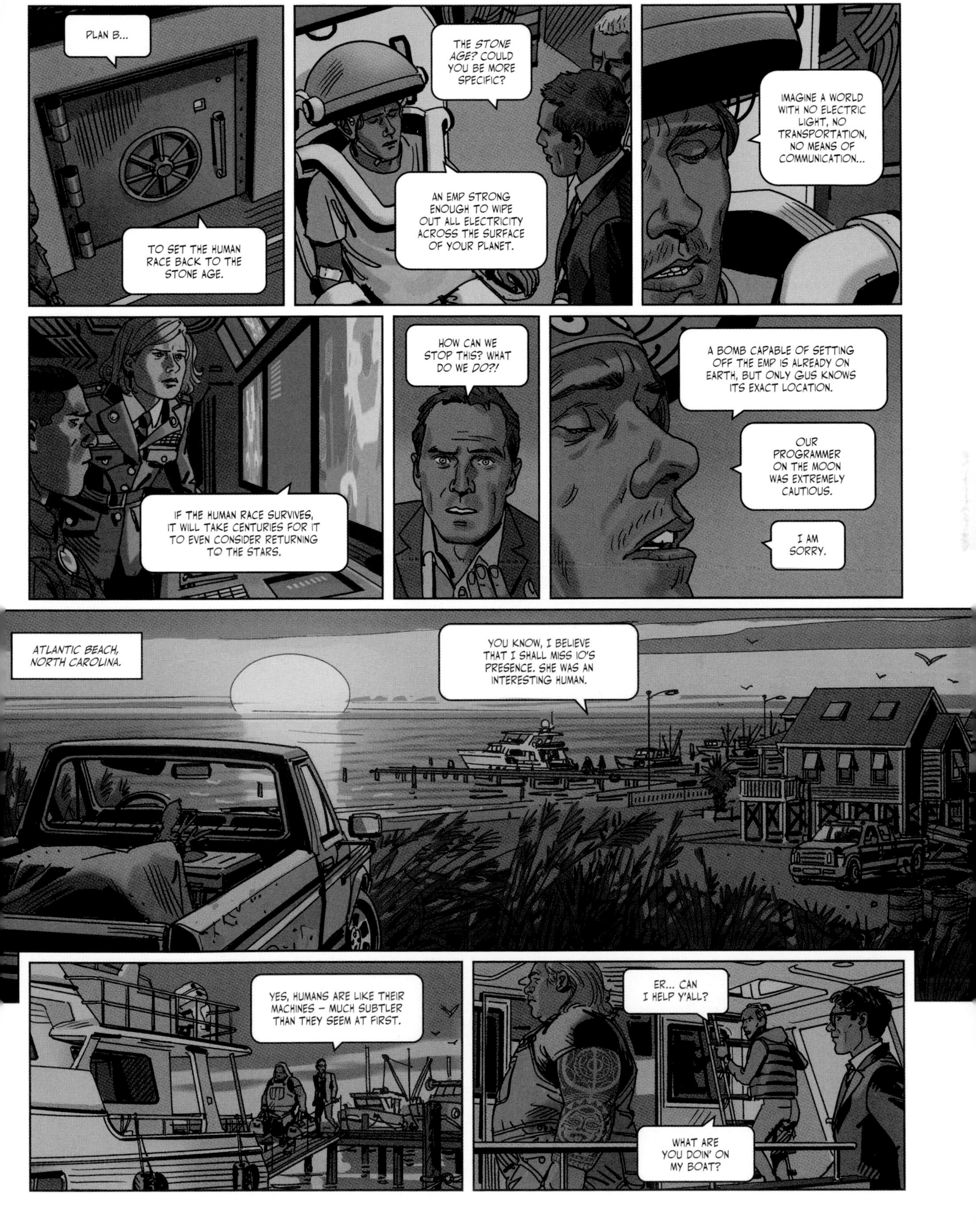
PLAN B...
TO SET THE HUMAN RACE BACK TO THE STONE AGE.
THE *STONE AGE*? COULD YOU BE MORE SPECIFIC?
AN EMP STRONG ENOUGH TO WIPE OUT ALL ELECTRICITY ACROSS THE SURFACE OF YOUR PLANET.
IMAGINE A WORLD WITH NO ELECTRIC LIGHT, NO TRANSPORTATION, NO MEANS OF COMMUNICATION...
IF THE HUMAN RACE SURVIVES, IT WILL TAKE CENTURIES FOR IT TO EVEN CONSIDER RETURNING TO THE STARS.
HOW CAN WE STOP THIS? WHAT DO WE *DO?!*
A BOMB CAPABLE OF SETTING OFF THE EMP IS ALREADY ON EARTH, BUT ONLY GUS KNOWS ITS EXACT LOCATION.
OUR PROGRAMMER ON THE MOON WAS EXTREMELY CAUTIOUS.
I AM SORRY.
ATLANTIC BEACH, NORTH CAROLINA.
YOU KNOW, I BELIEVE THAT I SHALL MISS IO'S PRESENCE. SHE WAS AN INTERESTING HUMAN.
YES, HUMANS ARE LIKE THEIR MACHINES – MUCH SUBTLER THAN THEY SEEM AT FIRST.
ER... CAN I HELP Y'ALL?
WHAT ARE YOU DOIN' ON MY BOAT?

LET US HOPE THAT THIS ONE WILL BE EQUALLY INTRIGUING.

YES, THAT WOULD BE MOST AGREEABLE.

I WILL SEARCH THE BOAT TO SEE IF THERE ARE ANY MORE.

HELLO, MA'AM.

START UP THE ENGINES. WE ARE LEAVING.

LEAVIN'? ER... WHERE TO?

MY COLLEAGUE WILL GIVE YOU THE EXACT COORDINATES.

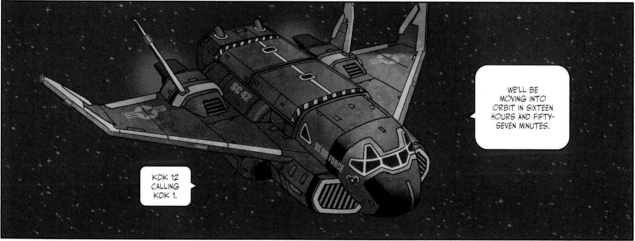

WE'LL BE MOVING INTO ORBIT IN SIXTEEN HOURS AND FIFTY-SEVEN MINUTES.

KDK 12 CALLING KDK 1.

THEN WE'LL REQUIRE ANOTHER HOUR AND FORTY-FIVE MINUTES TO REACH THE TARGET.

OK. ROGER THAT.

THE INFORMATION TO BE RELAYED TO THE COMMANDOS IS BEING UPLOADED TO YOU NOW.

IT MUST BE ACCOMPANIED BY AN IMMEDIATE CEASE-FIRE ORDER!

UNDERSTOOD, KDK 1.

OVER AND OUT.

ANOTHER TWENTY YARDS TO GO...

I CAN SEE HEAT SIGNATURES.

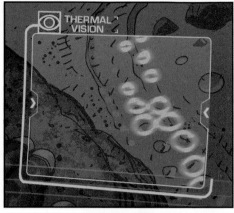

THERMAL VISION

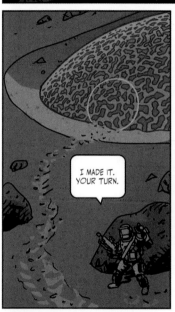

I MADE IT. YOUR TURN.

BUT? THE EARTH...

"IT...IT'S GONE DARK...THEY... THEY PLAN TO DESTROY IT!"

"WE MUST ACT... IMMEDIATELY!"

AGUILAR? AGUILAR? COME IN!

YES?

WHAT'S YOUR STATUS?

WE'VE LOCATED THE ENEMY BASE AND WE'RE PREPARING TO GO INSIDE.

NEGATIVE.

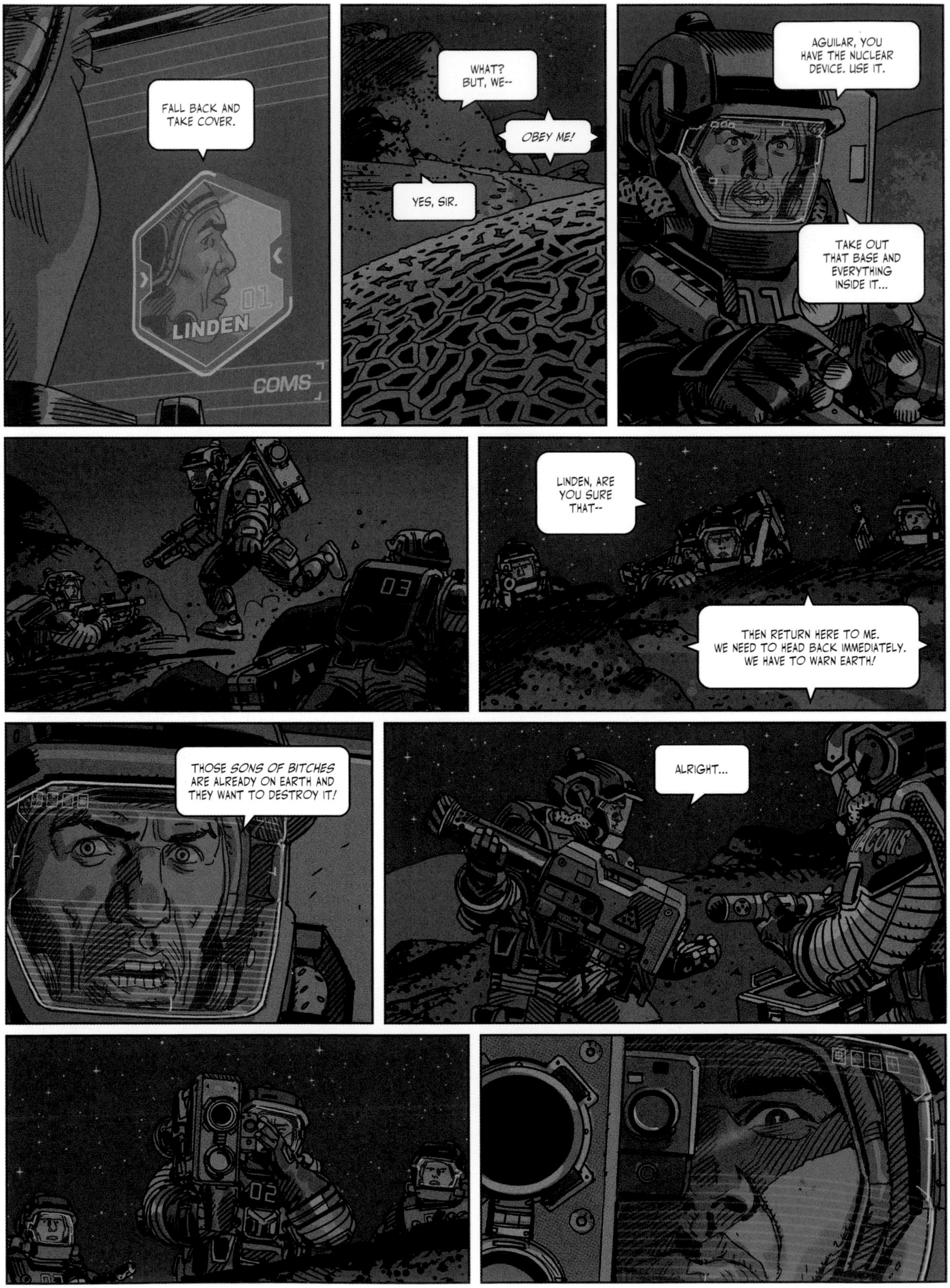
FALL BACK AND TAKE COVER.
LINDEN
COMS
WHAT? BUT, WE--
OBEY ME!
YES, SIR.
AGUILAR, YOU HAVE THE NUCLEAR DEVICE. USE IT.
TAKE OUT THAT BASE AND EVERYTHING INSIDE IT...
LINDEN, ARE YOU SURE THAT--
THEN RETURN HERE TO ME. WE NEED TO HEAD BACK IMMEDIATELY. WE HAVE TO WARN EARTH!
THOSE SONS OF BITCHES ARE ALREADY ON EARTH AND THEY WANT TO DESTROY IT!
ALRIGHT...

JAKOB. GO BACK TO LINDEN AND TAKE HIM TO THE BEACON.

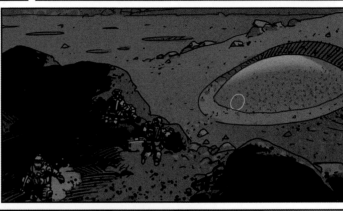

OK... AND YOU?

I DON'T KNOW YET...

I NEED TO THINK IT OVER.

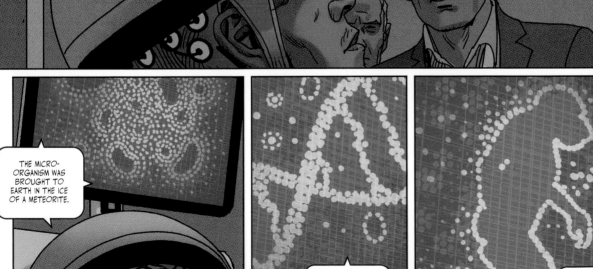

SAM, CAN YOU TELL ME ANYTHING ELSE ABOUT THIS VIRUS?

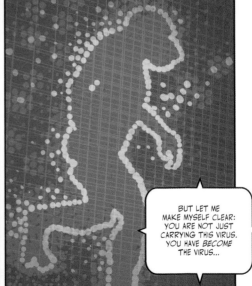

THE MICRO-ORGANISM WAS BROUGHT TO EARTH IN THE ICE OF A METEORITE.

ITS MATERIAL QUICKLY GRAFTED ONTO THE GENOME OF YOUR HOMINID ANCESTORS.

BUT LET ME MAKE MYSELF CLEAR: YOU ARE NOT JUST CARRYING THIS VIRUS. YOU HAVE *BECOME* THE VIRUS...

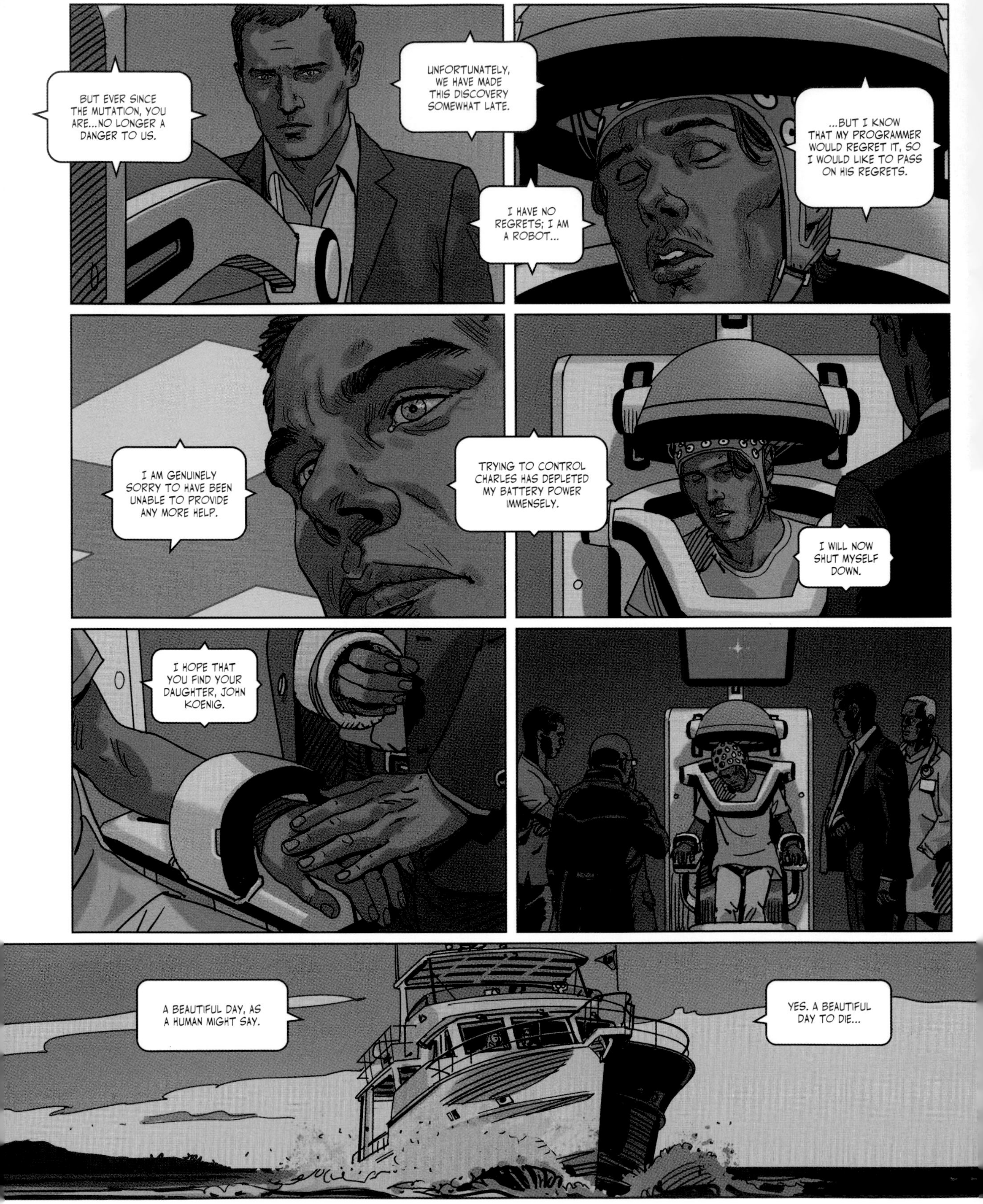
BUT EVER SINCE THE MUTATION, YOU ARE...NO LONGER A DANGER TO US.
UNFORTUNATELY, WE HAVE MADE THIS DISCOVERY SOMEWHAT LATE.
I HAVE NO REGRETS; I AM A ROBOT...
...BUT I KNOW THAT MY PROGRAMMER WOULD REGRET IT, SO I WOULD LIKE TO PASS ON HIS REGRETS.
I AM GENUINELY SORRY TO HAVE BEEN UNABLE TO PROVIDE ANY MORE HELP.
TRYING TO CONTROL CHARLES HAS DEPLETED MY BATTERY POWER IMMENSELY.
I WILL NOW SHUT MYSELF DOWN.
I HOPE THAT YOU FIND YOUR DAUGHTER, JOHN KOENIG.
A BEAUTIFUL DAY, AS A HUMAN MIGHT SAY.
YES. A BEAUTIFUL DAY TO DIE...

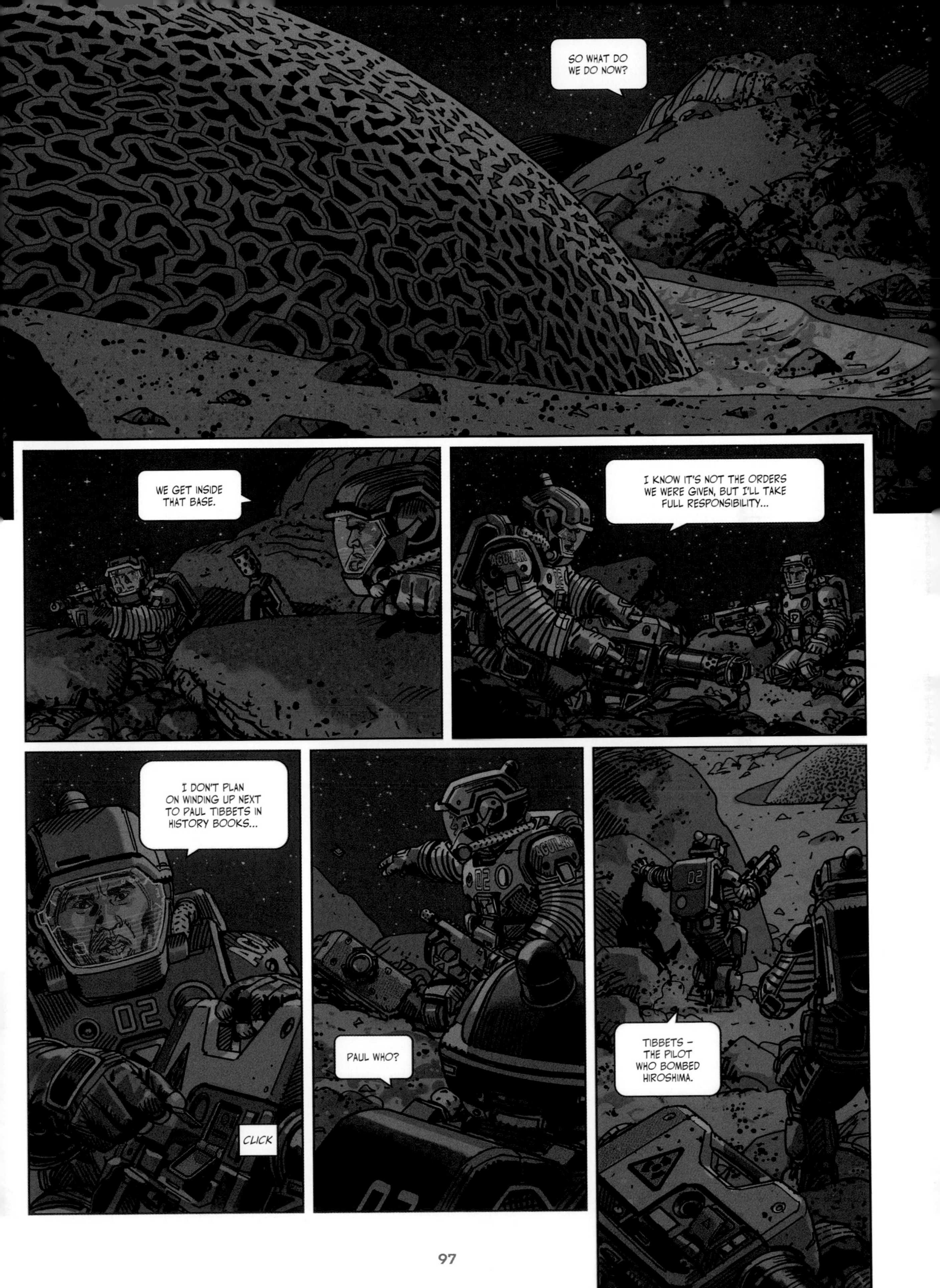
SO WHAT DO WE DO NOW?
WE GET INSIDE THAT BASE.
I KNOW IT'S NOT THE ORDERS WE WERE GIVEN, BUT I'LL TAKE FULL RESPONSIBILITY...
I DON'T PLAN ON WINDING UP NEXT TO PAUL TIBBETS IN HISTORY BOOKS...
CLICK
PAUL WHO?
TIBBETS – THE PILOT WHO BOMBED HIROSHIMA.

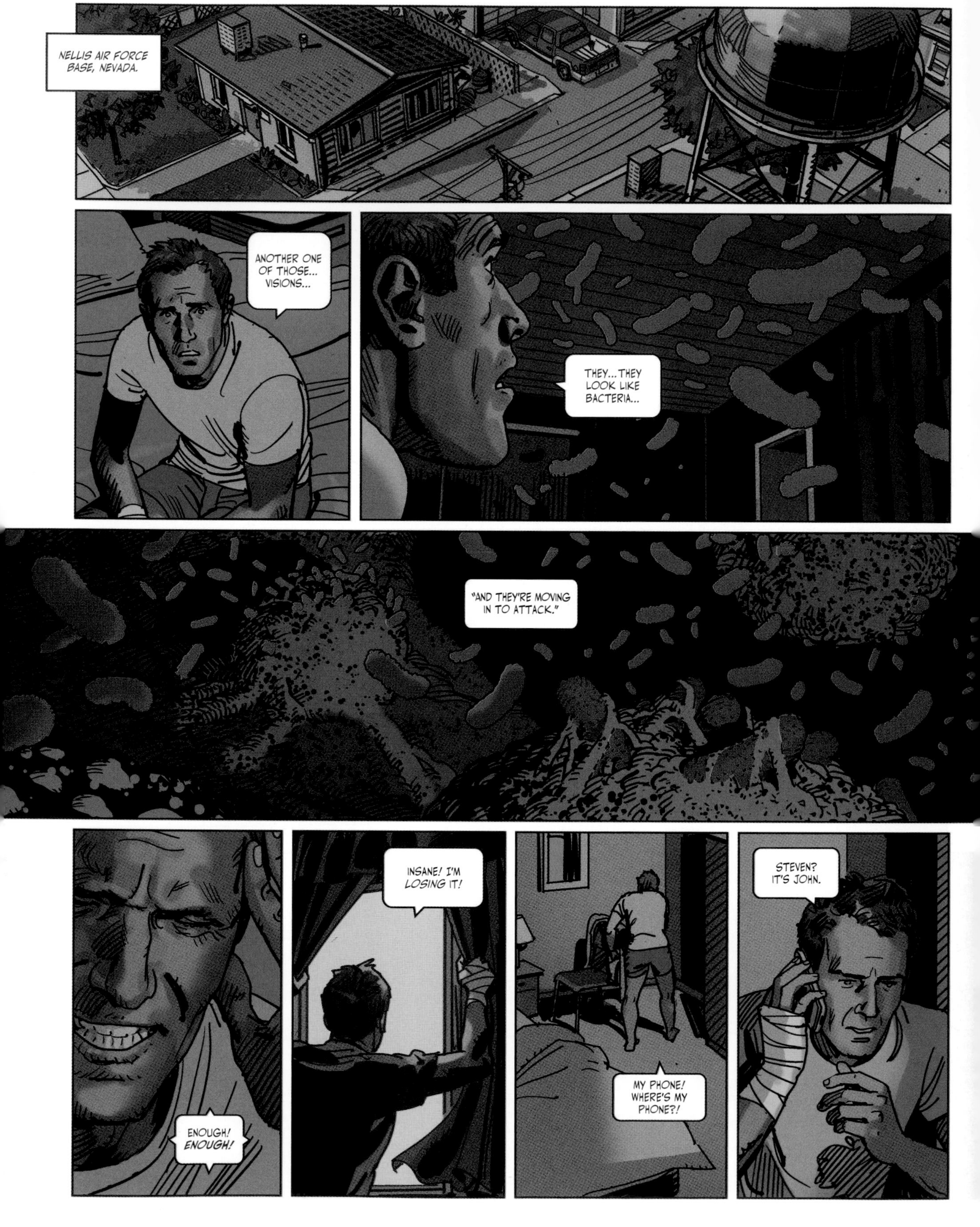
NELLIS AIR FORCE BASE, NEVADA.
ANOTHER ONE OF THOSE... VISIONS...
THEY... THEY LOOK LIKE BACTERIA...
"AND THEY'RE MOVING IN TO ATTACK."
ENOUGH! ENOUGH!
INSANE! I'M LOSING IT!
MY PHONE! WHERE'S MY PHONE?!
STEVEN? IT'S JOHN.

AGUILAR? AGUILAR? COME IN!

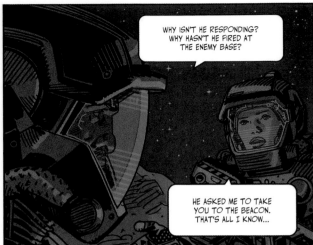

WHY ISN'T HE RESPONDING? WHY HASN'T HE FIRED AT THE ENEMY BASE?

HE ASKED ME TO TAKE YOU TO THE BEACON. THAT'S ALL I KNOW...

AGUILAR! YOU SON OF A BITCH, I KNOW YOU CAN HEAR ME!

I'LL GET YOU THROWN IN JAIL FOR TREASON!

THERE'S QUITE A LOT OF GROUND TO COVER.

WE REALLY NEED TO GET GOING, MR. LINDEN.

LINDEN?

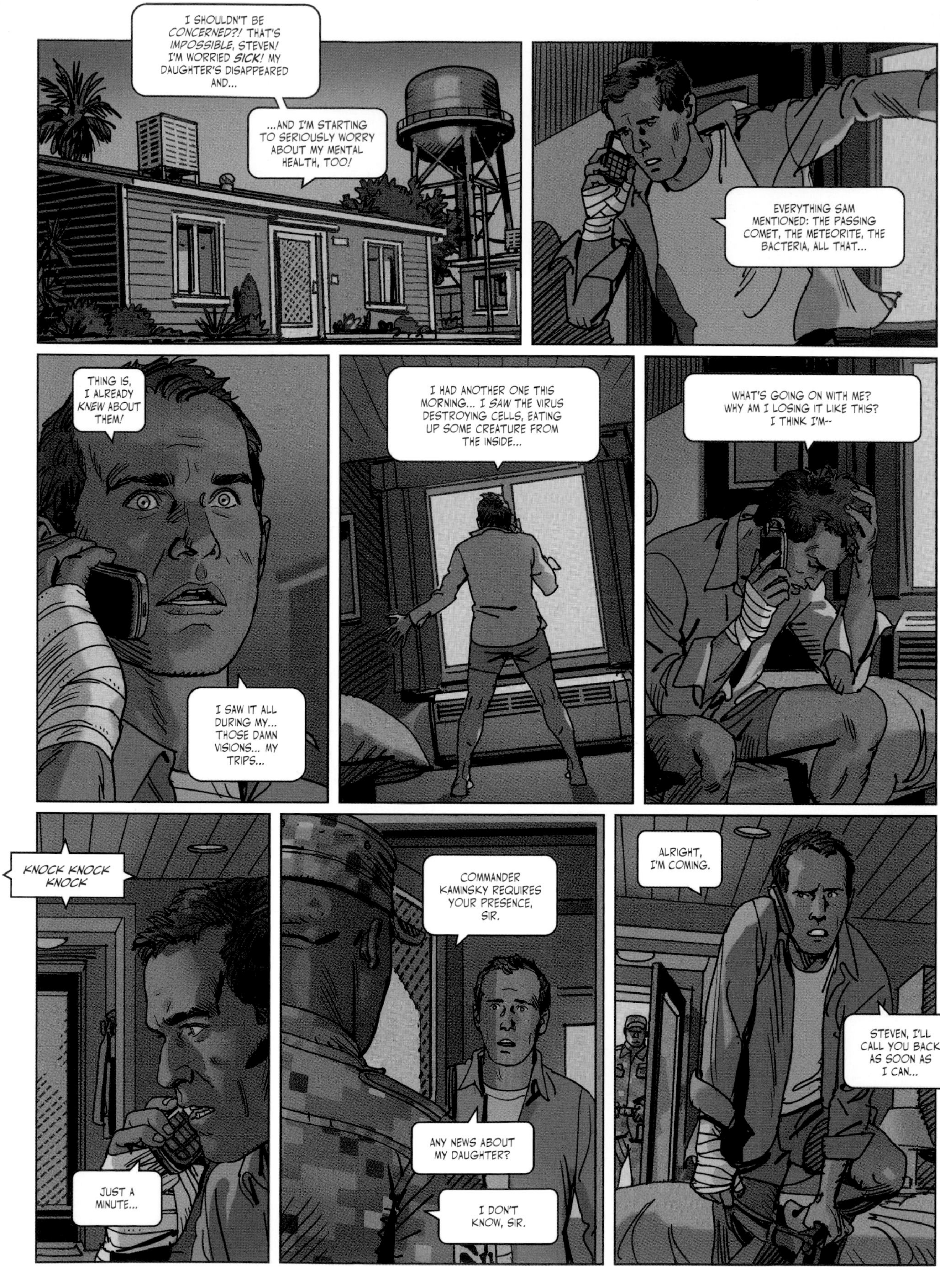

I SHOULDN'T BE CONCERNED?! THAT'S IMPOSSIBLE, STEVEN! I'M WORRIED SICK! MY DAUGHTER'S DISAPPEARED AND...
...AND I'M STARTING TO SERIOUSLY WORRY ABOUT MY MENTAL HEALTH, TOO!
EVERYTHING SAM MENTIONED: THE PASSING COMET, THE METEORITE, THE BACTERIA, ALL THAT...
THING IS, I ALREADY KNEW ABOUT THEM!
I SAW IT ALL DURING MY... THOSE DAMN VISIONS... MY TRIPS...
I HAD ANOTHER ONE THIS MORNING... I SAW THE VIRUS DESTROYING CELLS, EATING UP SOME CREATURE FROM THE INSIDE...
WHAT'S GOING ON WITH ME? WHY AM I LOSING IT LIKE THIS? I THINK I'M--
KNOCK KNOCK KNOCK
JUST A MINUTE...
COMMANDER KAMINSKY REQUIRES YOUR PRESENCE, SIR.
ANY NEWS ABOUT MY DAUGHTER?
I DON'T KNOW, SIR.
ALRIGHT, I'M COMING.
STEVEN, I'LL CALL YOU BACK AS SOON AS I CAN...

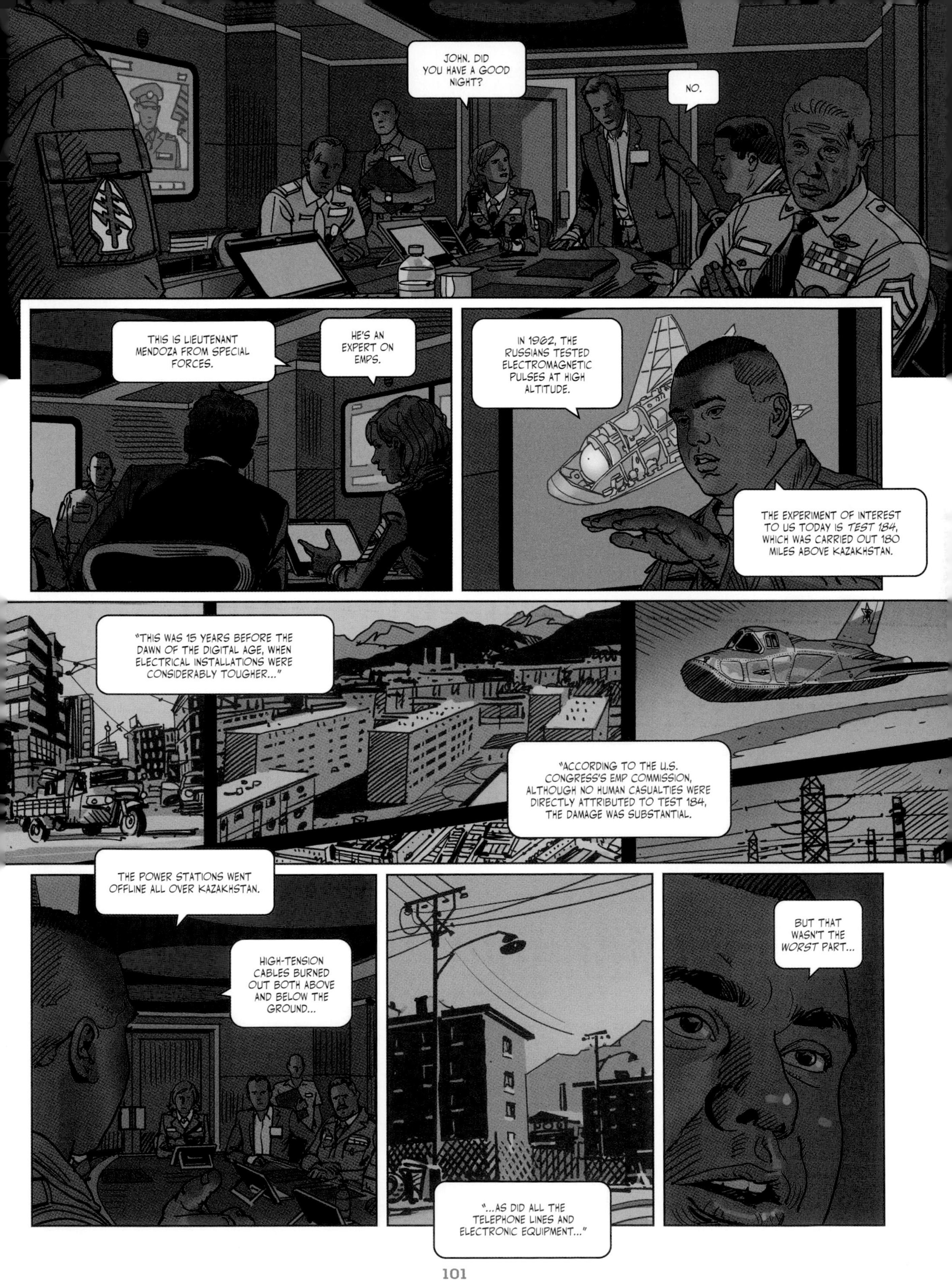

JOHN. DID YOU HAVE A GOOD NIGHT?
NO.
THIS IS LIEUTENANT MENDOZA FROM SPECIAL FORCES.
HE'S AN EXPERT ON EMPS.
IN 1962, THE RUSSIANS TESTED ELECTROMAGNETIC PULSES AT HIGH ALTITUDE.
THE EXPERIMENT OF INTEREST TO US TODAY IS *TEST 184*, WHICH WAS CARRIED OUT 180 MILES ABOVE KAZAKHSTAN.
"THIS WAS 15 YEARS BEFORE THE DAWN OF THE DIGITAL AGE, WHEN ELECTRICAL INSTALLATIONS WERE CONSIDERABLY TOUGHER..."
"ACCORDING TO THE U.S. CONGRESS'S EMP COMMISSION, ALTHOUGH NO HUMAN CASUALTIES WERE DIRECTLY ATTRIBUTED TO TEST 184, THE DAMAGE WAS SUBSTANTIAL.
THE POWER STATIONS WENT OFFLINE ALL OVER KAZAKHSTAN.
HIGH-TENSION CABLES BURNED OUT BOTH ABOVE AND BELOW THE GROUND...
"...AS DID ALL THE TELEPHONE LINES AND ELECTRONIC EQUIPMENT..."
BUT THAT WASN'T THE *WORST* PART...

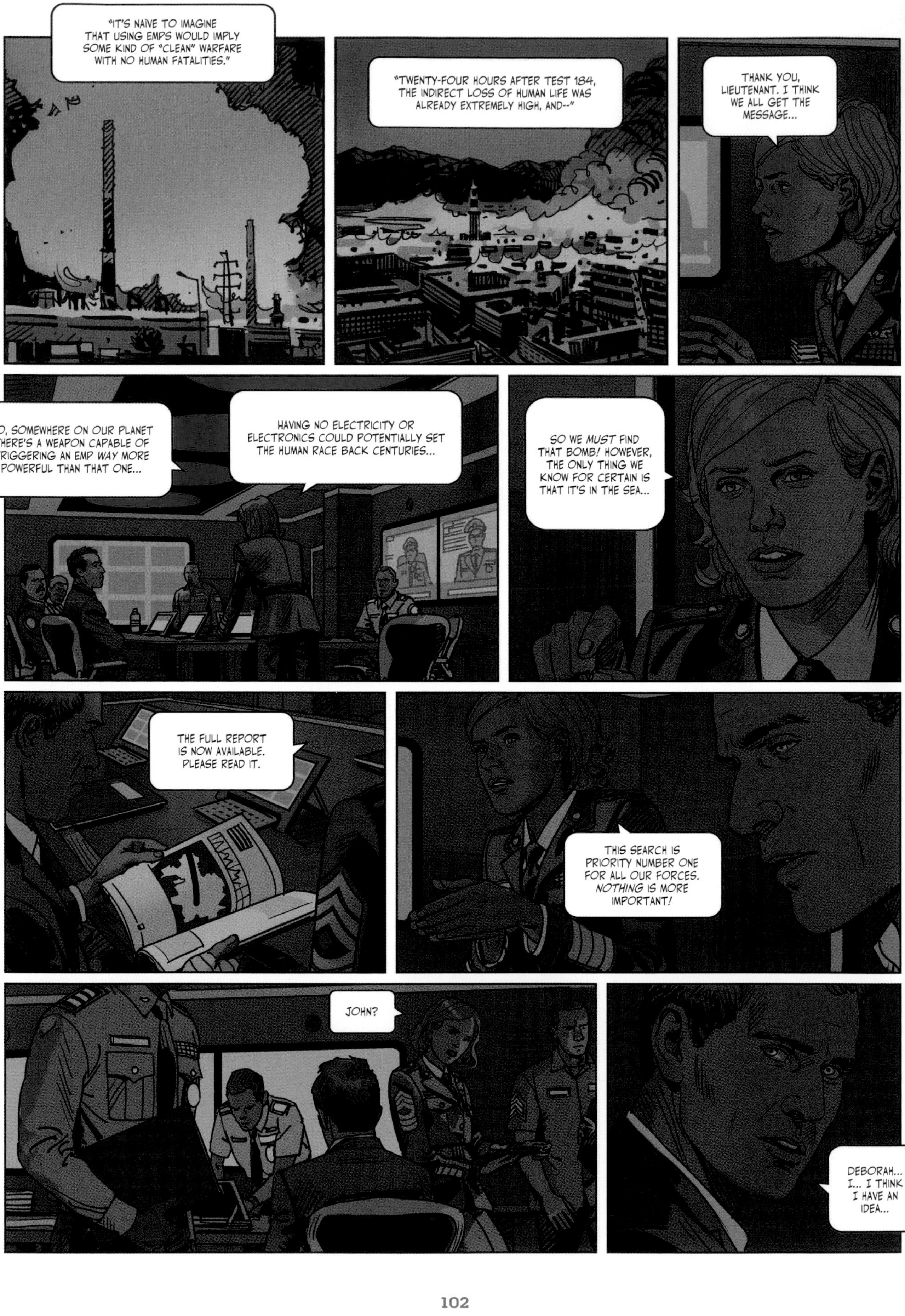
"IT'S NAÏVE TO IMAGINE THAT USING EMPS WOULD IMPLY SOME KIND OF "CLEAN" WARFARE WITH NO HUMAN FATALITIES."
"TWENTY-FOUR HOURS AFTER TEST 184, THE INDIRECT LOSS OF HUMAN LIFE WAS ALREADY EXTREMELY HIGH, AND--"
THANK YOU, LIEUTENANT. I THINK WE ALL GET THE MESSAGE...
SO, SOMEWHERE ON OUR PLANET THERE'S A WEAPON CAPABLE OF TRIGGERING AN EMP WAY MORE POWERFUL THAN THAT ONE...
HAVING NO ELECTRICITY OR ELECTRONICS COULD POTENTIALLY SET THE HUMAN RACE BACK CENTURIES...
SO WE MUST FIND THAT BOMB! HOWEVER, THE ONLY THING WE KNOW FOR CERTAIN IS THAT IT'S IN THE SEA...
THE FULL REPORT IS NOW AVAILABLE. PLEASE READ IT.
THIS SEARCH IS PRIORITY NUMBER ONE FOR ALL OUR FORCES. NOTHING IS MORE IMPORTANT!
JOHN?
DEBORAH... I... I THINK I HAVE AN IDEA...

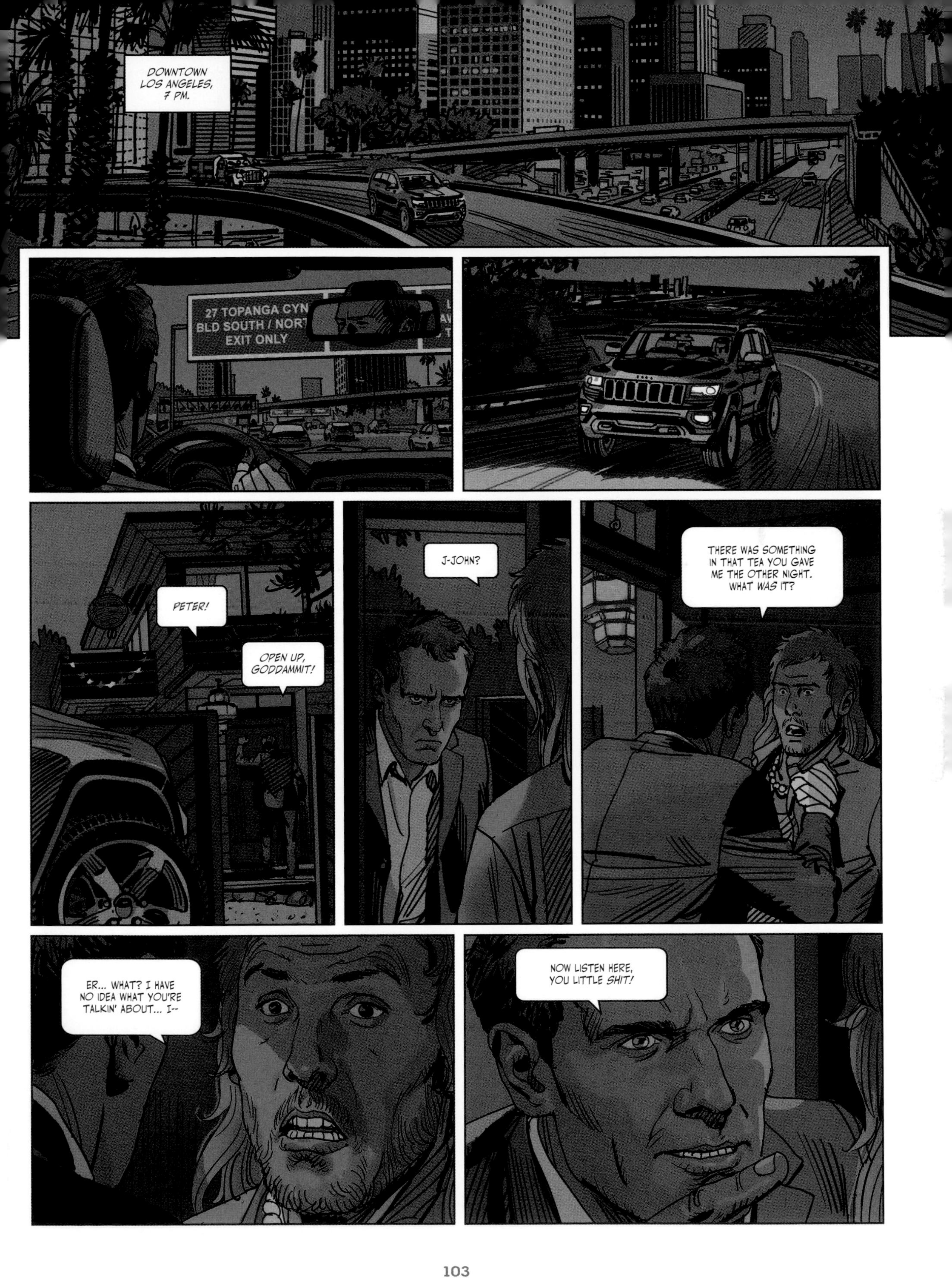
DOWNTOWN LOS ANGELES, 7 PM.
27 TOPANGA CYN
BLD SOUTH / NORT
EXIT ONLY
PETER!
OPEN UP, GODDAMMIT!
J-JOHN?
THERE WAS SOMETHING IN THAT TEA YOU GAVE ME THE OTHER NIGHT. WHAT WAS IT?
ER... WHAT? I HAVE NO IDEA WHAT YOU'RE TALKIN' ABOUT... I--
NOW LISTEN HERE, YOU LITTLE SHIT!

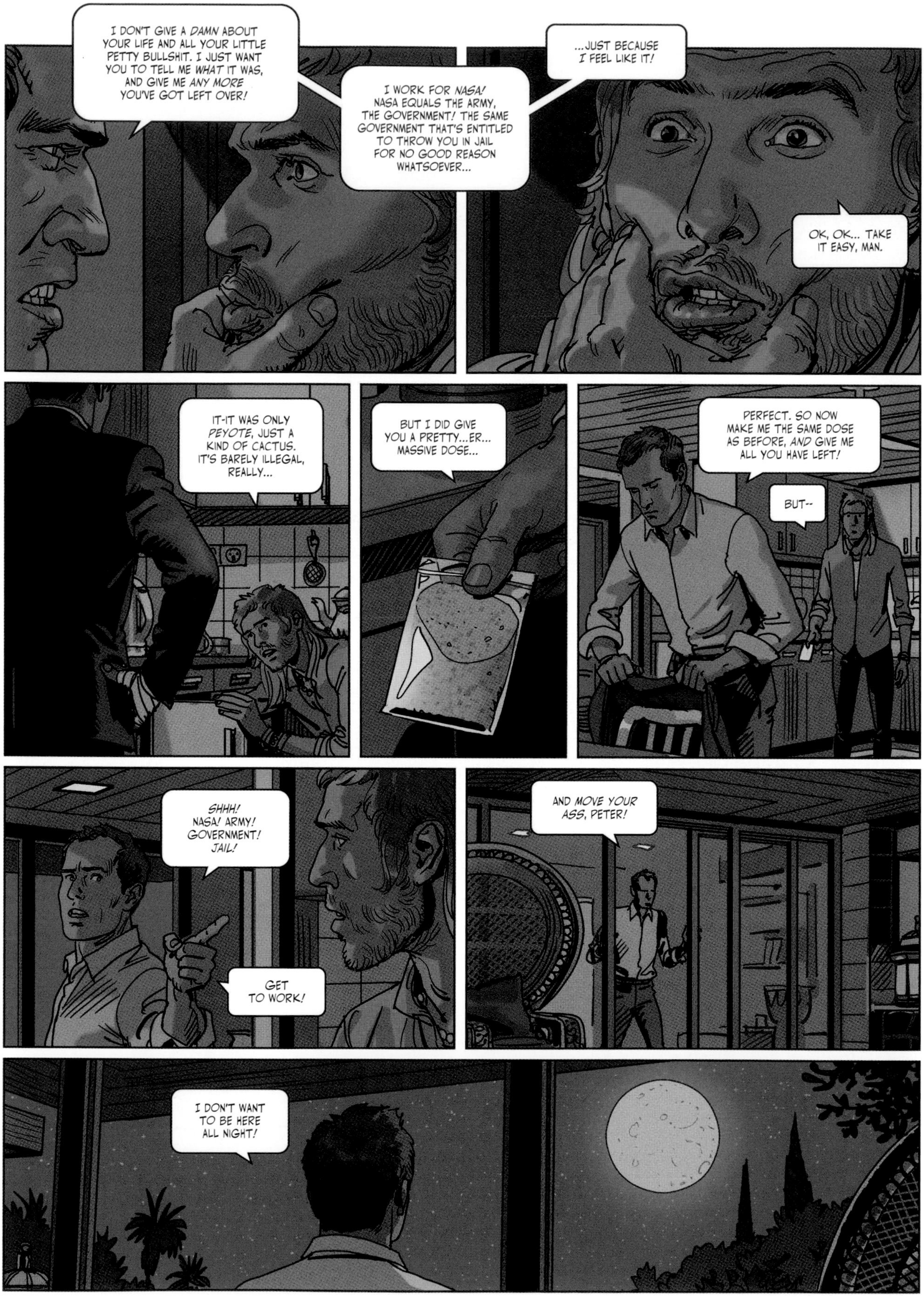
I DON'T GIVE A DAMN ABOUT YOUR LIFE AND ALL YOUR LITTLE PETTY BULLSHIT. I JUST WANT YOU TO TELL ME WHAT IT WAS, AND GIVE ME ANY MORE YOU'VE GOT LEFT OVER!
I WORK FOR NASA! NASA EQUALS THE ARMY, THE GOVERNMENT! THE SAME GOVERNMENT THAT'S ENTITLED TO THROW YOU IN JAIL FOR NO GOOD REASON WHATSOEVER...
...JUST BECAUSE I FEEL LIKE IT!
OK, OK... TAKE IT EASY, MAN.
IT-IT WAS ONLY PEYOTE, JUST A KIND OF CACTUS. IT'S BARELY ILLEGAL, REALLY...
BUT I DID GIVE YOU A PRETTY...ER... MASSIVE DOSE...
PERFECT. SO NOW MAKE ME THE SAME DOSE AS BEFORE, AND GIVE ME ALL YOU HAVE LEFT!
BUT--
SHHH! NASA! ARMY! GOVERNMENT! JAIL!
GET TO WORK!
AND MOVE YOUR ASS, PETER!
I DON'T WANT TO BE HERE ALL NIGHT!

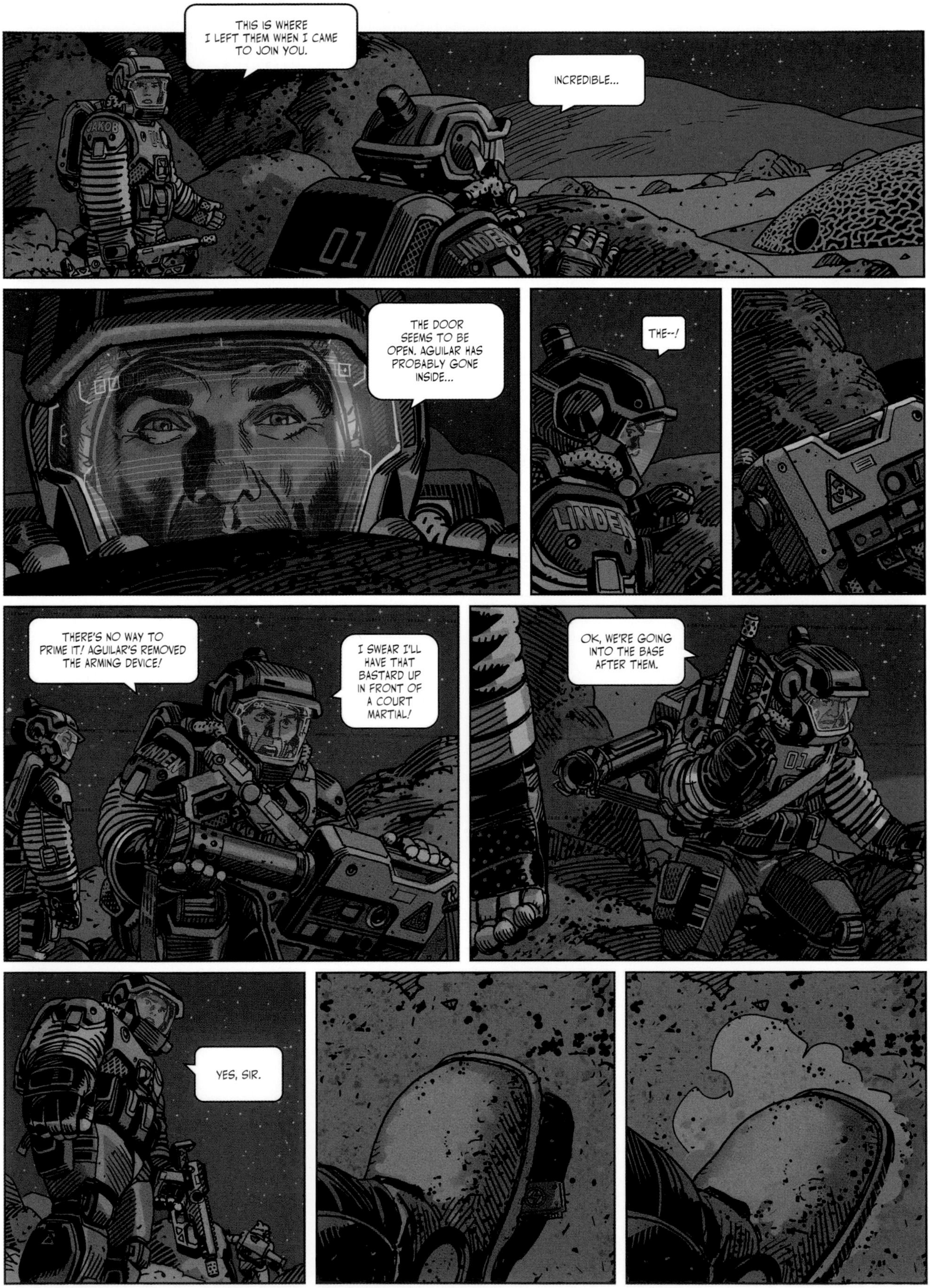
THIS IS WHERE I LEFT THEM WHEN I CAME TO JOIN YOU.
INCREDIBLE...
THE DOOR SEEMS TO BE OPEN. AGUILAR HAS PROBABLY GONE INSIDE...
THE--!
THERE'S NO WAY TO PRIME IT! AGUILAR'S REMOVED THE ARMING DEVICE!
I SWEAR I'LL HAVE THAT BASTARD UP IN FRONT OF A COURT MARTIAL!
OK, WE'RE GOING INTO THE BASE AFTER THEM.
YES, SIR.

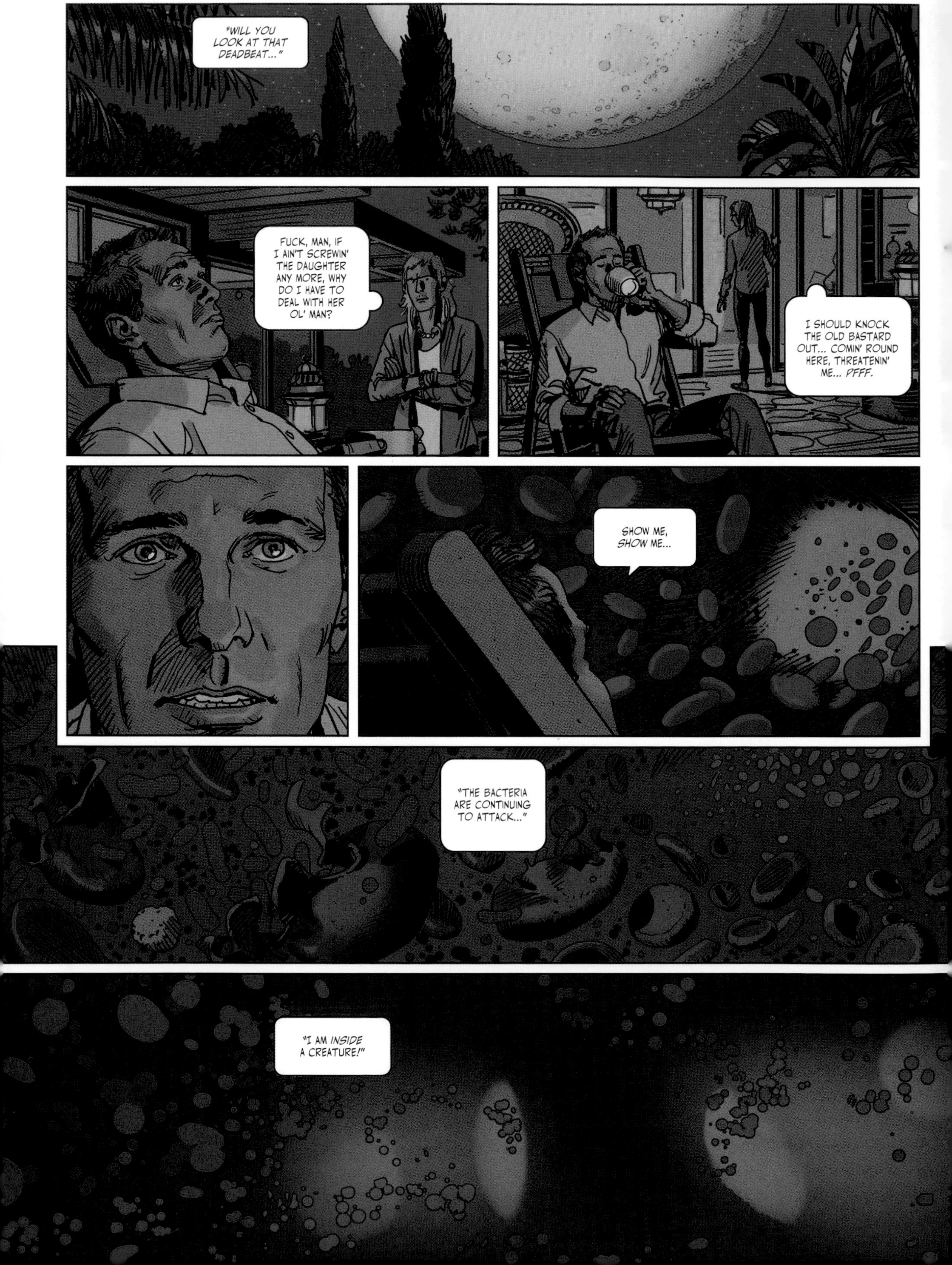
"WILL YOU LOOK AT THAT DEADBEAT..."
FUCK, MAN, IF I AIN'T SCREWIN' THE DAUGHTER ANY MORE, WHY DO I HAVE TO DEAL WITH HER OL' MAN?
I SHOULD KNOCK THE OLD BASTARD OUT... COMIN' ROUND HERE, THREATENIN' ME... *PFFF.*
SHOW ME, *SHOW* ME...
"THE BACTERIA ARE CONTINUING TO ATTACK..."
"I AM *INSIDE* A CREATURE!"

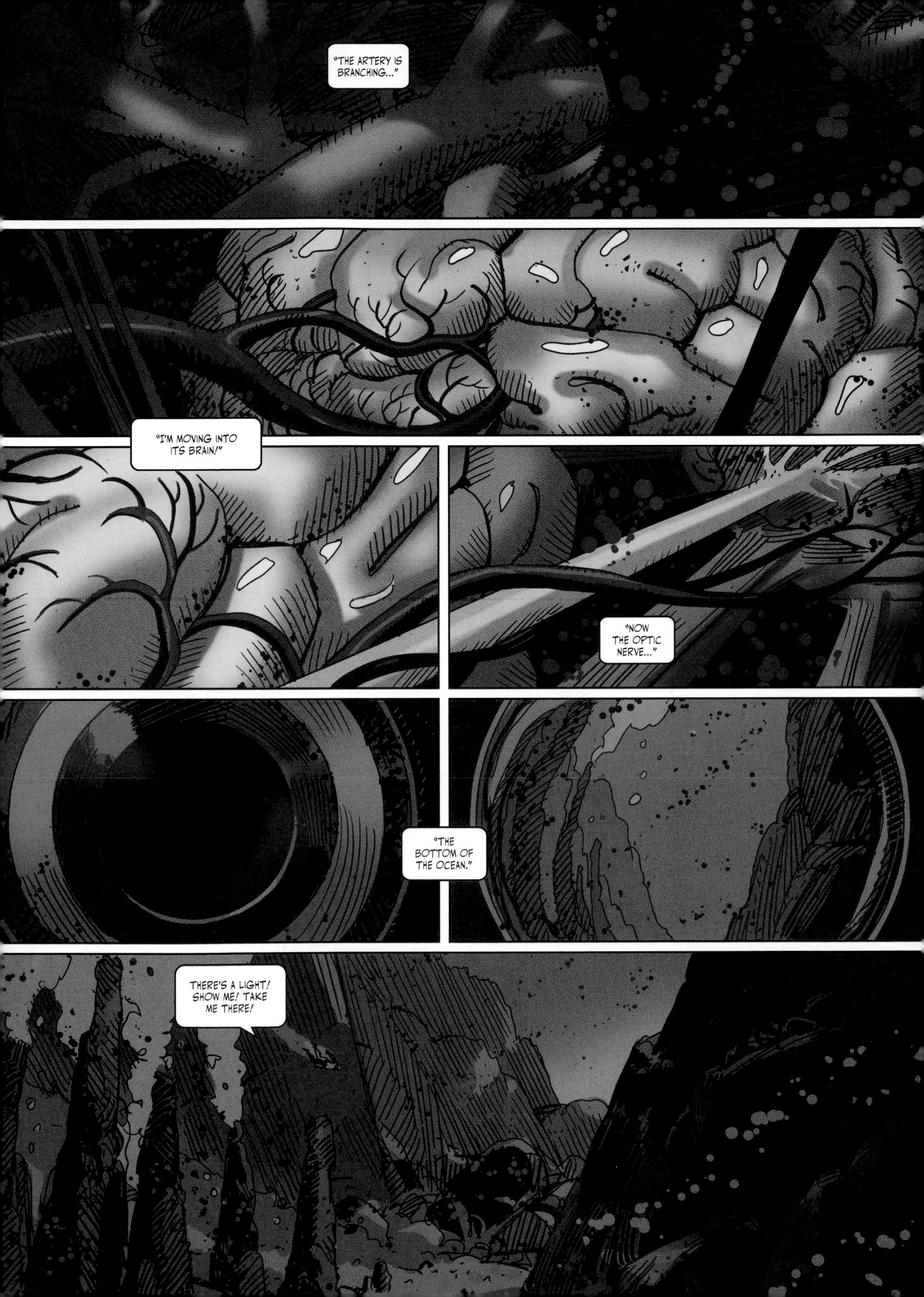
"THE ARTERY IS BRANCHING..."
"I'M MOVING INTO ITS BRAIN!"
"NOW THE OPTIC NERVE..."
"THE BOTTOM OF THE OCEAN."
THERE'S A LIGHT! SHOW ME! TAKE ME THERE!

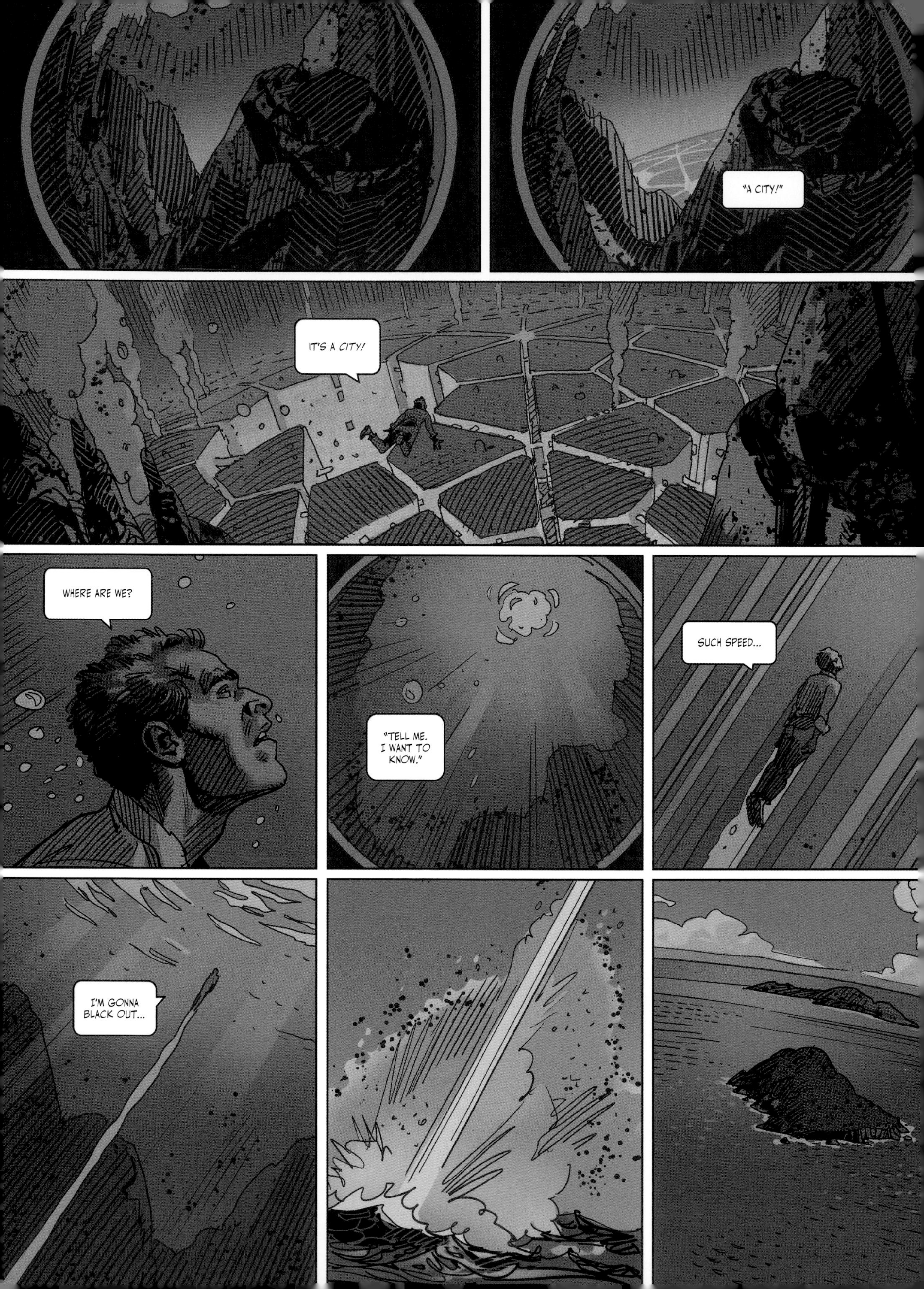
"A CITY!"
IT'S A CITY!
WHERE ARE WE?
"TELL ME. I WANT TO KNOW."
SUCH SPEED...
I'M GONNA BLACK OUT...

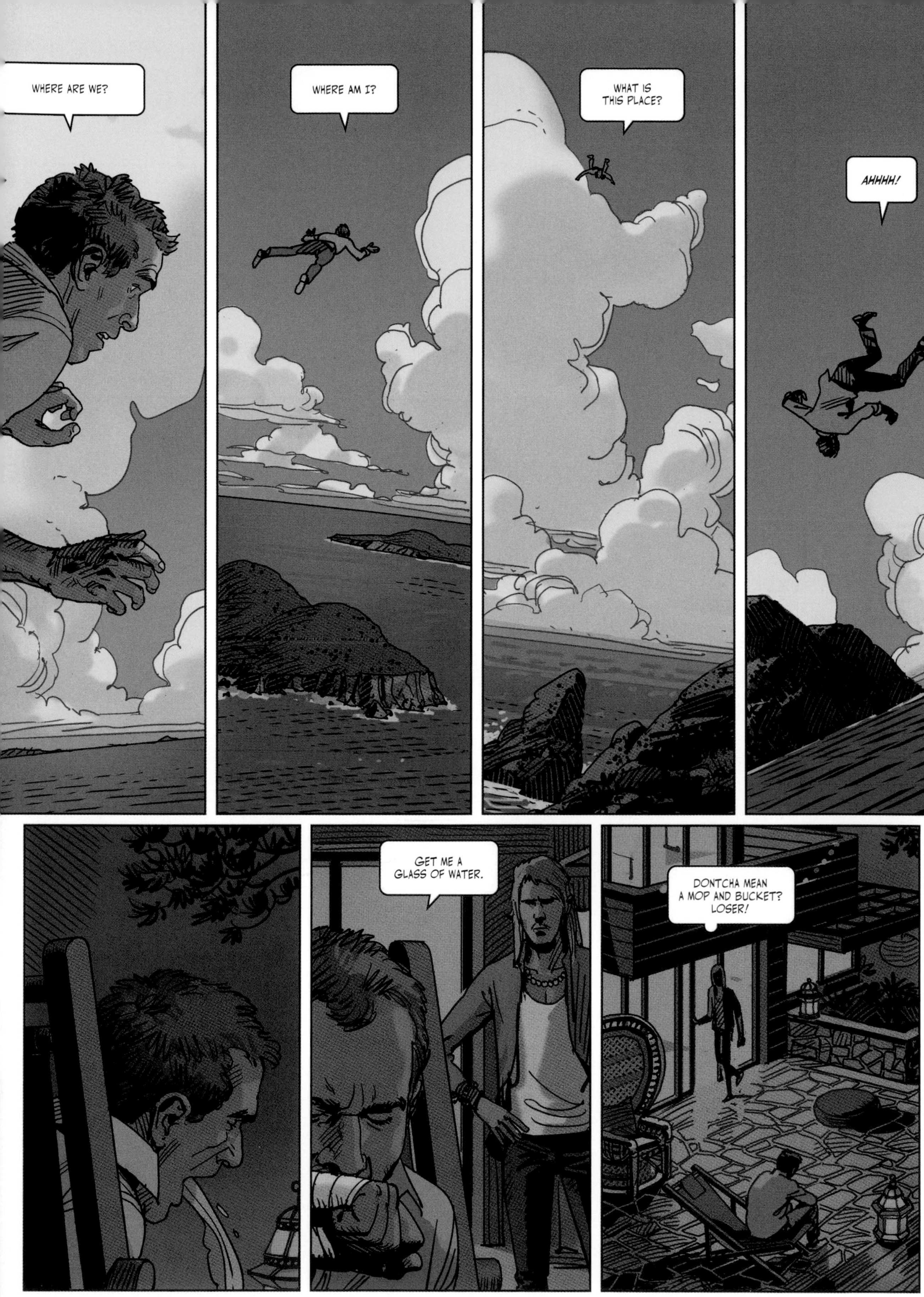
WHERE ARE WE?
WHERE AM I?
WHAT IS THIS PLACE?
AHHHH!
GET ME A GLASS OF WATER.
DONTCHA MEAN A MOP AND BUCKET? LOSER!

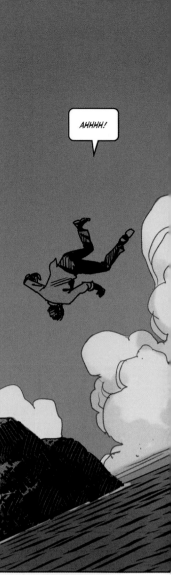

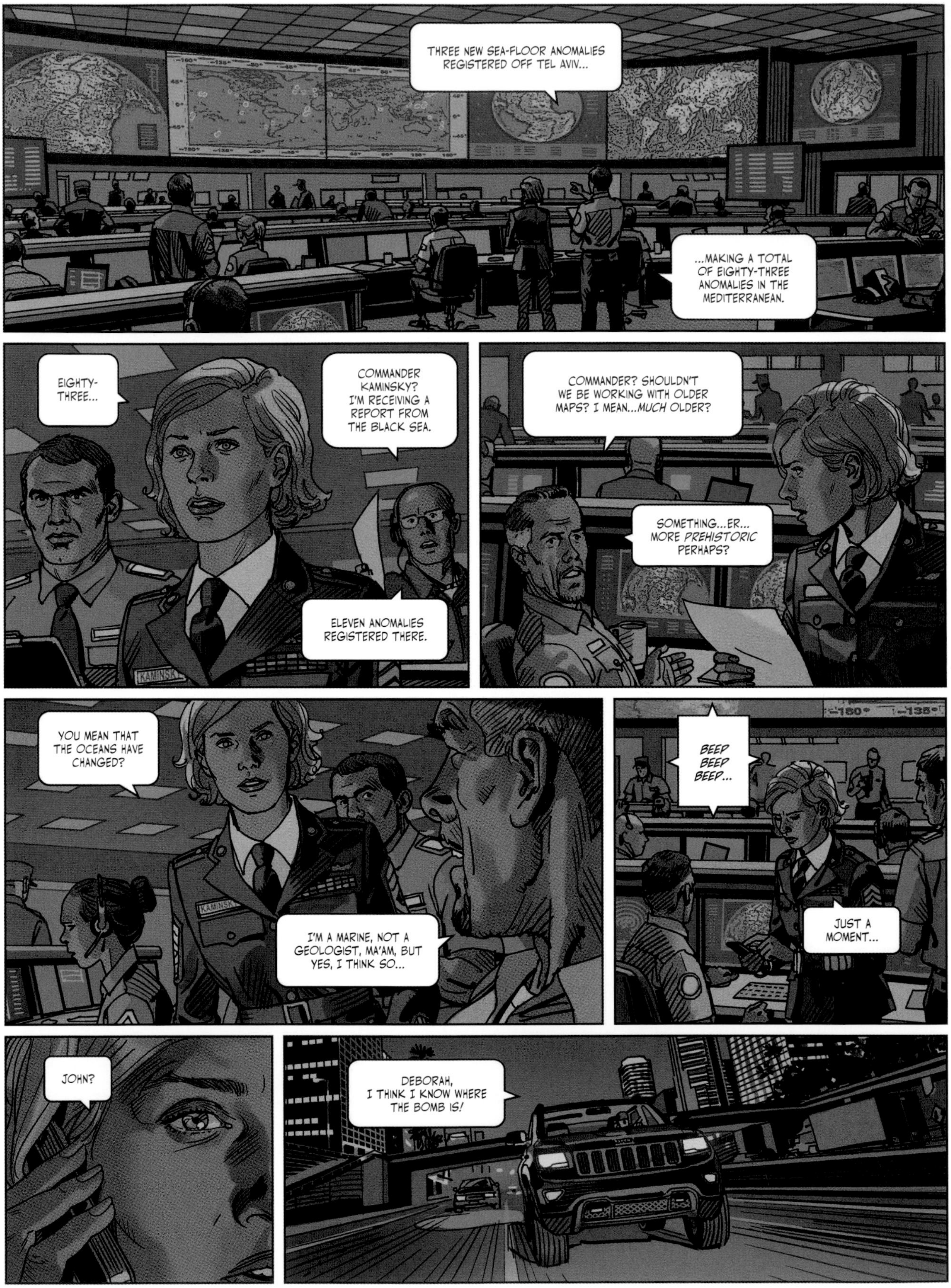
THREE NEW SEA-FLOOR ANOMALIES REGISTERED OFF TEL AVIV...
...MAKING A TOTAL OF EIGHTY-THREE ANOMALIES IN THE MEDITERRANEAN.
EIGHTY-THREE...
COMMANDER KAMINSKY? I'M RECEIVING A REPORT FROM THE BLACK SEA.
ELEVEN ANOMALIES REGISTERED THERE.
COMMANDER? SHOULDN'T WE BE WORKING WITH OLDER MAPS? I MEAN...*MUCH* OLDER?
SOMETHING...ER... MORE *PREHISTORIC* PERHAPS?
YOU MEAN THAT THE OCEANS HAVE CHANGED?
I'M A MARINE, NOT A GEOLOGIST, MA'AM, BUT YES, I THINK SO...
BEEP BEEP BEEP...
JUST A MOMENT...
JOHN?
DEBORAH, I THINK I KNOW WHERE THE BOMB IS!

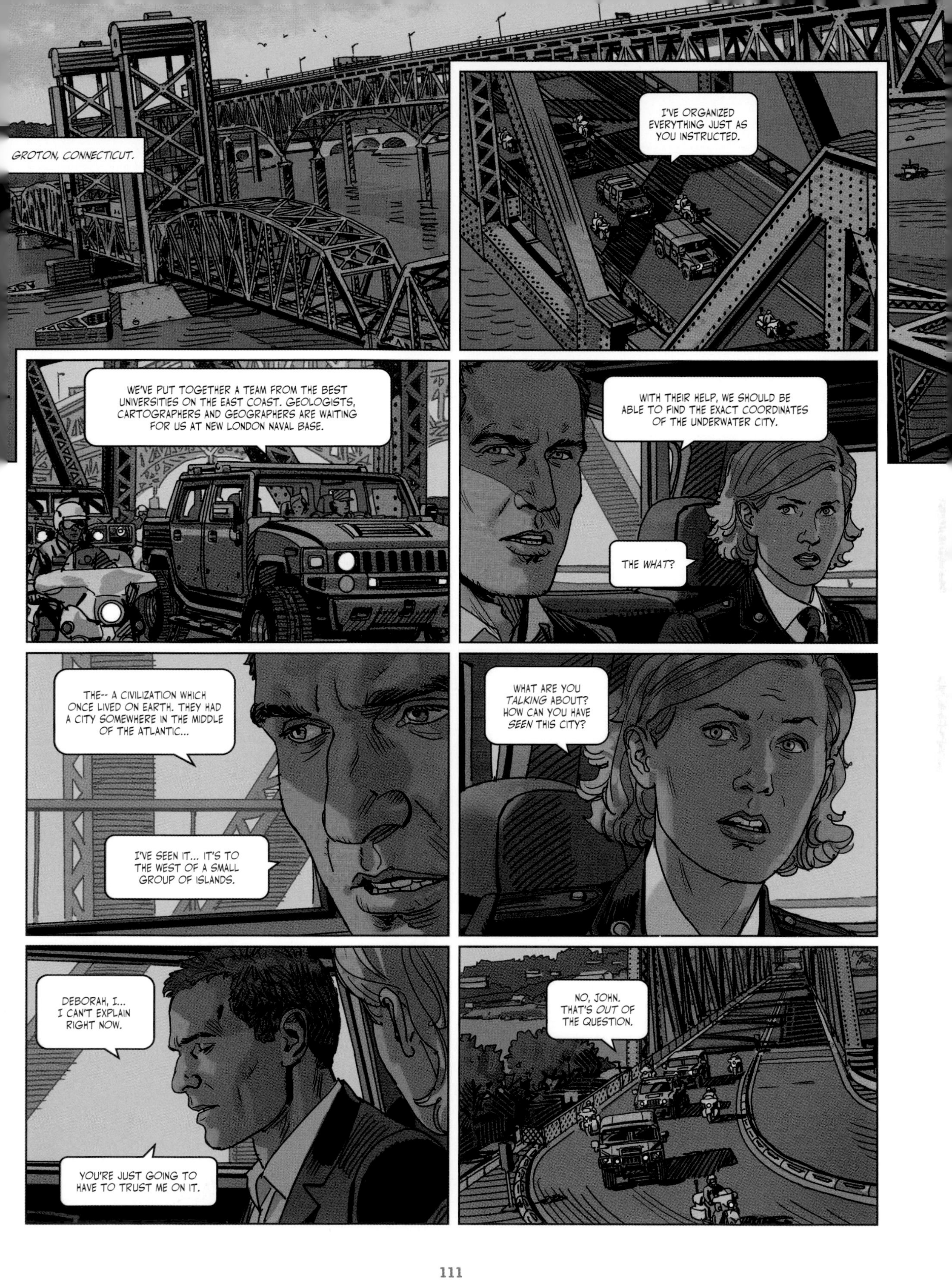
GROTON, CONNECTICUT.
I'VE ORGANIZED EVERYTHING JUST AS YOU INSTRUCTED.
WE'VE PUT TOGETHER A TEAM FROM THE BEST UNIVERSITIES ON THE EAST COAST. GEOLOGISTS, CARTOGRAPHERS AND GEOGRAPHERS ARE WAITING FOR US AT NEW LONDON NAVAL BASE.
WITH THEIR HELP, WE SHOULD BE ABLE TO FIND THE EXACT COORDINATES OF THE UNDERWATER CITY.
THE *WHAT*?
THE-- A CIVILIZATION WHICH ONCE LIVED ON EARTH. THEY HAD A CITY SOMEWHERE IN THE MIDDLE OF THE ATLANTIC...
I'VE SEEN IT... IT'S TO THE WEST OF A SMALL GROUP OF ISLANDS.
WHAT ARE YOU *TALKING* ABOUT? HOW CAN YOU HAVE *SEEN* THIS CITY?
DEBORAH, I... I CAN'T EXPLAIN RIGHT NOW.
YOU'RE JUST GOING TO HAVE TO TRUST ME ON IT.
NO, JOHN. THAT'S *OUT* OF THE QUESTION.

IT'S JUST... I'M AFRAID THAT YOU WON'T BELIEVE ME...

WELL, TRY ME...

YOU REMEMBER THOSE TRACES OF "NARCOTICS" THEY FOUND IN MY BLOOD?

YES, OF COURSE.

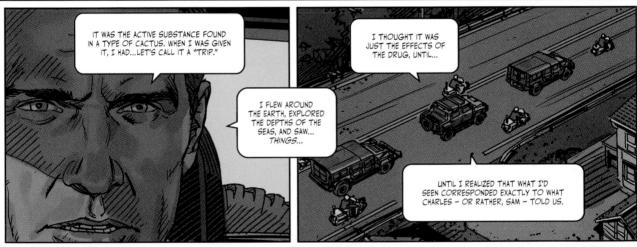

IT WAS THE ACTIVE SUBSTANCE FOUND IN A TYPE OF CACTUS. WHEN I WAS GIVEN IT, I HAD...LET'S CALL IT A "TRIP."

I FLEW AROUND THE EARTH, EXPLORED THE DEPTHS OF THE SEAS, AND SAW... THINGS...

I THOUGHT IT WAS JUST THE EFFECTS OF THE DRUG, UNTIL...

UNTIL I REALIZED THAT WHAT I'D SEEN CORRESPONDED EXACTLY TO WHAT CHARLES – OR RATHER, SAM – TOLD US.

I'M A SCIENTIST. I DON'T BELIEVE IN MAGIC. THERE MUST BE A RATIONAL EXPLANATION FOR ALL THIS...

BUT I JUST HAVEN'T FOUND IT YET...

YOU BELIEVE ME, DON'T YOU? TELL ME YOU BELIEVE ME...

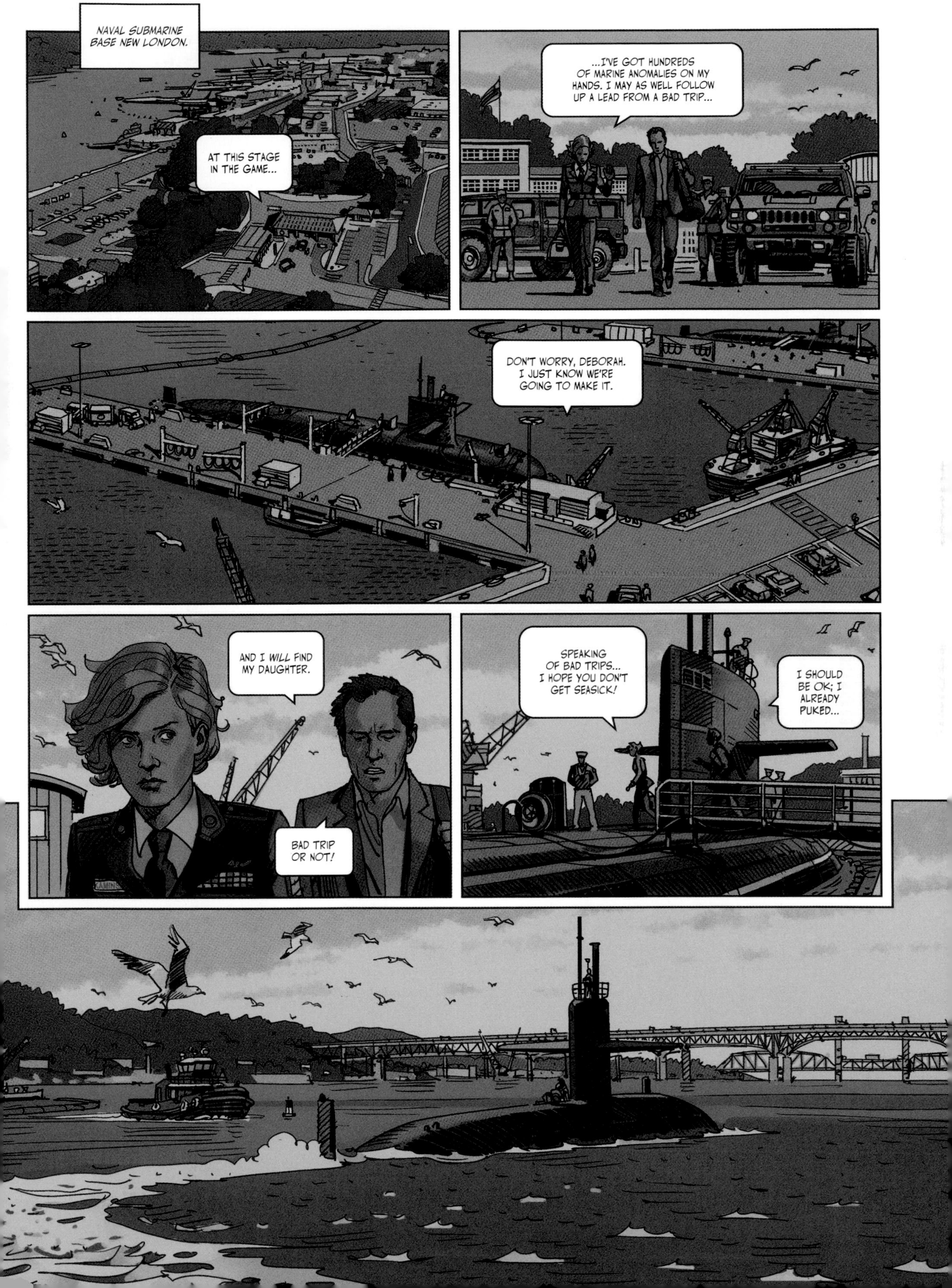
NAVAL SUBMARINE BASE NEW LONDON.
AT THIS STAGE IN THE GAME...
...I'VE GOT HUNDREDS OF MARINE ANOMALIES ON MY HANDS. I MAY AS WELL FOLLOW UP A LEAD FROM A BAD TRIP...
DON'T WORRY, DEBORAH. I JUST KNOW WE'RE GOING TO MAKE IT.
AND I *WILL* FIND MY DAUGHTER.
BAD TRIP OR NOT!
SPEAKING OF BAD TRIPS... I HOPE YOU DON'T GET SEASICK!
I SHOULD BE OK; I ALREADY PUKED...

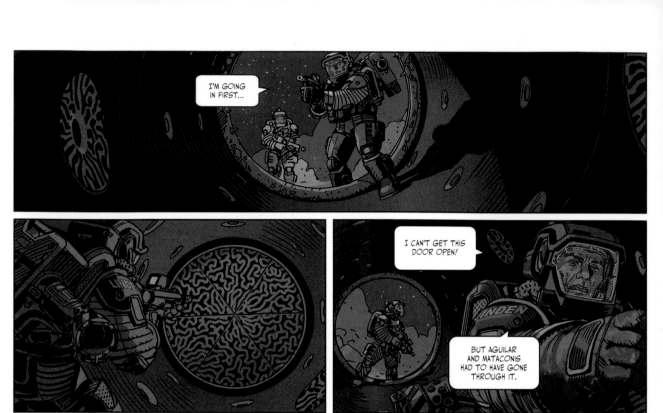

I'M GOING IN FIRST...

I CAN'T GET THIS DOOR OPEN!

BUT AGUILAR AND MATACONIS HAD TO HAVE GONE THROUGH IT.

I THINK WE'RE IN AN "AIRLOCK". THAT DOOR STAYS CLOSED WHEN THIS ONE IS OPEN.

DOORS ARE EITHER *OPEN* OR *CLOSED*. SHOULDN'T BE ALL THAT DIFFICULT TO FIGURE OUT.

THERE YOU GO...

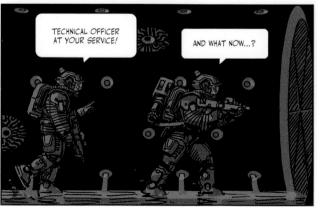

TECHNICAL OFFICER AT YOUR SERVICE!

AND WHAT NOW...?

THIS BASE MUST BE FILLED WITH LIQUID.

114

IT ISN'T WATER; IT'S MUCH DENSER...

I HOPE OUR WEAPONS WILL WORK IN IT...

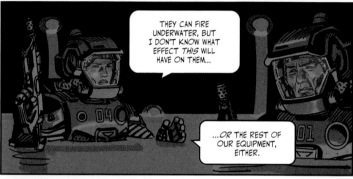

THEY CAN FIRE UNDERWATER, BUT I DON'T KNOW WHAT EFFECT *THIS* WILL HAVE ON THEM...

...OR THE REST OF OUR EQUIPMENT, EITHER.

DROWNING ON THE MOON... HOW PAINFULLY IRONIC.

OUR SUITS ARE WITHSTANDING IT PRETTY WELL. THE LIQUID ISN'T CORROSIVE...

ALTHOUGH NONE OF THE SENSORS CAN IDENTIFY IT.

THE DOOR'S OPENING!

AGUILAR, WE'RE INSIDE THE BASE. DO YOU *COPY?*

COPY!

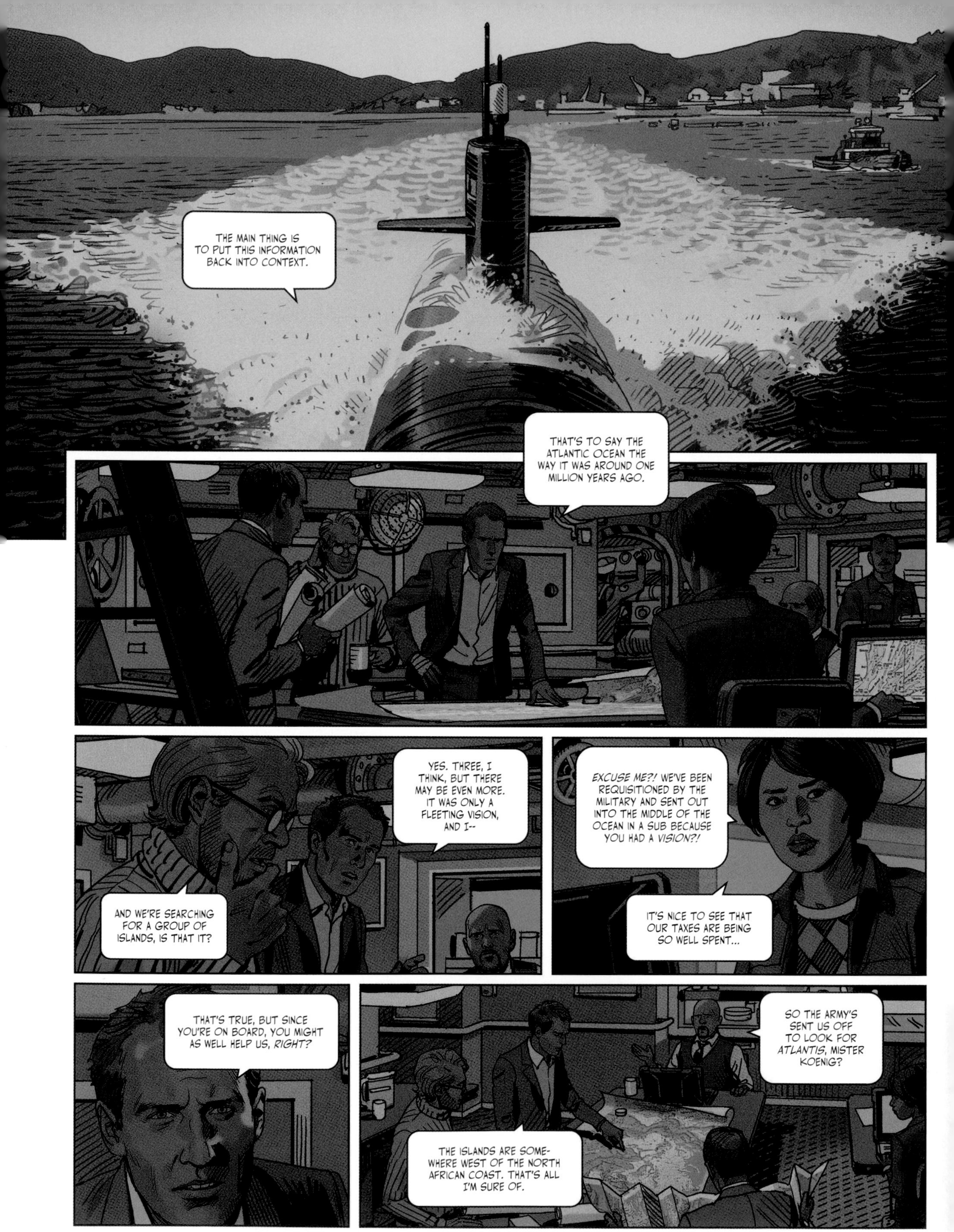
THE MAIN THING IS TO PUT THIS INFORMATION BACK INTO CONTEXT.
THAT'S TO SAY THE ATLANTIC OCEAN THE WAY IT WAS AROUND ONE MILLION YEARS AGO.
AND WE'RE SEARCHING FOR A GROUP OF ISLANDS, IS THAT IT?
YES. THREE, I THINK, BUT THERE MAY BE EVEN MORE. IT WAS ONLY A FLEETING VISION, AND I--
EXCUSE ME?! WE'VE BEEN REQUISITIONED BY THE MILITARY AND SENT OUT INTO THE MIDDLE OF THE OCEAN IN A SUB BECAUSE YOU HAD A *VISION?!*
IT'S NICE TO SEE THAT OUR TAXES ARE BEING SO WELL SPENT...
THAT'S TRUE, BUT SINCE YOU'RE ON BOARD, YOU MIGHT AS WELL HELP US, *RIGHT?*
SO THE ARMY'S SENT US OFF TO LOOK FOR *ATLANTIS*, MISTER KOENIG?
THE ISLANDS ARE SOME-WHERE WEST OF THE NORTH AFRICAN COAST. THAT'S ALL I'M SURE OF.

YES, EACH ANOMALY MUST BE ANALYZED IN DETAIL. ALL AVAILABLE RESOURCES CAN AND MUST BE USED.

YES, COMMANDER.

SO, HOW'S YOUR TEAM?

MY TEAM? A BUNCH OF MIDDLE-AGED NERDS WHO ARE HIGHLY SKILLED AT SNEERING... OH, THEY'RE *GREAT!*

DON'T BE OFFENDED; YOU'RE BETTER THAN THAT.

AND HOW ABOUT YOU?

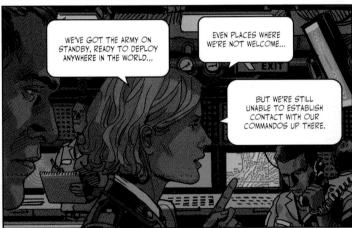

WE'VE GOT THE ARMY ON STANDBY, READY TO DEPLOY ANYWHERE IN THE WORLD...

EVEN PLACES WHERE WE'RE NOT WELCOME...

BUT WE'RE STILL UNABLE TO ESTABLISH CONTACT WITH OUR COMMANDOS UP THERE.

AND THERE'S NO NEWS OF MY DAUGHTER, I IMAGINE...

NO, NOTHING ABOUT HER EITHER. I'M SORRY, JOHN.

YEAH, I'M SORRY, TOO...

HEY, CAN I ASK YOU A QUESTION?

YES, OF COURSE.

IS THERE ANY ALCOHOL ON BOARD? I COULD *REALLY* USE A SHOT OF SOMETHING...

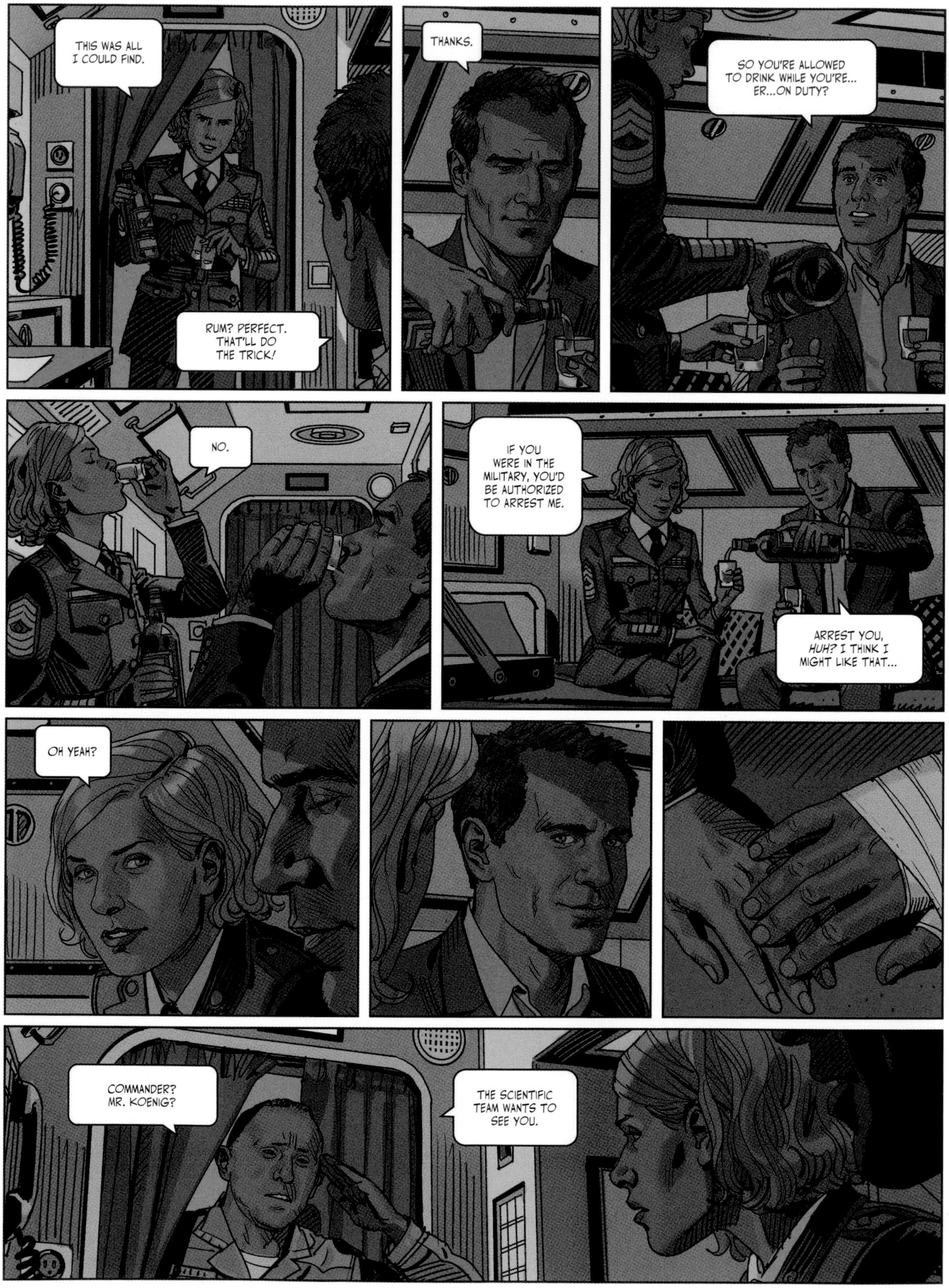
THIS WAS ALL I COULD FIND.
RUM? PERFECT. THAT'LL DO THE TRICK!
THANKS.
SO YOU'RE ALLOWED TO DRINK WHILE YOU'RE... ER...ON DUTY?
NO.
IF YOU WERE IN THE MILITARY, YOU'D BE AUTHORIZED TO ARREST ME.
ARREST YOU, *HUH?* I THINK I MIGHT LIKE THAT...
OH YEAH?
COMMANDER? MR. KOENIG?
THE SCIENTIFIC TEAM WANTS TO SEE YOU.

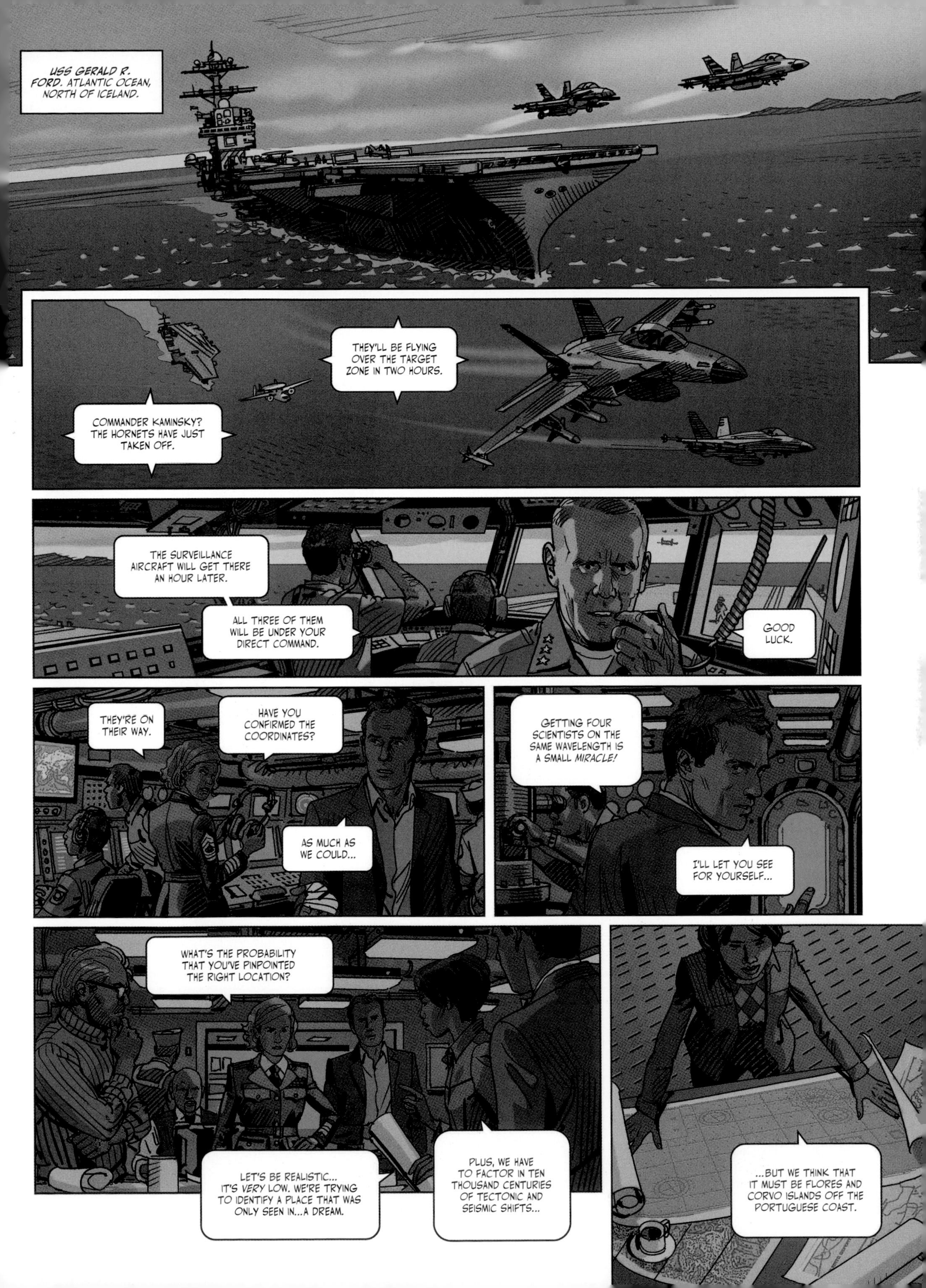
USS GERALD R. FORD. ATLANTIC OCEAN, NORTH OF ICELAND.
COMMANDER KAMINSKY? THE HORNETS HAVE JUST TAKEN OFF.
THEY'LL BE FLYING OVER THE TARGET ZONE IN TWO HOURS.
THE SURVEILLANCE AIRCRAFT WILL GET THERE AN HOUR LATER.
ALL THREE OF THEM WILL BE UNDER YOUR DIRECT COMMAND.
GOOD LUCK.
THEY'RE ON THEIR WAY.
HAVE YOU CONFIRMED THE COORDINATES?
AS MUCH AS WE COULD...
GETTING FOUR SCIENTISTS ON THE SAME WAVELENGTH IS A SMALL MIRACLE!
I'LL LET YOU SEE FOR YOURSELF...
WHAT'S THE PROBABILITY THAT YOU'VE PINPOINTED THE RIGHT LOCATION?
LET'S BE REALISTIC... IT'S VERY LOW. WE'RE TRYING TO IDENTIFY A PLACE THAT WAS ONLY SEEN IN...A DREAM.
PLUS, WE HAVE TO FACTOR IN TEN THOUSAND CENTURIES OF TECTONIC AND SEISMIC SHIFTS...
...BUT WE THINK THAT IT MUST BE FLORES AND CORVO ISLANDS OFF THE PORTUGUESE COAST.

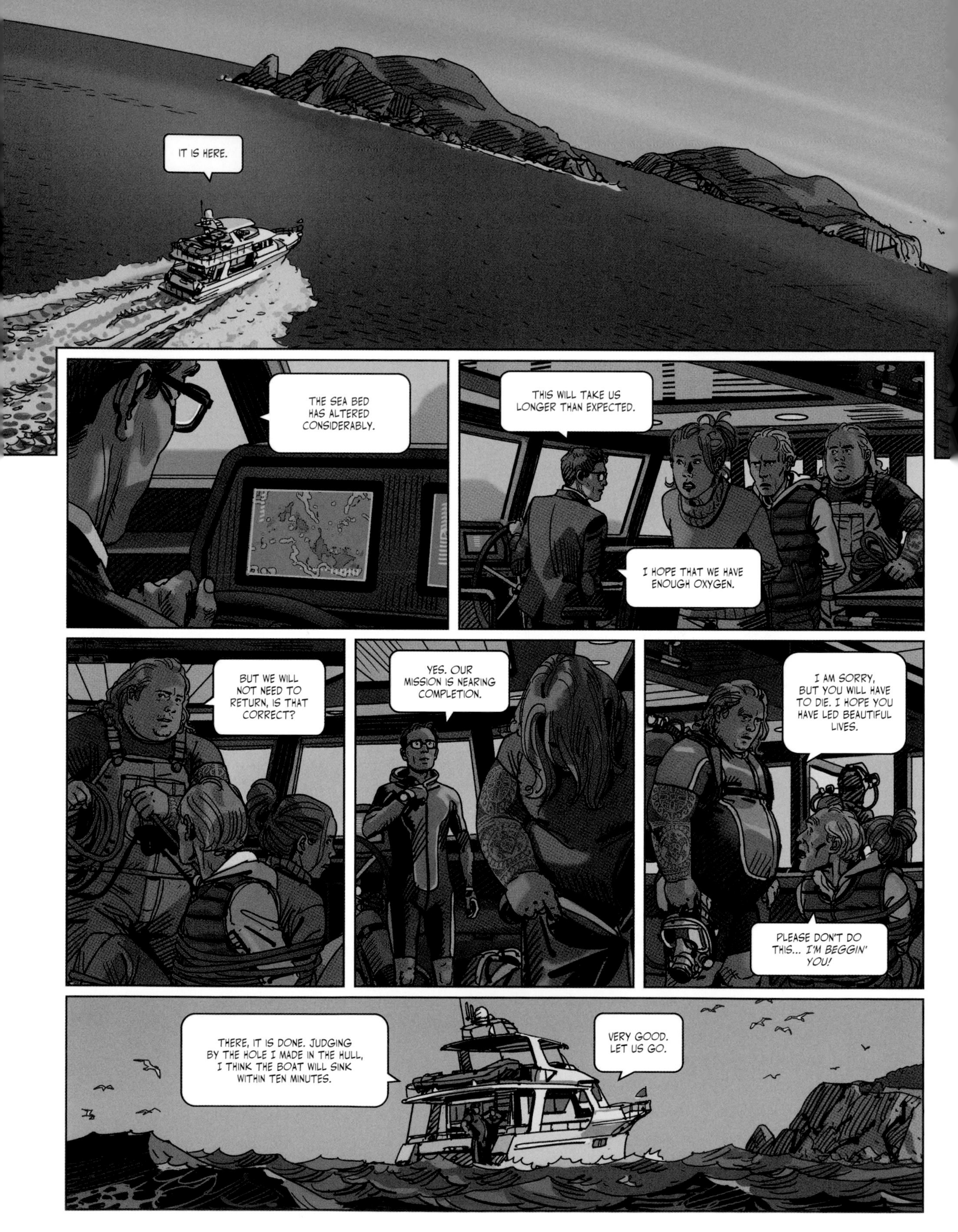
IT IS HERE.
THE SEA BED HAS ALTERED CONSIDERABLY.
THIS WILL TAKE US LONGER THAN EXPECTED.
I HOPE THAT WE HAVE ENOUGH OXYGEN.
BUT WE WILL NOT NEED TO RETURN, IS THAT CORRECT?
YES. OUR MISSION IS NEARING COMPLETION.
I AM SORRY, BUT YOU WILL HAVE TO DIE. I HOPE YOU HAVE LED BEAUTIFUL LIVES.
PLEASE DON'T DO THIS... *I'M BEGGIN' YOU!*
THERE, IT IS DONE. JUDGING BY THE HOLE I MADE IN THE HULL, I THINK THE BOAT WILL SINK WITHIN TEN MINUTES.
VERY GOOD. LET US GO.

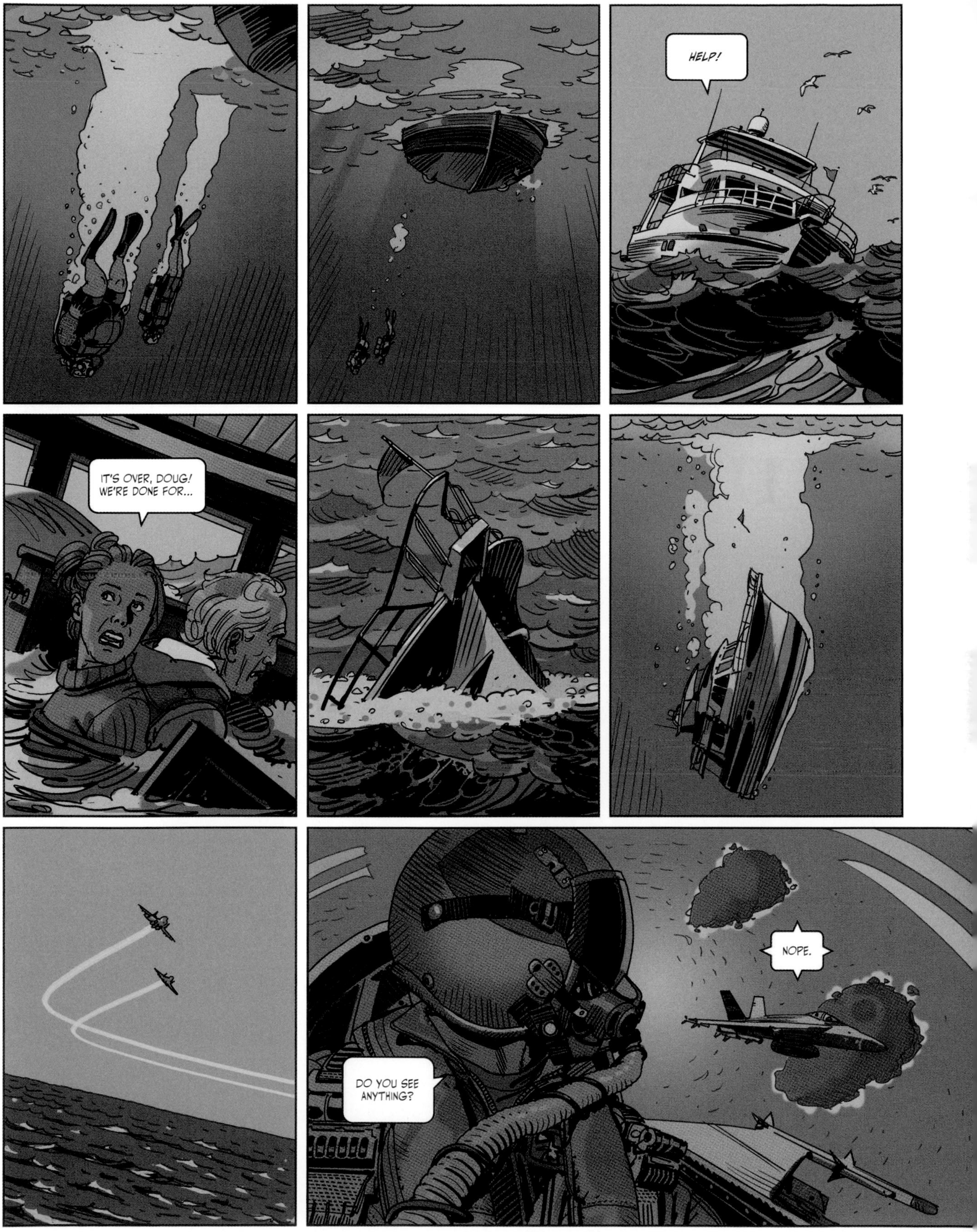
HELP!
IT'S OVER, DOUG! WE'RE DONE FOR...
NOPE.
DO YOU SEE ANYTHING?

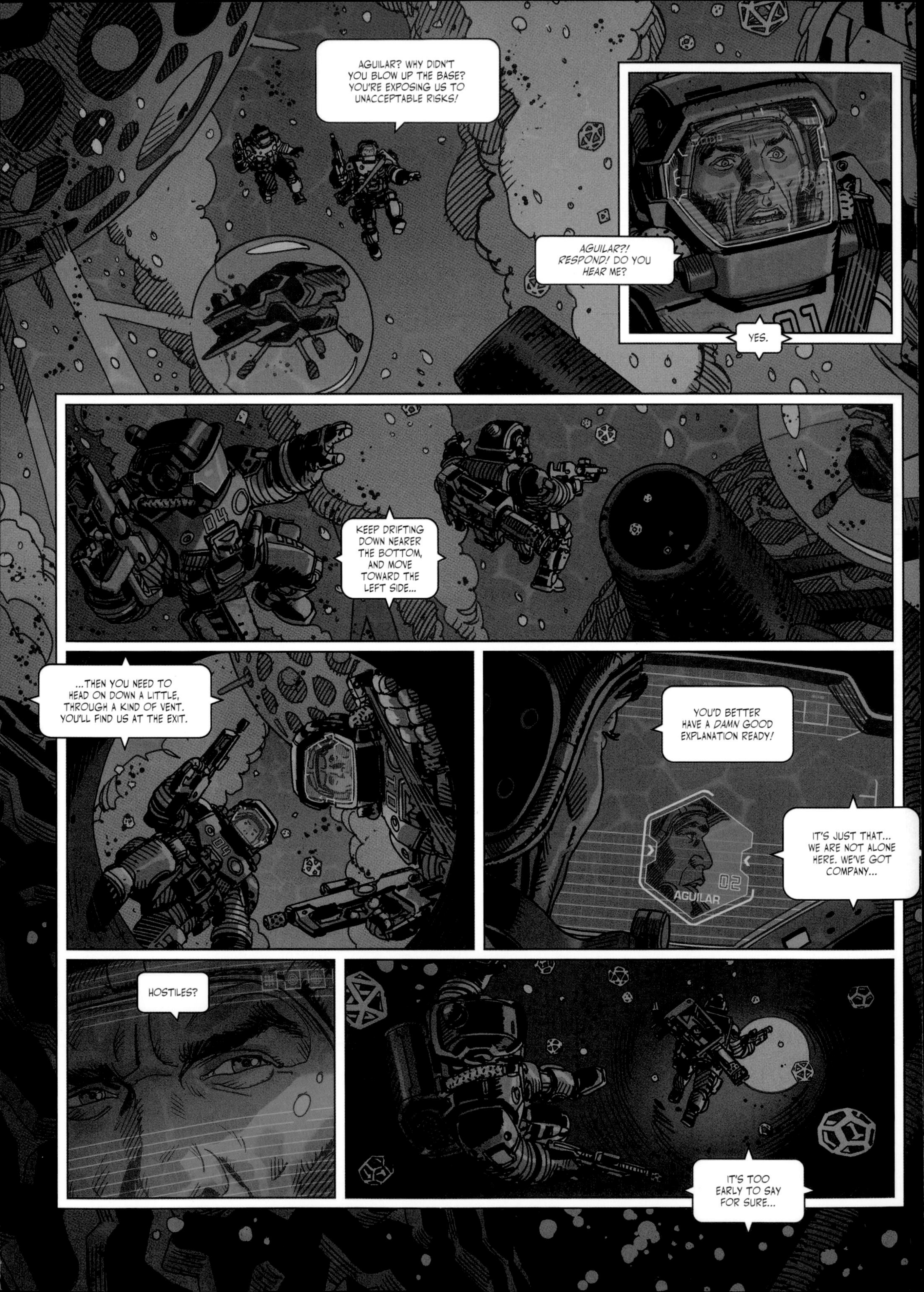
AGUILAR? WHY DIDN'T YOU BLOW UP THE BASE? YOU'RE EXPOSING US TO UNACCEPTABLE RISKS!
AGUILAR?! RESPOND! DO YOU HEAR ME?
YES.
KEEP DRIFTING DOWN NEARER THE BOTTOM, AND MOVE TOWARD THE LEFT SIDE...
...THEN YOU NEED TO HEAD ON DOWN A LITTLE, THROUGH A KIND OF VENT. YOU'LL FIND US AT THE EXIT.
YOU'D BETTER HAVE A DAMN GOOD EXPLANATION READY!
02
AGUILAR
IT'S JUST THAT... WE ARE NOT ALONE HERE. WE'VE GOT COMPANY...
HOSTILES?
IT'S TOO EARLY TO SAY FOR SURE...

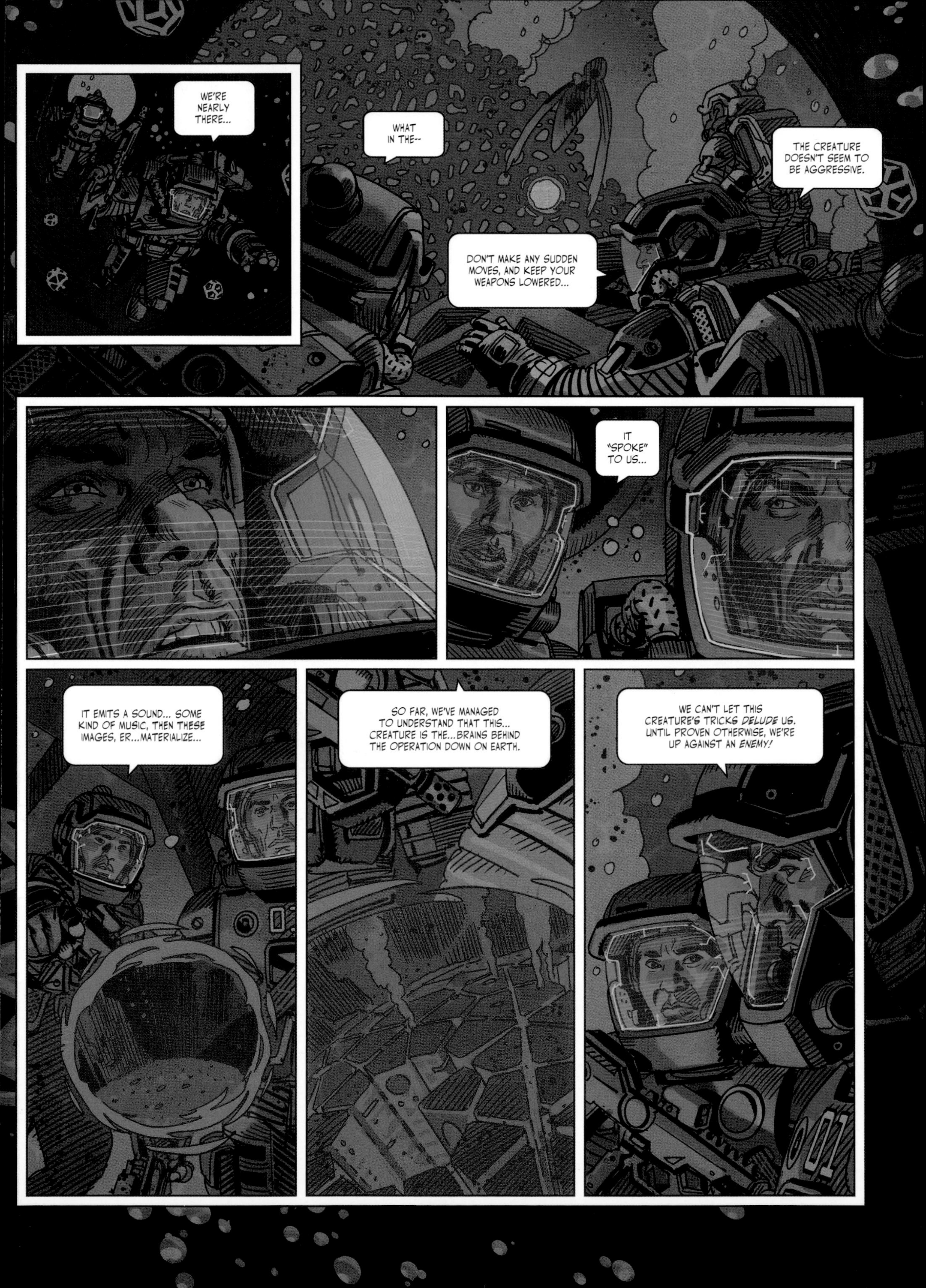
WE'RE NEARLY THERE...
WHAT IN THE--
THE CREATURE DOESN'T SEEM TO BE AGGRESSIVE.
DON'T MAKE ANY SUDDEN MOVES, AND KEEP YOUR WEAPONS LOWERED...
IT "SPOKE" TO US...
IT EMITS A SOUND... SOME KIND OF MUSIC, THEN THESE IMAGES, ER...MATERIALIZE...
SO FAR, WE'VE MANAGED TO UNDERSTAND THAT THIS... CREATURE IS THE...BRAINS BEHIND THE OPERATION DOWN ON EARTH.
WE CAN'T LET THIS CREATURE'S TRICKS *DELUDE* US. UNTIL PROVEN OTHERWISE, WE'RE UP AGAINST AN *ENEMY!*

THAT'S ON EARTH...
THEY HAVE A BASE
ON EARTH!

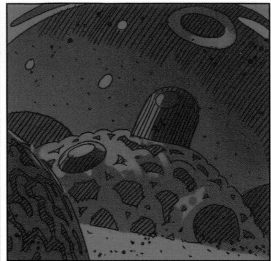

WE NEED TO
KNOW THAT BASE'S
COORDINATES
IMMEDIATELY!

LOOK! WHAT'S
IT DOING...?

I THINK I'M
BEGINNING TO
UNDERSTAND...

I THINK IT'S
GRATEFUL THAT
I DIDN'T FIRE THE
WEAPON...

I'D SAY WE'VE GOT A PEACE
PROCESS UNDERWAY HERE!

THAT THING IT
SHOWED US IN THE
BASE WAS A BOMB!
IT'S THREATENING
US, GODDAMNIT!

PEACE
PROCESS,
MY ASS!

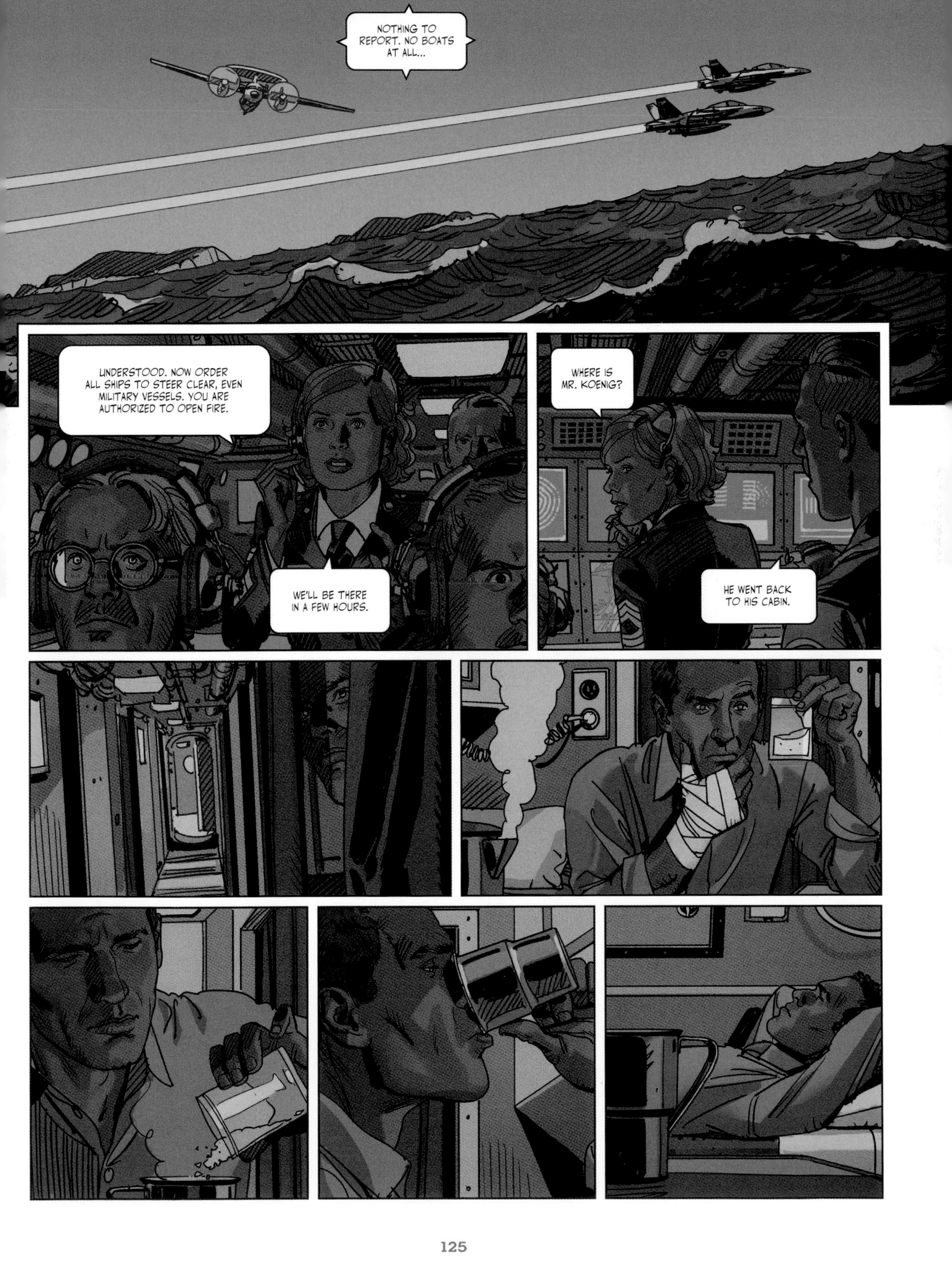
NOTHING TO REPORT. NO BOATS AT ALL...
UNDERSTOOD. NOW ORDER ALL SHIPS TO STEER CLEAR, EVEN MILITARY VESSELS. YOU ARE AUTHORIZED TO OPEN FIRE.
WE'LL BE THERE IN A FEW HOURS.
WHERE IS MR. KOENIG?
HE WENT BACK TO HIS CABIN.

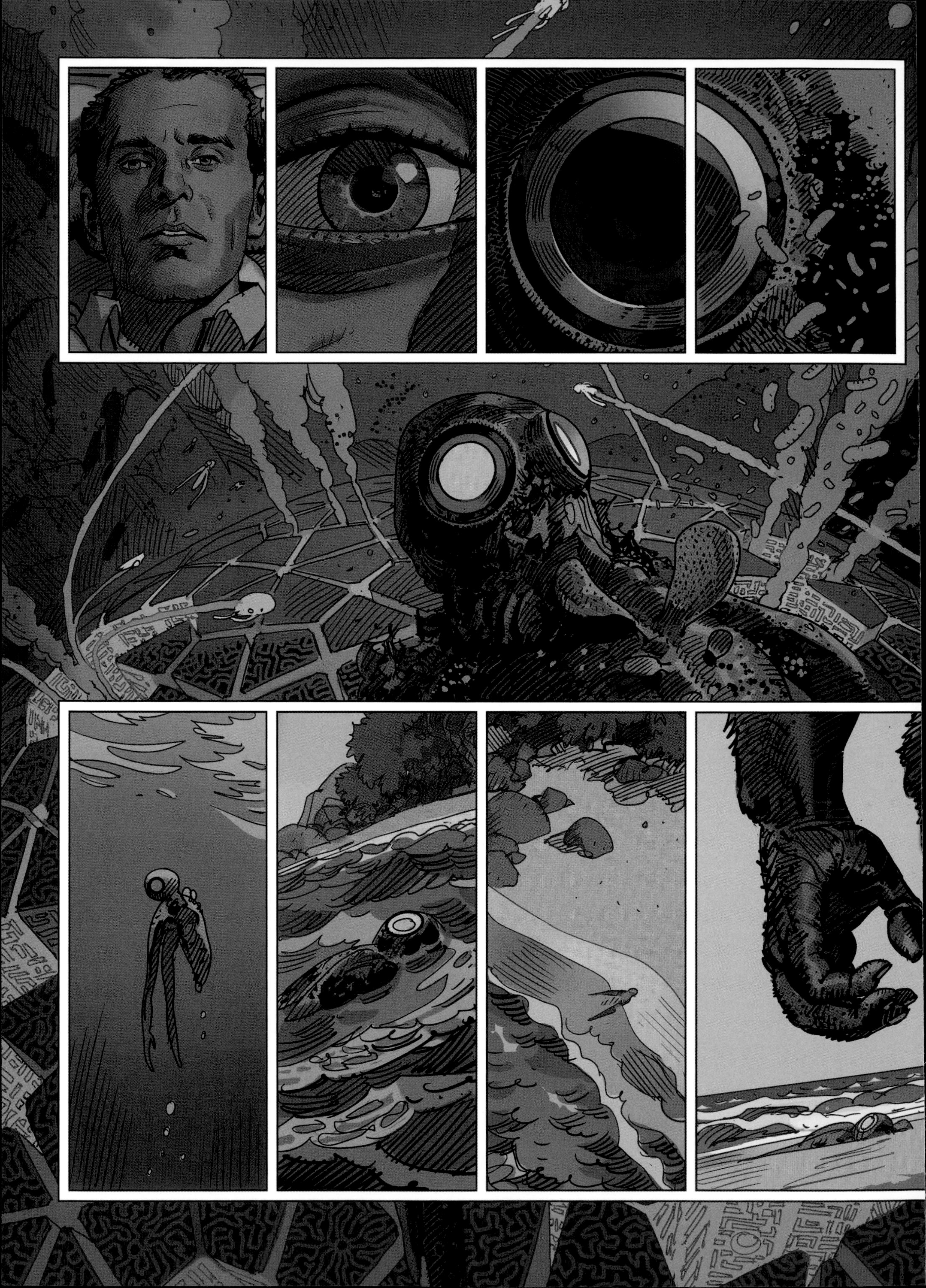

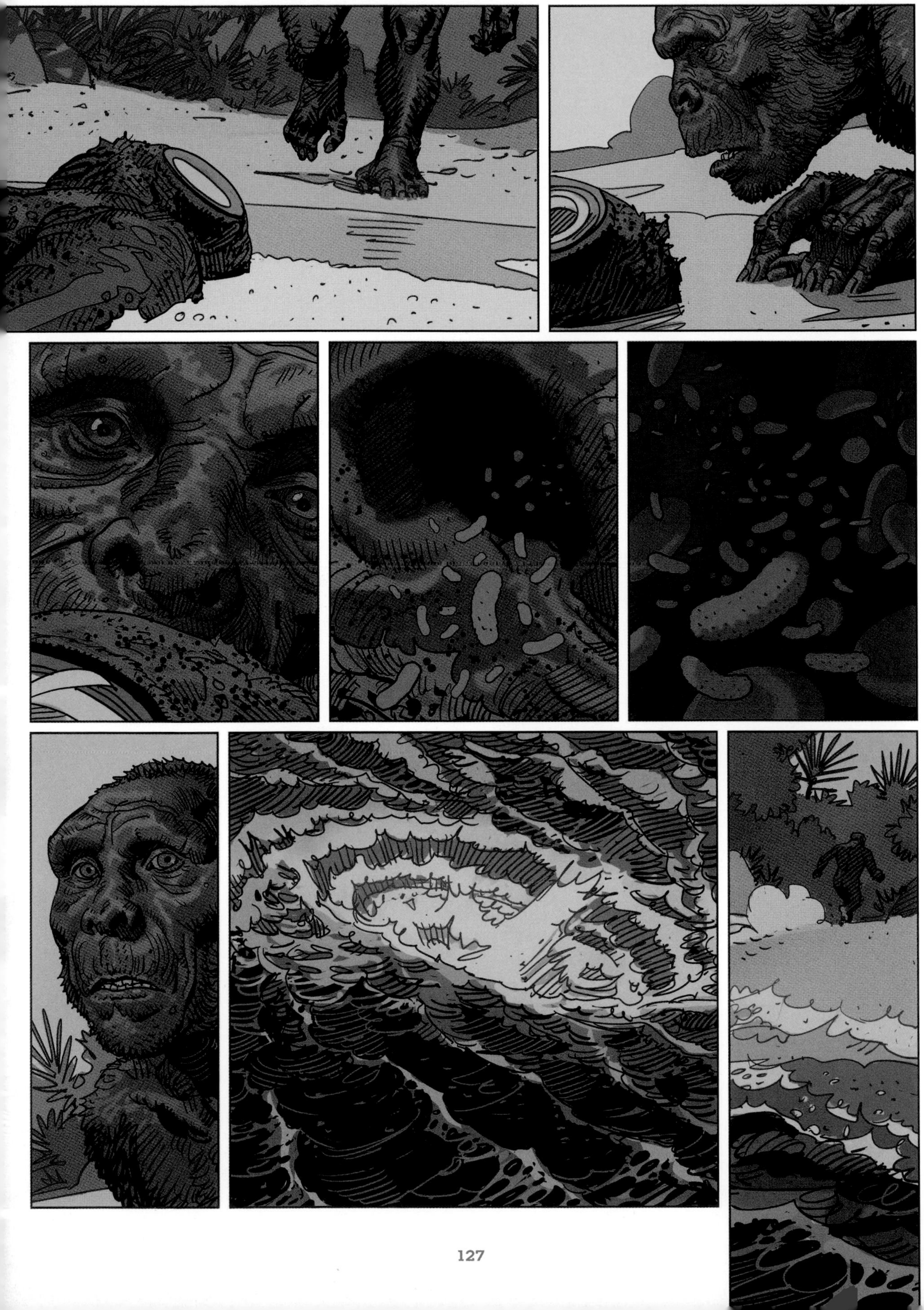

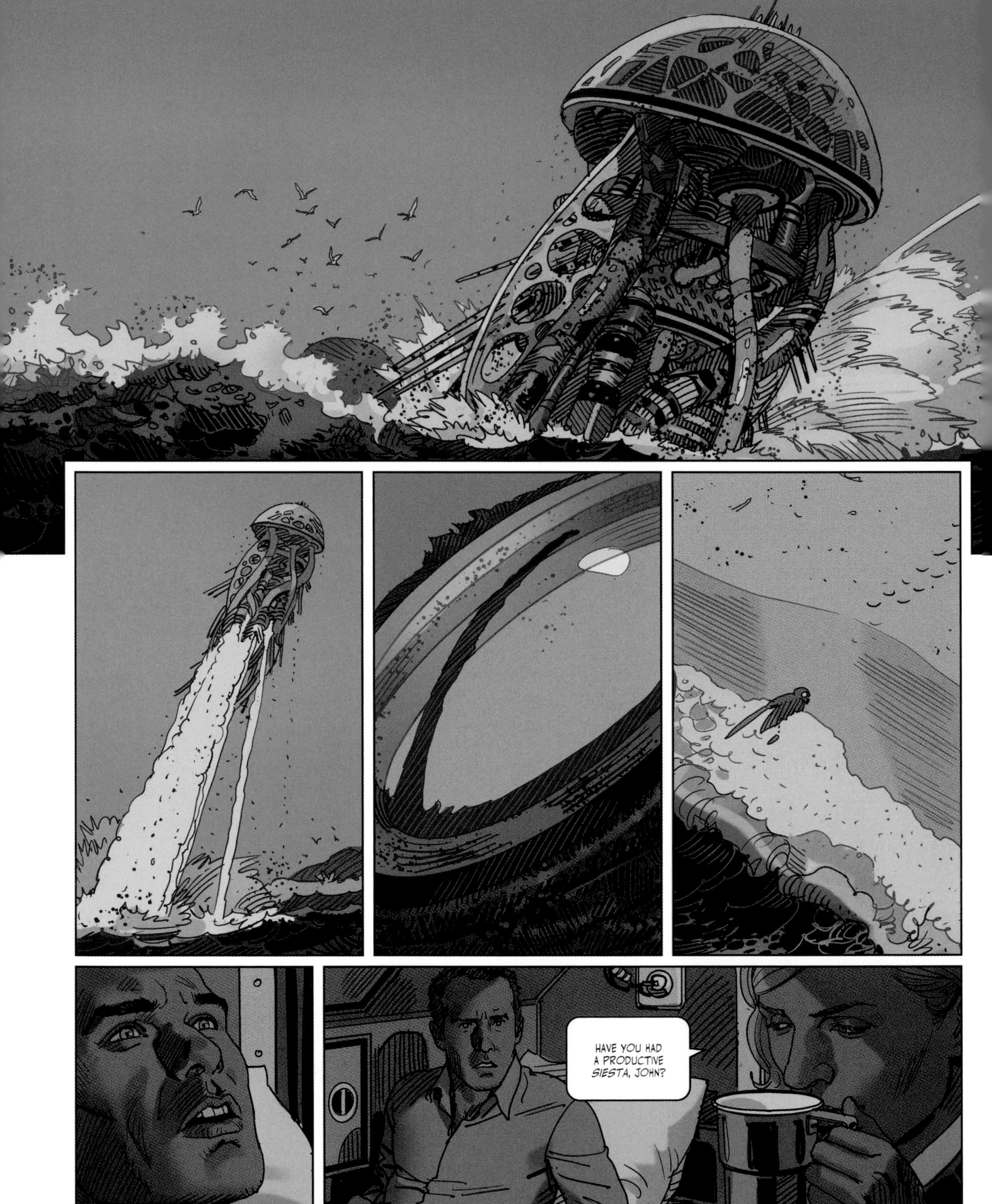
HAVE YOU HAD
A PRODUCTIVE
SIESTA, JOHN?

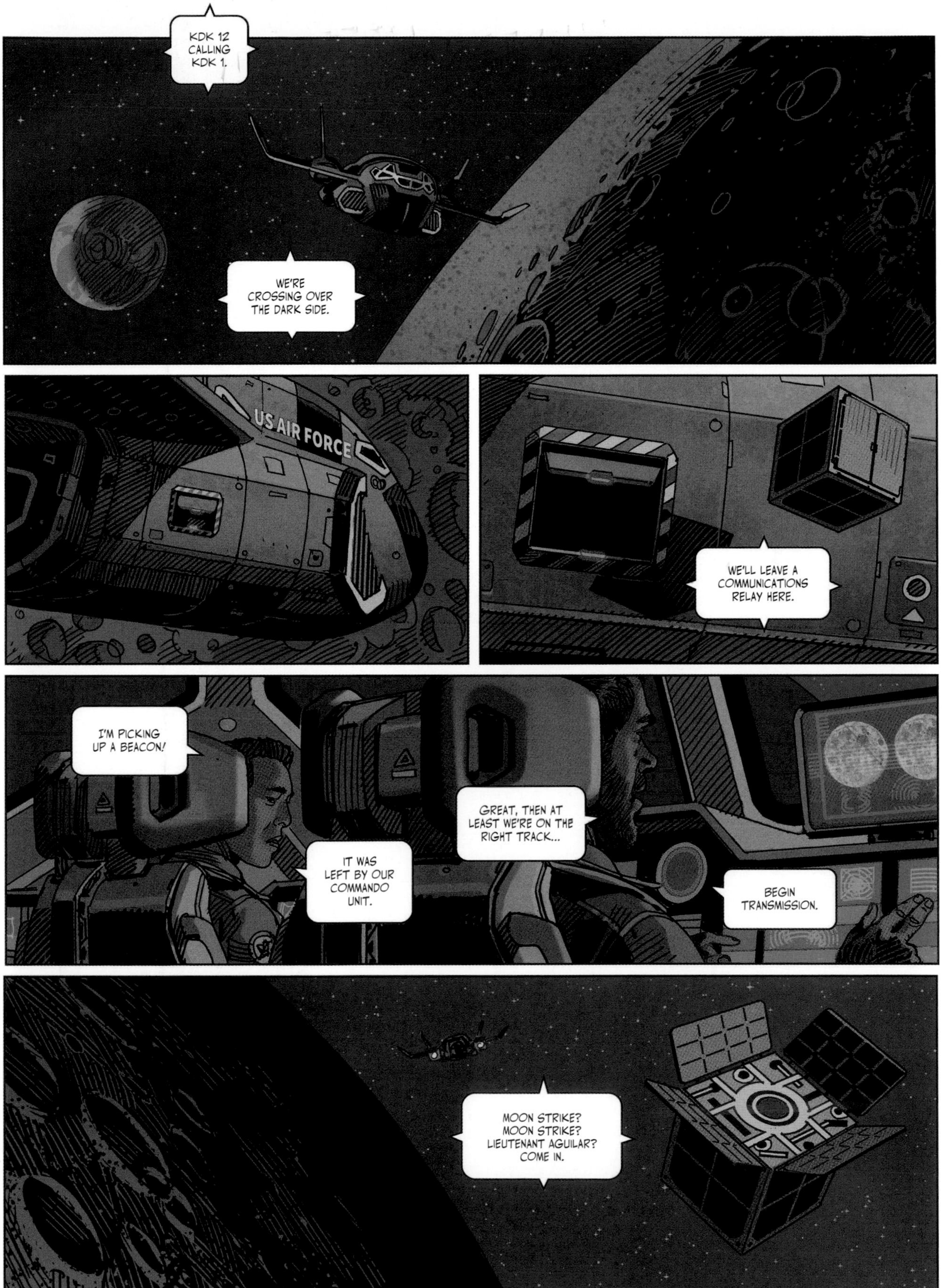
KDK 12 CALLING KDK 1.
WE'RE CROSSING OVER THE DARK SIDE.
US AIR FORCE
WE'LL LEAVE A COMMUNICATIONS RELAY HERE.
I'M PICKING UP A BEACON!
IT WAS LEFT BY OUR COMMANDO UNIT.
GREAT, THEN AT LEAST WE'RE ON THE RIGHT TRACK...
BEGIN TRANSMISSION.
MOON STRIKE? MOON STRIKE? LIEUTENANT AGUILAR? COME IN.

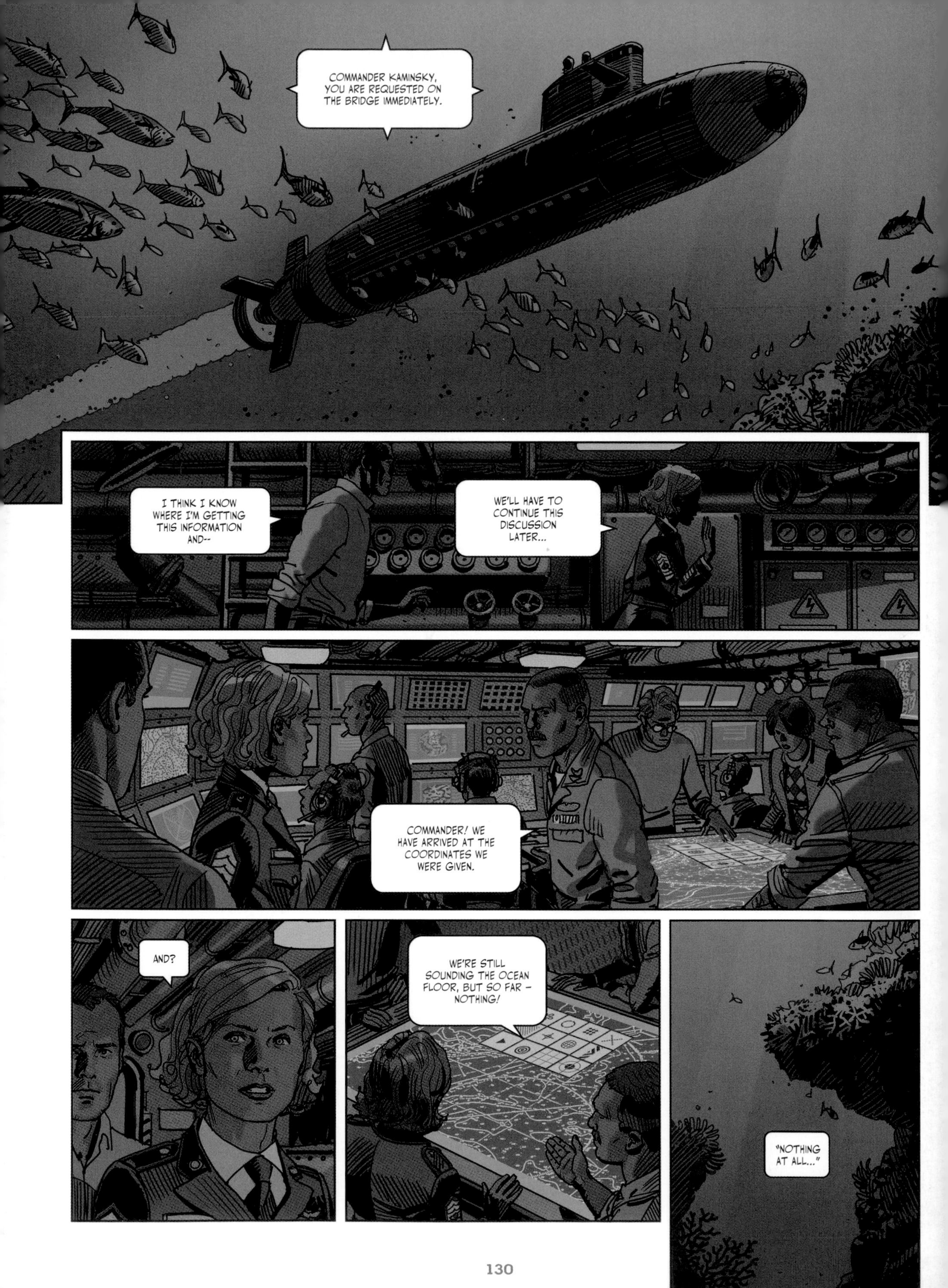
COMMANDER KAMINSKY, YOU ARE REQUESTED ON THE BRIDGE IMMEDIATELY.
I THINK I KNOW WHERE I'M GETTING THIS INFORMATION AND--
WE'LL HAVE TO CONTINUE THIS DISCUSSION LATER...
COMMANDER! WE HAVE ARRIVED AT THE COORDINATES WE WERE GIVEN.
AND?
WE'RE STILL SOUNDING THE OCEAN FLOOR, BUT SO FAR – NOTHING!
"NOTHING AT ALL..."

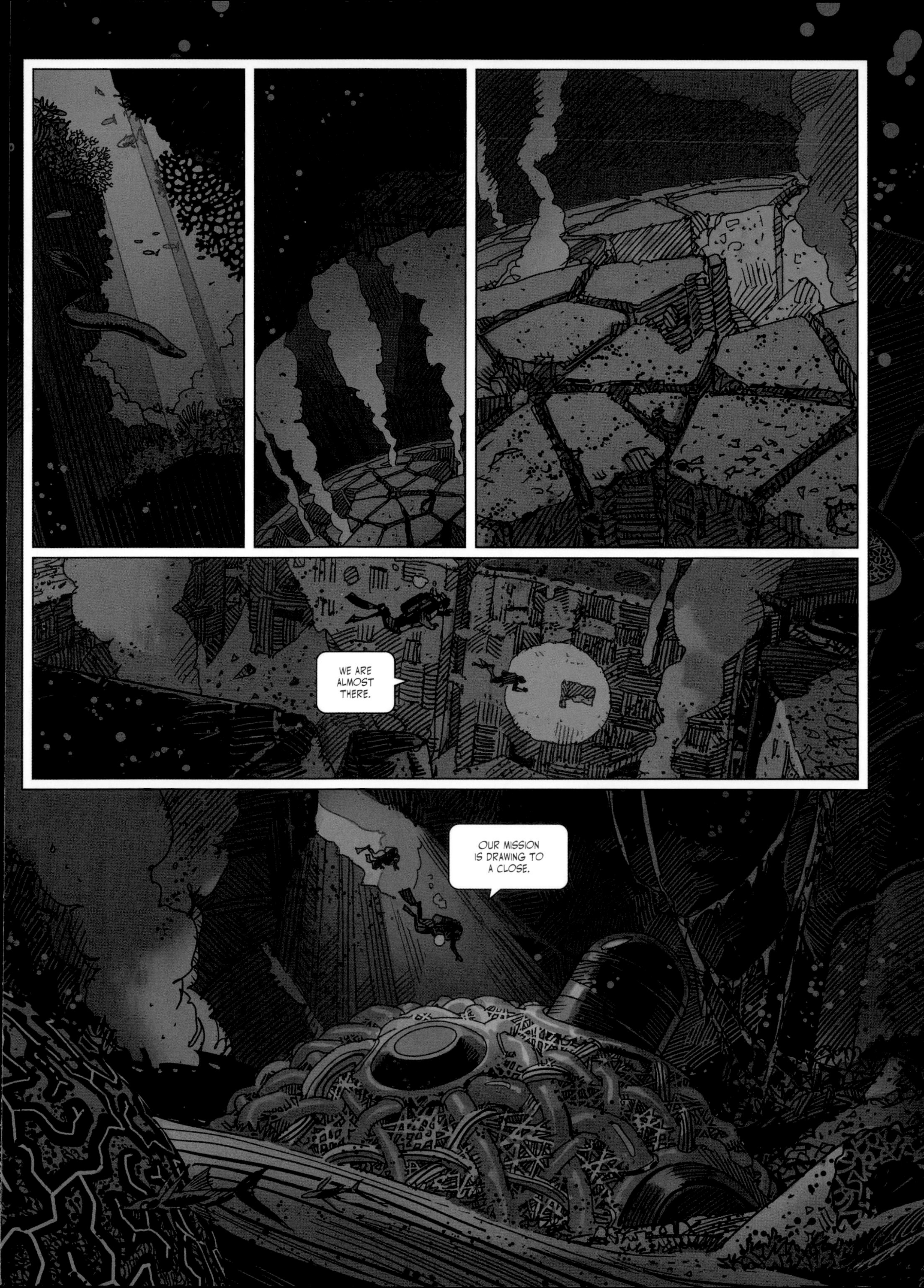
WE ARE ALMOST THERE.
OUR MISSION IS DRAWING TO A CLOSE.

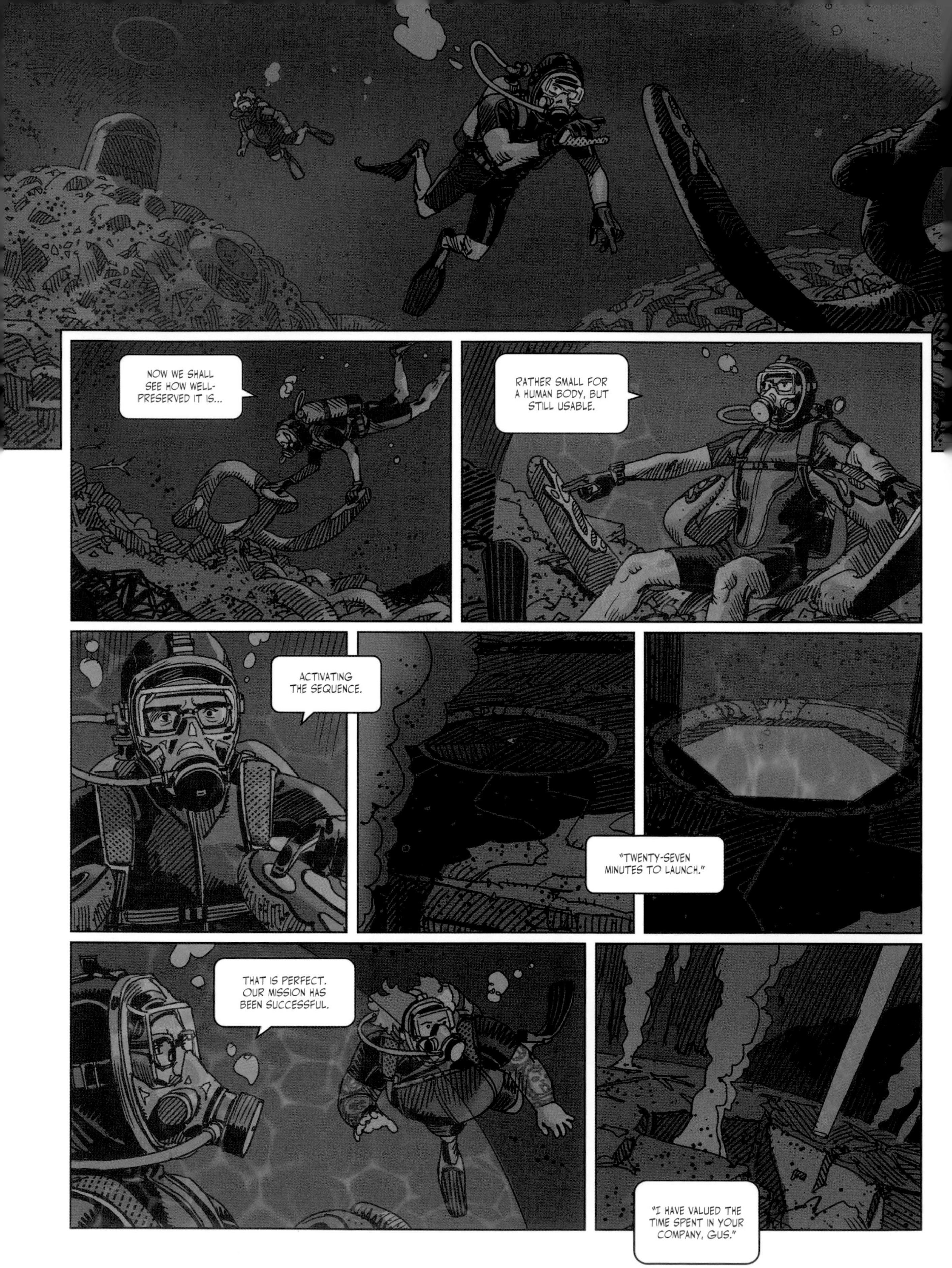

NOW WE SHALL SEE HOW WELL-PRESERVED IT IS...
RATHER SMALL FOR A HUMAN BODY, BUT STILL USABLE.
ACTIVATING THE SEQUENCE.
"TWENTY-SEVEN MINUTES TO LAUNCH."
THAT IS PERFECT. OUR MISSION HAS BEEN SUCCESSFUL.
"I HAVE VALUED THE TIME SPENT IN YOUR COMPANY, GUS."

I'M FED UP WITH THIS MONSTER'S THREATS.

LET'S END THIS *NOW!*

ENOUGH, LINDEN! *ENOUGH!*

WHAT'S GOTTEN INTO YOU?! ARE YOU *CRAZY?!*

SOME THINGS ARE MORE IMPORTANT THAN OBEYING *ORDERS,* LINDEN.

AGUILAR! YOU FUCKING *ASSHOLE!* YOU'LL BE COURT-MARTIALED!

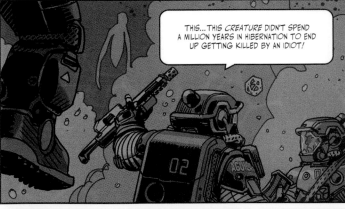

THIS...THIS *CREATURE* DIDN'T SPEND A MILLION YEARS IN HIBERNATION TO END UP GETTING KILLED BY AN IDIOT!

I'M TAKING COMMAND OF THIS MISSION, WHETHER YOU LIKE IT OR NOT!

LIEUTENANT?

YES?

I'M RECEIVING A MESSAGE FROM KDK 12! THEY'RE REAL CLOSE!

MOON STRIKE, WE'RE RELAYING A MESSAGE FROM COMMANDER KAMINSKY...

UPLOAD IN PROGRESS.

IT'S FROM KAMINSKY...

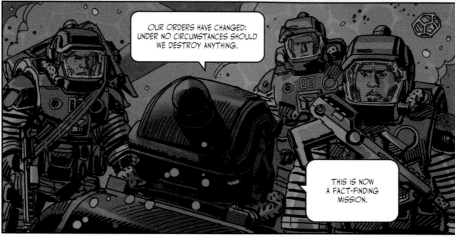

OUR ORDERS HAVE CHANGED: UNDER NO CIRCUMSTANCES SHOULD WE DESTROY ANYTHING.

THIS IS NOW A FACT-FINDING MISSION.

THEY KNOW ABOUT THE UNDERWATER BASE!

THEY WANT TO KNOW ITS LOCATION... AND URGENTLY!

THE SURVIVAL OF OUR PLANET IS AT STAKE!

THEN LET US BE CRYSTAL CLEAR WITH OUR INTENTIONS...

...WE ARE NOT ENEMIES.

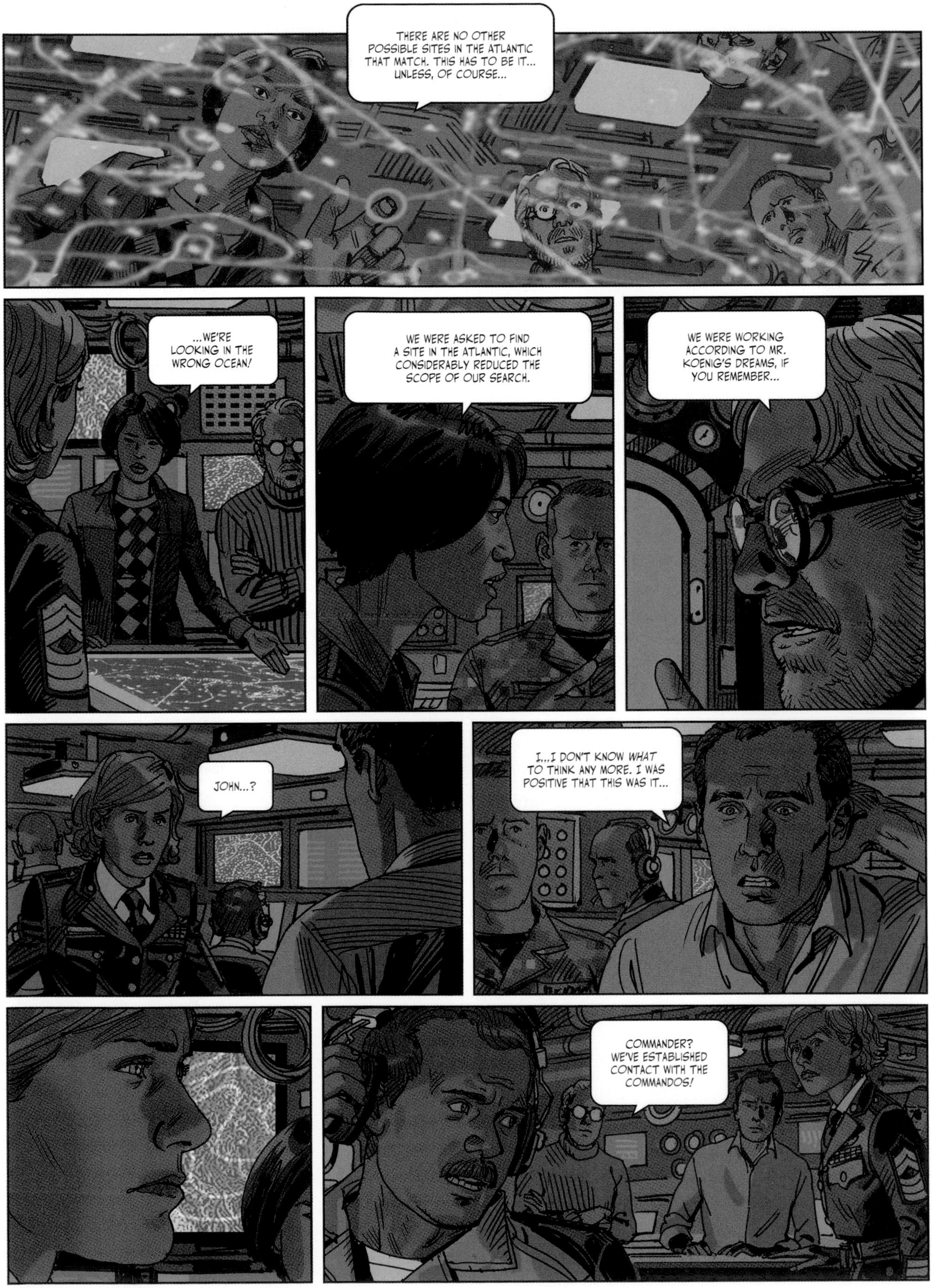
THERE ARE NO OTHER POSSIBLE SITES IN THE ATLANTIC THAT MATCH. THIS HAS TO BE IT... UNLESS, OF COURSE...
...WE'RE LOOKING IN THE WRONG OCEAN!
WE WERE ASKED TO FIND A SITE IN THE ATLANTIC, WHICH CONSIDERABLY REDUCED THE SCOPE OF OUR SEARCH.
WE WERE WORKING ACCORDING TO MR. KOENIG'S DREAMS, IF YOU REMEMBER...
JOHN...?
I...I DON'T KNOW *WHAT* TO THINK ANY MORE. I WAS POSITIVE THAT THIS WAS IT...
COMMANDER? WE'VE ESTABLISHED CONTACT WITH THE COMMANDOS!

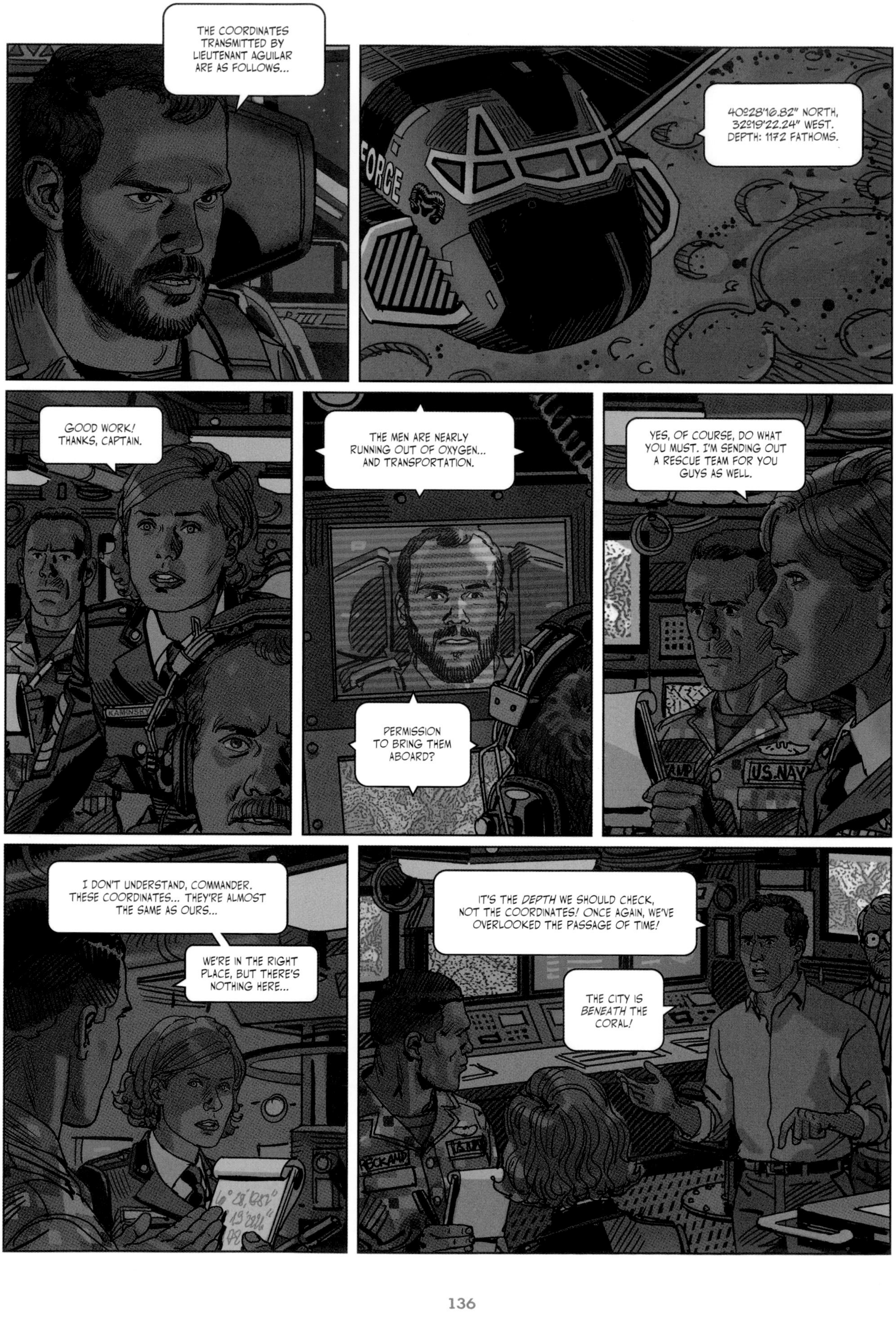
THE COORDINATES TRANSMITTED BY LIEUTENANT AGUILAR ARE AS FOLLOWS...
40º28'16.82" NORTH, 32º19'22.24" WEST. DEPTH: 1172 FATHOMS.
FORCE
GOOD WORK! THANKS, CAPTAIN.
KAMINSKY
THE MEN ARE NEARLY RUNNING OUT OF OXYGEN... AND TRANSPORTATION.
PERMISSION TO BRING THEM ABOARD?
YES, OF COURSE, DO WHAT YOU MUST. I'M SENDING OUT A RESCUE TEAM FOR YOU GUYS AS WELL.
U.S.NAVY
I DON'T UNDERSTAND, COMMANDER. THESE COORDINATES... THEY'RE ALMOST THE SAME AS OURS...
WE'RE IN THE RIGHT PLACE, BUT THERE'S NOTHING HERE...
IT'S THE *DEPTH* WE SHOULD CHECK, NOT THE COORDINATES! ONCE AGAIN, WE'VE OVERLOOKED THE PASSAGE OF TIME!
THE CITY IS *BENEATH* THE CORAL!
ECKARD

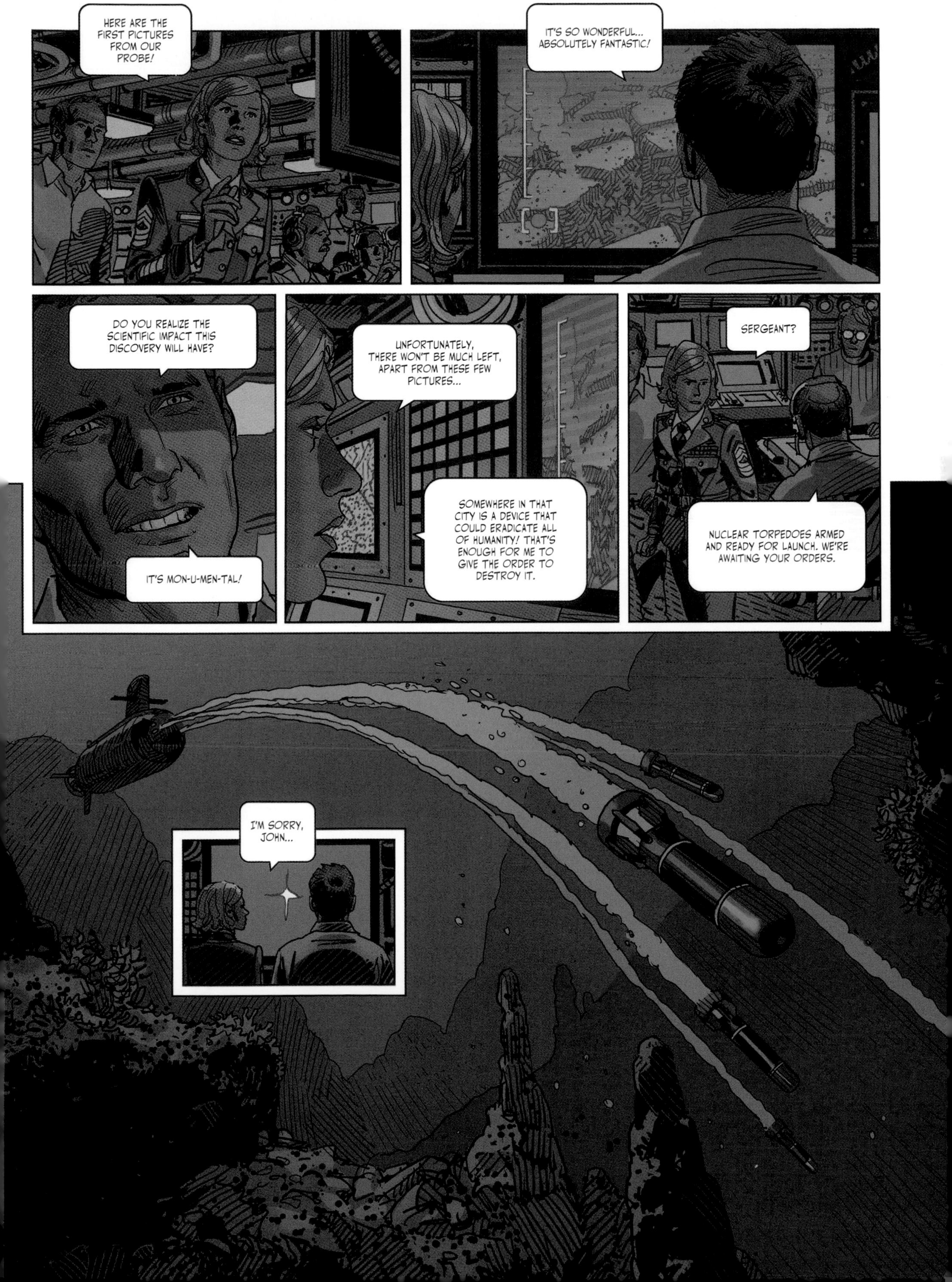
HERE ARE THE FIRST PICTURES FROM OUR PROBE!
IT'S SO WONDERFUL... ABSOLUTELY FANTASTIC!
DO YOU REALIZE THE SCIENTIFIC IMPACT THIS DISCOVERY WILL HAVE?
IT'S MON-U-MEN-TAL!
UNFORTUNATELY, THERE WON'T BE MUCH LEFT, APART FROM THESE FEW PICTURES...
SOMEWHERE IN THAT CITY IS A DEVICE THAT COULD ERADICATE ALL OF HUMANITY! THAT'S ENOUGH FOR ME TO GIVE THE ORDER TO DESTROY IT.
SERGEANT?
NUCLEAR TORPEDOES ARMED AND READY FOR LAUNCH. WE'RE AWAITING YOUR ORDERS.
I'M SORRY, JOHN...

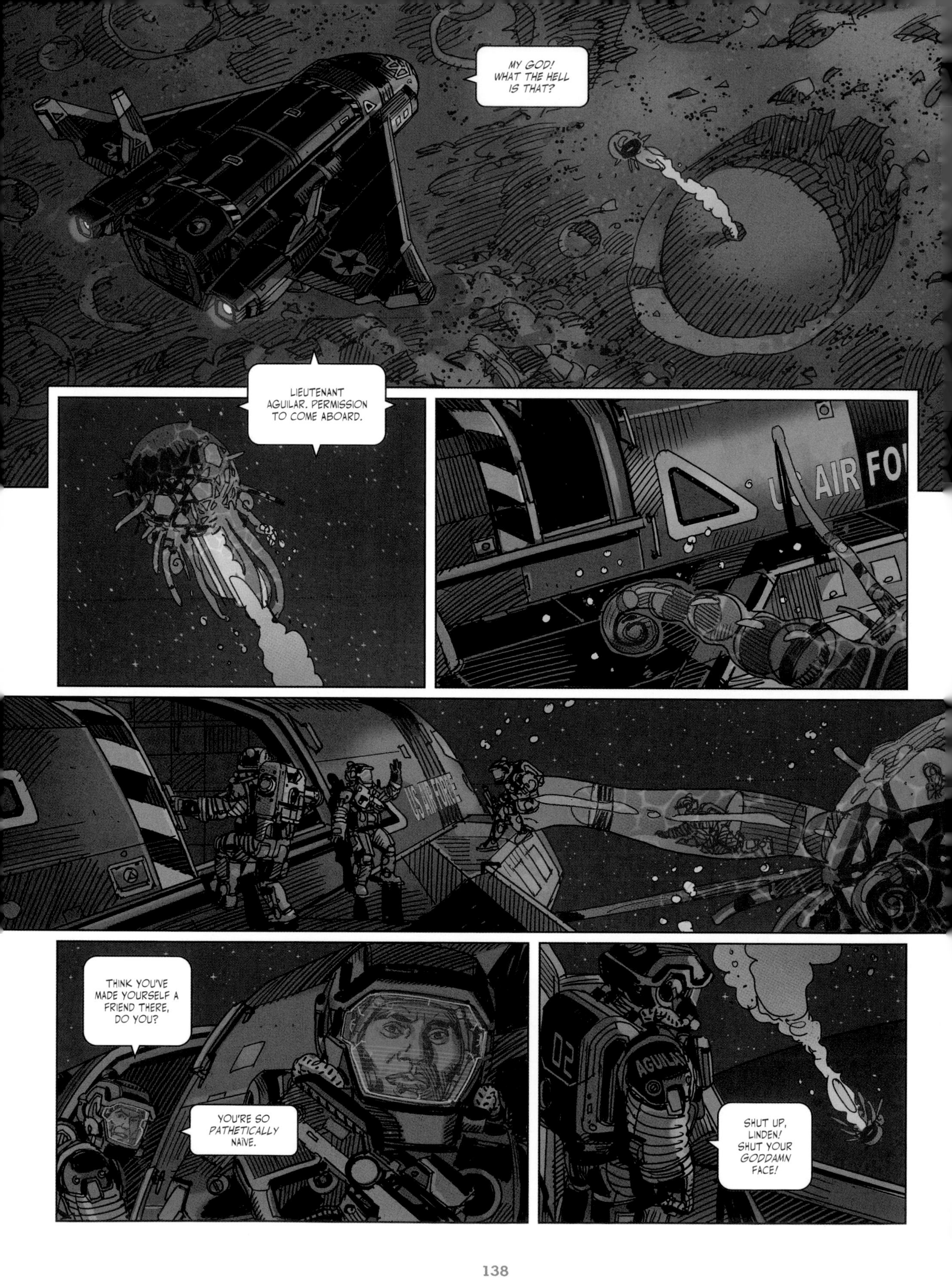
MY GOD! WHAT THE HELL IS THAT?
LIEUTENANT AGUILAR. PERMISSION TO COME ABOARD.
US AIR FO
US AIR FORCE
THINK YOU'VE MADE YOURSELF A FRIEND THERE, DO YOU?
YOU'RE SO PATHETICALLY NAÏVE.
AGUILAR
SHUT UP, LINDEN! SHUT YOUR GODDAMN FACE!

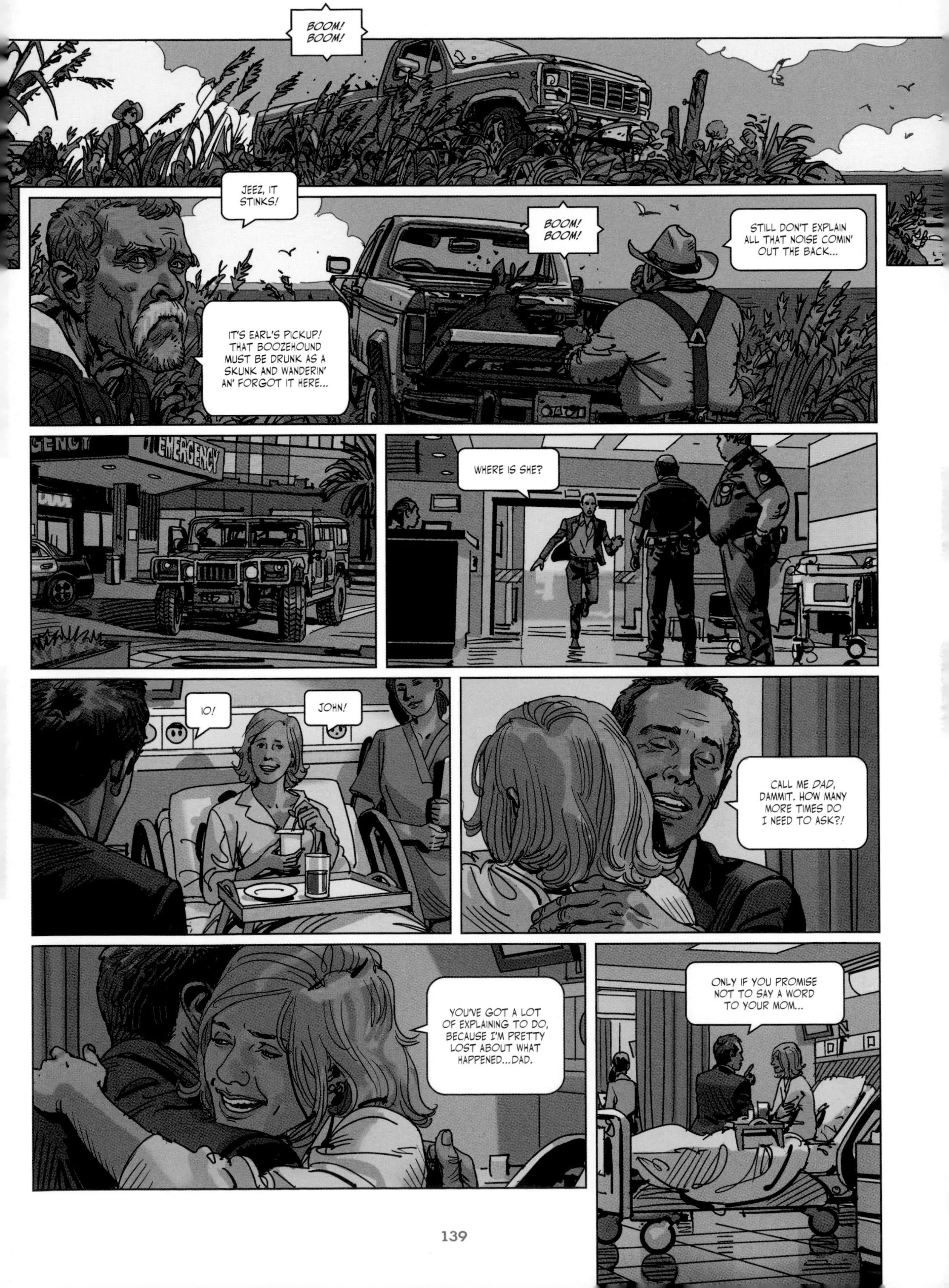
BOOM! BOOM!
JEEZ, IT STINKS!
IT'S EARL'S PICKUP! THAT BOOZEHOUND MUST BE DRUNK AS A SKUNK AND WANDERIN' AN' FORGOT IT HERE...
BOOM! BOOM!
STILL DON'T EXPLAIN ALL THAT NOISE COMIN' OUT THE BACK...
EMERGENCY
WHERE IS SHE?
IO!
JOHN!
CALL ME DAD, DAMMIT. HOW MANY MORE TIMES DO I NEED TO ASK?!
YOU'VE GOT A LOT OF EXPLAINING TO DO, BECAUSE I'M PRETTY LOST ABOUT WHAT HAPPENED...DAD.
ONLY IF YOU PROMISE NOT TO SAY A WORD TO YOUR MOM...

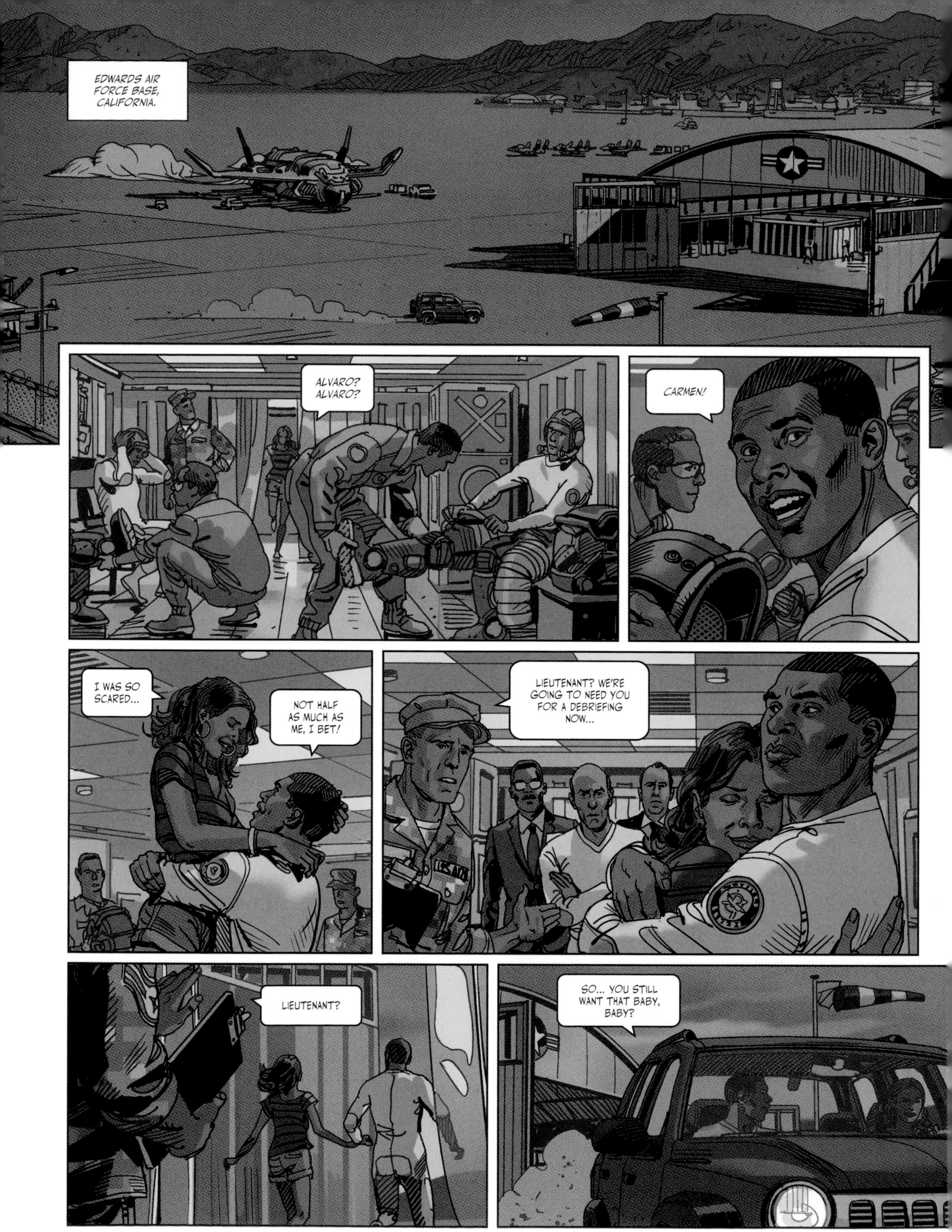
EDWARDS AIR FORCE BASE, CALIFORNIA.
ALVARO? ALVARO?
CARMEN!
I WAS SO SCARED...
NOT HALF AS MUCH AS ME, I BET!
LIEUTENANT? WE'RE GOING TO NEED YOU FOR A DEBRIEFING NOW...
LIEUTENANT?
SO... YOU STILL WANT THAT BABY, BABY?

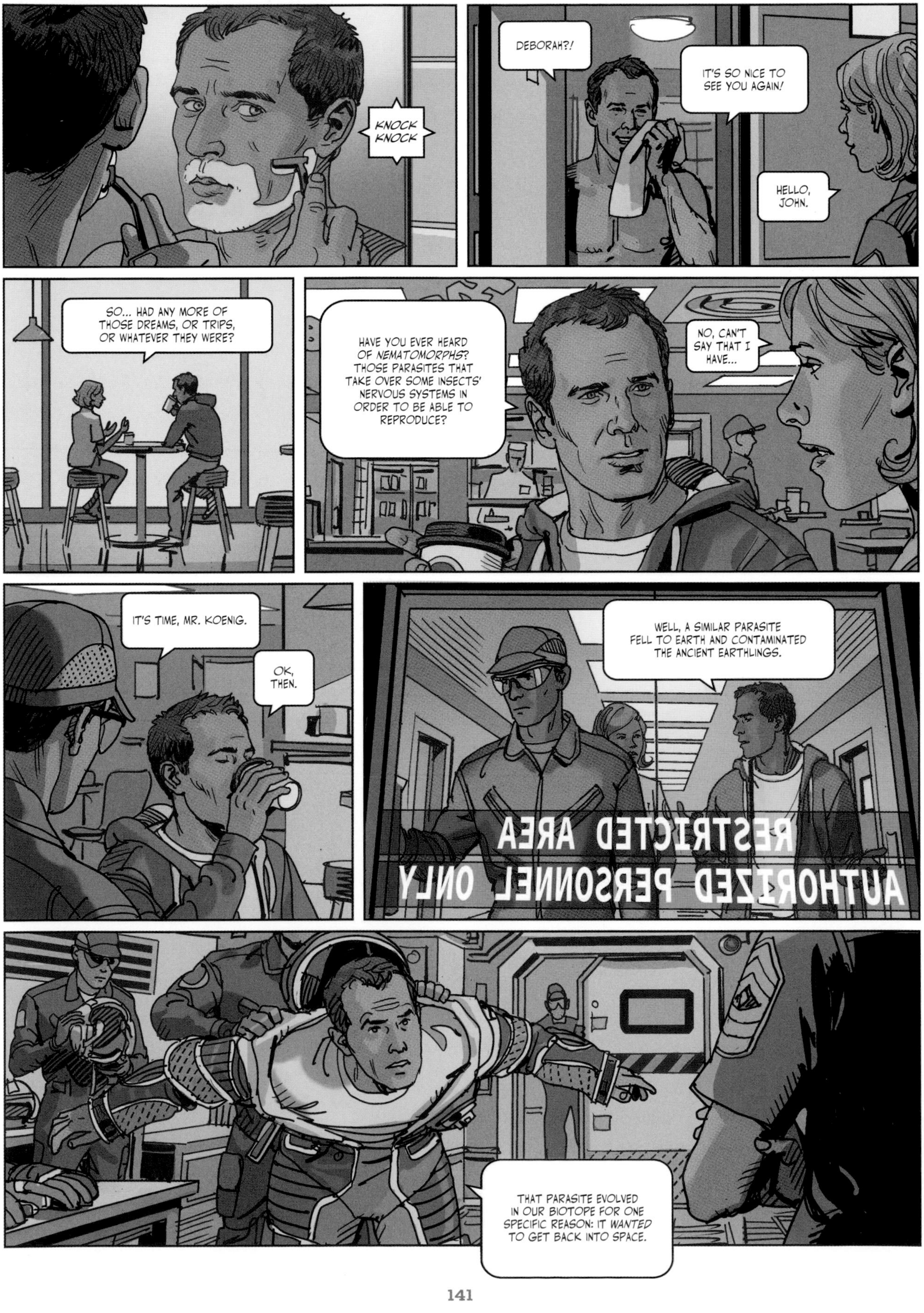

KNOCK KNOCK
DEBORAH?!
IT'S SO NICE TO SEE YOU AGAIN!
HELLO, JOHN.
SO... HAD ANY MORE OF THOSE DREAMS, OR TRIPS, OR WHATEVER THEY WERE?
HAVE YOU EVER HEARD OF *NEMATOMORPHS*? THOSE PARASITES THAT TAKE OVER SOME INSECTS' NERVOUS SYSTEMS IN ORDER TO BE ABLE TO REPRODUCE?
NO, CAN'T SAY THAT I HAVE...
IT'S TIME, MR. KOENIG.
OK, THEN.
WELL, A SIMILAR PARASITE FELL TO EARTH AND CONTAMINATED THE ANCIENT EARTHLINGS.
RESTRICTED AREA
AUTHORIZED PERSONNEL ONLY
THAT PARASITE EVOLVED IN OUR BIOTOPE FOR ONE SPECIFIC REASON: IT *WANTED* TO GET BACK INTO SPACE.

TO DO SO, IT INFECTED A SMALL ANIMAL SPECIES THAT WAS RESILIENT AND RESOURCEFUL...

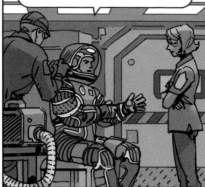

THE PARASITE SPLICED INTO ITS GENOME AND, THROUGHOUT THE CENTURIES, DROVE IT TO EVOLVE AND GROW INTELLIGENT. THAT RESULTED IN HOMO SAPIENS, WHOSE PROBES ARE NOW HEADING OUT INTO THE COSMOS...

THAT SPACE PARASITE IS IN *ME*, AND IN YOU, *TOO!* IT'S WHAT TURNED US INTO HUMAN BEINGS, DEBORAH!

IT SPEAKS TO ME... TO ALL OF US... AND ULTIMATELY IT WILL LEAD US TO THE STARS...

...OR IN THIS CASE — THE MOON!

YES, THE MOON... WHERE I'LL BE MEETING THE "CREATURE," THAT ANCIENT EARTHLING!

WHAT WOULD...WHAT WOULD YOU SAY TO HAVING A DRINK WITH ME WHEN I GET BACK?

I THINK YOU KNOW HOW TO REACH ME, RIGHT?

I SURE DO!

GOODBYE, DEBORAH. SEE YOU VERY SOON...

END

By the same writer (Jerry Frissen):

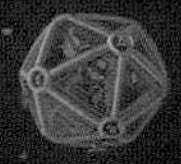

THE METABARON BOOK 1:
THE TECHNO-ADMIRAL & THE ANTI-BARON
with Alejandro Jodorowsky & Valentin Sécher
ISBN: 978-1-59465-153-3

THE METABARON BOOK 2:
THE TECHNO-CARDINAL & THE TRANSHUMAN
with Alejandro Jodorowsky & Niko Henrichon
ISBN: 978-1-59465-680-4

THE METABARON BOOK 3:
THE META-GUARDIANESS AND THE TECHNO-BARON
with Alejandro Jodorowsky & Valentin Sécher
ISBN: 978-1-59465-853-2

UNFABULOUS FIVE
with Bill
ISBN: 978-1-59465-082-6

THE ZOMBIES THAT ATE THE WORLD #1:
BRING ME BACK MY HEAD!
with Guy Davis
ISBN: 978-1-59465-083-3

THE ZOMBIES THAT ATE THE WORLD #2:
THE ELEVENTH COMMANDMENT
with Guy Davis
ISBN: 978-1-59465-013-0

THE ZOMBIES THAT ATE THE WORLD #3:
HOUSTON, WE HAVE A PROBLEM
with Jorge Miguel
ISBN: 978-1-59465-116-8

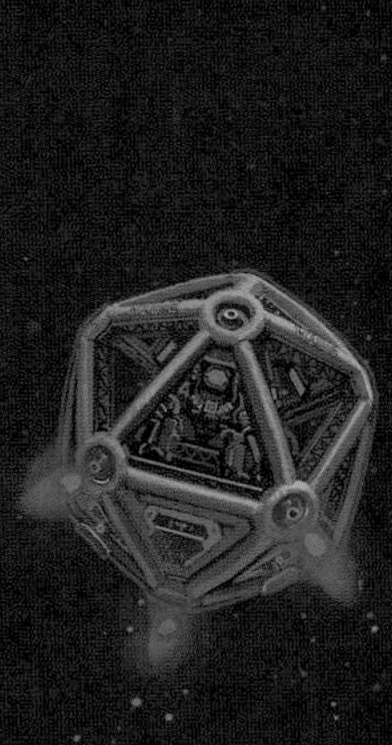

THE Z WORD
with Guy Davis & Jorge Miguel
ISBN: 978-1-59465-117-5

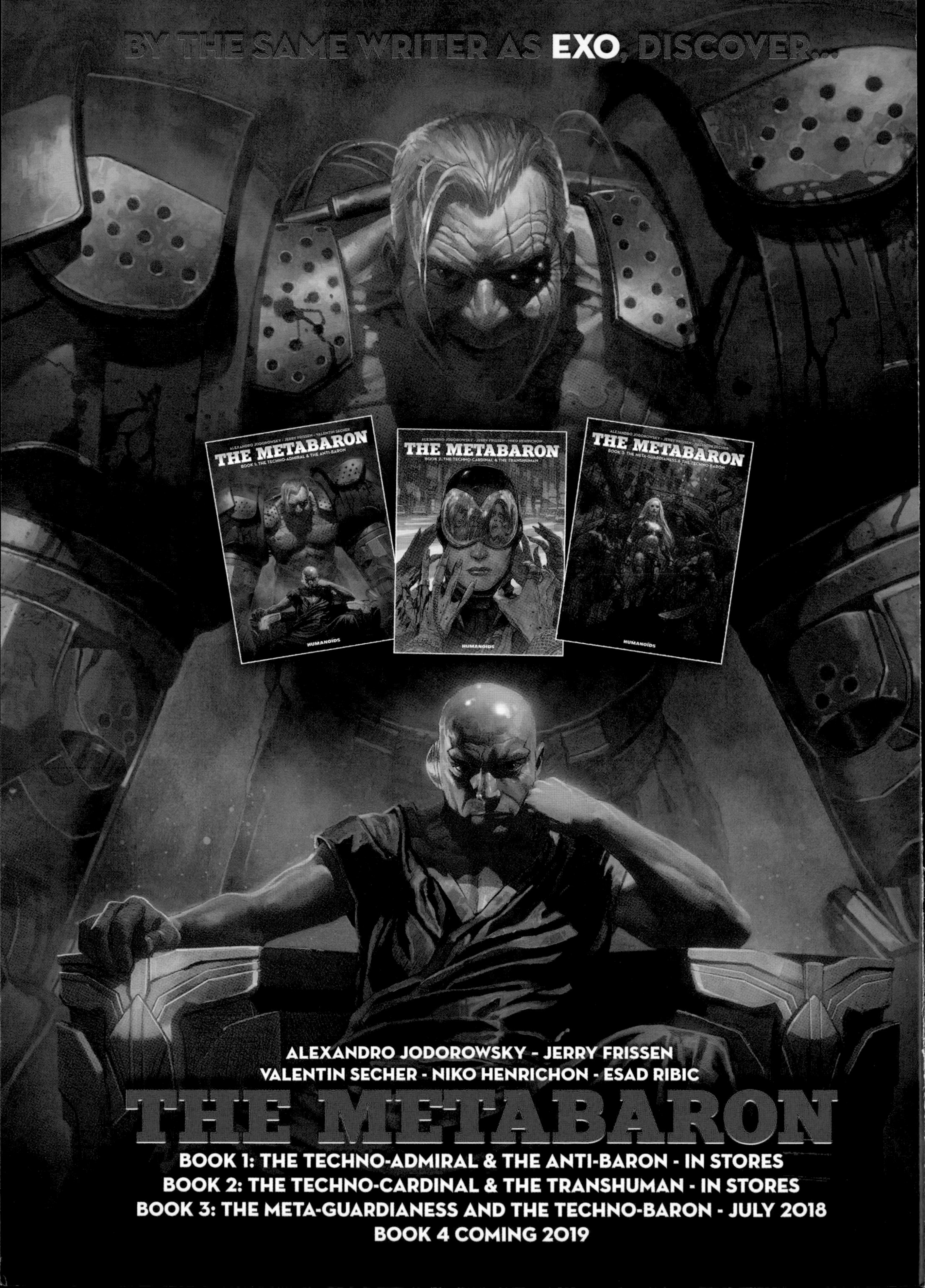
BY THE SAME WRITER AS EXO, DISCOVER...
THE METABARON
THE METABARON
THE METABARON
HUMANOIDS
HUMANOIDS
HUMANOIDS
ALEXANDRO JODOROWSKY - JERRY FRISSEN
VALENTIN SECHER - NIKO HENRICHON - ESAD RIBIC
THE METABARON
BOOK 1: THE TECHNO-ADMIRAL & THE ANTI-BARON - IN STORES
BOOK 2: THE TECHNO-CARDINAL & THE TRANSHUMAN - IN STORES
BOOK 3: THE META-GUARDIANESS AND THE TECHNO-BARON - JULY 2018
BOOK 4 COMING 2019